Schmidt Happens

Schmidt Happens

ROSS O'CARROLL-KELLY

(as told to Paul Howard)

Illustrated by ALAN CLARKE

PENGUIN

IRELAND

PENGUIN IRELAND

UK | USA | Canada | Ireland | Australia
India | New Zealand | South Africa

Penguin Ireland is part of the Penguin Random House group of companies
whose addresses can be found at global.penguinrandomhouse.com.

First published 2019
001

Penguin Ireland thanks O'Brien Press for its agreement to Penguin Ireland using the
same design approach and typography, and the same artist, as O'Brien Press used
in the first four Ross O'Carroll-Kelly titles

Set in 12/14.75 pt Dante MT Std
Typeset by Jouve (UK), Milton Keynes
Printed and bound in Great Britain by Clays Ltd, Elcograf S.p.A.

A CIP catalogue record for this book is available from the British Library

ISBN: 978–1–844–88451–3

www.greenpenguin.co.uk

MIX
Paper from
responsible sources
FSC
www.fsc.org   FSC® C018179

Penguin Random House is committed to a
sustainable future for our business, our readers
and our planet. This book is made from Forest
Stewardship Council® certified paper.

For Gerry Murtagh

Contents

Prologue: If You're New to This Channel, Welcome!   I

1. The Anti-Trump Fashion Item of the Season!   9

2. It's All about the Bag!   43

3. Unboxing This Year's Most Essential
   Lifestyle Accessory!   81

4. Faux Pas to Avoid on Your Confirmation Day!   116

5. What to Pack in Your Going-Away Bag!   153

6. A New and Exciting Interior Make-Over!   189

7. Outfit of the Day is a Canterbury Drill Top!   227

8. How to Style a Surgical Collar!   266

9. Every Woman's Absolute Must-Have!   301

10. The One Piece I Couldn't Live Without!   332

Epilogue: Don't Forget to Hit the Subscribe Button!   365

Prologue: If You're New to This Channel, Welcome!

I'm a sensitive man. It's one of the qualities I most love about myself, even though it doesn't get talked about as much as, say, my grapefruit biceps, my ravioli pecs and my handsome villain smile. But I'm definitely, definitely sensitive, especially when it comes to the needs of my children.

That's kind of how we've ended up in Horvey Nichs this afternoon. Sorcha is being dischorged from Holles Street tomorrow morning. She's going to be arriving home with a brand-new baby boy. Which is why it's important to let Honor and the triplets know that their mommy and daddy aren't going to love them any less, even though their mommy is going around having kids with other men who aren't their daddy. And the only way to let them know that it's business as usual is to bring them to Dundrum Town Centre to buy them shit.

Honor is checking herself out in the full-length mirror.

'I love it,' she goes – she's talking about a Gucci tulle dress with shooting stors, which she originally had on her Santa list but her old dear said it was too expensive.

'I love how it makes me look thinner,' she goes. 'How much is it?'

And I'm there, 'Well, it *was* fourteen hundred snots.'

'What do you mean it *was*?'

'As in, you know, it's been reduced – to *nine* hundred snots?'

'I don't want it if it's reduced.'

'Are you serious?'

'Does this *look* like the face of someone who's joking?'

It doesn't. But then it *never* does.

I'm there, 'But it's nine hundred snots, Honor – as opposed to, like, *fourteen* hundred?'

She goes, 'I want you to pay full price for it.'

'But why would I do that? It's on sale.'

'Because you said you were bringing us out today to show us that you still love us even though there's another baby coming into the house. And I don't think paying the sale price for my clothes is a good way of showing me that you love me.'

'But who's going to *know* that I paid the sale price for it?'

'*I'll* know.'

Daughters are complicated things.

'I'll tell you what,' I go. 'What if I pay the sale price for it, then give you the difference – however much that is – in cash?'

She's like, 'No, I want you to pay full price for it.'

About twenty seconds later one of the shop girls sticks her head into the dressing room and goes, 'Excuse me, are those your three boys pushing over all of the mannequins in the shop?'

'It definitely sounds like them,' I go. 'But, in better news, we've decided to take the dress.'

The woman looks at Honor and smiles. She's like, 'It really suits her!'

I'm there, 'Bit of a weird one this, but we were wondering would it be possible for you to chorge us *full* whack for it?'

She's there, 'Well, it's *actually* reduced at the moment.'

Honor goes, 'You're not listening. What my dad is trying to say is that he doesn't want it if it's reduced. He wants to pay the original, pre-sale price for it.'

The woman looks at me like I'm a donkey trying to explain Brexit. 'But why would you want to do that?' she goes.

And I'm there, 'You don't have children, do you?'

'No.'

'It's all ahead of you. Can you just tell me is it possible to chorge me what it would have cost if it *wasn't* in the sale?'

'I'll have to check with my manager first.'

She focks off to do that while Honor goes back into the cubicle to change out of the dress. And it's at that exact point that my *phone* ends up ringing? I can see from the screen that it's Kennet, the stuttering fock, who I would have been actually related to this morning if Ronan hadn't seen sense and bailed during the wedding rehearsal.

I answer by going, 'Why the fock are you ringing me? To reminisce about old times?' because – honestly? – I don't see any reason for us to be in touch now that my son is no longer engaged to his daughter.

'I think you know why Ine r . . . r . . . r . . . r . . . r . . . r . . . rigging,' he goes. 'Your sudden leabon my thaughter at the altodder.'

I'm there, 'I'd hordly say he left her at the altar. It was twenty-four hours before the wedding.'

'Th . . . th . . . th . . . that's irregeerdless. He's arthur breaking her b . . . b . . . b . . . b . . . bleaten heert, so he is. And Ine wanthon to know what you're p . . . p . . . p . . . proposing to do abourrut?'

'In terms of?'

'In teerms of c . . . c . . . c . . . c . . . c . . . c . . . compedden sayshidden?'

I actually laugh. I'm like, 'Compensation? Would you ever ask my orse?'

This is some day for being shaken down, it has to be said. First, Honor. Now, this clown.

'You listodden to me,' he goes. 'Sh . . . Sh . . . Sh . . . Shadden's veddy upset, so she is. Her m . . . m . . . m . . . mutter's throying to explain to her that a b . . . b . . . b . . . broken heert is no diffordent to a b . . . b . . . b . . . broken ankle or a s . . . s . . . s . . . sower neck – you're entitled to a few b . . . b . . . b . . . b . . . bob for it.'

I'm there, 'What a great mother D . . . D . . . D . . . D . . . D . . . D . . . Dordeen is!'

'S . . . S . . . S . . . S . . . Some wooden should pay – for what he's d . . . d . . . d . . . dudden to us as a f . . . f . . . f . . . f . . . famidy.'

'What's he done to your f . . . f . . . f . . . f . . . famidy? All he's done to *you* is denied you a free focking piss-up.'

Kennet laughs then. He goes, 'Oh, we *had* the piss-up – doatunt you w . . . w . . . w . . . woody about that. The whole bleaten lorruf us.'

For fock's sake! Ronan didn't cancel the reception? Three hundred people for dinner in Clontorf Castle – *and* a free bor. I don't

3

even want to think about what that's going to cost me slash my old man.

Kennet goes, 'We joost thought, Myra swell hab the p . . . p . . . p . . . p . . . peerty in addyhow. Shurden it's paid foe-er. W . . . w . . . w . . . waste not, want not – wha'? We deserb it arthur what that bleaten pox bottle did to eer Sh . . . Shadden. Although, I w . . . w . . . w . . . w . . . wouldn't luvven to be you, Rosser, when you get the b . . . b . . . b . . . b . . . b . . . biddle for the bar.'

I'll give him biddle for the focking bor.

I'm there, 'It'll be the last thing you ever get out of me.'

But he goes, 'S . . . S . . . S . . . S . . . Sebenty grand.'

'Excuse me?'

'Ine arthur discuston it wit Dordeen and we both feel that s . . . s . . . s . . . s . . . sebenty grand would j . . . j . . . joost about cubber the cost of the emotioniddle dabbage that your sudden is arthur doing to eer Sh . . . Sh . . . Sh . . . Sh . . . Shadden.'

'And why do you think *I* should pay?'

'Because Ronan dudn't hab addy muddy. And needer does he's mutter. And it was you what encoudaged him to be r . . . r . . . r . . . r . . . r . . . r . . . royden quare woodens out in that UC bleaten D– . . . D– . . . D– . . . D.'

'Dude, you're getting the sum total of fock-all out of me – and that's the rounded-up figure.'

'Ine wardon you, Rosser – you d . . . d . . . d . . . d . . . doatunt want to take me odden.'

'Dude, it's over. Breaking it off with Shadden and putting distance between himself and your family is the best decision Ronan ever made. Focking scum. Focking scumbags. Focking scummers.'

'You're a very s . . . s . . . s . . . s . . . siddy madden, Rosser. You're godda regret that.'

'I hordly think I will. As a matter of fact, there's no reason for me and you to ever have a conversation again.'

He goes, 'Doatunt hag up on me! Doatunt you deer hag –'

But I *do* hang up on him? Because the shop girl is suddenly coming back. She says that, yes, her manager said they are prepared to accept the full, pre-sale price for the dress.

Which is focking big of them.

Honor steps out of the dressing room and hands the dress to the woman, who removes the security tag from it, rings it up, then goes, 'That'll be one thousand, four hundred euros.'

I hand over my plastic.

'Thanks,' Honor goes. And it's actually a bit of a moment because it's not often that Honor uses that word. 'I still want that five hundred euros in cash that you mentioned as well.'

Seriously, who needs the Tuites for in-laws when you've got an eleven-year-old daughter bleeding you like a focking ATM on Christmas Eve?

Honor picks up her dress, then we go looking for Brian, Johnny and Leo. They're standing at the bottom of the escalator, kicking the ankles of a security gord, who is radioing for back-up.

'I'll take it from here,' I go.

The dude's like, 'Are these your children?'

I'm there, 'Trust me, I wouldn't be offering to take them off your hands if they weren't.'

He's like, 'They've pushed over all the dummies in the shop.'

'Not all of them,' I go, 'if you're still standing.'

Honor's there, 'Good one, Dad!' because she loves it when I'm being a dick to strangers.

'I know who these boys are,' the dude tries to go. 'They've been banned from Hamleys.'

What he obviously doesn't know is that there's also a photograph of them in the Build-A-Bear Workshop, warning the staff not to let them through the door of the place. Same with the Ort & Hobby shop.

He goes, 'I don't want you to bring them into this shop again.'

I'm like, 'Yeah, whatever,' then I grab Brian and Johnny by the hand, while Honor takes Leo, and we step onto the up escalator.

Honor is so good with the boys that it would actually put a smile on your face. She turns around to Leo and goes, 'Daddy bought me an amazing dress to make up for the fact that Mommy is a slut.'

I'm there, 'She's not a slut, Honor. She just had a baby that turned out to be someone else's other than her husband's. Although if that doesn't make her a slut, then I don't know what does.'

'Slut!' Leo shouts as we leave Horvey Nichs. 'Focking, focking slut!'

And it's at that point that I spot my old dear walking across the concourse towards us. Jesus Christ, she looks rough – try to imagine a fat Ronnie Wood in drag.

When she sees us, she tries to smile. But she's had so much work done to her face that she no longer has any command over her features and moving anything south of her hairline and north of her several chins would require major surgery.

'Oh, look,' she goes through frozen lips, 'it's you! Look at you . . . all!'

She seriously can't remember the names of any of her grandchildren.

'Hi, Fionnuala!' Honor goes – because the old dear has forbidden her from calling her Gran.

'Hello, you!' the old dear goes. 'And the other ones, look! One, two, three of them.'

I literally haven't set eyes on the woman since a few days before Christmas, when she was choking to death on a Kalamata olive and – yeah, no – I just stood by and watched, deciding that the world would be a better place without her in it. I want to make sure there's no awkwardness between us as a result.

I'm there, 'Honor, would you take the boys down to Gino's and get them whatever ice creams they want?'

I hand Honor a fifty and off she focks with the three boys running after her shouting, 'Focking ice cream! You focking motherfockers!'

I'm there, 'So how was your Christmas in the end?' just making small talk. 'Any plans to head back to Russia?'

She's been doing a lot of lectures over there to raise money for her charitable foundation, a not-for-profit organization that her and the old man set up with the mission of – get this – strengthening the capacity of people to meet the challenges of global interdependence.

A money-laundering operation, in other words.

'I have no plans to go back,' she goes. 'I don't think I'm going to be doing much travelling this year.'

'Just to let you know,' I go, 'Sorcha had her baby. A little boy.

And it turns out that Fionn is the father – just in case you're wondering.'

She wasn't wondering. She just shrugs. It's like I've told her how many alcohol units it's safe to drink in a week. It's of no focking relevance to the woman.

'Well,' I go, 'I thought I'd let you know anyway. Mother and baby doing fine – except, obviously, the kid is going to have to grow up knowing that his father is that goggle-eyed freak.'

She's there, 'I know what you're trying to do, Ross.'

'Hey, I'm just making pleasant chit-chat.'

'You're trying to find out how I feel about what happened before Christmas.'

'Before Christmas? Refresh my memory again?'

'I was lying on the floor of the kitchen, choking to death. And you just stood there, perfectly prepared to watch me die.'

'Oh, that!'

'Yes, Ross – that.'

'I was wondering were you going to bring that up.'

'If your father hadn't walked into the room when he did, I wouldn't be alive today.'

'Yeah, no, it'd be typical for you to hold a grudge.'

'You actually smiled, Ross, while I was clutching my throat and gasping for breath. You looked me straight in the eye and you smiled at me.'

'Like I said, it's so *you* not to be able to let that go. Come on, it's New Year's Eve. What do you say to you and me storting 2017 with a clean slate?'

She tries to smile. It's horrible. Her mouth looks like a plastic bucket filled with chopped liver with lipstick around the rim.

'Oh, there'll be no clean slate!' she goes – and she says it in a way that would have to be described as *chilling*?

I'm there, 'So what are you planning? You're obviously planning something for me.'

She goes, 'You'll just have to wait and see.'

I'm there, 'Wait and see? Is that a threat?'

'Yes, it is a threat – and not an idle one.'

7

'So you're threatening me – your only son?'

She just smiles at me and goes, 'You know, that might not *always* be the case, Ross.'

'So you're going to kill me? Or *have* me killed – is that it?'

But she just repeats what she originally said. She's like, 'Wait and see!' and she smiles at me again.

And I end up just gulping, because I know the woman is capable of literally anything.

She goes, 'Happy New Year, Ross,' then off she focks, the smell of Tanqueray Export Strength and Clarins *Eau Dynamisante* trailing after her like a Škoda Fabia with a focked exhaust.

The Anti-Trump Fashion Item of the Season!

'What about Gruffydd?' Sorcha's old man goes.

I end up just laughing out loud.

Sorcha's like, 'Gruffydd? Is that even a name?'

And *he's* there, 'Of course it's a name! It could be a nod to your Welsh heritage!'

Sorcha's there, 'I didn't know I was Welsh.'

I didn't know she was Welsh either. I *could* probably get an annulment – that's if I wanted to go down that route.

It's, like, New Year's Day, by the way. Sorcha has finally arrived home from the hospital with this famous – yeah, no – *baby* of hers? Her old dear has stuck balloons and bunting with the words 'Welcome Home, Sorcha and Baby!' all over the kitchen.

We're all sitting around the table. We're talking me, Sorcha, her old pair, Fionn and Honor.

'Your great-, great-, great-, great-grandfather came from Anglesey,' Sorcha's old man goes. 'And the name Gruffydd was passed down in our family from generation to generation.'

'Oh, like big noses?' Honor goes.

I laugh. No actual choice in the matter. Sorcha's old man has a ginormous hooter that looks like it's taken a few smacks from a wok.

I'm like, 'Great line, Honor! Great line!'

Sorcha's old dear tops up her own champagne flute and – definitely a bit hammered – goes, 'Does *she* have to be here?'

I'm about to remind her that Honor actually lives here – unlike her and her husband, who supposedly live in a Shomera in our gorden yet seem to spend all their time in my kitchen, eating my food and drinking my booze.

Sorcha goes, 'Of course she should be here, Mom! This is her little brother!'

Fionn – the proud dad – is holding the baby and making, I don't know, coochie-focking-coo noises at it.

Under her breath, Honor goes, 'He's not my little brother.'

Sorcha either doesn't hear it or chooses to ignore it because she goes, 'When it comes to names, I love nouns that are, like, suggestive of *virtue*? For instance, Sage, Truth and Valour.'

Sorcha's old dear looks at Honor and I can tell she's thinking, Yeah, that worked out so well for *her*, didn't it?

I turn around to Fionn and I go, 'You're being very quiet. What do *you* think of Gruffydd?' just trying to put the dude on the spot.

He goes, 'It's, em, definitely an *interesting* name. I just think I'd prefer something a bit more old Irish. I like names like Beathan. Ailpein. Mannix. Mogue. Tully. Caden. Roan. Winford. Merle. Tighe.'

Honor stands up from the table. 'I'm sorry,' she goes, 'I can't take any more of this bullshit. I'm going upstairs to vlog.'

Sorcha looks at me, then back at Honor – her mouth wide open. She goes, 'What are you talking about?'

Honor's there, 'I've become a fashion vlogger. It's none of your focking business anyway.'

'I didn't know you were interested in fashion.'

'Well, I wasn't interested before and I am now. It's not a big deal. I've storted my own YouTube channel – Love Honor and Obey – just putting up stuff about the kind of clothes I like to wear and my favourite beauty products.'

'Love Honor and Obey! Oh my God, that's a brilliant name! I'd love to work on it with you, Honor. It might be something we could do together. I've actually *worked* in fashion, remember?'

Sorcha had a boutique in the Powerscourt Townhouse Centre that was basically a tax write-off for her old man during the Celtic Tiger years.

Honor bitch-smiles her and goes, 'Yeah, if I'm ever doing a video about tragic clothes from the nineties, I might actually interview you.'

Then off upstairs she focks.

Sorcha stands up and takes the baby from Fionn. 'Look,' she goes, 'I realize that this is an unusual set of circumstances for everyone. We're all going to have to make certain compromises and adjustments. Can we all make it our New Year's Resolution to try to create a happy, stable home environment for this beautiful little baby, whatever we decide to call him?'

Cords on the table? He *is* a cute little thing, even if he does have Fionn's little moley eyes.

Her old man goes, 'Look at the way he's staring at you, Fionn! I don't think he's blinked in, oh, it must be sixty seconds. He's clearly got a high level of focus and concentration. And, of course, with your two sets of genes, I shouldn't be surprised.'

There's suddenly a loud thud upstairs and the sound of screaming and shouting. Brian and Leo are killing each other. Or maybe it's Leo and Johnny. Or maybe it's Johnny and Brian.

'Ross,' Sorcha goes, 'can you deal with that?' and it's as I'm leaving the kitchen that I hear Fionn say something that stops me dead in my tracks.

He goes, 'I'll go and get my things from the car.'

I turn around and I'm like, 'Your things? What things?'

And – I swear to fock – he's there, 'I'm moving in, Ross.'

I'm like, 'In? In where?' at the same time looking at Sorcha for an explanation.

She goes, 'Ross, we discussed this. I told you that if Fionn turned out to be the father, it was only fair that he should be allowed to play a full and active role in the baby's life.'

'I thought that meant he'd be dropping in once or twice a week to see him.'

Fionn goes, 'I actually did mention that I wanted to move in.'

And I'm there, 'But I didn't agree to it. It's my focking house.'

'The alternative is that I *could* apply for joint custody.'

Sorcha's old man goes, 'No one wants that, Fionn. I've worked in family law for forty years. Trust me, this is a much more sensible arrangement.'

I'm like, 'So where's he going to sleep?'

Sorcha goes, 'In the guest room – where you *were* sleeping?'

'And the baby?'

'The baby's going to be in our room with us.'

I end up just shaking my head. I knew it was going to take a lot of getting used to – but I had no idea just *how* much?

'No way,' I go. 'It's not happening.'

But Sorcha's old man goes, 'Come on, Fionn,' with a big, delighted smile on his face, 'I'll help you with your bags.'

The first thing that hits me is the smell of hash. I get it the second Tina opens the door to me – in her dressing gown, by the way, at three o'clock in the focking afternoon.

I'm like, 'How is he?'

She goes, ''Mon up – see for yisser self,' then she leads me up the stairs to his old bedroom, which I suppose is his *new* bedroom now?

Halfway up, I turn around to Tina and I go, 'Can you not smell that?' because she's supposed to be his mother.

'Ine arthur been asleep,' she tries to go.

I'm like, 'In the middle of the afternoon? Yeah, nice parenting, Tina.'

She's there, 'I was woorking the night shift. I oately fidished at sebben o'clock this morden.'

Yeah, no, she's a nurse in the Mater, which is a good enough excuse, I suppose.

I'm like, 'Hey, don't be so defensive. I was only commenting.'

She pushes the door and there's Ronan, lying on his old bed, listening to 'Amsterdam' by Coldplay – it was him and Shadden's song apparently – while sucking on a joint the size of a focking rolling pin.

The music is so loud and the hash so strong that he doesn't even notice us standing in the doorway and Tina ends up having to shout. She's like, 'Ro, your fadder's hee-or!'

She has a voice that could strip the enamel off your teeth. Ronan practically levitates off the bed with fright.

'Moy Jaysus!' he goes. 'You frightened the bleaten shire ourra me, Ma! Alreet, Rosser?'

I'm there, 'Alright, Ro?'

Tina walks into the room and storts picking his clothes up off the floor and folding them.

She's like, 'And what hab I toawult you about smoking that stuff in the house?'

He's there, 'Make shurden close the window.'

'Make shurden close the window,' she goes, at the same time closing the window. 'You *know* that Git Spence's young fedda is a tout.'

'Fooking informer,' he goes. 'Fooking rat bastard informer.'

'And you'd wanna think about getting up ourra that bed. It's not naturdoddle lying in bed all day listodden to the sayum song oaber and oaber.'

Ro looks at me and rolls his eyes. Or maybe they're rolling of their own accord. It smells like pretty strong hash – insofar as I'm a judge of working-class drugs.

He goes, 'Jaysus sakes, Ine still greebon, Ma.'

She's like, 'Greebon? What are you greebon foe-er?'

'Me maddidge is arthur enton.'

'You werdunt married.'

'Me engayuchmint, then.'

'Best thing that ebbor happened to you, getting away from that famidy. Now gerrup ourra that bed – you were apposed to be back at coddidge yestorthay.'

Tina focks off then and Ro tells me to sit down. I pork the old glutes on the edge of the bed while he lies down again and relights his joint.

I look at the walls. This room takes me back to the very first time I met my son a thousand unsupervised access days ago. His posters of Eminem, Henrik Larsson and the Ireland World Cup squad from 2002. Then photoshopped pictures of the Mona Lisa smoking a joint, Jesus at the Last Supper smoking a joint, Bob Morley smoking a joint. Actually, that last one might not be photoshopped – from what I've heard, the dude was pretty fond of the stuff.

I'm there, 'Your mother's right, Ro. What she said. About you calling off the *wedding*? It was the bravest thing you've ever done – although you could have saved me a fortune by cancelling the reception as well.'

He goes, 'Ine misson me thaughter teddible bad, Rosser,' and there's real sadness in his little yellow eyes.

I'm like, 'Rihanna-Brogan? Are you saying you haven't seen her?'

'Habn't seen her since I walked out of the choorch in the middle of the reheersoddle.'

'But you're entitled to see her, Ro. You're her old man.'

'Shadden's arthur thaken her away.'

'Away? Away where?'

'On the huddymoowunt.'

'The what?'

'The huddymoowunt.'

'Again?'

'The huddymoowunt.'

'Okay, I *think* you're trying to say honeymoon. Blink your eyes if you're trying to say honeymoon.'

He blinks his eyes.

Yeah, no, they were supposed to be going to Florida for two weeks – Ronan, Shadden and Rihanna-Brogan. We're talking Disney World, the whole works.

I'm there, 'Are you saying that she still went? Even though the wedding was called off?'

'She brought her mutter instead of me,' Ronan goes. 'I saw it on her Facebuke. She said she myras well – the thing was altreddy paid foe-er.'

I'm suddenly laughing, picturing Dordeen tripping over one of Goofy's big feet, then throwing in a claim. And that's when it suddenly hits me – like a focking snow shovel to the face.

'Hang on!' I go. 'I paid for that as well! Full-focking-board. Jesus Christ, Ro, why didn't you cancel all of these things?'

He's like, 'I'd a lot on me moyunt, Rosser.'

'These people are fock-all to do with us now and I've just sent them on a two-week holiday to Florida!'

'And the Cadda Beeyunt.'

The Caribbean! That's right! I paid for a focking cruise as well!

I'm like, 'Fock's sake,' feeling like a definite mug.

He goes quiet for a long time, then he goes, 'I hoort Shadden, Rosser.'

I'm there, 'People get hurt all the time, Ro. It's an unfortunate fact of life. But dumping her was a lot kinder than marrying her, then spending the rest of your life cheating on her. I should know.'

He hands me the joint. I take a blast from it. Fock, it's strong shit. I end up having an actual coughing fit.

'So how's *that* all going?' he goes, meaning my *own* domestic situation? He knows by now that Fionn is the father of Sorcha's baby and that me and Sorcha are back together.

I'm there, 'Hey, I'm just making the best of a shit state of affairs. *He's* moved in, by the way.'

'What? The funny-lookin' fedda with the glasses?'

I laugh.

I'm there, 'That's exactly him. I'm going to remember that quote. Focking sums him up.'

'So you're back sleeping in Sudeka's bed, the fadder of the babby is, what, across the lanthon? And where's the little babby sleeping?'

'In with us.'

He goes, 'Moy Jaysus!' and he just shakes his head.

I forget sometimes that Southsiders must seem as strange to Northsiders as Northsiders do to everyone else.

Tina knocks on the door, then sticks her head around it.

'Ro,' she goes, 'Shadden's da is dowunstayors.'

I'm up off the bed quickest. I'm like, 'Kennet?' my fists instantly tightening.

Ronan goes, 'Keep the head, Rosser.'

I'm there, 'What does he want?'

'I ast him to calt arowunt,' Ro goes.

I'm like, 'What? Why?'

'I caddent affowurt to fall out wirrum. Wetter I see me thaughter or not is dowun to him, Rosser. Utterwise, it's munts and munts going troo the cowurts, looking for access.'

'Right.'

'Ine godda throy and smoowit things oaber with the madden.'

Fock. I probably should mention the mouthful of abuse I gave him on New Year's Eve – except I *don't*?

We tip downstairs, Ro first, then me following closely behind. Ro opens the door and I think it's fair to say that neither of us is pre-pared for the shock that awaits us.

All of Ronan's worldly possessions have been dumped in the gor-den. I notice his Celtic jerseys. His collection of bongs. A framed poster of an alien – obviously smoking a joint. The kids from the neighbourhood are helping themselves to his shit and Kennet is standing there, just letting them. I end up chasing them off like crows in Ballyogan.

Ronan goes, 'What are you doing?'

Kennet's like, 'Joost returden yisser s . . . s . . . s . . . s . . . s . . . s . . . stuff.'

'Could you not hab let me collect it meself?'

'I doatunt want you addywhere nee-or that house. You hoort moy little p . . . p . . . p . . . p . . . p . . . p . . .'

I presume the word he's attempting to say is 'princess', but Ronan can't be orsed waiting for him to say it.

'Kennet,' he goes, 'I doatunt lub Shadden.'

He's there, 'So you said in the choorch. Well, now she's off on the croowuz wit her mutter. Hab you seen her p . . . p . . . p . . . pitchers on the Facebuke?'

Ro's like, 'I hab, yeah.'

'There's one of her wirra waiter, looking veddy cosy togetter. A big, b . . . b . . . b . . . b . . . b . . . b . . . big, muscly fedda. I says to Dadden, "I hope he's rooting her. She deserbs it arthur what that little bastard p . . . p . . . p . . . p . . . p . . . p . . . p . . . purrer troo."'

I'm like, 'Jesus Christ, Kennet, that's your focking daughter you're talking about.'

'Ah, the Rosser fedda,' he goes. 'I was w . . . w . . . w . . . w . . . w . . . wontherdin when you'd throw your p . . . p . . . p . . . peddy's woort in.'

Ronan goes, 'Look, Kennet, Ine soddy it ditn't woork out between

Shadden and me. Alls Ine inthordested in now is being a good fadder to Rihatta-Barrogan.'

Kennet's like, 'Yeah, that w . . . w . . . w . . . w . . . woatunt be happoden, Ronan, Ine afrayut.'

'I've rights, Kennet.'

'You've *no* bleaten rights. You geb up your bleaten rights the m . . . m . . . m . . . m . . . midute you walked out on her m . . . m . . . m . . . mutter.'

Ro storts literally pleading with the dude. 'Kennet,' he goes, 'you caddent stop me seeing me owunt thaughter!'

Kennet looks at me and he smiles. 'See, I was morten happy for you to hab a r . . . r . . . r . . . r . . . r . . . relashiddenship wirrer,' he goes. 'That was until your fadder hee-or opened he's m . . . m . . . m . . . m . . . mowt last week.'

Ro looks at me. He's like, 'What's he thalken about, Rosser?'

Kennet goes, 'He geb me a m . . . m . . . m . . . m . . . owt fuddle of abuse on the phowunt. I oately rag him up to say, no heerd f . . . f . . . f . . . f . . . f . . . feelons – important we all gerron for the sake of the young wooden.'

I'm there, 'That's not exactly how the conversation went, Kennet. You asked me for seventy focking Ks.'

'N . . . N . . . N . . . N . . . Next thing I know,' he goes, 'he's c . . . c . . . c . . . c . . . cawding us all s . . . s . . . s . . . scuddem bags. The wholet famidy – me, Dordeen, Shadden, Dadden, Kadden. Saying the best thing you ebber did was p . . . p . . . p . . . put distiddence between you and us.'

Ronan looks at me. He's like, 'Did you say that, Rosser?'

I can't deny it. I give it a shot, though. I'm there, 'He's making it up.'

Kennet goes, 'Ine making you're a probiss hee-or today, Ronan. You're nebber godda see your th . . . th . . . th . . . th . . . th . . . th . . . th . . . th . . . th . . . th . . . th . . . th . . . thaughter again. And you've your f . . . f . . . f . . . f . . . fadder theer to thank for that.'

Kennet walks away then – focking ridiculous pigeon-walk on him. Ronan just looks at me with tears in his eyes. He goes, 'You bleaten flute, Rosser.'

I'm there, 'Ro, I'll fix it. Don't worry.'

But he turns his back on me, then he disappears into the gaff, before shouting, 'You're arthur boddicksing evoddy thing up!' then slamming the door behind him.

Sorcha's already in bed when I walk into the room wearing my Leinster rugby base layer, which does me a lot of favours in terms of showcasing the abdominals in a flattering light. She doesn't take the hint, though.

She goes, 'What do you think of either Braddock or Legion?'

I'm like, 'Are they paint colours for the walls of the nursery?'

She goes, 'They're boys' names, Ross. Those are the latest ones we're thinking in *terms* of?'

'Oh,' I go, trying to sound like I actually care, but falling someway short. 'Hmmm.'

She's there, 'So how was Ronan?'

I'm like, 'Yeah, no, he's struggling, to be honest. Kennet says he's going to stop him seeing Rihanna-Brogan.'

'He can't do that, can he?'

'It's Finglas, Sorcha. Who knows what's legal out there?'

'Could you maybe have a word with Kennet for him?'

'I, er, kind of did that already. I don't want to be too critical of myself, but I think I may have actually made things worse.'

'Oh, well, at least you tried. Are you flexing there, Ross?'

'Flexing?'

'Er, your *stomach* muscles?'

'Not really.'

'You look like you're flexing your stomach muscles.'

'I'm not. But, in fairness to me, I *have* been doing a lot of sit-ups recently.'

She yawns twice – one straight after the other – then she goes, 'Oh my God, *all* the yawns!'

I'm there, 'I hope that's not your way of saying you're tired,' and I give her one of my famous smiles.

She instantly goes, 'Forget it, Ross. We're not doing *that*.'

I nod in a hopefully understanding way.

I'm there, 'How long did the midwife say it would be before you were, you know – I hate to use the phrase – but back in the saddle?'

She goes, 'Ross, in case you haven't noticed, there's a *baby* in the room?'

I'm there, 'He's asleep, though.'

I look into the crib and I click my fingers three times.

'Yeah, no, look,' I go, 'he's totally out of it.'

She's there, 'It doesn't matter. Ross, I'm not having sex with you when the baby is in the room.'

'How long is he going to be focking sleeping in here, then?'

'Excuse me?'

'I'm asking the question, Sorcha. When you said you wanted us to get back together, I took it for granted that sex was going to be included in the deal.'

'So what do you want me to do, Ross? Do you want me to put the baby outside on the landing, then bring him back in when you've had your five minutes of fun?'

Five minutes. That's a dig. That's a definite dig.

I'm there, 'I'm pretty sure I can last longer than five minutes, Sorcha. If you want, I can take off this Leinster rugby base layer and prove it to you.'

'No. And keep your voice down. Fionn can hear everything we're saying.'

'No, he can't. He's across the landing.'

'Yes,' she goes, 'but he can hear us through the baby monitor.'

I feel my jaw just drop.

'The baby monitor?' I go. 'You're telling me that Fionn can hear everything that's said and hopefully done in this room?'

'He has to have ears in here, Ross. He's going to be doing all the night feeds.'

'What, so he's going to be popping in and out as well?'

'I told you that he wants to play a full and active role in his son's life. It's important that they have that bonding time to let the baby know who his father is. Fionn's been reading all the books, Ross. He doesn't want his son growing up confused about his role in this house.'

'Well, I'm kind of confused about my *own* role, to be honest?'

'Stop being melodramatic,' she goes, then she switches off her bedside lamp.

And that's when I end up having one of my famous ideas. I tell her that I'm going for a dump, then on the way into the *en suite*, I pretend to stub my toe off the leg of the crib – when, in fact, I give it a fairly hefty kick.

The thing actually moves and the baby wakes up straight away, screaming his head off. Sorcha's there, 'Oh! My God, Ross!'

But I'm like, 'It was an accident, Sorcha. It was a genuine accident.'

The baby is seriously squawking now. And, of course, ten seconds later the door opens and in runs Fionn – no knock or anything.

'What happened?' he goes, still putting on his glasses.

I'm there, 'I don't know. I think your baby needs feeding.'

Sorcha goes, 'He doesn't. Ross kicked the crib.'

I'm there, 'Either way, you better get him out of here. I'm not going to be able to sleep with that focking racket.'

Fionn picks the baby out of the crib, puts his tiny little head to his hort and walks out of the room, bouncing him up and down lightly and making soothing noises.

He's like, 'Shhh, shhh, shhh – it's okay, Baby. It's okay.'

Sorcha yawns again, then turns over in the bed. When I'm sure she's not looking, I reach into the crib and I switch off the baby monitor.

A second later, I think, Okay, why am I switching if off? Let Fionn hear our sweaty goings-on! So I switch it back on again and I turn the volume way up high.

I take off my famous base layer and I climb into the bed. I touch Sorcha on the shoulder, then, in my sexy voice, I whisper, 'Father Fehily used to say that we should try to view every setback as an actual opportunity.'

But she just goes, 'Seriously, Ross, I have zero interest in having sex with you right now.'

And I'm suddenly remembering what marriage feels like.

★

I walk into the Horseshoe Bor and every set of eyes in the place is fixed on the TV in the corner. The old man isn't hord to find. As usual, his is the loudest voice in the room.

'Look . . . at . . . that . . . *hair!*' he goes. 'People say it's a wig, but I can tell you, most assuredly, that it's real! Would you believe me if I told you that I touched it once? Oh, yes! I was lucky enough to play nine holes with the chap – in the famous Doonbeg, if you don't mind!'

The old man runs his hand through his own hair, which most definitely isn't his own.

I notice quite a few familiar faces dotted around the bor. Then I realize that it's basically the entire New Republic porliamentary porty and they're watching the inauguration of Donald Trump.

'Of course, that was back in 2014,' the old man goes, 'when the world considered him an idiot – me included! He gave me his private number! But would you believe I threw it in the bin that Christmas when I did my annual, end-of-year, business cord cull?'

Hennessy is standing beside him. He goes, 'You should have kept that card, Charlie. I said it to you at the time.'

I morch over to the old man and I'm like, 'You wanted to see me?' because that's what his voice message said.

He's there, 'Ah, Kicker! Delighted you could make it! What a day, eh, Ross? I'm reminded of the words of the great Machiavelli: "Something, something . . . Something, something else." You'll take a drink surely?'

I'm there, 'No, thanks. I'm actually *picky* about who I drink with?'

He knows I don't mean that. I'd have a pint with Chris Ashton if the dude was paying.

God, I hate Chris Ashton.

The old man catches the borman's eye and silently mouths the word 'Heineken.'

This Trump dude is up on the screen and he's going, 'Today, January 20, 2017, will be remembered as the day the people became the rulers of this nation again! The forgotten men and women of our country will be forgotten no longer! Everyone is listening to you now!'

The old man picks his phone up off the bor and – I swear to fock – storts tweeting, leaving me standing there like a knob.

Charles O'Carroll-Kelly √ @realCOCK – 9m

Who is looking out for OUR citizens? Certainly not Petty Officer Enda Kenny TD, the man who put the interests of Europe's banks AHEAD of the interests of his own people! We will be paying back debts that had NOTHING to do with us for CENTURIES to come! Terrible deal!

Reply 17　Retweet 36　Like 202　✉

Seriously, he's worse than Honor.

So I whip out *my* phone then and check my messages. Still nothing from Ronan. I feel bad for focking things up for him, but I *was* only trying to help.

'You said in your voicemail that it was *important?*' I go, picking up my pint and knocking back a mouthful.

'Oh, yes!' the old man goes, finally putting his phone back down on the bor. 'There *was* something I wanted to discuss with you! Your mother's birthday is coming up next month – and it's a significant one!'

I'm there, 'Yeah, no, she's seventy.'

'Well, as it happens, she's decided not to reveal the exact number!'

'I've just done it for her. It's seventy.'

'You know how sensitive she is about her age! But I want to throw a surprise porty for her in the house – just to mork the occasion, as it were!'

'Yeah, no, I'm *busy* that night?'

'I haven't even told you when it is yet, Ross!'

'Hey, the last time I clapped eyes on that woman was New Year's Eve in Dundrum when she accused me of trying to kill her.'

'I've tried to explain that to her, Ross! I told her that what you were *actually* doing was sizing up the situation – as was your wont on the rugby field, lest we forget! I told her it was your job to decide tactics and to call the shots – inverted commas! I said, "It's Kicker's natural instinct to stand back and weigh up a situation before throwing himself into the fray – not unlike his good pal, Mister Jonathan Sexton Esquire!"'

'And what did she say to that?'

'Well, you know your mother! You and I have both tried to explain the laws of the great game to her with little or no success! I fear the metaphor was rather lost on her!'

Up on the screen, Trump is all, 'America will start winning again! America will start winning like never before! We will bring back our jobs! We will bring back our borders! We will bring back our wealth! We will bring back our dreams!'

A cheer goes up from all the old man's mates.

He goes, 'How's, em, Sorcha, by the way?'

I just shrug my shoulders. I'm there, 'Fine, I suppose.'

'And the little baby?' he goes. 'What this she's called again? I'm terrible at remembering names!'

'It's a *he*,' I go. 'And they haven't come up with a name yet. They're thinking in terms of Legion and something else.'

He's like, 'Oh, those are *both* beautiful names! I must go and visit her, Ross! Offer her my good wishes and those of all the porty!'

I'm there, 'I wouldn't if I were you. She literally hates your guts.'

'Hates my guts? That can't be right! We've known each for twenty years! Yes, we've had our political differences –!'

'She liked you until you became –'

'What?'

'I don't know – whatever the fock you are these days. A racist.'

'It's not racist to say that Cork people are lazy and refuse to pay their fair share of taxes in society! They're not an ethnic group, Ross, no matter how much they like to think they are!'

'Then you're, I don't know, misogynistical – whatever the actual word is?'

'Women can't parallel park! I'm pointing out something that's a genetic fact.'

Hennessy goes, 'Their brains are smaller.'

'Of course they are, Old Scout! But you're not allowed to point that out nowadays! You can't say anything for fear of causing offence!'

Donald Trump goes, 'A national pride will stir ourselves, lift our sights and heal our divisions! It's time to remember that old wisdom our soldiers will never forget, that whether we are black or brown or white, we all bleed the same red blood of patriots!'

The old man reaches for his phone again. He's un-focking-believable and I don't mean that in a *good* way?

Charles O'Carroll-Kelly √ @realCOCK – 18m

Where are OUR patriots? They're certainly not in Leinster House! We are ruled by men who gave away our sovereignty and squandered the future prosperity of our country in the interests of propping up a FAILING European super state! Sad!

Reply 360 Retweet 940 Like 6,070 ✉

I'm there, 'Can you leave your phone alone for even five minutes? Seriously, you're worse than my daughter.'

He goes, 'Sorry, Kicker! You see, Twitter is my megaphone! It allows me to speak directly to the people without the so-called mainstream media distorting my message!'

Hennessy is staring at his own phone.

'You're trending in Ireland right now,' he goes.

The old man's like, 'You see what I mean, Kicker? So, anyway, will you come? To your mother's surprise *sixtieth* – inverted commas – birthday?'

I tell him possibly – mainly because I'm hoping to get the sponds off him to settle the bor bill in Clontorf Castle.

Nine focking grand, by the way.

Donald Trump's giving it, 'We stand at the birth of a new millennium, ready to unlock the mysteries of space, to free the Earth from the miseries of disease, to harvest the energies, industries and technologies of tomorrow! So, to all Americans, in every city, near and far, small and large, from mountain to mountain, from ocean to ocean, hear these words: you will never be ignored again! Your voice, your hopes and dreams will define your American destiny! Your courage, goodness and love will forever guide us along the way! Together, we will make America strong again! We will make America wealthy again! We will make America safe again! And, yes, together, we will make America great again! Thank you! God bless you! And God bless America!'

Hennessy raises his brandy to the old man. He's there, '*Za zdorovie!*'

And the old man smiles, raises his own glass and goes, '*Za zdorovie!*'

So – yeah, no – I'm in Honor's room and she's filling me in on what happened in school this week. It's important to stay up to date with what's going on in your children's lives. That's what you always hear people say.

'Oh my God,' she goes, 'Sincerity Matthews got a dog for Christmas!'

And I'm like, 'Okay, which one is Sincerity Matthews again?'

'Dad, you *know* who Sincerity Matthews is.'

I do. I rode her mother.

I'm like, 'Yeah, no, is she the one we beat to win the *Strictly Mount Anville* father-and-daughter ballroom dancing competition?'

She goes, 'Exactly! Are you going to let me finish my focking story or not?'

I'm there, 'Sorry, Honor.'

'So Sister Dave asked her what breed of dog it was. And Sincerity was like, "Er, it's a rescue dog!" and I was like, "Okay, *why* do people always say that? As in, a rescue dog isn't an actual breed!"'

'It sounds like you really put her in her place.'

'She was just saying it to be a virtue-signalling bitch.'

'I love the way you're not afraid to call people out. There needs to be more people like us in the world, Honor.'

'But now Sister Dave wants to see you. To talk to you about my behaviour. And my language.'

'Okay, that's good information for me to have. I'll make sure to avoid her for a few weeks and she'll hopefully forget.'

'A focking *rescue* dog!'

'The nerve of the girl. The focking nerve.'

'Anyway,' she goes, 'if you don't mind, I'm about to do a Ten Key Items You Need In Your Wardrobe video for my channel?'

I'm there, 'Cool,' wondering what she's getting at.

'So, er, get the fock out of my *room*?' she goes.

I'm like, 'Okay, I can take a hint.'

I tip back out onto the landing and she slams her door in my face. I can hear suddenly women's voices downstairs and I remember that Sorcha is having all of her mates over today to meet the baby. So I head downstairs, just to see who's there and – being honest – how they're looking.

It ends up being just the usual crew of Sophie, Chloe and Amie with an ie, plus, of course, Lauren, who's brought her two boys – Ross Junior and little Oliver – with her.

This look of fear crosses Ross Junior's face when he sees me. He goes, 'Roth, where are the boyth?' obviously meaning Brian, Johnny and Leo.

I'm like, 'They're upstairs, presumably killing each other. Do you want to go up to see them?'

And – I swear to fock – he goes, '*No!*' then he runs over to his old dear and storts hanging onto her like a drowning man. This kid is, like, ten years old and the boys have just turned four – and *he's* focking terrified of *them*?

He goes, 'Mommy, what if they come thown the thtairth?'

Lauren's like, 'They can't get you – Mommy promises. Do your butterfly pose like Doctor Ellis showed you.'

I'm not making this shit up. Ross Junior uses his two hands to make a butterfly, then he places them in the middle of his chest.

Lauren goes, 'Now just sit quietly like that for two minutes and think about your breathing,' then she turns around to Sorcha and goes, 'He's been diagnosed with anxiety issues.'

'Oh! My God!' Amie with an ie goes. 'My niece suffers with anxiety!' and she sounds like she's focking delighted for the girl. 'She has to go to a Cognitive Behavioural Therapist and everything!'

Ross Junior doesn't have anxiety issues. He's over-focking-mothered – that's the kid's only problem, although I resist the urge to say something by quickly changing the subject. I'm there, 'So what are you lot watching?' because there's, like, some kind of protest on the TV, mostly women, looking seriously pissed off about something.

'It's the Women's Morch on Washington,' Amie with an ie goes. 'There are, like, a million women out on the streets.'

'What do they want?' I go. 'Do we know yet?'

Lauren goes, 'A president who *isn't* a racist, misogynistic Nazi who mocks people with disabilities and brags about sexually assaulting women.'

And I just nod as if to say, 'Yeah, no, good answer.'

Sophie's there, 'I still can't believe he won. Like, does anyone *else* here still have moments where they're just like, "Oh! My God!"?'

'All the time,' Sorcha goes. 'I keep waking up in the middle of the night thinking it's all been a terrible nightmare.'

Amie with an ie points at the screen and goes, 'Oh my God, look at those Hashtag Not My President t-shirts! OMG! Want!' and she whips out her phone, presumably to try to buy one online.

Sophie goes, 'I just keep reminding myself that Hillary won the *actual* popular vote.'

'That's why I don't consider him my president,' Amie with an ie goes.

I'm like, 'Well, there's also the fact that you're not actually American – as in, you don't actually *live* there?'

She looks up from her phone and gives me *the* most unbelievable filthy. 'Actually,' she goes, 'there's a slight, slight chance that I was conceived in the States, when my mom and dad were on honeymoon in, like, *Hawaii*? Even though the dates don't actually add up.'

Someone's brought pink champagne and someone else has brought those sea salt caramel truffles that you get in BTs. I grab a chocolate and go to pour myself a glass of bubbly, except Sorcha goes, 'Er, Ross, we're actually having a *girlie* day here?'

I'm there, 'I don't mind. Where's the baby, by the way?' because he's the reason they're all supposedly here.

'Fionn has taken him out for a walk. He should be back any minute.'

Sophie goes, 'It must be *so* weird for you, Ross, is it?'

I'm like, 'Weird? As in?'

'I don't know – as in, like, *random?*'

'It's not random,' I try to go. 'It's not random at all.'

It's totally focking random.

She's there, 'A lot of goys would be, like, totally weirded out by the situation – no offence, Sorcha.'

All of a sudden, the front door slams, then a second or two later Fionn arrives in, carrying the baby in one of those – I don't exactly know what they're called – but *sling* things that you wear on your front.

'Oh my God,' Chloe goes, 'I love your papoose.'

A papoose! That's it!

I just laugh and shake my head. He really is a ridiculous person.

All the girls get up and stort crowding around him and the baby, going, 'Oh my God! Oh my God! Oh my God!'

Fionn takes off the – hilarious – papoose and hands the little lad to Lauren, who goes, 'Oh my God, Fionn, he's *so* like you!'

He's like, 'Thanks,' even though she never said it was a compliment. Fionn's no scene-stealer, bear in mind.

He squints his eyes – focking glasses – and he looks at the TV. He's like, 'How's the morch going?'

'Amazing,' Sophie goes. 'Scorlett Johansson is there. And we *think* we saw America Ferrera?'

He's like, 'They said on Newstalk that there's a million people on the streets of Washington alone.'

Chloe is like, 'That's, like, ten times more than were at the inauguration yesterday. I just hope Hillary is watching this and thinking, "Oh! My God!"'

Sophie looks at her phone and goes, 'Shit! They only have the Hashtag Not My President t-shirts left in grey! And grey *totally* washes me out!'

Ross Junior is instantly jealous of the baby, of course. He hates not being the centre of attention, so he storts – I swear to fock – literally crying, going, 'Mommy, I'm thcared! What if they ethcape from their room and come thown thtairth?'

Lauren catches me shaking my head. She looks at me and goes, 'Have you got a problem?'

I'm like, 'How about telling your son to stop being such a focking wuss, Lauren?'

Her face just drops. She's like, 'What did you just say?'

I'm there, 'I'm sorry, Lauren, I'm just making the point. He's not anxious, he's just over-mothered.'

'How *dare* you?'

'You wrap a kid up in cotton wool and this is what ends up happening. He's scared of his own shadow, Lauren.'

'You stand there and lecture me about raising children? You've got three boys upstairs who've been banned from the Disney Store –'

'They're banned from Hamleys – get your facts right. They got focked out of the Disney Store. Big difference.'

'– who've been banned from the Stillorgan Bowl, Imaginosity and God knows where else.'

The Aquazone Waterpork in Blanchardstown.

She goes, 'Everyone in this town is talking about those boys and how they're three little Antichrists.'

Sorcha goes, 'Lauren, this is a day for women to support each other, not fall out.'

But Lauren's on a roll now. 'And as for your daughter,' she goes, 'where do I even begin? You have no control over her whatsoever.'

It's funny, I actually don't give a shit about her slagging off the boys. I know half the town is talking about them. They've been mentioned two or three times on *Liveline* and poor Joe Duffy was speechless listening to some of the stories. The three of them are dicks. But I won't have Lauren or anyone else talking shit about Honor.

I'm like, 'You're out of order, Lauren. I'd go even further and say you're *bang* out of order?'

She goes, 'Lecturing *me* on how to raise children!'

Some dude on the TV goes, 'Hillary Clinton is not at the march, but she *has* tweeted her support,' and Sorcha shushes everyone.

She's like, 'Oh my God, she *does* know it's happening!'

The dude goes, 'Just a moment ago, she posted the following message to her Twitter account: Thanks for standing, speaking & marching for our values @womensmarch. Important as ever. I truly believe we're always Stronger Together.'

Sorcha suddenly stands up.

'Oh! My! God!' she goes. 'Why didn't I think of it before? That's what we're going to name our little boy, Fionn!'

Fionn's like, 'What are you talking about?'

And Sorcha goes, 'We're going to call him Hillary!'

I'm driving Sorcha home from Holles Street. She had a follow-up appointment to discuss, let's just say, *women's* stuff? I'm never too interested in the details because of my famously weak stomach, but I ask her how it went anyway – the whole loving husband routine.

'Obviously I don't want you to go into specifics,' I go, 'but is everything okay – I don't know – in that general area?'

Sorcha laughs. She goes, 'Yes, Ross, everything's fine – *in that general area*. They're very happy with how my scars are healing.'

I'm like, 'Okay, T.M.I., Sorcha! Definite T.M.I.!'

And then she says something that puts an instant smile on my face.

'The doctor said I can go back to having sex,' she goes, 'as soon as I want.'

I'm like, 'That's great news,' and I'm suddenly grinning so hord that my face actually hurts. 'So when do you want it and we'll schedule it in?'

'Would you think it was weird if I said now?'

'Now?'

'I don't know why but I'm, like – oh my God – *so* horny all of a sudden.'

'It could be my *Acqua di Parma*.'

'You *do* smell great.'

'Or my Canterbury Vaposhield Hybrid Padded Zip Top. It's new.'

'Maybe it's a bit of both.'

'Hey, we'll be home in a few minutes – we can do something about it then.'

'I don't think I can wait.'

I'm like, 'What?'

She laughs. She's like, 'Seriously, Ross. I actually *don't?*'

I'm there, 'What do you want me to do?'

'Pull in!'

'Pull in? Pull in where?'

'Pull in here!'

Here ends up being a little layby at the Dalkey end of the Vico Road. It's pretty public, it has to be said, but Sorcha doesn't seem to *give* a shit? The second I pull in, the girl is literally all over me. She grabs me by the back of the head and forces my mouth onto hers, then with her other hand, she storts going at the buttons on my chinos like she's rummaging for her shopping trolley token in a pocketful of change.

I'm not going to go into any more detail than that because it's private, husband-and-wife stuff. All I will say is that she manages to pull my – okay, there's no easy way of saying it – *penis* out of my trousers while I unzip her Canada Goose jacket, pull up her jumper and have a bit of fun with the Knowles sisters.

'Oh! My God!' she goes, kicking off her Uggs, then pulling off her jeans with her knickers still inside, 'I have to have it, Ross! I have to have it now!' then she throws her left leg over me, so that she's suddenly sitting astride me, and I tell her that I haven't seen her this horny since the night she drank half a bottle of Advocaat at a charity table quiz to send the Three Rock Rovers women's thirds to a blitz in Eindhoven.

With her face filled with concentration, she moves our pieces into position and she goes, 'Oh my God, this is going to feel so good. Oh my God, this is going to feel so good. Oh my God, this is going to feel so . . .'

Oh, fock!

I've woken up. Yeah, no, I'm lying in bed, covered in sweat, with Sorcha nowhere to be seen. I focking hate when that happens in movies, never mind in real life when I think I'm just about to get some. I end up just putting a pillow over my face and screaming into it. It's been, like, six or seven weeks since I rode Sincerity's mother – my longest losing run in years – and I think it's genuinely beginning to affect me. Backed up doesn't even begin to describe it.

I decide then to just – the usual – rub one out and I stort looking around the room for Sorcha's MacBook. Fun fact about me, I can't actually do it using *just* my imagination? Yeah, no, I've always needed a visual. But I can't find Sorcha's laptop anywhere and it's quite possible she hid it after the last time I borrowed it and forgot to clear the search history.

It doesn't matter because I end up finding a stack of women's magazines on the floor beside the bed, one of which is *Irish Tatler*. There's a sort of hot MILF on the cover of the thing and she's wearing a black, sort of, like, cashmere jumper dress with suede, thigh-high boots. I stort thinking about slowly hitching that dress up around her waist, inch by inch, while kissing that long, slender neck and suddenly my – again – penis is throbbing like a toad's throat.

So I'm lying there, leaning on one elbow, staring at the cover of the magazine while beating one out. And, just as I'm shutting my eyes to bring the horse home, I hear this sudden piercing scream and I open them again to discover that Sorcha has walked into the room.

She's like, 'Oh my God! What the fock are you doing?'

Which I personally think is a little bit of an *overreaction*? I totally get that she's shocked, but she's walked in on me having sex with her actual friends in the past. At least this is only a wank.

I say that to her as well – although obviously in a nicer way.

'I can't help it if I'm backed up!' I go. 'Jesus Christ, Sorcha, I've got balls like focking Galias here!'

And that's when she says something that makes me instantly lose my horn. 'Ross,' she goes, her hand over her mouth, 'that's your mother!'

I'm like, 'What?'

'On the cover of *Irish Tatler*, Ross! It's Fionnuala!'

I look at the picture more closely. Oh, Jesus Christ, she's right.

In my defence, I *could* say that her face has been heavily airbrushed – but, at the same time, like I said, Jesus focking Christ.

Sorcha goes, 'What the fock is wrong with you, Ross?' because

I'm still lying there on my side, my dick draped limply across my thigh now, looking like an empty pop sock.

I'm there, 'There's nothing *wrong* with me, Sorcha. I thought it was just some random MILF. The woman's a disgrace, dressing like that at her age.'

Sorcha just shakes her head – she's seriously disgusted with me – then she turns around and walks out of the room.

I'm about to get up and throw the magazine in the bin, but that's when I notice what it says next to her picture. It's like, 'Fionnuala O'Carroll-Kelly at 60!' and I genuinely laugh.

She's managed to lose a decade somewhere.

I open the magazine and I flick through it, looking for the feature on her. There ends up being fifteen or sixteen pages on the woman and then loads of photographs of her wearing various clothes provided by Brown Thomas, none of which can disguise the fact that the woman is pure trogfilth.

None of the outfits she's wearing does anything for me. There's no reason why they should, of course, and I don't even know why I'm mentioning it.

I read down through the orticle. It's the usual horseshit. Her charity work. All of the causes she's raised awareness – but no actual money! – for. The strength of character it took to forgive after she was wrongly – yeah, spare me! – accused of murdering her second husband. The pride she feels at being described as a – hilarious! – strong, feminist role model. Her 'second shot at love' with the man some people are predicting will be Ireland's next Taoiseach. And her regrets about not having had any . . .

I actually stop dead when I read it. Then I end up having to read it again and again and again. I can't believe it. But at the same time it's there in actual quotes – my old dear going, 'My only real regret in life . . . is that I never had children.'

I end up ringing my old man in a rage. From the dial tone, it's obvious that he's away somewhere. He answers after six rings. He goes, 'Hello there, Kicker!'

I'm like, 'Where the fock are you?'

He's there, 'Hennessy and I are in Moscow, Ross! Little bit of business! And don't worry, I know why you're ringing!'

'Do you?'

'Of course! Enda Kenny's announcement!'

I'm there, 'Excuse me?'

He goes, 'He's promised to deal with his future effectively *and* conclusively – *his* words, Kicker – after his Saint Patrick's Day visit to the White House!'

I'm like, 'That's not why I'm ringing! I'm ringing because that bag of dolphin semen and illegally sourced donor organs who used to call herself my mother is suddenly telling *Tatler* magazine that her one regret in life was not having children.'

He's there, 'I'm sure she didn't say that, Ross!' always prepared to see the good in her. 'What's this our friend calls it? Fake news – quote-unquote!'

I'm there, 'She focking said it. I'm looking at the magazine now: "My only real regret in life is that I never had children." And she looks bet-down in all the photographs, by the way – including the cover.'

He goes, 'She must have meant *more* children! "My only real regret in life is that I never had *more* children!" Yes, that makes sense! I expect it's one of these famous misprints that sometimes happen!'

There's, like, a knock on the bedroom door then and I hear Sorcha go, 'Ross, are you decent?'

I end up just hanging up on the old man and I go, 'Of course I'm decent!'

Sorcha walks into the room after first peeping around the door to make sure.

I'm there, 'I said I was decent, Sorcha. You don't have to turn this into a thing.'

She's like, 'You can't blame me for being shocked, Ross.'

'I told you,' I go, 'I thought it was some random middle-aged looker, like Mary Kennedy or Celia Holman Lee. The photographs have been doctored, Sorcha. I've a good mind to sue – who was it again? – *Irish Tatler?*'

She sits down on the side of the bed. 'Ross, I want to talk to you about something,' she goes. 'I want to clear the air between us.'

I'm like, 'Er, okay?'

God, I love Celia Holman Lee.

'Ross,' she goes, 'I know you're, let's just say, *frustrated* at the moment.'

I'm like, 'Blue balls, Sorcha. Blue focking balls.'

'Which is why I want to address the issue. Look, I know we're back together and everything, but I'm definitely not ready for us to be, you know, intimate yet.'

'By not ready to be intimate you obviously mean not ready to have sex,' I go.

'I need to learn to trust you again.'

'How long is that going to take?'

'It'll take as long as it takes, Ross.'

'That long, huh?'

'But in the meantime, while we're rebuilding our relationship . . .'

'Go on.'

'What would you think of the idea of us going back dating again?'

Naturally enough, I'm like, 'Dating?' wondering is it possibly a trap? 'Are you being serious?'

She laughs. She goes, 'A lot of married couples go on dates, Ross.'

I'm there, 'Do they?'

'Of course they do. Everyday life is, like, so stressful, with work and family and blah, blah, blah. I was reading in a magazine – it might even have *been* that *Irish Tatler* – where this relationship counsellor was saying that all married couples should do it, whether it's once a month or once a week . . .'

I'm there, 'And you'd be totally cool with that?'

She actually laughs. She's there, 'Why wouldn't I be cool with it?'

I don't know is the answer. It's just that she used to be the jealous type – especially when I rode other women.

She's like, 'Do you remember my friend Maoilíosa spelt the Irish way? I met her coming out of Platinum Pilates in Stillorgan the other day and she said that going on date nights was how she and her husband have kept the actual magic in their marriage.'

I'm there, 'Yeah, no, I can see how it'd definitely make things interesting. And if it leads to something else – as in, sex – you're saying that you'd be totally cool with that?'

She goes, 'I kind of *want* it to lead to something else, Ross? That's the whole point going back dating again. Do you want to think about it?'

I'm like, 'No! I mean, I already have. And the answer is yes. Big time.'

I check the time. Fock. It's after two o'clock. I tell Sorcha that I have to go and collect Honor from school.

As I'm passing Fionn's room, I notice that his door is open. I look inside and he's lying on the bed, with Hillary resting on his chest. He's also reading a book, like the attention seeker that he is. I suddenly remember that the baby monitor was probably on in our room. So I stick my head into the room and I go, 'You heard every word of that, I presume?'

He's like, 'Ross, what goes on in your marriage is none of my business.'

'As a matter of interest, did you hear the bit about me wanking off while looking at Sorcha's *Irish Tatler*?'

'Ross, I've got more important things to do than listen to your conversations.'

'What, like reading books? What is it, by the way? Not that I've any interest.'

'It's a book about how communicating with babies in a myriad of different languages can encourage faster brain development.'

'Yeah, good luck with that.'

'You asked me what I was reading.'

'That was just to make the point,' I go, 'that not everything worth knowing can be found in books.'

There's, like, silence between us then.

I'm there, 'And keep that thing about me accidentally wanking over a picture of my mother to yourself.'

*

I'm like, 'Okay, *say* that again?'

JP laughs. He's there, 'You've got to see it, Dude. She opened a bottle of champagne . . . using a focking sword! Well, a sabre. She hit the bottle with the blunt side of it and the top of the bottle separated from the actual neck.'

'And you're saying this is something that's going on in the Shelbourne?'

'The woman is on the actual staff there now. Let me see can I find the video.'

He storts looking through his phone while all the rest of us can do is just shake our heads.

I'm there, 'Ten years ago, I was worried about this country. But then I hear shit like that and it suddenly feels like it's 2003 again.'

This ends up sending us all on a trip down memory lane, where we're suddenly remembering our favourite things about the Celtic Tiger.

'Hey,' Oisinn goes, 'do you remember that oxygen bor in Brown Thomas?'

And I actually laugh because Sorcha used to use it at least twice a week. They basically pumped air up your nose for fifty squids an hour.

'That'sh hilarioush!' Magnus goes. 'You guysh were happy to pay for fresh air and now you refushe to pay for water?'

We *all* laugh. Oisinn's – it still sounds so random – *husband* has been a great addition to the group, even though he knows fock-all about rugby.

JP manages to find the video. He's like, 'Here you go,' and we all end up just watching it, totally mesmerized.

Fionn comes back from the jacks halfway through and looks over JP's shoulder. 'Is that the woman in the Shelbourne?'

And JP's there, 'Yeah, she opens bottles with a sword! Watch!'

And of course, Fionn can't resist rubbing his knowledge in our faces. 'Yeah, it was actually Napoleon's army who started it,' he goes. 'The Hussars would take over a town, find the nearest inn and open all the champagne bottles using their sabres.'

He has to ruin everything with his facts and focking figures. I'm going to be honest with you, I didn't realize that Napoleon was an actual person. I thought he was one of those mythological characters, like Cú Chulainn or Henry the Eighth. Fionn knows a lot more about history than I do, but I'm definitely going to google the focker the next time I'm in the jacks.

I decide to change the subject. I ask Oisinn how work's going. He lost his business, Gaycation Ireland – a tour operator specializing in LGBTQ stag and hen porties – in the same fire that destroyed Erika's ort gallery.

'It's going to take about a year for the building to be rebuilt,' Oisinn goes. 'In the meantime, I'm just working out of the aportment, trying to keep the business going as best I can.'

Magnus goes, 'Alsho, I have applied for a job!'

I'm there, 'A job? Jesus, are things really that bad?'

'Well, there ishn't enough work right now for ush both to take a shalary from the bishnish. Alsho, much ash we love each other, I don't think it'sh shuch good idea for ush to be shtuck in the apartment all day together! Sho I have a job interview on Monday – with Fashebook!'

He means Facebook, and I tell him fair focks.

Christian arrives then. Late as usual. Lauren probably giving him a hord time. I order him a 7-Up. He's nearly two years sober in fairness to the dude. But the first thing he does when he arrives is he storts talking to Fionn about the baby like it's perfectly okay to do so in front of me.

He goes, 'Lauren said you and Sorcha finally settled on a name?'

Fionn's there, 'Yeah, we've decided to call him Hillary,' and he says 'we' like *he* had an actual *say* in the matter?

Of course, he uses this as a cue to whip out his phone and stort showing everyone his photographs, totally forgetting that other people's baby pictures are dull as shit.

'Hillary?' Oisinn goes, looking over his shoulder – *pretending* to be interested? And you can tell that what he's thinking is, Isn't that a bird's name? He's there, 'Hillary after –'

'Hillary Clinton,' Fionn goes. 'But I've also got a great-, great-grandfather on my mother's side whose second name was Hilary with one L.'

Focking spare me, I think. He had fock-all to do with it and now he's just trying to put a positive spin on the story.

Christian goes, 'Hillary de Barra. I have to admit, it does sound very distinguished, doesn't it? Chief Justice Hillary de Barra! President Hillary de Barra!'

It pisses me off in a major way, but I say nothing.

All of a sudden, two absolute honeys walk into Kielys. The one on the left looks like Kate Upton, except with a crooked mouth, and the one on the right looks like, I'm going to say, Chrissy Teigen, except with swimmer's shoulders.

As they walk past, I look the two of them up and down and I go, 'All those curves – and me with no brakes!' and even though the two of them keep walking, the one with the big shoulders definitely smiles.

She's the only focking one, by the way. When I turn around, the goys are all looking at me like I've, I don't know, walked into the Aquazone Waterpork in Blanchardstown and done a shit in the kiddies' pool.

Okay, full disclosure – that's what they were actually talking about the last time I heard the triplets mentioned on *Liveline*. It was Leo who did the deed. He climbed up the mast of the pirate ship, whipped down his trunks and crimped one off into the water below. Poor Joe Duffy, having to listen to that straight after his lunch. He apparently had to go to an ad break while he vomited his tuna melt into a wastepaper basket.

I'm like, 'What? What's everyone's problem?' because they're definitely looks of *disapproval* that I'm getting?

JP goes, 'You can't actually talk to women like that any more, Ross.'

I'm there, 'What do you mean? Do you know how many times that line has worked for me? Focking three! Including once coming out of the Kilkenny Design Shop on a girl who turned out to be a second cousin of Vogue Williams. Twice removed.'

Fionn – it would *have* to be him, of course – goes, 'Ross, haven't you heard about the whole Hashtag Me Too and Hashtag Time's Up thing?'

I'm like, 'Er, yeah – how does that affect me?'

'Well, you can't say things like that any more. It's not appropriate.'

'Who says so?'

'Women say so.'

'Maybe the women *you* know. I've met one or two of them over the years, remember? And I wouldn't bother wasting good lines on them anyway.'

'I'm talking about women all over the world, Ross. They're standing up and they're saying that the predatory behaviour of people like Donald Trump is not acceptable any more.'

'So you're saying that males and females aren't allowed to find each other attractive now?'

'Of course we're allowed to find each other attractive.'

'Because the continuation of the species kind of depends on it, Fionn. That's no offence to you, Oisinn. Or you, Magnus.'

'You can find women attractive, but you're not allowed to talk to them in a way that objectifies them.'

It all ends up spilling out of us then. Let's be honest, the tension between us has been building up ever since I saw that baby's face in the incubator and realized it was too ugly to be mine.

I'm there, 'And you're the expert on what women want to hear now, are you, Fionn? A focking virgin until you were how old?'

'Now you're being childish,' he goes.

'Am I? Why don't you say what this is *really* about?'

'What is it *really* about, Ross?'

'You're still bulling because Sorcha picked me over you.'

'Sorcha and I tried to make a go of it – it didn't work out.'

'Because she's still in love with me and you can't get over that fact.'

'Hey, I've always said it. I don't think you're worthy of her.'

'And that's why you're giving me filthies just for paying another girl a compliment.'

'I just think Sorcha deserves better. She's taken you back and you're already up to your old tricks.'

'That's where you're wrong, Dude. Sorcha is happy for us to have an open relationship.'

He's there, 'An open relationship?'

'Don't pretend you didn't hear what we were talking about the other day in the bedroom. We're both going back dating again. She was the one who actually suggested it.'

He actually laughs in my face, then he goes, 'Ross, when Sorcha said she wanted you to go back dating, I think she meant –'

I'm like, 'What? What do *you* think she meant, Fionn – you with all your experience of women?'

But he just goes, 'Nothing. You're right,' which is weak from him.

I'm there, 'Rides my wife while we're on a break, then tries to lecture me about what is and isn't appropriate? Yeah, thanks for that, Fionn, you Specsavers-bothering fock.'

I look across the pub and I notice that the two birds – Kate Upton and Chrissy Teigen – are looking over in my direction.

So I'm like, 'I'm going to go and talk to these two beautiful ladies over here. Unless, of course, me being physically attracted to them offends them on some level. I'm sure they'll let me know.'

It's a cracking line to leave on.

I tip over to the two girls and I'm like, 'Hey, how the hell are you?'

They're both like, 'Yeah, no, great.'

I go, 'The name's Ross, by the way. I'm sorry about what I said – I hope you didn't find it offensive.'

Chrissy Teigen goes, 'I thought it was funny.'

I'm like, 'Funny? That's interesting,' staring across the bor at Fionn. 'Very interesting.'

Then they introduce themselves to me. Kate Upton's name is Faolan Fitzgerald and Chrissy Teigen's name is Eabha Barnes.

I've decided that Faolan is the one whose number I'm going to be leaving here with tonight. I look her in the eye and I'm there, 'When I saw you walk in here tonight – I swear to God – my knees actually *buckled*?'

Faolan goes, 'Er, *I'm* actually engaged to someone. Eabha is the single one.'

So I look at Eabha and I go, 'When I saw you walk in here tonight – blah, blah, blah.'

She laughs and she's there, 'I'll have a glass of Cab Sav, if you're offering.'

And I'm there, 'Oh, I'm offering,' making it sound dirty. 'I'm definitely, definitely offering.'

'Oh my God,' she goes, 'you're actually *really* cute!'

And it's nice to know that *I* haven't lost *my* touch – even if everyone else has lost *theirs*?

2

It's All about the Bag!

Honor hands me her phone and she goes, 'Here!'

And I'm like, 'Okay, *why* are you giving me your phone?'

'Because,' she goes, 'you're going to film a video for my YouTube channel.'

I'm like, 'Really?'

'Oh my God,' she goes, 'why are you making such a big deal out of it?'

I'm there, 'Because it *is* a big deal, Honor. I love when we do shit together.'

Honor goes, 'Whatever. The only reason I'm asking you is because my tripod hasn't arrived yet and I need both of my hands free to do an unboxing.'

'Okay,' I go, 'what's an unboxing?'

'Watch and you'll find out. Just point the camera at me and stort recording, okay?'

So I do what I'm told. I've kind of made that a general rule in my dealings with my daughter.

She goes, 'Hi, goys, welcome back to my channel!' in this really sweet voice that I've – *honestly?* – *never* heard her use before. 'Now, last week on Love Honor and Obey, it was *all* about the bag! It's a favourite topic of mine and I know from your comments that it's literally a favourite topic of yours, too!'

Seriously, it's like she's had a personality transplant or something.

She goes, 'We covered investment bags and I showed you some pieces from my collection, everything from my medium Chanel classic flap to my Hermès So Black Birkin! Today, I'm going to show you ten style hacks to make any bag look AH-MAZING – even if all you can afford is High Street! But first, I'm going to stort today's video with an unboxing! Yay!'

She claps her two hands together and I keep filming her as she reaches under her bed and pulls out a lorge cordboard box.

'And what I'm going to be unboxing,' she goes, 'is not a bag but something that's been on my wish list for – oh my God – ages! And it's something that my amazing, amazing dad bought for me! Dad, turn the camera on yourself and say hello to everyone!'

I turn the phone around and I stort waving, going, 'Hey, goys!' probably getting a bit carried away if I'm being honest.

Honor goes, 'So this is Ross, everyone! And he's my dad! So, Dad, why don't you tell my viewers what *you're* wearing today?'

'Excuse me?'

'Come on, why don't you talk us through your Outfit of the Day? We'll stort with the top! Describe that top you're wearing!'

'This? This is, like, the new Leinster home jersey.'

'The new Leinster home jersey! And who's it by?'

'Er, Canterbury.'

'So describe it to us! What is it about this top that you love?'

'I don't know. They're my team. I mean, if their new jersey was a black bin-liner, I'd walk around wearing it.'

'That is *so* funny! And what are those three stors above the crest?'

'Oh, that's, like, how many times Leinster have won the Heineken slash European Cup. Actually, you asked me what I loved about this top? I think what I love most about it is that they've left room for a fourth stor – there, look! A lot of people would consider that arrogant. Not me.'

'And what about the trousers? Tell us about the trousers!'

I point the camera down at my trousers. I'm there, 'The trousers are just, like, beige chinos. I should say classic beige chinos.'

She goes, 'By?'

'Dockers. They're basically the only trousers I ever wear. And that's for the last, like, twenty years.'

'If it's not broke, don't fix it, right? And the shoes – show us the shoes!'

I point the camera at my feet.

I'm there, 'These are, like, Dubarry Docksiders – otherwise known as Dubes.'

'And they're, like, boat shoes, aren't they?'

'That's right, yeah.'

'And do you *own* a boat?'

I actually laugh.

I'm like, 'No, but I'm also wearing boxer shorts – and I've no intention of getting into a fight.'

Honor bursts her hole laughing. And, even after she *stops* laughing, I can see the absolute delight in her face. She's obviously thinking, Oh! My God! This is pure gold!

She goes, 'Okay, camera back on me now! So that was my dad, everyone! As you can see, he's actually hilarious! He's also *the* best father in the world – even though I'm obviously biased – and also a really, really cool person! For instance, he buys me absolutely everything I ever ask for, no questions asked, including this lovely surprise, which I'm about to unbox and which he insisted on paying full price for, even though it was supposedly in the sale!'

It's a definite moment for me, hearing my daughter talk about me in such gushing terms. I actually don't know how I manage to keep the phone steady.

'Now,' she goes, 'camera on the box please, Dad!'

I have to admit, it's a bit random that people actually want to watch this shit – basically a stranger opening a box with a dress in it.

Anyway, she pulls the ribbon off the thing.

'It's so exciting!' she goes. 'And I'm *so* glad to be sharing this moment with all of you!'

She lifts the lid off the box and there's all this, like, pink tissue paper inside. She pushes it to one side and goes, 'Here it is! O! M! G! Love! Dad, are you getting this?'

I'm like, 'Yes, I am.'

'Could you maybe get a close-up of it?'

I do.

She goes, 'This is my brand-new Gucci tulle dress with shooting stors! The print was inspired by Creative Director Alessandro Michele's fascination with outer space! But this is the first time that the famous shooting stor motif has featured in a children's collection! And I have to say, I love, love, LOVE these embellishments – the sporkling crystals and the multi-coloured sequins!'

And that's when, all of a sudden, I hear Sorcha calling me from our bedroom down the landing. She's like, 'ROSS? ROOOSSS???'

'Ignore her,' Honor goes. 'Now, I absolutely adore this fabric, even though it's man-made, but the quality is still ah-mazing! Goys, this dress is SO stunning! I can't lie!'

But Sorcha keeps going, 'ROOOSSS??? ROOOSSS??? ROOOSSS???'

I'm there, 'I better go and see what she wants,' and I stop filming.

'Just open the door and tell her to go fock herself,' Honor goes. 'That's what *I* always do?'

I'm there, 'You can't really get away with that kind of thing when you're married to someone, Honor. It's hord to explain.'

'Let the father of her focking baby go instead, then.'

'Again, that'd be my usual instinct, but it's complicated. Look, we'll finish this in a few minutes, okay?'

'Fock's sake,' she goes as I'm leaving the room. 'Why does she have to be such a needy bitch?'

I tip down the landing to our bedroom. Sorcha is sitting on the edge of the bed, breastfeeding Hillary.

She's there, 'I was calling you for ages.'

I'm like, 'Yeah, no, I was just doing a bit of vlogging with Honor.'

'You?'

'Yeah, no, she asked me to film her while she was doing an unboxing.'

'Did she?' she goes, sounding definitely jealous. 'I was watching her YouTube channel this morning. You know she's already got two hundred subscribers?'

I'm there, 'I'm not surprised. She's an absolute natural in front of the camera. She got me to do a bit as well. My Outfit of the Day.'

I notice the hurt look on Sorcha's face.

She goes, 'She was obviously taking the piss out of you.'

I'm there, 'I don't think she was. You seem definitely jealous.'

'It's just I genuinely believed that fashion was the thing that would eventually bring me and Honor closer together. I'm not being a bitch, Ross, but the only reason she's involving you in this thing is to hurt me.'

'Right.'

'Again, that's not me being a bitch.'

'So you said. What did you want, by the way?'

'Oh, yeah, the reason I called you – do you remember we were talking about the two of us going on dates again?'

'I certainly do.'

'Well, have you arranged anything yet?'

I'm like, 'Errr,' because it still feels *weird* talking about it? As it happens, I got Eabha's number and there's been quite a bit of texting back and forth – filthy, a lot of it. I think she might be a fockaholic. I'm there, 'Er, yeah, no, *kind* of?'

'Right,' she goes.

'And you're still cool with that, are you?'

'Absolutely. Why wouldn't I be?'

'No reason.'

She finishes feeding – *such* a random name – Hillary, then storts burping the dude.

'So what about you?' I go. 'Have you arranged anything yourself?'

She's like, 'No, I'll let you take the lead on this one.'

In fairness, I think she's going to have a lot more difficulty finding dates than I will. I'm not being a dick, but she's a mother of five these days – and even though she's talking about going back to yogalates, she's never going to get her body back to its original factory setting.

She goes, 'I'm so glad we're doing this, Ross.'

I'm there, 'Yeah, no, I am, too. I can't believe my luck, in fact.'

'So when's it happening?'

'You want to know?'

'Of course I want to know!'

'Well, I was going to suggest maybe Monday night?'

'Great! And *where* were you thinking in terms of? Hey, what about that new Japanese-American fusion restaurant on Camden Street?'

'Everybody Loves Ramen?'

'It's supposed to be amazing.'

'Yeah, no, I've heard good things myself. That's actually a good call.'

'What time were you thinking?'

'Well, I'm supposed to be meeting Devin Toner in Grogan's at seven. He's trying to sell me his old Bodymax Ab Cruncher. I'll probably head for the restaurant straight from there.'

'So what do you think – eight o'clock?'

'Sounds about right, yeah.'

'Do you want me to book it?'

'You? Would that not be a bit weird for you?'

'No, I don't think so.'

'I think I'd find it a bit weird if the roles were reversed. I might just book it myself if that's okay?'

'Whatever you think, Ross. Oh, speaking of restaurants, we're going to Roly's for Sunday lunch tomorrow.'

'What? Who?'

'You, me, Honor and the boys. Mom and Dad are treating us.'

'I focking *hate* your mom and dad!'

'Ross!'

'I do, though. And so does Honor.'

'Monday is the first day of Dad's release from bankruptcy – and he wants to bring us out to say thank you for putting a roof over their heads for the last two years.'

'Focking dickhead.'

'Ross, he's being nice.'

'He's incapable of being nice. Anyway, I'd better go back to Honor's room. We're doing ten style hacks to make any bag look AH-MAZING – even if all you can afford is High Street!'

Sorcha's old man is full of it. And when I say *it*, I obviously mean *shit*?

He goes, 'It's just our little way of saying thank you, Sorcha – for putting up with us.'

He doesn't thank *me*, by the way. *Or* Honor? There's not a word of appreciation for Brian, Johnny and Leo – although they're not actually sitting here. They're running wild around the restaurant.

Sorcha goes, 'It's like I said to you this morning, Dad. You can go on living in the Shomera for as long as you like.'

I'm there, 'Obviously we don't mean that literally.'

'Yes, we *actually* do, Ross.'

'I thought it was more a figure of speech, like, Have a nice day! or, Drink responsibly!'

Sorcha's old man goes, 'It'll be one more year, then we'll be out of your hair, Sorcha.'

I end up nearly choking on a mouthful of Pomme Anna. I'm like, 'A year?'

Honor says it at the exact same time. She's like, 'You must be focking joking.'

He goes, 'I'm hoping to go back into practice soon. We'll get some savings together and rent a little apartment – maybe somewhere in Dalkey, so we can be close to Hillary.'

Honor looks at me. 'A year?' she goes. 'Can you believe this shit?'

I don't get a chance to call the focker out on it because all of a sudden some dude passes our table on the way back from the jacks and goes, 'Edmund Lalor! How the hell are you?'

He's a big, fat focker with a voice that's about twenty decibels louder than it needs to be. The kind of dude you'd see playing golf in Milltown with my old man and nodding in agreement when my old man says shit like, I don't know, women shouldn't be allowed to use credit cords while they're premenstrual.

The dude goes, 'How the hell are you? Are you looking forward to the Six Nations?'

And Sorcha's old man goes, 'Yes, it, em, should be a good one this year. A lot of interesting match-ups.'

There are few funnier things in life than Sorcha's old man trying to pretend that he knows anything about rugby. He quickly changes the subject by introducing the orsehole to his wife and daughter.

'This is Hugh Hess,' he goes. 'Specializes in Family Law. Hugh, you know my wife. And this is my daughter, Sorcha.'

He says fock-all about me and Honor, by the way.

'Ah,' this Hugh dude goes, 'you're the famous Senator!'

Sorcha's like, 'Yes, I was one of An Taoiseach's nominees to Seanad Éireann – although, at the moment, I'm on, like, *maternity leave?*'

You can see the dude's eyes immediately glaze over.

'That's, er, great,' he goes. 'Edmund, when are we going to see you back in the Courts again?'

'As it happens,' Sorcha's old man goes, 'I was just discussing that very thing. From today, I am officially no longer a bankrupt!'

'Well, then I'm going to get the waiter to send you over a bottle of champagne!'

'You don't need to do that, Hugh.'

'I'm doing it! No arguments!'

'Actually, I was just telling my daughter that I'm hoping to return to practising in the coming months – maybe start looking at office space by the summer.'

The dude fishes about in the inside pocket of his suit jacket and whips out his business cord. 'Ring me,' he goes, 'as soon as you want to come back. I can send a lot of work your way. I've got way more cases than I can handle.'

Sorcha's old man goes, 'Thanks, Hugh. Thank you so much.'

The dude eventually focks off back to his table and Sorcha's old man stares at the cord like it's, I don't know – name some famous painting? He's there, 'I think my luck is changing at long last!'

He's delighted with himself. The proverbial dog with a boner.

Sorcha's old dear goes, 'It's fate, Edmund! That's what it is!'

He's like, 'Hugh was right, by the way, Sorcha. It's maybe time you started thinking about returning to the Upper House of the Oireachtas and the vital business of governance!'

It's weird because I didn't hear the dude say anything *like* that?

Sorcha goes, 'Er, I've just had a *baby*, Dad!'

But her old man's like, 'Fionn's more than capable of looking after Hillary. Haven't you seen how he is with him? Besides, you've got a country to run.'

A country to run? Wind your focking neck in, I think. It's only the Seanad!

He goes, 'Such a pity that he couldn't make it today. Where did you say he was again?'

Sorcha's there, 'He's having lunch with his own family. His sister is home from Vancouver. She's meeting Hillary for the first time.'

I rode his sister. Several times. I don't mention it, though. I suppose there's no real reason to.

The dude goes, 'He was chatting away to Hillary this morning in French, would you believe? Not only French but German, too. Did you know that children born to multilingual parents perform better in IQ tests? It's in this book he's reading.'

'Absolutely fascinating!' Sorcha's old dear goes – and she seems to genuinely mean it.

'Fionn speaks seven different languages fluently. Were you aware of that, Sorcha?'

There's a bit of him that will never forgive her for getting back together with me. I'm about to call him a focking knob-end when Honor all of a sudden looks up from her phone and goes, 'Oh my God, Dad, you are *so* popular!'

I'm like, 'Me? What are you talking about? Is it rugby-related?'

'People – oh my God – *love* you,' she goes. 'The video with your Outfit of the Day in it has got, like, 526 views!'

Sorcha tries to get in on the act then. She's there, 'Oh my God, I was going to suggest doing a video on juxtaposing metallics with pastels! I've always said I can't believe it's not an actual thing, Honor!'

But Honor totally burns her. She just goes, 'They love our chemistry, Dad. Listen to the comments they left underneath my unboxing video: "You are so lucky to have a dad who buys you everything you want! My dad is a stingy focking prick who doesn't buy me shit!" And then this one: "Oh! My! God! You two are like a comedy act! Your dad is HILARIOUS! Boxer shorts! Lol! And I love that funny voice he does!"'

I'm thinking, What funny voice?

Honor goes, 'And then – oh my God – this one: "I hope my dad and your mom both die, then I hope my mom and your dad get married, because then you'll be my sister and I'll have LOADS of clothes AND a cool dad!"'

It's all good stuff for me to hear. But what's even nicer for me is the *reason* Honor's reading the comments out? She's reminding me that I'm a great father, despite the fact that I can't speak any languages other than English – and that not especially well.

I'm there, 'Did you hear all of that, Sorcha? Maybe read out some more, Honor. It'd be interesting to get a few other people's takes on what kind of a father I am.'

Sorcha goes, 'Yeah, I think we've maybe heard *enough*, Ross?'

A waiter arrives at our table then. Brian, Johnny and Leo are with him and their faces are covered with what looks very much to me like chocolate ice cream. The dude goes, 'Can I ask you to please keep a closer eye on your children? We don't allow guests into the kitchen to help themselves to dessert.'

And that's when the shouting suddenly storts. It's coming from the far side of the restaurant – someone going, 'Are you deaf or just fucking stupid? I said my lunch is cold!'

It's Hugh Hess – and he's absolutely rinsing some poor waitress. She's trying to argue back, except he's shouting over her with his big focking Law Library voice. He's going, 'I'm not interested in *when* you brought the food or how long it's been sitting here. It should have been sufficiently hot to allow me to go to the bathroom, then talk to an old colleague on the way back to the table. But it wasn't. And now it's lukewarm – at best. It's fucking unacceptable.'

Everyone in the restaurant just freezes. Out of the corner of his mouth, Sorcha's old man goes, 'Hugh has a terrible temper. He's famous for it.'

The waitress storts crying then, but the dude doesn't let up. He's like, 'Oh, here come the tears! The fucking snowflake generation! Can't accept criticism!'

People are just, like, staring with their mouths open, feeling sorry for the poor girl but at the same time not wanting to get involved. And that's when Honor suddenly stands up.

'Will you *shut* the fock up?' she goes.

There's, like, gasps in the restaurant. It's Roly's, bear in mind.

The dude goes, 'I beg your pardon?' like he's in court or something.

Honor's there, 'No one actually *gives* a fock whether your lunch is cold or not! So sit the fock down and shut the fock up, you fat, pompous wanker!'

You can hear people all over the restaurant struggling to hold the laughter in. Sorcha's old man is obviously thinking about all the work he's been promised because he turns suddenly pale. He looks at Honor with genuine hatred in his eyes and goes, 'That's enough from you!'

And I'm like, 'No, it isn't,' and then *I* stand up? 'You heard what the girl said – pipe the fock down.'

'Who the hell are you?' Hugh Hess goes, proving that *he* knows fock-all about rugby as well.

I'm there, 'I'm her father.'

'Well,' he goes, 'may I suggest that you take a firmer hand in parenting that child?'

But I'm like, 'No, you may not. Because Honor has turned out just fine. And I'm proud to have raised a daughter who's prepared to stand up to men like you.'

He stands up then? He's there, 'Men like me? Perhaps you'd like to explain what you mean by that phrase? But I'd advise you to be solicitous in your choice of words – there *are* witnesses present.'

'Er, bullying a *waitress*?' I go. 'It's the easiest thing in the world to pick on someone who's not allowed to answer back – and tell you what you actually are. Which is a prick, in case you were wondering.'

It's un-focking-believable! Everyone in the restaurant storts suddenly *clapping*? It's, like, a full-on round of applause. Then the cheering storts. I pick my napkin up off the floor and I throw it on the table, then I walk out of the place, stopping only to shout, 'End of!' at this Hugh Hess tool. 'End! Of!'

I walk down the stairs and out onto Ballsbridge Terrace. I stand there for a seconds, then I realize I left my focking jacket behind. But then a few seconds later, Honor comes out carrying it.

She's like, 'You forgot this.'

And I'm there, 'Thanks. I didn't want to have to walk back in?'

'Why did you even leave?'

'I actually don't know. It felt like a real mic drop moment. I think I just got swept along by all the clapping and cheering. I'd barely even touched my venison.'

'Do you want to go back in?'

'Not really, no.'

'Neither do I.'

'Let's just go home, will we? Sorcha can bring the boys.'

I'm about to stort walking back to the cor.

'Wait a minute,' Honor goes. 'Did you mean what you said?'

I'm there, 'In terms of?'

'What you said about being proud of the way I am.'

'Hey, I definitely meant it. I love that you're not afraid to call it.'

'You're the only one. Everyone else thinks I'm horrible.'

'You're not horrible. Not all the time. Plus, you've other qualities.'

'Did you see *his* face?'

She means Sorcha's old man.

I'm like, 'Yeah, no, it *was* funny. No work for him, I'm presuming.'

She goes, 'Dad, I know I'm not always nice to you, but I want you to know that I think all those people who left comments under my unboxing video are right. You *are* the best dad in the world.'

She throws her orms around me and I kiss her on the top of her head. The best dad in the world. I'll take that. But then suddenly my phone rings. It's a number I don't recognize, but I end up taking the call anyway. I'm like, 'You've got Ross!' which is a thing I've gone back to saying when I answer the phone.

It ends up being a woman's voice. She's like, 'Ross? Ross O'Carroll-Kelly, is it?'

And I'm like, 'Depends. Who wants to know?'

She goes, 'I'm Garda Sheila Ní Fhloinn from Finglas station. I just wanted to let you know that your son has been arrested.'

I hear Ronan before I see him. I'm standing in the gorda station on Mellowes Road and I can hear him roaring from the area of the cells.

'Let me ourra hee-or!' he's going. 'I'll fooken moorder evoddy

54

last one of you doorty Fascist bastards – smell of bleaten bacon off the lot of yous!'

I haven't heard him talk like this since he was ten years old and a Gorda Youth Diversion Officer seized his imitation Glock. I apologize to the woman.

'Sorry,' I go. 'He obviously learned that from his mother's side of the family.'

She smiles at me. She's not great. And that's with the greatest will in the world.

'We know Ronan of old,' she goes and she says it in, like, a *fond* way? 'Tina used to bring him in here – he couldn't have been more than five – and she'd ask us to lock him up for the weekend. Scare him straight, she said. He'd refuse food for forty-eight hours, then he'd walk out of here on Sunday night, shouting, "You didn't break me, you dirty pig fucks!"'

I laugh. I shouldn't, but I do.

I'm there, 'He was very funny as a kid. I thought he'd left those days behind him, though. So what did he do?'

She goes, 'We arrested him last night outside the home of his wife. I believe they're separated?'

'Yeah, no, they were never actually *married*? Thanks be to fock.'

'We received a complaint. There was an allegation that he was planning to snatch his daughter.'

'Let me guess who the allegator was. Did he have a st . . . st . . . st . . . st . . . stutter?'

She laughs. I think she genuinely likes me. It's such a pity she's horrendous.

She goes, 'Let's just say we know Kennet Tuite of old as well.'

I'm there, 'There's no way Ronan would have tried to snatch Rihanna-Brogan. He probably just wanted to see her.'

'Look, the lads all love Ronan in here. But we have to take these reports seriously. Plus, he was drunk and abusive.'

From the cells, I can hear him shout, 'I'll thrag evoddy last one of yous bastoords up in front of fooken GSOC . . . Yous fooken bastoords!'

I'm there, 'Has he been chorged with anything?'

She goes, 'Nothing. We hoped he might just sleep it off. If you can calm him down, he can go now.'

She presses some buttons on a keypad on the wall, then leads me into a corridor where all the cells are. Ronan's in the last one. She unlocks the door and in I walk.

He goes, 'They took the laces out of me bleaten rudders, Rosser!'

He looks like shit. I say it to him as well. I'm like, 'You look like shit.'

Then he stares at me as if he's seeing me for the first time. He goes, 'You doorty, bleaten collaborator, Rosser! You doorty, bleaten collaborating fook!'

I'm there, 'Ro, calm down!'

'Let me ourra hee-or!' he shouts. 'I want to speak to Nordeen O'Suddivan!'

I'm like, 'Ronan, you need to –'

'Doatunt ted me what I neeyut, Rosser. It was you what fooked it up for me. You're the readon Kennet woatunt let me see me thaughter. You're the readon Ine not godda see her grow up.'

Then he storts hammering on the cell door with his fists, going, 'I want evoddy bleaten one of yisser identification numbers! I'll have yous all up in front of the fooken Ombudsmadden . . . you fooken . . . fooks!'

That ends up being the last straw. I grab him by the front of his shirt and I swing him round and slam him up against the wall.

He's like, 'Get yisser hands off me, you fooken Fascist! I want your PPS number!'

And I'm there, 'Ro, will you shut the fock up?' and I say it in such a way that he knows I'm suddenly serious. 'Just do yourself a favour and listen, okay? They're happy to release you now if you promise to calm down. Come on, I've got your sister waiting outside in the cor.'

He's like, 'Hodor?'

Oh, that brings him to his senses. He worships her like she worships him.

I'm there, 'Honor, exactly. And I know she's looking forward to seeing you. So what do you say?'

He stares at me for a good ten seconds without saying a word, then he puts his forehead on my shoulder and storts literally just *sobbing*?

He goes, 'I joost wanthed to see me beauriful thaughter. Me lubbly little R&B. I habn't seen her in a munt, Rosser. It's killing me.'

I'm there, 'You *will* see her. You've just got to be patient. In the meantime, you've got to keep going, Ro. I rang Tina on the way here. She said you haven't gone back to college since Christmas.'

'I've no inthordest in coddidge addy mower.'

'Well, how are you going to provide for your daughter if you don't get a good job?'

I know I'm on shaky ground here myself.

I'm like, 'You want her to be proud of you, don't you?'

He's there, 'Of course I bleaten do!'

'Well, she's not going to be proud of you if you end up with a criminal record and you're on the literally dole. Now, look, I know I focked things up for you, Ro, but I'm going to put it right.'

I bang on the door three times to summon the famous Sheila.

She opens the door. 'Have you calmed down?' she goes.

And Ro's like, 'Ine soddy, Sheila. Ine soddy for all the thrubble Ine arthur causing and Ine soddy for saying you were ugly.'

There's no point in telling her that she's not because that would just come across as insincere. So instead I go, 'Everyone's a critic, huh?'

Sheila's there, 'Don't worry about it, Ronan. I hope the next time we see you in here, you'll be a solicitor, representing Nudger or Buckets of Blood or one of that crowd.'

He goes, 'Thanks for being so wontherstanding, Sheila.'

I tell her the same thing, then I lead Ro outside to the cor pork. We're halfway to the cor when the woman calls me back. She goes, 'Can I have a quick word with you?' and it's all very cloak-and-dagger.

I tell Ronan to get into the cor and talk to Honor. I'll be with him in a minute. Then I walk back to Sheila.

'If this is what I think it is,' I go, trying to let the woman down gently, 'I think it's only fair to point out that I'm kind of married.'

She goes, 'What?' and it's straight away obvious that I've got the wrong end of the stick.

I'm there, 'Sorry, what were you about to say?'

She goes, 'I was just going to tell you that there's something interesting you might like to know about Kennet Tuite.'

'I call him K . . . K . . . K . . . K . . . Kennet. The stuttering fock.'

'He's having an affair with his wife's sister.'

Okay, *now* she has my attention. I'm like, 'You are shitting me! Are you talking about Mordeen?'

She's there, 'Dordeen's sister, yeah.'

'How do you know that?'

'You hear all sorts of things in here,' she goes. 'They've been at it for years. Every Friday afternoon. Out near the airport.'

I'm there, 'My old man gives him Friday afternoons off work to let him sign on.'

'I don't know whether he signs on or not. But between three o'clock and four o'clock you'll find him on Collinstown Road – near where all the plane-spotters hang out – having sex with Mordeen in the back of a black Bentley.'

I laugh. I'm there, 'That's actually my old man's cor. Between three and four o'clock, you say?'

'Every Friday,' she goes.

I'm so happy, I could nearly kiss the woman. But – yeah, no – I manage to restrain myself.

Jesus Christ, Eabha can talk. I mean, the girl hasn't shut the fock up since she sat down at the table and that's not me being sexist.

'I'd describe myself as religious,' she goes, 'but I wouldn't be, like, *super* religious? As in, I'd be definitely spiritual – never walk under ladders, never open an umbrella indoors – but then I also like different bits from different, I suppose, belief systems, as in I'd go to Mass, mostly if someone died, but at the same time I've also read bits of the Koran – well, I've got a collection of memes from it on my phone – but then I'm also into, like, Far Eastern philosophy – incense, candles, all of that, like I actually *own* seven oil burners, as in, I literally can't see an oil burner without literally buying it. By the way, have you ever read *The Secret*?'

She's been talking like this for the last fifteen minutes. She's either very, very nervous or – more likely – coked off her tits.

'Speaking of the whole spirituality thing,' she goes, 'did you see that guy in California who's going to court to try to change his star sign – oh my God, you *must* have heard about it because it was, like, all over social media this week, as in, he was born Capricorn but he identifies as Taurus – no, it might have actually been Virgo, and I was saying to my friend Faolan, who you met in Kielys that night, I think it'd be amazing if that came in here as well, as in, if there was a referendum, I would definitely vote yes, as someone who's always felt like a Sagittarian trapped in a Pisces body.'

I'm there, 'Eabha, are you, like, *on* something?'

'Er, *yeah*?' she goes, like it's the most ridiculous question she's ever heard. It suddenly feels like it's 2003 again.

She's like, 'Do you want some?'

I'm there, 'No, you're good. It's just, you know, I'm trying to read the menu here and I can't concentrate because you're . . .'

Gibbering away like a focking Rhesus monkey.

But she *looks* fantastic, in her defence. Like I said, Chrissy Teigen, except with the humungous shoulders that I've mentioned once or twice and also – I didn't cop this the night I met her in Kielys – but very blinky eyes, although that's possibly down to all the cola she's been stuffing up her hooter.

'I'm sorry,' she goes, 'I haven't asked you a single thing about you, oh my God, I love Udon noodles if they're what I think they are, you mentioned that night in Kielys that you're a rugby player, I have to say I've never really been into rugby, as in, I'm not your typical rugger-hugger, although I did have sex with a Leinster player once, even though he turned out to be a Leinster *hockey* player?'

She stands up from the table. She goes, 'I just have to, you know . . .'

I'm like, 'Jesus Christ, can we maybe order first, Eabha? I'm focking storving here.'

She's there, 'I won't be long,' even though she was gone fifteen focking minutes the last time.

Off she focks anyway. I'm sitting there thinking, I honestly thought dating was going to be more fun than this. I order another bowl of prawn crackers and I whip out my phone. I notice that I've had three missed calls from Sorcha and also two text messages.

'Been trying to ring u,' the first one says. 'So sorry, couldnt get Hillary to settle, running 20 mins late,' and then the second one is like, 'Nearly there, go ahead and order if u want, im not going to have a storter, can u order me the dry-aged angus wantons in hot and sour kimchi soup which everyone says are amazing!!!' and I'm obviously thinking, What the fock is she talking about?

And that's when I look up to see her walking through the door of the restaurant. I'm up off the chair and straight across the floor, going, 'Er, what the fock are you doing here?'

The question seems to confuse her.

She's like, 'What am I doing here? We're on a date night! Have you been drinking?'

My entire body turns cold and I'm suddenly replaying our conversation in my head. And then the penny finally drops. When she suggested we stort dating again – Jesus Christ! – she obviously meant dating each other!

God, I'm so focking thick. As Aoibhinn Ní Shúilleabháin once said of me, during the course of a withering put-down in Gleesons of Booterstown: 'If you showed Dermot Bannon the inside of your head, he'd say the design was focking minimalist.'

Sorcha goes, 'I'm so sorry I'm late. Fionn was good enough to drive me in,' and I'm remembering my conversation with him when, I suddenly realize, he was actually going to tell me that I got the wrong end of the stick, but then he obviously changed his mind.

She's there, 'How's Devin Toner?'

And I'm like, 'Er, not happy,' and at the same time I'm looking over my shoulder at the door of the Ladies'.

She's there, 'Did you *buy* the Ab Cruncher in the end?'

And I'm like, 'Er, no. It didn't have adjustable resistance settings and he wanted eighty snots for the thing. Like I said, he called me a focking timewaster. Do you know what, Sorcha? I think we might actually go somewhere else?'

'Somewhere else? No way! I've heard *so* much about this place!'

And then she spots my famous Henri Lloyd hanging on the back of my chair. She goes, 'Oh my God, you got an amazing table!' and she storts making her way across the restaurant to where me and Eabha have been sitting.

I have to think fast. Cometh the hour, blah, blah, blah.

I spot a waiter – a Chinese slash Japanese dude, if that doesn't sound too racist – walking towards me. I stop him, pull him to one side and go, 'Excuse me, I don't want to cause a scene but my wife says there's a girl snorting coke in the Ladies'.'

The dude looks back at me like he doesn't really know what to do with this information.

So I go, 'I'm only mentioning it because my wife is actually a cop – and you could be closed down for allowing your premises to be used as a basic *drug* den?'

Oh, that shakes him. He suddenly storts shouting something in Chinese – slash Japanese – then he storts running in the direction of the jacks, followed by three or four other waiters, again, all Chinese slash Japanese.

Sorcha watches the scene open-mouthed, along with everyone else in the restaurant. I make my way over to the table and I sit down.

Sorcha goes, 'Oh my God, I wonder what's going on?'

I'm like, 'Yeah, no, it's very hord to know, isn't it?'

Five seconds later, the door of the Ladies' flies open and the waiters emerge, literally carrying Eabha and running towards the door with her like she's a focking battering ram.

Sorcha goes, 'Oh! My God!'

Everyone does, in fact.

And I'm like, 'The drama, huh?'

But then suddenly – right out of left field – she goes, 'Whose coat is this on the back of my chair?'

And I'm thinking, Oh, fockety, fockety, fock-fock!

I'm like, 'Sorry, Sorcha?' somehow managing to keep my cool.

'There's a coat on the back of my chair,' she goes. 'It's H&M. I actually own it in camel.'

I stand up and I'm like, 'Someone must have left it behind – whoever was here before us. I'll give it to the old Maitre Dude.'

I grab the coat and I make my way to the door. Eabha is outside on Camden Street and she's making a bit of a scene. She's, like, roaring at the waiters, going, 'I'm going to sue your focking orses! Do you have any idea who my father is?'

They wouldn't. Like I said, they're not from round here – again, *not* racist.

When she sees me, she goes, 'Come on, Ross, let's go!'

But I'm there, 'Er, I think I'm going to stay.'

'Stay? What the fock?'

'You know, I'm storting to wonder are me and you even suited, Eabha? The other thing is that I'm actually storving. And I've heard good things about the dry-aged angus wantons in hot and sour kimchi soup.'

'Are you focking seriously telling me you're going to eat in there? After these fockers accused me of snorting cocaine?'

The waiter I tipped off ends up letting me down in a big-time way then. He points at me and he goes, 'He tell us!'

Eabha's there, 'Excuse me?' and she looks at me then, expecting an explanation.

'His wife see you!' the dude goes. 'She police lady!'

Jesus Christ. Who'd be a whistleblower, huh?

'Your wife?' she goes, then she storts looking over my shoulder into the restaurant. She obviously sees Sorcha sitting in her old seat because she goes, 'You never said you were married.'

I'm like, 'It was all a major misunderstanding,' and I throw her coat to her. She doesn't catch it and it lands in a puddle on the ground.

'You focking wanker!' she goes and she makes a run at me, except the waiters grab her. They hold her back and they threaten to ring the Feds unless she focks off pronto.

'Anyway,' I go, 'it was nice meeting you, Eabha,' even though it was about as much fun as a lapdancer with a cough.

I give her a wink, then I tip back inside to my second date of the evening. I sit back down opposite Sorcha, then I stort looking through the menu again. I'm there, 'I might end up having the Thai red chicken curry.'

Sorcha smiles at me, but then she's suddenly looking over my shoulder, going, 'Oh! My God! *What* is that girl doing?'

I look around. Through the window, I can see Eabha holding above her head what looks very much to me like a Dublin Rental Bike. And she's ranting and raving.

I'm thinking, She's not going to throw that through the window, is she? She wouldn't. There's no actual way.

But then she does. There's, like, a humungous crash as the window shatters in a million pieces and the people sitting next to it scream and run for cover.

Eabha shouts, 'You focking orsehole, Ross! I'll focking get you for this!'

A second or two later – much to my relief – I notice two Gords arrive and they drag her, kicking and screaming, into the back of a squad cor.

Sorcha goes, 'The poor girl! I wonder what's wrong with her?'

I'm like, 'Who knows what goes through women's heads sometimes?'

Sorcha smiles at me. 'I know you're going to say I'm being paranoid,' she goes, 'but for a second there I thought she actually said your name!'

I can't look her in the eye, so I keep staring down at the menu.

'Like you said yourself,' I go, 'it's all about you learning to trust me again.'

'Oh! My God!' Honor goes.

I'm like, 'What's wrong?'

Because I'm collecting her from school and those are literally her first words when she opens the door of the cor.

She's there, 'Someone *filmed* what happened in Roly's the other day? On their actual phone? It's all over social media, Dad! We've gone viral!'

I'm not a fan of that expression and I'm saying that as someone who's had a few scares in the old STD area over the years.

She's there, 'Everyone's putting up links to Love Honor and Obey and saying, "This is the father and daughter in that video! They have their own style vlog!" Dad, I had, like, two hundred and fifty subscribers yesterday. Now I've got, like, seven and a half thousand!'

She checks her phone, then goes, 'Oh my God, it's nearly eight thousand now! And everyone's talking about the amazing dynamic between us – how we're more like best friends than father and daughter.'

I stort the cor – and that's when I spot Sister Dave waving at me across the yord. I can tell straight away that she wants a word.

I'm like, 'Fock, she's seen me.'

Honor goes, 'Just drive off, Dad.'

'I can't drive off. Like I said, I accidentally made eye contact with the woman.'

Five seconds later, she's standing next to the cor. I wind down the front passenger window, although I keep the engine running.

I'm like, 'What seems to be the problem, Sister Dave?' like I've been pulled over for a breathalyser test.

The woman goes, 'I wanted to talk to you about Honor.'

Honor's there, 'Tell her to fock off, Dad.'

Of course that gets the boys going.

Brian's like, 'Fock off!'

And Leo's like, 'Stupid focking bitch!'

I do the usual and pretend I can't hear it. I'm there, 'Is this about what Honor said to Sincerity Matthews? Because I actually agree with her. A rescue dog isn't a breed. Unless it was *literally* a rescue dog – as in, one of those dogs they use to find people who are lost in the snow. A little barrel of brandy tied to his neck. Is it called a Saint Bernard or something? Sorry, I'm a deep thinker sometimes. It comes out of nowhere.'

But Sister Dave isn't interested in talking about dogs – or *any* pets. She goes, 'Oh, we've moved on from that. I want to talk to you about a different matter.'

I'm like, 'Namely?'

'Your daughter informed me this morning that she doesn't wish to make her Confirmation.'

Honor's there, 'Yeah, what I actually said was that you can shove your Confirmation up your orse.'

I'm just, like, nodding along, as if the point that Honor just made was both reasonable and valid.

I'm there, 'And can I just ask you, Honor – in terms of background – why don't you want to make your Confirmation?'

She goes, 'Er, because I don't believe in *God*?'

I'm there, 'Don't you?' because it comes as a genuine shock to me. I thought all kids believed in God.

She goes, 'Of course I don't believe in him! Because there's no such focking thing! It's just a bullshit story that someone made up two thousand years ago to make poor people happy with having nothing!'

I turn around to Sister Dave and I'm like, 'Is this true?'

She says fock-all. She's obviously a company woman.

'Yeah, right!' Honor goes. 'A fairy visited a virgin and told her she was pregnant with God's baby!'

I actually laugh. I'm there, 'Whoa, give me that again, Honor?'

'A fairy,' she goes. 'Visited a woman. Who'd never had sex before. And said she was going to have God's baby.'

'Who's claiming that?'

'It's in the Bible, Dad.'

'Is it?'

'Er, it's kind of the whole *point* of the book?'

'Well, I don't remember that storyline. But, now that you say it, it does sound like total horseshit.'

I look at Sister Dave.

'And presumably,' I go, '*you're* saying it's *not* horseshit?' because I'm still prepared to hear both sides.

She's there, 'I am not here to discuss the issue of faith with you. I'm here to tell you that Honor is *expected* to make her Confirmation along with all of the other girls in her class.'

In the rear-view mirror, I watch Brian put his hand down the back of his trousers, fart into his hand and then – this is definitely new – blow it, like a kiss, at Sister Dave. Honor cracks up laughing. I'm wondering, where the fock did he learn that?

Sister Dave tries to just ignore it. She's there, 'When Honor's mother was a student in this school, she was a member of the St Madeleine Sophie Barat Prayer Circle.'

'Yeah,' Honor goes, 'just because *she* was a gullible sap doesn't mean *I* have to be?'

I look at Sister Dave and go, 'You heard the girl. If she's not into it, she's not into it.'

But Sister Dave goes, 'You haven't heard the last of this,' and she turns on her heel – lace-up brogues never went out of style with that lot – and she walks back into the school.

'Ugly bitch!' Leo shouts after her.

I put the cor into Drive and we're suddenly out of there. I'm thinking about Sorcha, though. I'm like, 'You know your old dear is going to go ballistic when she finds out you don't believe in God?'

Honor goes, 'I don't care. When was the last time you saw *her* go to Mass on a Sunday? When was the last time you saw her actually pray?'

'That's true. The word hypocrite comes to mind. Well, let's not tell her about the whole you-not-making-your-Confirmation thing. I think it's the kind of thing we should maybe spring on her at the last minute – maybe even the morning *of*? It'll be too late for her to do anything about it then.'

Sorcha's in bad form and I know what it's about. Yeah, no, people have been texting her and WhatsApping her and Facebook messaging her all week about the video of me and Honor calling out that dude in Roly's. They're saying – I'm guessing – fair focks to your husband and fair focks to your daughter, who's very much a chip off the old block.

So it's understandable that she's a little bit jealous about all the attention we've been getting, especially because she just sat there with her mouth open while the dude was ripping the waitress – I'm going to use the phrase – a *new* one?

She goes, 'Seriously, Ross, I've had, like, five times more messages about this than I did about Hillary being born.'

I'm there, 'I have to admit, I can't believe how huge this thing has suddenly become. Three people said it to me this morning when I was in Cavistons. I'm talking about three people separately. The word hero is being bandied about online. Not to rub your nose in it.'

She's doing her yogalates exercises in the bedroom, by the way, and she's so irritated that she ends up having to pull out of a pose, mid-pigeon.

'Don't get me wrong,' she goes, 'I'm actually really proud of Honor for daring to speak truth to power.'

She wouldn't be saying that if she heard the way she spoke to Sister Dave yesterday.

She goes, 'It's just that Dad is very upset, Ross.'

I'm there, 'Only because she cost him work. Her vlog is suddenly massive, by the way. You know she's got, like, nine thousand subscribers now? Although I *should* say *we*?'

Sorcha pulls a face like she's not impressed, but I can tell that she definitely is.

She goes, 'I still say she's only using you to punish me.'

I'm there, 'Why would she want to punish you?'

'Er, for having another *baby*?'

'I don't know about that, Sorcha.'

'Ross, Honor never had *any* interest in clothes. And she knows I've always talked about having my own style vlog – that was before I went into politics. Seriously, she's doing it to make me jealous. And you're being totally used, by the way. You just can't see it.'

She asks me then if I've seen her noise-cancelling headphones and I tell her they're under the bed. She grabs them and she puts them on – presumably to drown me out, because I've spent the last twenty minutes reading her out some of the comments about our video on style hacks to make any bag look AH-MAZING – even if all you can afford is High Street! My favourite description of us is still 'a father and daughter act with a very funny but beautifully touching dynamic' or 'a sort of foul-mouthed Ant and Dec'.

That's when I hear cor doors slamming outside. I look out the window and it ends up being Fionn's old pair and his sister, Eleanor, who used to look like Carolyn Lilipaly but sadly *doesn't* any more? They're getting out of a silver Renault Megane and the girl is carrying a present, which is presumably for Hillary, and a bunch of flowers, which are presumably for Sorcha.

Fionn steps out of the house to greet them, carrying the baby in that famous focking papoose of his. He goes, '*Regarde, Hillary! C'est ta grand-mère! Et ton grand-père! Et ta tante! Elle s'appelle Eleanor!*'

I have literally no idea what language he's attempting to speak. But I stort thinking about him trying to fock me over – yeah, no, driving Sorcha to the restaurant where he *knew* I was having dinner with another bird? And I suddenly have an idea.

I turn around and Sorcha's doing the plough pose with her headphones on and her eyes shut tight. I open the window a crack and a second later – okay, this is going to sound *possibly* childish? – but I shout, 'OH, THAT'S FANTASTIC, SORCHA – KEEP DOING THAT!'

She can't hear me. God, those headphones are unbelievable. But Fionn *definitely* hears me – and so do his old pair and his sister, because when I peek at them through the closed curtains I can see them looking up at the window in shock.

I go, 'THAT'S IT, SORCHA! YEAH! YEAH! YEAH! YEAH! THAT'S IT, DIG YOUR NAILS INTO MY ACTUAL BACK!'

This must all come as a massive disappointment to Fionn, who presumably heard Sorcha tell me a couple of weeks ago that she's not ready to let me put my P in her V – and now here we are, in the middle of the day, going at it like farm dogs.

'HOME STRETCH NOW!' I shout. I look at Sorcha – still oblivious. 'THAT'S IT! BRING IT HOME, GIRL! GO ON, SORCHA! BRING IT HOME! ATTAGIRL! BRING IT HOME! BRING IT HOME!'

It's hilarious. They're all just, like, staring at each other in shock. I keep the commentary going while Fionn invites his old pair into the house. I can hear his old man downstairs in the hall, suddenly talking very loudly, either trying to drown out my shouting or trying to alert us to the fact that there's someone in the gaff.

He's going, 'DID YOU HEAR ENDA KENNY'S BREXIT SPEECH?' at the top of his voice. 'SAID A LOT OF THINGS THAT NEEDED TO BE SAID, I THOUGHT. I ESPECIALLY AGREED WITH WHAT HE HAD TO SAY ABOUT THE IMPORTANCE OF PROTECTING THE GOOD FRIDAY AGREEMENT, AS WELL AS ENSURING FREE MOVE-MENT ON THESE ISLANDS AS PART OF THE COMMON TRAVEL AREA.'

I really let them have it then. I move over to the bed and I stort banging the headboard off the wall really hord, going, 'SLOW DOWN, HORSEY! SLOW DOWN, HORSEY! OH MY GOD, HERE IT COMES! OH MY GOD, HERE IT COMES! OH MY GOD, HERE IT COOOMMMEEESSS!!!'

And it's hilarious because Sorcha is still lying on her back with her feet around her ears, not a clue what's going on.

I tip downstairs then – at the same time opening my trousers and unbuttoning my shirt. I can hear voices coming from the kitchen. Again, Fionn's old man is trying to warn me of their presence. 'IRELAND'S MEMBERSHIP OF THE SINGLE MARKET AND THE CUSTOMS UNION HAS BEEN THE CORNER-STONE OF MUCH OF OUR SOCIAL PROGRESS OVER THE LAST GENERATION!'

I walk into the kitchen, buttoning my chinos. And – holy fock! – what are the chances? Sorcha's old pair are in there as well.

I'm there, 'Hey, Fionn, I didn't hear you come in!' and I pretend to be all out of breath. 'Nice to see you, Mr and Mrs de Barra. Hey, you too, Eleanor. I hear you're still with your husband. What was his name again?'

She doesn't answer me. Like the rest of them, she's in shock. It's one o'clock in the day, bear in mind.

I go to the fridge, grab the milk and drink it straight from the corton, shirt still open. Sorcha's old man is just, like, staring at me with total and utter hatred in his eyes.

I can honestly say it's the angriest anyone has been with me since two summers ago when I took Sean O'Brien's brand-new Massey Ferguson out for a spin without his permission and managed to turn the thing over while performing a three-point turn outside the entrance to Tullow Business Pork.

'In the name of God,' Sorcha's old man goes, 'would you *please* button up your shirt?'

But I'm like, 'Hey, it's my house. No one asked you to keep dropping in unannounced. And you're more than welcome to fock off at any point – especially now that you're not bankrupt any more.'

A second or two later – hilarious – Sorcha comes downstairs and into the kitchen and, I swear to God, she's actually *limping*?

'Oh my God, hi!' she goes, talking to Fionn's old pair and sister. 'I didn't hear you come in!'

Sorcha's old man goes, 'Clearly!'

Sorcha's there, '*Hola, Hillary! ¿Cómo estás?*' and then she limps across the kitchen and switches on the Nespresso. 'Oh my God,' she goes, 'I think I actually injured myself upstairs, Ross! I know I shouldn't put my back under so much pressure, but it just felt so good! Actually, my toes are still tingling!'

I can't even begin to describe the faces in the kitchen – Fionn's especially. I can't even look at them in case I laugh in their faces. Instead, I whip out my phone and pretend to look at that. I've got a text message from the old man, reminding me about the old dear's surprise birthday porty this weekend.

I take another long drink from the milk corton.

'Oh my God,' Sorcha goes, 'it literally feels like the ground is still moving.'

There's a look of definite jealousy on Eleanor's face. Like I said, she's had the pleasure.

Sorcha's old dear goes, 'Perhaps this is a case of – what's this phrase your daughter sometimes uses? – T.M.O.?'

Sorcha goes, 'Oh, it's hordly that, Mom. Why shouldn't I talk about it? Even though I know you're not into it yourself, I *was* actually going to recommend it to Fionn's mom.'

Fionn's old dear's jaw practically hits the floor. It's Fionn who ends up having to go, 'Sorcha, I really don't think –'

She's like, 'I think it'd be good for you, Mrs de Barra! It would definitely help loosen you up a bit!'

Jesus Christ!

'Sorcha!' Fionn's old dear goes.

'No, seriously,' Sorcha goes. 'I'm trying out this new position where I put my two legs in the air, my legs slightly open and then –'

Sorcha's old man goes, 'Darling, do you *really* think this is something you should be telling us?' and he sounds angry enough to kill me.

Sorcha laughs. She's like, 'I know it's not your kind of thing, Dad, but when you get into it – as in, *really* into it? – you want to do it all the time. *And* everywhere you go. Ross and I used to do it – obviously discreetly – while we were queuing for the checkout in Superquinn.'

I end up having to leave the room then because I'm about to herniate myself trying *not* to laugh?

Behind me Sorcha goes, 'Now, who's for a cappuccino?'

It feels like Friday will never come around – but obviously it eventually *does*? It's, like, just after lunchtime when I text Ronan and tell him not to worry – he's going to see his daughter very, very soon. Then I stick the address into the satnav and hit the M50.

Half an hour later, I'm crawling along Collinstown Road, with my eyes peeled for the old man's matte-black Bentley Mulsanne, my hort beating in double-time with the excitement of it all.

I drive past little groups of people – sad focks mostly – looking up at the sky for planes coming in to land, passing the binoculars between them. That'll be Fionn in about twenty years, I think to myself, then I have a little chuckle at the idea. Him and Hillary – plane-spotting. The poor kid.

Then I spot the cor. It's porked at the end of a laneway to my right. I'm looking at the rear end of the thing. And even from this distance, I can see that they're giving the suspension a real workout. The thing is going up and down like Mel Gibson on a three-day bender.

I pork up about twenty yords behind them, then I get out of the cor and close the door as quietly as I can. In the boot, I've got the megaphone that Sorcha used to bring everywhere with her when she ran for election in Dublin Bay South.

I whip it out – I'm talking about the megaphone – then I creep up behind the cor.

The windows are all steamed up. Inside, I can hear them going hord at it and the conversation is comical. *He's* there, 'Your t . . . t . . . t . . . t . . . t . . . t . . . t . . . t . . . tits are l . . . l . . . l . . . l . . . l . . . l . . . l . . . l . . . l . . . l . . . lubbly, so thee are.'

And *she's* going, 'Jaysus, you hab me bleaten sweating, so you do.'

'Throy not to get addy f . . . f . . . f . . . f . . . fake tadden on the seats. Ch . . . Ch . . . Cheerdles woatunt be happy abourrit.'

'Ine lubben what you're doing to me, Kennet.'

'Ine l . . . l . . . l . . . lubben it as weddle, Mordeen.'

'Say sometin romaddentic.'

'Wh . . . wh . . . wh . . . what are you wanton me to say?'

'Call me that nayum.'

'What nayum?'

'The nayum you used to call me.'

'Geebag?'

'No – *arthur* you realized that you ditn't hate me, that you reedy lubbed me and you wished you'd maddied me instead of Dordeen.'

'Oh, yeah – th . . . th . . . th . . . th . . . th . . . the Rowuz of Finglas West.'

'The Rowuz of Finglas West! I lub that Kennet, so I do. Call me it again – while you're riding me.'

'The Rowuz of Finglas West.'

'No, woork it into a seddentence!'

'Ine lubbing riding you – the R . . . R . . . R . . . R . . . R . . . Rowuz of Finglas West.'

Much as I hate to break up this romantic scene, I've got actual shit to do, so I put the megaphone up to my mouth and – in my best bogger accent – I go, 'Eermed Gyardai! We have you surrounded, you filty animals! Gesh oush of thet vehickle with your hends in the eer!'

I can hear Kennet in the cor going, 'W . . . W . . . W . . . W . . . W . . . W . . . W . . . What in the nayum of J . . . J . . . J . . . J . . . J . . . J . . . Jaysus!'

Then I can hear Mordeen going, 'Will you gerroff of me, you bleaten dope!' and Kennet's like, 'Ine th . . . th . . . th . . . th . . . throying, ardent I?'

I decide to up the stakes.

I'm there, 'Gesh oush of thet vehickle with your hends in the eer – or we will open fire in five seconds. Five . . . four . . . three . . . two . . .'

The back door suddenly flies open. *She* gets out first – totally storkers except for Kennet's chauffeur hat, which she's using to cover her money box. Her flabby, fake-tan-covered body is glistening with sweat – she looks like something you'd see on a blind potter's wheel.

A few seconds later, the other door opens and out climbs Kennet, again, totally naked except for his shoes and socks and his mickey sticking out like the little peg on the front of a bird box.

His opening line is a cracker. He goes, 'It's n . . . n . . . n . . . n . . . n . . . not whorrit l . . . l . . . l . . . l . . . l . . . looks like, Geerd.'

That's when he suddenly cops that it's not a Gord at all, that it's me.

He's there, 'What in the nayum of J . . . J . . . J . . . J . . . J . . . ?' and, as he's saying it, I whip out my phone and I stort filming the two of them – focking Skobeo and Juliet.

He's like, 'R . . . R . . . R . . . R . . . Rosser? What are you bleaten playing at?'

He's slower on the uptake than even me. I'm there, 'I'm blackmailing you, Kennet.'

I keep filming him, capturing the moment when the penny finally drops.

He goes, 'You d . . . d . . . d . . . d . . . d . . . d . . .'

And I'm like, 'I'm going to stop you there, Kennet – before you say something you regret.'

The two of them are, like, shivering with the cold. It's the end of January, bear in mind, and they're both in the focking raw.

I'm like, 'Here's what's going to happen now. You're going to ring Ronan right this second and you're going to tell him that he can see Rihanna-Brogan any time he wants. Day or night.'

'Ast me b . . . b . . . b . . . b . . . b . . . boddicks.'

'You either do it or Dordeen finds out about you and the focking Rowuz of F . . . F . . . F . . . F . . . Finglas West here.'

He stares at me for a long time. But he knows he's beaten. He goes, 'I'll rig him when I get howum arthur woork.'

But I'm there, 'No, you'll ring him right now – while I'm standing here. Go and get your phone.'

He just shakes his head, then reaches into the back of the cor for his trousers. He takes the phone out of his sky rocket, then dials Ronan's number.

'He's not answerdon,' he straight away goes.

I'm there, 'Let it ring.'

Eventually, Ronan answers.

Kennet goes, 'S . . . S . . . S . . . S . . . Stordee, Ro?'

I'm there, 'Tell him you're ringing to apologize for the way you acted.'

He goes, 'Ine, er, rigging to apodogize for the way I acted. You hoort Shadden and I'll n . . . n . . . n . . . nebber forgib you for that.'

I'm like, 'Stop adding your own line in. Tell him you acted like a prick. Tell him or I'm sending this to Dordeen right now.'

He goes, 'Look, I acted like a p . . . p . . . p . . . p . . . p . . .'

I'm like, 'Yeah, this week, Kennet.'

'. . . p . . . p . . . p . . . p . . . p . . . prick.'

'Tell him he's a great father.'

'You're a gr . . . gr . . . gr . . . gr . . . great fadder.'

'Say, "Unlike me."'

'Uddenlike m . . . m . . . m . . . me.'

'Tell him you're a terrible father.'

'Ine a t . . . t . . . t . . . t . . . t . . . teddible fadder.'

'And a stuttering fock.'

'And a st . . . st . . . st . . . st . . . stutterdon fook.'

'Now tell him he can see his daughter any time he wants.'

'You can see yisser thaughter addy toyum you waddant.'

'Now tell him you're a stuttering fock again.'

'Ine a st . . . st . . . st . . . st . . . stutterdon fook.'

'Now hang up.'

He hangs up.

And I'm like, 'Good work, Kennet! Good work! Now, I'm going to leave you two love birds to get back to doing whatever sick shit you were doing to each other!' then I turn away with the intention of just making my way back to the cor.

But then I notice all the plane-spotters staring up at Ryanair Flight Whatever-the-Fock coming in to land and I think to myself, Why not give those poor fockers a *real* thrill?

So I hold the megaphone up to my mouth and I go, 'ATTEN- TION! THERE IS A NAKED MAN AND WOMAN OVER HERE AND THEY'RE HAVING SEX IN A CAR! REPEAT! THERE IS A NAKED MAN AND WOMAN AND THEY'RE HAVING SEX IN A CAR!'

And suddenly they're all looking over in *our* direction – one or two of them through their binoculars. Kennet and Mordeen dive back into the cor.

Kennet goes, 'Ine godda get you b . . . b . . . b . . . b . . . back for this, Rosser!'

Then he pulls the door shut.

Delma tells us all to shush. She's there, 'They've just pulled into the driveway!'

There's, like, eighty or ninety of us crammed into the kitchen. Most of them the old dear knows from her various campaigns to stop things coming to Foxrock – Travellers, the Luas, German supermorkets.

Delma asks me to switch off the lights, which I do. A few seconds later, the front door opens, then it slams shut and I hear voices in the hallway.

The old dear's going, 'I really can't *abide* poor people! Can't you do something about them, Charles?'

'Unfortunately,' the old man goes, 'a lot of them are my voters, Fionnuala! Come down to the kitchen for a moment, will you, Dorling!'

She's like, 'Why?'

'Just come with me! There's something I want you to see!'

Then a few seconds after that, the kitchen door opens and the light is switched on. All of the old dear's mates shout, 'SURPRISE!' and the old dear just stands there with her mouth open so wide you could paddle a focking canoe into it if you were brave enough.

She turns to the old man and she says the most hilarious thing. She goes, 'Is this about my drinking?'

Seriously? She sees all of her friends in her kitchen and automatically assumes it's an intervention.

She's there, 'If this is going to be a lecture, I can tell you now that you're wasting your time.'

I haven't laughed so much at my old dear since the time in O'Brien's on Newtownpork Avenue when she walked up to a cordboard cut-out of Tom Doorley and asked if it could recommend a really good First Growth Bordeaux.

The old man goes, 'It's a porty, Fionnuala! Look at the balloons and the bunting there!'

She sees the banner stretched across the kitchen with 'Happy 60th Birthday, Fionnuala!' on it and she seems suddenly happy. Or at least she manages to arrange her features in such a way that it could *pass* for a smile, although a dog would probably consider it an attack grimace.

Delma throws on the music – Bublé, obviously – then everyone storts knocking back the gin and the Veuve Clicquot and telling the old dear that she doesn't look anything like sixty. Which is true. She looks her *actual* age. Which is seventy.

I spend the next hour trying to get her on her own, but instead I've got the old man in my ear, going, 'Scotland – eh, Ross?'

Yeah, no, Ireland lost to Scotland today.

I'm like, 'What?'

He goes, 'You know, I still can't believe, with all your knowledge, that Joe Schmidt isn't banging your door down! It's not like he's so well off for assistant coaches! I don't blame you for looking a bit down in the proverbial dumps! It's either that or you've suddenly realized that it's only eight weeks until Theresa May is due to trigger Article 50 of the Treaty of Lisbon! Don't be nervous, Kicker! Leaving the European Union will be the best decision

Britain has ever made – just as it will be for Ireland when the time comes!'

I'm just like, 'Yeah, shut the fock up,' because I notice the old dear on the far side of the kitchen. She's hugging Delma, who's obviously hammered herself because she's crying her eyes out and telling her that she loves her and she's so happy for her.

The old dear's going, 'Thank you, Delma. Charles and I wanted you to be the first to know.'

I walk over to her and I'm like, 'Let me guess – you've finally found a surgeon who can remove your forked tail?'

She just goes, 'Hello, Ross! Aren't you going to wish me a happy sixtieth?'

I'm there, 'If this was ten years ago, I might. Delma, would you maybe fock off and let me speak to my supposed mother alone?'

Delma's like, 'How rude!' but she thankfully *does* fock off?

'I saw the magazine,' I go.

She's like, 'Which magazine are you talking about?'

'You *know* the one I'm talking about. The one with you on the cover in the dress and the boots. It did nothing for me, just to let you know.'

She has the actual gall to laugh. She goes, 'What a strange thing to say! Why would it *do* anything for you?'

'I'm saying it didn't, thankfully.'

'I'm your mother!'

'You wouldn't have known that reading the orticle. Yeah, no, I loved your line about how you regretted that you never had children. And don't deny it. It was on the same page as the picture of you lying on the bed in the red Heidi Higgins dress, the white faux-fur stole and the pink ballerina-style court shoes.'

'Yes, I loved that dress!'

'Again – I can't see any man getting turned on by it. I suppose you're going to deny saying what you said? You're going to claim it was, like, a misprint?'

'It wasn't a misprint, Dorling.'

She actually *smiles* when she says it? Her mouth is disgusting – like someone sat on a punnet of raspberries.

I'm there, 'Really? I was hoping you were going to say you were maybe misquoted.'

She's like, 'I wasn't misquoted either.'

'So that was your revenge, was it? The thing you were banging on about in Dundrum that day?'

Again, she smiles. I'll never eat raspberries again in my life.

She goes, 'Oh, that's only the beginning of it, Dorling.'

I'm like, 'Meaning?'

But she doesn't answer me. Instead, she storts tapping the side of her champagne flute with a pastry fork to let everyone know that she's about to make a speech.

'This should be good,' I go, meaning the opposite. It'll be shit.

She's there, 'I just wanted to say thank you all for this wonderful, wonderful birthday surprise!' loving being the centre of attention, of course. 'Thank you to Charles, the love of my life, for arranging it. I was born in 1957 . . .'

I shout, 'Was that the number of the room in the hospital?' and I end up being shushed by everyone – Delma the loudest of all.

The old dear goes, 'And during my sixty years on this planet, it's fair to say that I have lived through quite a bit.'

'The Famine!' I go. 'The dinosaurs!'

'There have been good times and bad times. And by my side, through it all, have been you – my dearest, dearest friends. And that's why I'm delighted that you are all here tonight, not just to share my birthday with me but to hear my wonderful news. Charles and I have an announcement to make.'

She's going to say they're getting married again. She'll have to focking wait. It'll be years before his divorce from Helen comes through. But she doesn't say that at all. That's *not* her big announcement. It's something else. It's something that, when I hear it, makes me feel like I've just fallen from a great height. She looks me dead in the eye when she says it as well.

She goes, 'Charles and I . . . have decided to have a baby!'

3.

Unboxing This Year's Most Essential Lifestyle Accessory!

The old man's secretary tells me that he's busy and he doesn't wish to be disturbed. This is in, like, the *Dáil*, by the way? So I'm obviously wondering what the fock he could be doing that's so important?

I just morch straight past her and into his office. The secretary – who's not great – comes pegging it in behind me, going, 'I'm sorry, Charles! He just burst in!'

'Who is it?' I hear him go.

Yeah, no, his voice is coming from the other side of a door to the right. It could *possibly* be a jacks?

She goes, 'He *claims* to be your son.'

'Ah,' the old man goes, 'that'll be the famous Ross!'

'I didn't know whether to let him in or not. It's just, I didn't know you *had* a son.'

I'm like, 'For fock's sake!'

He goes, 'It's quite alright, Francine! His story checks out! I'll be out in a moment, Ross! I'm just finishing up here!'

'I haven't come for a pleasant chat,' I go. 'I want to talk to you. About what the old dear said the other night. In her speech. The drunken sow.'

This Francine one focks off and leaves me talking to the dude through the door.

'Refresh my memory,' he has the actual balls to go. 'What was it she said again?'

'Er, she said you two dopes were having another baby?'

'Oh, yes – well, I was as surprised as you were, Kicker!'

'So she *was* just shit-faced?'

'No, what I mean is that we *were* planning to keep the entire

81

thing *entre nous* – pardon the French – until we had a pregnancy to confirm!'

'What?'

'I don't know what possessed her to tell everyone! She was probably – as you said – very excited!'

'Sorry, did I miss something in Biology when I was at school?'

I missed everything in Biology when I was at school. I was on the S, I shouldn't need to keep reminding people.

He goes, 'What are you talking about, Kicker?'

I'm there, 'I'm saying she's too old to have a baby. As in, she's been through the focking menopause and she's out the other side.'

'Well, a few years ago, Kicker, when your mother began to feel the slow advance of age, it seems she decided to have some of her eggs frozen!'

'You're shitting me. Please tell me you're shitting me.'

'Totally unbeknownst to me, of course! You see, I think it was *always* Fionnuala's intention to give you a little brother or sister one day!'

'And she's waited until now – when I'm thirty-focking-seven?'

'She's had a very busy life, Ross! Her writing career! Her humanitarian work!'

'I can't believe you're actually entertaining this?'

'Look, I'm not going to claim I was ecstatic about the idea! I mean, I didn't even know she'd *gone* to this – inverted commas – clinic! It happened back in 1988, it seems! She told me she was going to Switzerland to have something done to the lines around her eyes! Well, it turns out she went to this pioneering fertility expert in the Ukraine, who claimed he could freeze her eggs and guarantee their viability for up to forty years!'

'This is like a focking nightmare.'

'She rang the clinic just after Christmas to find out how they were – inverted commas – *doing*! And, well, the answer turned out to be very well indeed!'

'You know why she's doing this, don't you? It's to get me back for the whole me-possibly-letting-her-choke-to-death thing. That's how petty the woman is. I *could* even use the word vindictive.'

'I'm sure it's nothing of the sort, Kicker! No, your mother has just reached that point of her life where she's looking back on all of her achievements –'

'She's achieved fock-all. I want that noted.'

'– and she's wondering, What's next? Just like I am! We both have our bucket lists, Ross! One more achievement to chalk down before we shuffle off this mortal coil! Quote-unquote! Mine, as you know, is to become the Taoiseach and lead Ireland out of its disastrous relationship with the European Union! Your mother's is to have another baby! And who am I to deny her that?'

'I think you've lost it. I think the two of you have totally lost it. So when is this supposedly happening?'

'Well, the next step is to test my, em, *seed*!'

'Jesus Christ, I think I'm going to vom on your focking corpet.'

'I have to send a sample away! Make sure all my little swimmers are healthy and robust!'

'Seriously, I can actually feel it in the back of my throat.'

'Then we're going to try to find a host – a *surrogate*, I believe it's called, in the parlance – to carry the chap, *or* girl, to term!'

'And what's going to happen to the kid when you two fall off the perch? Have you thought about that?'

'Hopefully that won't be happening any time soon, Kicker! I still have unfinished business with your friend and mine – Monsieur Michel Barnier!'

He suddenly opens the door of the jacks. And that's when I notice – in the name of all that is focking sacred – he's holding what looks like a little medication bottle. And inside the bottle is his . . . Okay, you don't even need me to finish that sentence.

I'm talking about jizz. I'm talking about *his* focking jizz.

I'm like, 'What the –? When did you –? Is that what –?' but I'm too shocked to even talk.

He goes, 'You look rather pale, Ross! I think that defeat to Scotland has hit you horder than you're prepared to admit!'

'Thank you all,' Honor goes, 'for the ah-mazing responses we've had to our last video on Love Honor and Obey, which was

83

Transitioning Your Wardrobe from Autumn/Winter to Spring/ Summer! It has 7,700 views and counting, so thank you *so*, so much for that! And welcome to all my new subscribers this week! We're up to 20,000 now and that's, like, *so* exciting! Today, I want to show you a pair of boots, which are pretty much my *life* at the moment – as in, like, *literally?* – and I'm also going to be doing a Zara haul and a LuisaViaRoma unboxing, which I'm – oh my God! – so, so excited about! But first I want to show you *my* Outfit of the Day! Move back, Dad, so you get the whole thing in. It's a red-and-white-candy-striped jumpsuit by Stella McCortney. What do you think of it, Dad?'

I'm there, 'I don't know. I'd have to see it with the red nose and clown make-up to properly judge.'

Honor laughs, hits me a playful slap, then goes, 'Oh! My! God! See? This is what I have to put up with – all the time! He really is hilarious, as well as an amazing father, who, as some of you know, taught me to stand up to bullies and orseholes! Now, this jumpsuit is super, super fun! And, quite literally, there is nothing *not* to love about it! It also comes in other colours, including black and white, and also coffee and cream, which I – oh my God – *also* love?'

I'm just like, 'Get them, then.'

Honor goes, 'What?' and her face lights up – and it's lovely because I manage to capture the moment on camera.

I'm there, 'If you like it in those other colours, then you should have it in those other colours,' and I make a big show of handing her my credit cord.

'Oh! My God!' she goes. 'Okay, you can all see what a cool person my dad is!'

I'm like, 'Not a problem, Honor.'

She's there, 'That's, like, six grand –'

Fock! Did she say six *grand*?

'– and he gives it to me,' she goes, 'no questions asked! Thanks, Dad!'

I'm like, 'Er, not a problem, Honor.'

That's when Sorcha – again – storts calling me from our bed-room. She's like, 'ROSS? ROOOSSS???'

Honor goes, 'What the fock is that woman's problem now?'

I stop filming.

I'm there, 'Yeah, no, it sounds quite urgent – as in, she seems pretty upset about something?'

'She *is* upset,' she goes. 'Because I'm doing something that *she's* always dreamed of doing? And I'm doing it with you and not her. That's why she keeps trying to drag you away every time we're filming – haven't you noticed?'

'It could be that. Or – shit! – maybe Sister Dave rang her and told her about the whole you-not-making-your-Confirmation thing?'

'Dad, trust me, she's just a focking manipulative bitch!'

Suddenly, Sorcha bursts into the room. She's holding the baby in her orms and he is screaming.

'Ross,' Sorcha goes, clearly upset, 'there's something wrong with Hillary!'

Honor just rolls her eyes.

I'm there, 'What are you talking about?'

'He's vomiting constantly!' she goes. 'His stomach's empty but he's still, like, dry-retching?'

I'm like, 'Oookaaay,' wondering what she wants me to do.

She goes, 'Can you drive us to Tallaght?'

I'm there, 'Tallaght? Fock!'

Honor's there, 'What about the baby's father? What's *he* doing tonight?'

I honestly think she hates Fionn more than I do.

'He's at the National Concert Hall,' Sorcha goes. 'He went to the Johann Strauss Gala with Mom and Dad . . . Ross, can you *please* drive us to the hospital? I'm really scared!'

I'm looking at this tiny little baby and I feel instantly sorry for him. He looks genuinely sick – as in, his face has turned, like, green.

I'm like, 'Yeah, no, problem,' and Sorcha runs downstairs.

I turn around to Honor and I'm like, 'Do you think you could stay here and look after your brothers? We'll be as quick as we can.'

And, as I'm leaving the room, Honor goes, 'The woman is playing you for a fool, Dad!'

We end up hitting the road. Hillary dry-retches the entire way to Tallaght Hospital. Sorcha is sitting in the back of the cor, cradling him in her orms, going, *'Alles wird gut! Bitte, Hillary! Shush, shush, shush! Hab dich liebe, Hillary! Mein kleiner Prinz!'*

Fionn finally decides to ring Sorcha back as we're pulling into the hospital cor pork. He stepped outside the Concert Hall at the interval and discovered that he's got, like, twenty missed calls from Sorcha. All I end up hearing is *her* side of the conversation?

She's all, 'There's something wrong with Hillary . . . He's sick, Fionn . . . I don't *know* what kind of sick, just that he's vomiting . . . We've just arrived in Tallaght . . . Ross drove me . . . Yes, Fionn, Ross . . .'

She hangs up then. She's like, 'Of course, I'll have to deal with *his* guilt now over not being at home when it happened.'

I say nothing. She made her bed. And he got into it and got her pregnant.

Sorcha gets out of the cor and runs into the hospital with Hillary. I pork, then I follow her inside. The waiting room is pretty rammers, but she ends up being seen pretty much straight away.

I'm like, 'Good luck, Sorcha. I'm sure it's going to be fine.'

And she smiles at me and goes, 'Thanks, Ross,' and I know that she genuinely appreciates it.

The nurse takes her and Hillary inside.

Half an hour later, Fionn comes racing into the waiting area, going, 'Where is he?' meaning obviously Hillary. 'WHERE IS HE?'

I don't even get a chance to go, 'You took your focking time!' because he runs straight past the reception desk and into the actual hospital bit where all the doctors and nurses hang out. A few seconds later, Sorcha's old man comes running in, wearing – I shit you not – a tuxedo! A man who puts on a focking tuxedo to listen to an orchestra in the National Concert Hall. That's the kind of man we're talking about.

He goes, 'Where is she?' meaning obviously Sorcha. 'WHERE IS SHE?'

Again, he doesn't wait for me to answer, just chases after Fionn, as does Sorcha's old dear, who arrives a second or two after that.

I end up sitting there for another fifteen minutes. I check the old man's Twitter feed.

Then, a few minutes after that, Sorcha walks back into the reception area with Hillary, who seems alright now, and Fionn and her old pair.

Sorcha goes, 'Come on, Ross, we're going.'

I'm like, 'What's the Jack? Is he okay?'

'They think it's gastroenteritis.'

I nod my head like I know what she's talking about, even though I don't. I'm like, 'That sounds bad.'

She goes, 'He's going to be fine. They gave him something to calm him down,' and then – this is hilarious – she turns around to Fionn and goes, 'I should have asked them to give *you* something as well!'

It's hilarious. They end up having this major borney then in front of the entire *waiting* room?

He's there, 'Yeah, I was asking questions, Sorcha!'

But Sorcha's like, 'No, Fionn, you were demanding answers! There's a big difference!'

'I was worried about my son!'

'Just go back to your concert!'

'What's that supposed to mean?'

'Well, you're obviously feeling guilty about going out tonight and leaving me to look after Hillary, but now you know he's fine – so you can go back to your Johann Strauss whatever-the-fock-it-was!'

Sorcha's old man tries to stick his beak in then. He goes, 'Let's all calm down. Your mother and I invited him along, Sorcha. We had a spare ticket, which we did offer to you.'

Dressed like he was conducting the orchestra. What a focking tool.

There's no calming Fionn down, though, and it's soon pretty clear that his *real* issue here is obviously me.

He goes, 'I'm not going to have *you* judging *me* on my parenting skills.'

Sorcha's like, 'Okay, what the fock is that supposed to mean?'

He's there, 'I'm talking about you two, going at it like I don't know what in the middle of the afternoon, with the triplets in the house – and my parents and sister downstairs!'

'*And* us!' Sorcha's old dear goes.

Oh, fock!

I'm suddenly there, 'Let's all just calm down – like Sorcha's old man said. The full-tux wanker.'

But Sorcha has a confused look on her face. She's there, '*Going* at it? What are you talking about?'

Fionn's like, 'You were having sex, Sorcha!'

'What? When?'

'The other day. When my mum and dad and Eleanor called around to see Hillary.'

'We weren't having sex. Ross and I haven't *had* sex since we got back together.'

As pissed off as he is, there's a little bit of Fionn that'll be delighted to hear that.

He goes, 'Sorcha, you walked into the kitchen and announced that you were trying out a new position upstairs. This was in front of my parents. You said you had your legs up in the air.'

I can only imagine what the people in the waiting room are making of this. They'll have some story to tell when they finally get out of here.

'I was talking about a new yoga position,' Sorcha goes.

He's like, 'What?'

'As in, like, *plough* pose?'

'But you told my mum that it might loosen her up . . . Okay, that part of the conversation suddenly makes sense. But we heard you up in the room doing it. Ross was certainly making noises like he was having sex with someone.'

88

I'm there, 'I'm wondering did someone have a drink or two in the Concert Hall tonight?'

But then Sorcha's old dear has to throw her thoughts into the mix. She goes, 'Yes, *we* heard it, too! He was making the most disgusting noises!'

I'm thinking, I wouldn't say you're a whole lot of fun between the sheets yourself, love.

'Noises?' Sorcha goes. 'Well, I didn't hear anything because I had my noise cancelling headphones on.'

Sorcha's old man has to go, 'He was shouting, if memory serves: "BRING IT HOME, GIRL! GO ON, SORCHA, BRING IT HOME!"'

Of course, Sorcha straight away recognizes it as port of my whole script. She turns around to me and goes, 'Ross, what the fock is going on?'

And I'm like, 'It was a joke, Sorcha.'

'Oh! My God!' she goes, 'I'm a member of the Upper House of the Oireachtas and I'm married to a child!'

I'm there, 'I genuinely thought it was something you'd eventually hopefully laugh at!'

But she just shakes her head and goes, 'Dad, will you drive me home, please?'

So – yeah, no – I'm sitting in Finnegan's in Dalkey, having a cheeky lunchtime pint and playing a game that I call 'Being Joe Schmidt'. I've got my famous Rugby Tactics Book open on the bor in front of me and I'm writing down the fifteen players I'd choose to stort against Italy in the Six Nations this weekend.

The borman goes, 'Have you it picked yet?' because this would be a pretty regular sight – me sitting at the bor, jotting down my thoughts. There's so much knowledge between the covers of this book that it sometimes terrifies me. I'm always telling Honor that I'm going to hand it to Joe Schmidt himself one day and go, 'We're going to win the next World Cup – here's how to do it!'

Can you imagine?

'Yeah, no,' I go, 'I've got my storting fifteen pretty much decided.

Except I can hear the complaints already. The phrase "Leinster bias" being thrown at me. I'll just have to take it on the chin, though. That's the job.'

The borman turns the book around, throws his eyes over it, then sucks air in through his teeth.

'One or two big calls there,' he goes.

I'm there, 'I have to put out what I consider the best team.'

'I don't envy you the job.'

I'm like, 'Thanks, Dude,' because I love the way they indulge you in Finnegan's. 'You know, I might actually have another pint.'

He picks up a glass and goes, 'Heineken, is it?'

And I'm there, 'I'm not even going to dignify that with a response.'

It's at that exact point that my *phone* all of a sudden rings? I consider not answering it – I'm working here – but when I look at the screen, I see that it's Ronan.

I answer, going, 'Hey, Ro, how the hell are you?'

He's like, 'You'll nebber guess what, Rosser!' and I can hear the excitement in his voice.

I'm there, 'What is it, Ro?' pretending not to know.

'Ine joost arthur seeing Rihatta-Barrogan!'

'No!'

'Ine seerdious. Kennet reng me the utter day and says he, "I was wrong to stop you seeing yisser thaughter." I've got fuddle access, Rosser, addy toyum I waddant.'

'All's well that ends well, huh?'

'That's reet.'

'Look, can I let you into a little secret, Ro? Even though I'm sort of patting myself on the back here. The reason Kennet is letting you see your daughter again is because I'm blackmailing him.'

'Blackmayult? Oaber what?'

'Let's just say I found out something and we'll leave it at that. Okay, I'll tell you – he's riding Dordeen's sister.'

'Which wood are you thalken about, Rosser? Nordeen?'

'No, the other one.'

'Mordeen?'

90

'That's the one. She's some focking catch, by the way!'

'You're habbon me on. You're pudding me woyer, Rosser.'

'I'm not pulling your wire, Ro. I caught them going at each other like teenagers on a Leaving Cert trip in Magaluf.'

'Moy Jaysus.'

'They do it every Friday afternoon on that road out by the airport where people look at planes and jack off.'

'Kennet and Mordeen!'

'Your t . . . t . . . t . . . t . . . t . . . t . . . t . . . t . . . tits are l . . . l . . . l . . . lubbly, so thee are.'

He laughs. He's like, 'Jaysus, Rosser.'

I'm there, 'Like I said, I'm not claiming the credit, but it *was* down to actual me. It's nice to get that recognition. Where are you, by the way?'

'Ine thriving troo Clodden Ski.'

'Where?'

'Clodden Ski.'

He must mean Clonskeagh – Skeagh Town! – because he then goes, 'Ine on me way into coddidge.'

I can feel my face instantly burst into a smile. I'm there, 'College? You're going back to UCD?'

He's like, 'Of course Ine going back. I hab to get me Law thegree to make me thaughter proud of me. And so's I can buy her alt the things she waddants.'

'Daughters are very expensive to run. Trust me, I know.'

'Rosser, can I ted you sometin?'

'Yeah, no, fire ahead, Ro. I'm just having a couple of pints here, trying to make some difficult decisions.'

'Tanks.'

'What are you thanking me for?'

'For cubbing to get me when I was addested. And for thalken sense to me in the ceddle that day. You toalt me it'd woork out and you were reet, Rosser.'

'Hey, it was nothing, Ro.'

'Doatunt fooken do that, Rosser. You're altways fooken doing that.'

'What?'

'Thalken yisser self dowun. Joost learden to take a bleaten compliment.'

'Yeah, no, the only compliments I'm good at taking are the ones that relate to obviously rugby.'

'You're an unbeliebable fadder, Rosser.'

It's an amazing thing to hear and it immediately makes me want to be a better person. In the same way that seeing all those humungous TVs when you're in Horvey Norman makes you want to watch more nature documentaries.

I'm like, 'Thanks, Ro.'

He's there, 'You're a great fadder, Rosser. And Ine nebber godda let you forgerrit.'

So Sorcha ends up not talking to me for, like, a week after the whole making-sex-noises-out-the-window-while-she-was-doing-her-yogalates thing. Yeah, no, she gives me the full-on silent treatment until I remember that Valentine's Day is coming up and I suggest that we should maybe do something nice together.

She goes, 'What were you thinking in terms of?' and I can sense that her anger is at last beginning to thaw.

I'm there, 'I was thinking in terms of something romantic,' knowing what buttons to press with the girl.

'But what specifically?' she goes, still making me go through the phases.

And I'm there, 'That'd be telling. Let's just say that I have a nice surprise in mind.'

Which I don't, of course – and, worse, I then end up forgetting to even *organize* one? All this business about my old dear having a sprog has totally thrown me. So Valentine's Night rolls around and we're in the cor and I'm driving in the direction of Donnybrook without a clue where I'm actually taking her.

And Sorcha is letting me know, in no uncertain terms, that I haven't fully wormed my way back in there yet. She's going, 'You humiliated me, Ross!'

And I'm all, 'What are you talking about, Sorcha?'

'Er, you pretending that we were having sex?' she goes. 'Oh my God, I keep having flashbacks to the things I said in that kitchen. I told Fionn's mom that it might help loosen her up a bit.'

'You might have accidentally stumbled on something there. I've always thought that woman had one or two itches that needed scratching.'

'Yeah, you can't say things like that any more, Ross.'

'Hey, I've *always* said it, though. I used to say it to Fionn in school. I even offered to take on the job – joking, obviously.'

'Well, you can't talk like that now – whether you're joking or not.'

'Whatever.'

'Oh my God, I told her that I sometimes did it while I was queuing to pay in Donnybrook Fair.'

'I think you said Superquinn.'

'The actual shop isn't the issue. I had to ring her to apologize. Can you imagine how embarrassing that was for me?'

'Hey, I only did it as a joke. Well, it was mainly to piss off Fionn.'

She shakes her head and sighs and I'm suddenly picking up on the fact that she might be happy to finally let it go.

She goes, 'Erika used to say to me all the time that my problem was I married a rugby wanker and then I couldn't believe it when he turned out to be a rugby wanker.'

I'm there, 'She has to defend me. She's my sister. Slash half-sister.'

'So where are we going, Ross? Oh my God, it's not Chapter One, is it?'

That's not a bad call. But then I'm thinking, There's no way we could just rock up there on Valentine's Night without a booking. So I end up having to go, 'No, it's not Chapter One.'

'Because I've heard amazing things,' she goes, 'about their rehydrated crapaudine beetroot.'

'Like I said, it's not Chapter One.'

'Oh my God, it's not Dylan McGrath's new place, is it? The blow-torched scallops are supposed to be divine! Or is it Forest & Morcy on Upper Leeson Street, which – oh my God – *everyone* is talking about?'

'Sorcha, will you please stop guessing? It's supposed to be a surprise!'

'I'm sorry. It's just I'm really excited.'

I'm like, 'Are you? Genuinely?' at the same time thinking, Shit! I've set her up for a major disappointment here.

She goes, 'Do you know what's funny? When we were leaving Honalee tonight, it actually felt like 1998 again.'

I'm there, 'Fionn reading a book and watching us drive off with tears in his eyes. Your old man threatening me out of the corner of his mouth. I know what you mean.'

She laughs, in fairness to her.

We pass Donnybrook gorda station and I indicate left and that's when Sorcha's mood suddenly takes a turn.

'Oh my God,' she goes, 'you're not bringing me to Kielys, are you?' and she doesn't mean it in a good way.

I laugh. I'm there, 'Of course I'm not bringing you to Kielys!'

I *was* bringing her to Kielys. It's the only place I could think of and she's always been a fan of the lamb shank. Obviously, though, I can't bring her there now. Which means I have to come up with an alternative – and fast. I pull into the cor pork opposite the pub.

And that's when Sorcha becomes suddenly excited. She puts her hand over her mouth and goes, 'Oh my God! Oh my God! Oh my God! I *know* where you're taking me!'

I'm like, 'Yeah? Okay, let me hear where *you* think it is, then I'll tell you if you've guessed right.'

'We're going to Eddie Rocket's!'

'Eddie Rocket's? Okay, why would we be going there, do you think?'

'It's where we first met each other all those years ago!'

'Absolutely. Exactly. Ta-dah!'

'Oh my God, I remember finally plucking up the courage to tell you that I thought you played an amazing game and you bought me a vanilla malt and asked me for my number!'

I'm there, 'You're definitely taking me back now. Talk about nostalgia.'

I've no focking memory of any of that.

'Dear, oh dear!' I go. 'Dear, oh dear!'

She goes, 'Ross, that is *so* romantic. And it's such a *you* thing to do – when you're being yourself, that is.'

We get out of the cor, then she links my orm as we tip around to Empty Pockets.

The place ends up being rammers. There's, like, no tables, but we're offered a seat at the counter, which Sorcha gets very excited about because we're shown to the exact same spot – apparently – where we were sitting when we first spoke to each other all those years ago.

We sit down.

'So how *are* you?' she goes as I throw my eyes over the menu. 'I know that's such a random question to ask but we've kind of felt like ships in the night recently, haven't we?'

I'm there, 'Er, that's because you've been giving me the *silent* treatment?'

'I mean, even before that. Obviously, Hillary is taking up so much of my attention at the moment. It feels like we still haven't, you know, connected yet.'

'Why did they feel the need to change this menu?'

'Ross, are you listening to me?'

'Yeah, no, I am.'

'So what's happening in your life right now?'

'I don't know. Not a huge amount. Oh, except my old pair are planning to have another baby.'

'Excuse me?'

'Yeah, no, that's what *I* said.'

'Ross, your mother's just turned seventy.'

'My exact words.'

'I presume they're talking about adopting, then? Is she thinking in terms of Africa – as in, going down the whole Madonna route?'

'Listen to what I'm saying, Sorcha. They're *having* a baby. It turns out that she froze some of her . . . bits.'

'Her eggs?'

'Eggs were definitely mentioned. I don't know the ins and outs of how it works. But she went somewhere. I called into the Dáil to ask

my old man what the fock they were playing at and I caught him –
God, I can't even bring myself to say the words – wanking into a
tablet bottle.'

'Oh! My! God!'

'Wanking into a tablet bottle, Sorcha! Wanking into a tablet
bottle!'

'Okay, stop saying that.'

'Sorry, I know we're about to eat.'

'That's, like, so random. Is it not, I don't know, *irresponsible* to
bring a child into the world at her age?'

'Exactly! Why didn't she do it, like, thirty years ago? The focking dog.'

Sorcha asks me if she can order for both of us. She wants us to
have the exact same thing we had the first night we met in here. It
turns out that I'm having a Classic with bacon and cheese fries and
a side of chicken tenders.

I'm there, 'So what about you? How has *your* week been? I'm just
making conversation here.'

'Oh, stressful,' she goes. 'Fionn and I are looking at schools at the
moment.'

'Schools?'

'For Hillary.'

'He's not even two months old, Sorcha.'

'Believe it or not, that's actually quite *late* to be enrolling these
days? That's if you want to get your son into a genuinely good
school.'

We haven't put Brian, Johnny and Leo's name down anywhere,
by the way. I suppose it'd be just throwing good money after bad.

I'm there, 'It'd be interesting to hear what Fionn considers a genuinely good school.'

'Well,' Sorcha goes, 'he likes the idea of Coláiste Eoin.'

I actually laugh.

I'm like, 'In Stillorgan?'

'Yeah,' she goes, 'the whole Irish culture thing is obviously
important to Fionn.'

'It's a focking Gaelic football school.'

'Okay, I don't even know what that means.'

'As in, I've met people who went there and they left at eighteen not knowing what rugby even was.'

'I don't think rugby is a priority for Fionn.'

'I'm tempted to say that it never was.'

Which is actually horsh, because Fionn was a great player. He should have made the Ireland schools team – even though I'd never give him the pleasure of saying it to his face.

'Anyway,' I go, 'I don't know why I'm getting upset here. He's not my kid. I'm just pointing out that it's a Gaelic football school. Just make sure you have all the facts before you come to a decision. I'll leave it at that.'

Our food arrives. The waitress who puts it down in front of us is possibly Spanish and she looks like a young Catalina Sandino Moreno. I mill into my burger. I keep catching Sorcha looking at me out of the corner of my eye and smiling to herself.

I'm like, 'What?'

She goes, 'I think that waitress fancies you!'

I actually thought the same thing myself.

I'm there, 'No way. I certainly didn't do anything to encourage it.'

She goes, 'You actually look quite well at the moment,' and she storts picking at her Chicken Caesar Salad.

'By the way, speaking of schools,' she goes, 'have you heard anything from Mount Anville about Honor's Confirmation?'

I'm there, 'Errr,' not wanting to tell her about my conversation with Sister Dave because I'm picking up a vibe here that tonight might be the night when we finally have sex. 'When you say "heard anything", what are you thinking in terms of?'

'Well, it's only, like, eight weeks away,' she goes. 'I just thought there'd be a lot more about it. Letters home. Prayer meetings. Do we even know what name she's planning to choose yet?'

'She definitely hasn't mentioned it to me.'

'You two are too busy with your vlog, of course. Thick as thieves, the two of you. That's not me being jealous. I'm just commenting on the fact that, when I made my Confirmation, it was this, like, major, major deal.'

'Maybe it's not a big thing any more. Like Arthur's Day. I mean, that died a death, didn't it?'

'It's hordly the same thing, Ross. I just think, in this day and age, the whole Confirmation thing is more important than ever. What with Brexit and Trump and – I'm sorry to say it – but your dad, it's actually vital that young people have a moral compass. And I still think that the Catholic Church can hopefully *be* that moral compass? I heard Michelle Obama say the other day that the only way to defeat Fascism is to raise a generation of children to know better.'

'That's actually a good point.'

I catch her smiling at me again.

She goes, 'Hey, do you know where we should go after this?'

I'm there, 'I'm listening,' and I feel a smile forming on my face.

She puts her hand on my knee and she whispers in my ear, 'We should go where we used to always go to have sex.'

I'm there, 'Are you talking about Claire's granny's bed with the waterproof mattress protector?'

'No, Ross, I'm talking about Killiney Hill cor pork.'

Jesus Christ, I focking hope I'm not dreaming again!

I'm there, 'Are you serious?'

She just nods and goes, 'I feel like I'm finally ready to be –'

'Ridden?'

'I was going to say intimate.'

She smiles at me and I smile back at her. I ask for the bill straight away. Catalina Sandino Moreno is going home with a massive tip tonight, I think.

And that's when I hear a woman's voice behind me go, 'You . . . focking . . . WANKER!'

I actually laugh because I'm thinking, I wonder what poor focker is about to get a serious earful – and on Valentine's Night of all nights?

And that's when I notice the suddenly serious expression on Sorcha's face.

She goes, 'Oh my God, Ross, it's that girl who threw the Dublin Rent a Bike through the window of Everybody Loves Ramen!'

Oh, shit! Oh, shit! Oh shitty, shitty, bang, bang!

She goes, 'Oh my God, Ross, she's coming over here!'

The next thing I feel is, like, a tap on my shoulder. I turn around and standing there is Eabha. She doesn't look overjoyed to see me.

I'm there, 'Sorry, can I help you?' still thinking I can bluff my way out of this one.

'You focking orsehole,' she goes. 'You focking . . . WANKER!'

I honestly haven't heard that kind of language from a woman since three Christmas Eves ago in Dunnes Stores in Cornelscourt, when I threw my cor into a porking space that Mary Mitchell O'Connor had been eyeing up for the best port of twenty minutes. She tried to let me know how pissed off she was by leaning on her horn, but she had a set of reindeer antlers and a big red nose fixed to her Toyota Avensis, which meant I probably didn't take her annoyance as seriously as I *should* have? But then she wound down the window and let me have it.

My God! Seriously. My God!

I stand up. I'm there, 'You've obviously mistaken me for someone else. Sorcha, let's hit the road.'

But Eabha goes, 'Ross. O'Carroll. Kelly.'

Sorcha's like, 'Ross, do you know this girl?' because everyone in Ed's has stopped talking at this point and is glued to the conversation.

I'm there, 'I'm just trying to place her, Sorcha.'

'Let me jog your focking memory,' Eabha goes. 'A few weeks ago. In Everybody Loves Ramen. We were on a date.'

Sorcha's there, 'Okay, what's she talking about, Ross?'

I'm like, 'I don't know. It's definitely news to me, Babes.'

'We were on a date,' Eabha goes. 'And then his wife showed up. I presume *you're* his wife?'

Sorcha's there, 'Yes, I am,' and she says it in a really, like, *defensive* way?

I'm like, 'Sorcha, when you said you thought we should stort dating, I thought you meant other people.'

'We've only just got back together. Why would I suggest we date other people?'

'That's why I thought it was so random. You've never been a fan of me playing the field.'

'I actually don't believe this.'

'It was a definite misunderstanding, Sorcha. And, by the way, Fionn knew I'd got the wrong end of the stick and he never told me. As a matter of fact, he let you walk into the restaurant, knowing your husband was sitting in there with another woman. It was only my quick thinking that saved you from having to see that. So if anyone's to blame, it's Fionn.'

Eabha has more to say on the subject, though. I sort of *suspected* that she would?

She goes, 'Do you know what your husband did to get rid of me?'

Sorcha's like, 'What?' prepared to believe literally anything of me at this stage.

Eabha's there, 'He told the waiter that I was doing coke in the toilets.'

I'm like, 'You *were* doing coke in the toilets.'

'I got focking chorged. With possession. And causing criminal damage.'

'Hey, you focked a bike through a restaurant window.'

'Do you have any idea who my dad is?'

'No,' I go, 'we never got that far. You were banging on about some dude in the States who's one stor sign but identifies as another.'

'I've had to sign up for counselling.'

'Personally, I think I did you a favour there. You are one seriously boring bitch when you're on that shit.'

Suddenly, without any pre-warning, she picks up Sorcha's vanilla malt, grabs the waistband of my beige chinos and tips the entire contents of the steel container down the front of my boxers.

I'm like, 'JEEESSSUUUSSS!!!' because my nuts instantly freeze.

Eabha turns around and walks out the door. And while I put my hand down into my boxers to try to massage some feeling back into my balls, Sorcha takes the cor keys out of my jacket pocket.

I'm like, 'Sorcha, wait! It was a genuine misunderstanding!'

But she just goes, 'I'm taking the cor, Ross. You can get a taxi.'

And I take it for granted that she means a taxi home and not to Killiney Hill cor pork.

Were you ever sorry that you asked someone a simple question?

Yeah, no, me and the goys are in the Aviva Stadium, where Ireland are beating France by seven points to six. But I've managed to miss Conor Murray's try, Johnny Sexton's conversion and pretty much everything that's happened in the ten minutes since – and all because I made the mistake of turning around to Magnus during a break in play to ask him how the job in Facebook was going?

It was a figure of speech more than anything. I wasn't looking for an answer. But he was suddenly boring the ears off me, going, 'It'sh absholutely fantashtic, Rosh. The people who work there are *sho* nyshe. But thish ish becaush Fashebook ish a company that knowsh how to keep itsh shtaff happy and motivated.'

I was thinking, Jesus Christ, I didn't ask you for your focking life story. But the dude was suddenly on a roll. He was like, 'There ish a fantashtic canteen,' even though the match has restorted, 'where all the food ish free! Jusht think about that for a minute, Rosh! Your breakfasht, lunch and dinner – *if* you want it – ish free! Plush, nobody'sh deshk ish more than one hundred feet away from a micro-kitchen, where you can make coffee, make tea, make herbal tea – alsho there ish shparkling water on tap! Alsho, there ish fridgesh everywhere, which are full of cansh of Coke – alsho free, Rosh!'

I had my famous Rugby Tactics Book open on my lap and I storted scribbling a few notes in it, hoping he'd take the hint that I had fock-all interest in what he was saying – except he *didn't*? He just kept banging on.

He was like, 'Alsho, the fashilities are shecond to none. There ish a shwimming pool and a gym, which ish open twenty-four hoursh a day! There ish a pool table, air hockey, fushball – I love fushball! There ish alsho – thish ish amashing – a mushic room! Can you believe that, Rosh? A room that ish full of, like, mushical instrumentsh – sho if you're having a streshful day, you can go in there with the other guysh on your team and you can have, like, jamsh!'

Like I said, I missed the try and I missed Johnny adding the cheese and biscuits, which is the bit I'm most annoyed about, because I like to really study him and look for tiny glitches in his pre-kick routine that wouldn't be *obvious* to the untrained eye?

We're heading for the bor at half-time and the dude is still in my focking ear. He's going, 'I honeshtly haven't played the electric guitar shinsh I wash, like, sheventeen yearsh old. But there I wash yeshterday, in the middle of the afternoon, playing 'Shweet Child of Mine' – I'm shuddenly like Shlash from *Gunsh and Roshes*! – with my Team Leader shinging vocalsh with hish tie around hish head – it wash hilarioush! – and a girl from Human Reshorshesh playing the drumsh!'

A couple of minutes later, I'm standing at the bor, getting the pints in. I turn around to Christian, who's going to help me carry them, and I'm like, 'Dude, you have to swap seats with me.'

He laughs.

'There's not a chance,' he goes. 'I got stuck with him for an hour in Kielys. Telling me how he beat the Emerging Business Operations and Strategy manager in a game of Fussball.'

I'm there, 'I do like the dude.'

'I like him as well.'

'It's just, I barely took a note in that first half. *How's the new job going?* It's fine. Or it's shit. That's all he had to say.'

'He talked me through every goal in that Fussball match.'

'I'll swap with Oisinn. I mean, he's the one who married him, right?'

We grab the drinks and we make our way through the crowd to where the goys are waiting – we're talking Oisinn and Magnus, we're talking Fionn and JP, and also JP's old man, who I haven't seen for a long time.

I'm like, 'Alright, Mr Conroy? How the hell are you?'

He goes, 'I'm pretty focking great, Ross!'

I'm there, 'I hear you're getting out of the property business?' because JP mentioned that he was thinking of possibly retiring.

'That's right,' he goes. 'Time to pass the business on to my successor!'

I take a quick glance at JP, who's looking all pleased with himself. Fair focks to him, I think. He'll make a very good Managing Director of Hook, Lyon and Sinker.

JP's old man goes, 'Here, Ross, what do *you* think of this invention I've come up with?'

But JP just rolls his eyes. He's like, 'Dad, not this again!' and he seems kind of *embarrassed* by him?

I'm there, 'What kind of invention are we talking?'

JP goes, 'He's come up with an idea to help slum landlords squeeze even *more* tenants into their flats and aportments.'

'All I'm saying is that we're living in a time of record homelessness,' his old man goes. 'And we need to start maximizing our existing living space.'

JP's like, 'Tell him your idea, Dad. No, actually, *I'll* tell him. My old man thinks the solution to Dublin's accommodation crisis is for people to sleep vertically.'

The guys all laugh. I don't – mainly because I don't know what the word vertically means.

'It's more diagonally,' JP's old man goes. 'The mattress would be set at a ninety-degree angle, with a footboard to stop you sliding off. The beauty of it is that it takes up exactly half the space of a standard single bed, turning a six-bed living space into a twelve-bed living space instantly.'

JP goes, 'And tell them what you're calling this invention of yours.'

His old man's like, 'The Vampire Bed.'

Oisinn thinks this is hilarious, as does Magnus, who goes, 'You Irish and your shenshes of humour!'

Fionn has to throw his thoughts into the mix, of course.

'Actually,' he goes, 'there *is* an evolutionary rationale behind the idea. There's evidence to suggest that early man slept standing up, being a creature given to flight rather than fight. And in Ancient Egypt, people of noble birth often slept on beds that were slanted because they associated lying down with death.'

What a focking conversation killer than ends up being. I genuinely don't know how Sorcha let him anywhere near her.

I'm like, 'Fock's sake, Fionn. Why do you have to bring every-thing back to shit you've read in probably books? As my daughter would say, you're yucking my yum here.'

He goes, 'Sorry, Ross, if I've inadvertently educated you in some way.'

That's poor from him. Poor.

I'm there, 'Coláiste focking *Eoin*, by the way? If Father Fehily was alive today, he'd turn in his focking grave.'

I realize then that I need a slash before the second half storts, so I head for the reptile house. I'm actually standing at the urinal – my Rugby Tactics Book under my orm – when JP's old man comes in and stands next to me. He whips it out.

'You didn't laugh,' he goes.

I'm there, 'I wasn't actually looking. I'm trying to make sure I don't get any splash-back on my chinos here.'

'I meant you didn't laugh when I was talking about the vertical bed.'

'Yeah, no, that's because I didn't know what the word –'

'You know, for a long time now, I've been having doubts about the boy.'

The boy is what he calls JP.

I'm like, 'What kind of doubts are you talking about?'

He goes, 'I'm not sure he's the man to steer Hook, Lyon and Sinker through the next economic boom. As a matter of fact, I'm sure he's not.'

'You don't mean that.'

'He lacks imagination. He can't see that the so-called housing crisis is essentially a storage problem. How do we store this amount of people in the accommodation that we've got? He's also – I can't believe I'm saying this about a son of mine – but *nice*.'

'There's no doubt he's nice.'

'Do you know where nice guys finish?'

'Is it last?'

'You're damn right it's last! Ever since he was a kid, he's had a streak of human decency in him that I always thought would hold him back in business. His instinct is always to do the honourable thing. And I've worked too hard to make Hook, Lyon and Sinker what it is today, only to watch him sign up to the Property Services Regulatory Authority Code of Conduct.'

'So you're not going to retire, then?'

'Oh, I'm retiring.'

'So who's going to run the estate agency when you retire?'

He smiles at me – with his dick in his hand, remember – and he goes, 'You are.'

I end up saying nothing for the next ten seconds. I finish having a slash. I give the thing a shake, then I put it away and walk over to the sink to wash my hands.

A second or two later, JP's old man joins me again, although he doesn't wash his hands. He's not that kind of man.

I'm there, 'Are you actually serious?'

He's like, 'You're damn right I'm serious.'

'I need to maybe think about it.'

'What's there to think about? I'm offering you the opportunity of a lifetime here.'

'I'm just thinking about what JP's reaction would be?'

'No, you're not.'

'Excuse me?'

'Do you know *why* you were the best estate agent I ever worked with, Ross?'

'You always said it was my lack of basic human feeling.'

'Yes, it was that. But it was also your ability to detect weakness. Now, tell me this, when you look at JP, do you see a strong character who's capable of leading Hook, Lyon and Sinker through the next period of prosperity, however long it lasts?'

'I don't know.'

'Yes, you do. You just don't want to say it.'

'He has his hort set on taking over from you. I honestly don't think I could do it to the dude. We played rugby together. I can't stress that enough.'

'What if I offered you a million a year?'

'Sorry, I don't think I heard you right.'

'Oh, you heard me right. A million a year – plus the usual bonuses and commissions. What do you say?'

'I don't know *what* to say.'

'So think about it. Only don't take too long.'

So it's, like, Monday morning and I manage to track the old man down to Hennessy's office in Fitzwilliam Square. The two of them are sitting around chatting to this five-foot-nothing bald dude, who turns out to be a Russian called Fyodor.

'This is my son!' the old man goes, introducing us. 'Remember I told you about rugby? Well, this is the chap I was talking about! Ross, this is Fyodor – he's come over from Moscow to do some, em, work for us!'

I just shrug. I *could* pretend to give a fock but the truth is, I don't.

I'm there, 'Can I have a word with you?'

The old man goes, 'I know what this is about, Kicker!'

I'm like, 'Do you?'

He goes, 'You're looking for a news update on this putative brother or sister of yours! Well, I'm sad to tell you, Ross, that it's bad news! It turns out the clinic were disappointed with the quality of my – inverted commas – sperm!'

'For fock's sake.'

'Like Renua in the last General Election, it seems I have an extremely low count! So it looks like the entire thing is off! Your mother's devastated, naturally enough!'

'Well, *I'm* focking delighted. The two of you carrying on like dopes. Anyway, I didn't come here to talk to you about your sperm. I came here to talk to you about something else.'

Hennessy looks at Fyodor and goes, 'Tell the team to concentrate on the fake Facebook accounts today – and to make sure to retweet anything that Charlie posts on Twitter.'

Fyodor goes, 'Is good, yes,' then off he focks.

I'm there, 'I've been offered a job.'

The old man goes, 'A job? Good Lord, Ross, you haven't worked in years!'

'Nor have those oestrogen patches that the old dear buys on the dark web. What's your point?'

'My point is, why on Earth would you want a job? I provide for you, don't I? The direct debits!'

'JP's old man has decided to retire and he thinks I might be the man to take over as the Managing Director of Hook, Lyon and Sinker.'

'Well, he has been drinking rather a lot lately!'

'Excuse me?'

'There was an incident in Sandyford before Christmas, Ross! He drove a Renault Espace into a stationary Luas in Sandyford! The chap could have lost his licence – if he wasn't already banned from driving for ten years!'

Then he whips out his phone, goes, 'I've just remembered, I haven't posted anything derogatory about our wonderful leader for three or four days!' and storts suddenly tweeting.

Charles O'Carroll-Kelly √ @realCOCK – 17m

Petty Officer Enda Kenny TD will be forever remembered as the man who visited austerity on our country at the behest of Europe's political and banking elite. People are still SUFFERING! Why wait any longer, Enda? Go now!

Reply 470 Retweet 1k Like 8.2k ✉

I'm there, 'You don't think I could do it, do you?'

He goes, 'What's that, Kicker?'

'You not-so-subtly changed the subject there. You don't think I'm capable of running Hook, Lyon and Sinker.'

'It's not that you wouldn't be capable, Ross! I just wonder would you be playing to your strengths?'

'Meaning?'

'Well, I've always thought of you as having a rugby brain, Ross!'

Under his breath, Hennessy goes, 'I blame myself for dropping him on his head when he was a baby.'

The old man's there, 'I told you to forget about it, Hennessy. Water under the bridge.'

I'm like, 'A rugby brain? I've just realized, after all these years, that's your way of saying I'm focking stupid, isn't it?'

'You know, in some company,' he tries to go, 'that would be considered a compliment!'

'Yeah, the company of *other* rugby players who *also* failed the Leaving Cert! You know something? I'm going to say yes to him. I'm going to prove you hopefully wrong.'

'Did you hear me telling that focking prick to shut the fock up?' Honor goes.

She's lying on her bed, talking to her Auntie Erika over Face-Time. I love that they have so much in common.

'I did,' I hear Erika go. 'He kind of deserved it, I thought. He was *so* rude to that waitress.'

Yeah, like *she* can afford to talk. Making waiting staff cry used to be her speciality – especially the men.

She goes, 'I'm absolutely loving your channel, Honor. You're a natural in front of the camera. I loved the one you did about Transitioning Your Wardrobe from Autumn/Winter to Spring/Summer.'

'I've got, like, 47,000 subscribers.'

'Oh my God, my niece is a social media influencer! Sorcha must be so proud!'

'I know she's definitely *jealous*?'

I'm there, 'Say hi to Erika for me, will you?'

Honor goes, 'Dad says hi!'

I'm like, 'What's she wearing?'

'What?'

'Doesn't matter.'

Erika goes, 'So when are you coming out to Australia, Honor?'

Honor's like, 'Oh! My God! I would *love* to go to Australia!'

'Well, maybe your mom and dad will bring you out here one day. I think you'd really love Perth. It'd be great to hang out again – like we used to!'

'I wish *you* were my mom.'

'You shouldn't say things like that, Honor.'

'I do, though. My mom's a jealous slut who doesn't know how to dress and keeps having babies by different men.'

I decide to leave them to their little gossip. I look in on the boys – they're kicking the shit out of each other, they're fine – then I tip downstairs because I need to talk to Sorcha.

Relations between us have been, let's just say, pretty strained since the incident on Valley's Day, but I need to have a word with her about the whole me possibly taking over Hook, Lyon and Sinker situation.

I walk into the kitchen and her and Fionn are playing a game – so-called – with Hillary. The two of them are sitting opposite each other. Sorcha is holding Hillary and Fionn is holding up – I shit you not – a succession of basically *cue* cords? Each one is a different colour and Sorcha is going, 'What is it, Hillary? *Qu'est-ce que c'est? Was ist das?*'

Then Fionn is like, 'Blue. *Bleu. Blau. Gorm. Blu. Azul. Lán sè.*'

At least Sorcha has the decency to look embarrassed when I walk in on them. She goes, 'It's this book Fionn's reading. The author says that babies are capable of retaining up to one hundred times more information in their unconscious minds than was previously believed!'

What's wrong with pulling funny faces? Or even playing Peek-a-boo? I decide not to get involved, though. It's their child whose life they're destroying.

I'm there, 'Can I have a word?'

And Sorcha goes, 'Yeah, what's wrong?'

'Er, in *private*? It's a family matter – meaning he's not family. Meaning *he* needs to leave.'

Fionn sighs, then takes Hillary from her and says they're going to go for a walk. When he's focked off, I turn around to Sorcha and I go, 'JP's old man has asked me to take over the management of Hook, Lyon and Sinker.'

Sorcha's like, 'What?'

'Yeah, no, when he retires. He thinks I'm the man to lead the company through the Celtic Phoenix.'

'He *has* been drinking a lot lately. Did you hear about the incident with the Luas before Christmas?'

'Why is that everyone's automatic reaction?'

'I'm not trying to rain on your parade, Ross.'

'Jesus Christ, the man drives his cor into a stationary tram while pissed and suddenly he's not capable of making rational decisions? No one was killed, Sorcha!'

'You *were* a great estate agent. He did always say that.'

'Yeah, no, thanks for that recognition – finally. The thing is, I'm also thinking about the future here.'

'The future?'

'Yeah, no, the boys will be storting Montessori soon enough – provided we can find a school willing to take them. You're going to be going back to the presumably Seanad. It might be time for *me* to actually do something with my life.'

'So have you said yes to him?'

'No. The thing is, JP has his hort set on the job. Except his old man thinks he's not ruthless or emotionally numb enough to do it.'

'So what's the problem? If Mr Conroy wants you to do it –?'

'Rugby is the problem, Sorcha. As in, me and JP played rugby together.'

'You can't use rugby as an excuse for everything, Ross.'

'Now you're talking like a crazy person.'

'Why don't you just talk to JP? I'm sure he'll understand.'

'I'll give him a ring now.'

It's at that exact moment that Honor arrives down the stairs. 'Oh my God,' she goes, 'I just *love* Erika!'

Sorcha's there, 'Oh my God, were you talking to your Auntie Erika? How is she?'

'I was saying to her I'd love to do a video of just me in her walk-in wardrobe,' she goes. 'She has – oh my God! – amazing fashion sense,' and I can tell she's only saying it to piss Sorcha off.

Sorcha ends up taking the bait, of course.

She goes, 'You're welcome to do one in my walk-in wardrobe as well, Honor.'

'What,' Honor goes, 'with all your Ugg boots and your Juicy tracksuits? You dress like Britney when she got fat.'

Sorcha – stupidly – decides to try to put her foot down. She's there, 'Honor, that is no way for a girl to speak to her mother – especially a girl who's about to make her Confirmation.'

Honor laughs. She's like, 'Er, I'm *not* making my Confirmation.'

I'm there, 'Okay, let's pork this for another day, will we?'

Sorcha goes, 'What do you mean, you're not making your Confirmation?' and then she looks at me. 'Ross, what's she talking about?'

I'm there, 'I've no idea, Sorcha. It's the first I'm hearing about it.'

Honor ends up totally hanging me, of course.

She's like, 'No, it's not, Dad. Sister Dave told you what I said – that she could shove her Confirmation up her focking hole.'

Sorcha's like, 'Oh my God, is this true, Ross?' and I decide to just come clean.

I'm there, 'I don't know what exact words were used, but – yeah, no – Sister Dave *may* have mentioned to me that Honor was considering sitting out the big day.'

She goes, 'She's not sitting anything out.'

'Maybe you should just listen to her reasons first.'

'What reason could she possibly have for not wanting to make her Confirmation?'

And Honor looks Sorcha dead in the eye and goes, 'Er, because there's no such thing as God?'

She delivers this line just as Sorcha's old pair are stepping into the kitchen from outside – and from the shocked looks on their faces, it's pretty obvious that they heard it.

'What's going on?' Sorcha's old dear asks.

Sorcha's there, 'Honor says she's not making her Confirmation.'

I try to lighten the atmos. I'm like, 'Why is it so important that she makes it? I'm genuinely wondering.'

Sorcha goes, 'Because I was a member of the St Madeleine Sophie Barat Prayer Circle when I was in Mount Anville, Ross.'

Sorcha's old dear goes, 'And because Edmund and I are both Ministers of the Eucharist.'

'Exactly,' Sorcha goes. 'How would it look for us if it suddenly came out that my daughter – and their actual granddaughter – was refusing to affirm the promises that we made for her at her Baptism?'

I'm there, 'Is that not *her* choice, though?'

'Of course it's not *her* choice! She's far too young to decide that there's no such thing as God.'

'It's just we had the big chat – didn't we, Honor? – about religion and I thought a lot of the points she made were interesting. Tell her what you told me, Honor, about the fairy going to see the virgin. Listen to this one, Sorcha.'

Sorcha's old man is fuming. His face is literally purple. Like Sorcha said, him and his wife would be regular Mass-goers. I can see why he'd hate having this shit pointed out to him. All those Sunday lie-ins he could have had. He must feel like a right mug.

He goes, 'Are you referring to the Annunciation of the Blessed Virgin Mary?'

I'm there, 'I don't know what the exact chapter is called. Have *you* heard this story, Sorcha?'

He goes, 'Of course she's heard it! It's one of keystones of the Catholic faith!'

I'm like, 'Well, it was definitely a new one on me. A fairy going to see a virgin and telling her – what was it again, Honor?'

'She was going to give birth to the Son of God!' Honor goes, at the same time laughing.

I laugh as well. No choice. I'm there, 'I mean, come on! Does it not sound ridiculous when you hear it put like that?'

'And what about dead people coming back to life?' Honor goes.

I'm like, 'Whoa, gimme that again?'

'It says in the Bible that Jesus was put to death, then three days later he was walking around with fock-all wrong with him.'

I laugh.

I'm like, 'That's definitely in there, is it? You're not making that up?'

'No,' she goes, 'I'm not making it up.'

Sorcha's old man lets a roar out of him then. He's like, 'That's the story of the Resurrection of Christ! And how dare you speak about it in such a flippant manner!'

Honor laughs in his face.

She's like, 'Okay, I'm going to have to leave you all to self-soothe,' and she sort of, like, swans out of the kitchen with her nose in the air.

Actually, she's getting more and more like Erika every day.

Sorcha gives me the filthiest of filthies. She goes, 'Ross, she is making her Confirmation and that's all there is to it!'

I step out into the gorden and I ring JP's mobile. He answers on the second ring.

He goes, 'Rossmeister!' and he sounds – yeah, no – in great form.

I'm there, 'Hey, Dude. Where are you?'

'I'm just setting off for Wexford,' he goes. 'We're the official agents for a new scheme of commuter homes they're building in Oilgate. They're not due to go on the morket until the summer, but people are already queuing to put deposits down on them. They've pitched tents and everything.'

'We seem to be doing all the same things as a society that we did fifteen years ago. Thanks be to God.'

'Dad thinks we should just leave the people there. You know, good for the image – economy booming, demand for houses never higher. But I'm just going to go down there, take their contact details and tell them they can go home.'

'That's, em, very nice of you. And that isn't meant to sound like a criticism.'

It is a criticism.

He's like, 'So, what's up?'

'Yeah, no,' I go, 'there's something I need to talk to you about.'

'Do you fancy a spin?'

'Down to Oilgate?'

'Yeah, I can swing by and pick you up if you want.'

So that's what ends up happening. Twenty minutes later, I'm sitting in the front passenger seat of his X5, wondering how I'm going to break the news to him. And he's not making it easy for me because he won't shut the fock up about his plans for Hook, Lyon and Sinker once his old man retires.

'There's going to be a lot of changes,' he goes. 'For thirty years,

Hook, Lyon and Sinker has been a byword for unscrupulous practices in the areas of selling and letting property.'

I'm there, 'Your old man worked hord to build up that reputation.'

'Well, I want to end all of that. I want people to think of Hook, Lyon and Sinker as the ethical estate agency. I want us to be one hundred percent straight and above board in our dealings with customers. When I take over, it's going to be all different. We're going to stop using flowery language to exaggerate the merits of our properties. We're going to stop inflating prices to over and above what our properties are actually worth. We're going to stop lying to prospective buyers about the level of interest in a property and pretending they're in an auction situation when they're actually not.'

'That's, em, a lot of changes.'

'I want the behaviour of our staff to change as well. For instance, I'm banning chest-bumping in the office.'

Jesus Christ. If he's mad enough to think he can take the chest-bump out of selling houses, he's mad enough to do anything.

He goes, 'The first thing I'm going to change, though, is the name. Hook, Lyon and Sinker has too many associations with the bad old days of the Celtic Tiger. I was thinking of something like Green Homes. Or New Stort.'

We're on the M11, approaching the exit for Brittas Bay, when I decide to just blurt it out. I'm there, 'Your old man wants me to take over Hook, Lyon and Sinker when he retires.'

He goes, 'What?'

'He asked me, Dude. I said I'd have to have a think about it. But obviously I wanted to say it to you first.'

He's like, 'You?' and I can already see that he's devastated.

I'm there, 'For what it's worth, he thinks you're too nice to take over from him.'

'When?'

'What?'

'When did he make you this offer?'

'Last Saturday. At the French match. When we were in the jacks.'

'I can't believe you're actually considering it. For fock's sake, Ross, we played rugby together.'

'Rugby is the reason I was scared to bring it up with you. Rugby is the reason I haven't had a proper night's sleep all week.'

'This is because you didn't laugh at his stupid Vampire Bed idea. You were the *only* one who didn't laugh.'

'He just thinks I'd do a better job steering Hook, Lyon and Sinker through the next bubble.'

He suddenly steps on the brake and swerves into the hord shoulder. He's like, 'Get out.'

I'm like, 'What? We're in the middle of focking nowhere.'

'I said get out.'

'How am I supposed to get home?'

'Not my focking problem.'

'Dude, this is crazy.'

'Plotting behind my old man's back to shaft me. Get the fock out of my cor!'

He basically roars it at me, so I end up having no choice in the matter. Out I get. And with a screech of tyres he drives off, leaving me – like I said – out in the literally sticks.

I'm just thinking, He'll calm down eventually. And that's when I notice, in the foraway distance, JP's X5 pulling into the hord shoulder again. He's seen sense, I think. He's thought about all the orguments: (a) it's business; (b) it's not personal; (c) he wouldn't have won a Leinster Schools Senior Cup medal if it wasn't for me.

I actually break into a run and it only takes me a minute or two to reach his cor. I open the front passenger door and I go, 'Dumping me in the middle of Wicklow – I knew you couldn't go through with it!'

But I notice straight away that he's crying – as in, like *seriously* bawling?

I'm like, 'Dude, I'll keep you on the staff. There's no question of me letting you go, if that's what you're worried about.'

But he goes, 'Ross, I just had a phone call. My dad is dead.'

4.

Faux Pas to Avoid on Your Confirmation Day!

'There's a standard test,' JP goes, 'that estate agents use to decide whether or not a house is situated in what can be called a "desirable area".' It works like this. First, you ring the Feds and you tell them that a man wearing a balaclava and carrying a knife is climbing through your kitchen window. Then, when you've hung up, you ring Domino's and you order a twelve-inch pizza with everything on it. The rule is that if the pizza shows up before the Feds – as is almost always the case in Terenure, I'm reliably told – then you couldn't in all honesty describe the area as desirable.'

The entire congregation laughs.

He's like, 'The so-called Conroy Test is used throughout the property industry and was named in honour of the man who invented it, the man whose life we have come here this morning to celebrate – the man lying in a wooden box, here in Our Lady Queen of Peace Church on the Merrion Road.'

It has to be said that JP is holding it together unbelievably well. Actually, he's doing more than just holding it together. He's delivering a eulogy that is doing his old man definite justice.

'Inventing the Conroy Test,' he tells the packed church, 'was something of which my old man was justifiably proud – even though he wasn't above exaggerating the chorms of a property himself!'

Everyone laughs. The man was a focking crook, in fairness to him.

He goes, 'It was Dad, for instance, who first christened Stoneybatter "Dublin's Notting Hill" and who came up with the idea of calling Greystones "Ireland's very own Hamptons".'

Again, there's more laughter – probably at the idea that anyone would actually *choose* to live in Greystones.

He goes, 'I'm also reminded that it was my old man who, in 2007, took a court case to try to establish the right of estate agents, when quoting the measurements of a property, to include the width of the bricks and the cavity wall space in their calculations. And while the High Court threw out the case – and subsequently his application for costs – I know he was enormously proud when the *Sunday Business Post* described it as one of the twenty moments that defined the Celtic Tiger era – along with Seán FitzPatrick calling on the Government to tackle the sacred cows of children's allowance, old age pensions and medical cords for the over seventies, and Gerald Kean dressed as Louis XIV.'

Oisinn leans over to me. He goes, 'He's knocking it out of the ball pork up there.'

And I'm like, 'Yeah, no, he definitely is,' but at the same time I can't help but feel like shit. If only I'd kept my mouth shut for even ten minutes longer, then JP wouldn't know the truth about what his old man really thought of him, which wasn't much – certainly in terms of work.

'My dad was obviously a brilliant, brilliant man,' JP goes. 'But his greatest gift – you might even call it the *real* Conroy Test – was for fatherhood.'

Everyone claps, even though it's basically bollocks. He was much better at selling houses than he was at being a dad. He's probably spinning in that box right now at being dissed like this.

'Because whatever else he was,' JP goes, his voice cracking with emotion, 'he was my daddy,' and he looks down at little Isa, sitting on Chloe's lap, directly in front of me. 'And I would consider it my greatest achievement in life if I could be the kind of father to my son that my father was to me.'

Well, he's certainly that – in the sense that he's no longer in a relationship with the boy's mother and he only sees the kid at weekends. Still, everyone claps, then the choir sings 'In My Father's House (Are Many Mansions)' as JP and a bunch of Mr Conroy's mates from the Fitzwilliam Casino & Cord Club carry the coffin down the aisle and out of the church.

We all shuffle outside to the cor pork and we do the whole

sympathizing with the rellys thing. I tip over to JP's old dear and I'm there, 'Hey, Mrs Conroy, I'm really sorry and blah, blah, blah.'

And she goes, 'He was a focking prick, Ross,' which makes me laugh out loud because it's not the kind of thing you *expect* to hear at a South Dublin funeral? Especially from the widow. 'If you want to sympathize with someone, do it with that Slovakian whore he left me for.'

She flicks her thumb at Madlenka, who's standing, like, three feet away from us. It's like, *awks* much? The girl is literally bawling her eyes out. I've never been especially comfortable around crying women, despite my long years of exposure to them, so I give her a sort of sad face, head cocked to one side, bottom lip turned down – the same face that Sorcha pulls when she hears about, say, a polar bear who's been found dead with four hundred used Nespresso capsules in its stomach – then I move quickly along.

The cor pork ends up being rammers. Half of South Dublin must be here. Everyone is standing around, telling their favourite stories about the man. I hear one dude say that Barry Conroy sold him his very first house in 1974 – and, despite that, they managed to remain friends for more than forty years.

I tip over to JP, who's chatting to Christian, Oisinn and Fionn. There's no sign of Magnus, by the way. He's apparently – and this is the exact word that gets used – *working*?

JP is telling the goys how his old man died. It turns out it was, like, a massive hort attack. No real surprise there. The dude's orteries were so furry, you could give them to your kids to cuddle.

'I mean, literally five minutes before he hit the deck,' he goes, 'he managed to sell a two-bedroom house in Dortry for €640,000.'

Oisinn just shakes his head. He's there, 'Six hundred and forty thousand euros for Dortry! And they said this country was finished?'

'He put the phone down, walked out of his office into the middle of the floor and said, "Can you believe they actually bought it? The walls are so thin that the neighbours will be finishing their fucking sentences!" And those were the last words he ever spoke.'

'I suppose there's some consolation,' Christian goes, 'in knowing that he died doing what he loved.'

That's Christian for you. He always knows the right thing to say.

'Good point,' I go. 'Stiffing some dope with more money than sense is definitely how he would have wanted to go.'

My old man and Hennessy tip over to us then. The old man shakes JP's hand and tells him that Shanahan's won't be Shanahan's without Barry Conroy sitting in his usual seat, telling some filthy joke or other.

'I was talking to the chap only a few days ago!' he goes. 'In Peterson of Dublin, where, as you know, he always bought his cigors! He told me one about a woman who turned out to be a fishmonger's daughter of all things! A fishmonger's daughter! Have you ever heard the like of it? And that is how I shall remember your father!'

JP's like, 'Thanks, Charles. We're having a few drinks in his honour in the M1 later on, if you fancy popping in.'

'I shall certainly show my face,' the old man goes, 'although I shan't be drinking!' And then he turns to me. 'The doctor has put me on this new diet, Ross! No alcohol! A lot of red meat and green vegetables – try to improve the quality of my –'

I'm like, 'Okay, don't even *think* about finishing that sentence.'

'I'm just mentioning it in dispatches, Ross, that your mother and I haven't quite given up hope yet!'

The goys are all looking at each other, thinking, what the fock is he even talking about? But I'm just looking at JP, who's still refusing to make eye contact with me.

The last man I hurt this deeply was, believe it or not, Felix Jones. Long story. But back in the day, my old man had this deal with the Leinster Branch of the IRFU where he agreed – on the QT – to pay the release chorge for any current player unlucky enough to have his cor clamped. Cian Healy, for instance, would be basically skint today if it wasn't for my old man.

Anyway, about a week after he signed for Munster, Felix rang me to say that his Kia Sorento had been clamped after he threw it in a loading bay outside Supermac's in Dooradoyle and could he have my old man's credit cord details? I should have just given him the number – the goy worshipped me – but instead I told him that since he was no longer a Leinster player, he wasn't covered by the terms of the deal any more.

Let's just say that angry words were exchanged. He said one or two things about my rugby career – or, more specifically, lack thereof – which he definitely didn't mean, while it was possibly childish of me looking back to suggest that he put his complaint in writing and send it to Conor Pope via the *Irish Times*.

In my defence, he'd gone to play for the enemy and I was hurt. But I lost a friend that day.

The next time I heard from Felix was about a month later, when he asked me to return his copy of Paddy Casey's *Living*, which I remembered borrowing from him but just couldn't find. Then about two years later, I tried to Like a Vine that he posted on Twitter of a man skiing into a tree, only to discover that he'd blocked me.

Yeah, no, I hurt Felix badly – just like I've hurt JP now.

I sort of, like, steer the dude away from the rest of the goys and I'm like, 'I just wanted to say – again – sorry.'

'What for?' he goes. 'Plotting with my old man behind my back to shaft me?'

'No . . . Well, yeah . . . But mostly I'm just sorry for opening my mouth.'

'For telling me that my old man thought I was useless?'

'He didn't think you were useless, Dude. He just thought you had too much human decency to run a successful estate agency. In a way, if you think about it, that's sort of a compliment.'

'Don't try to dress it up as something it's not, Ross. My own father didn't trust me to take over the family business. You've no idea how it feels, Ross, to know that no matter what I achieve in life now, I'll never be in a position to prove my old man wrong.'

'Dude, I'm sorry I even opened my mouth.'

'So am I, Ross. Believe me. So am I.'

I spot Ronan coming out of the Orts Block. He's surprised to see me.

'Rosser?' he goes. 'What are you doing hee-or?'

I'm there, 'Yeah, no, I was just passing – thought I'd swing in and see did you fancy grabbing a bit of lunch slash a few pints?'

He's like, ''Mon, so, we'll go to the restordoddent.'

'So you're choosing the lunch option over the pints option?' I go, unable to hide my disappointment. 'Is everything okay?'

He laughs. He's like, 'I've leckchodders this arthur noon, you bleaten mad thing!'

We stort walking along the side of the lake. It's great to see him back in college and back in cracking form. I say it to him as well.

He goes, 'Thanks, Rosser. Me and Shadden ardent at war with each udder addy mower. And Ine getting to see me thaughter pretty much evoddy utter day. Hee-or, do you know what we should do? We should arrange a playdate between Rihatta-Barrogan and the boyuz.'

I'm there, 'My boys?'

'The thriplets, yeah.'

'I don't know, Ro, they're banned from pretty much every-where.'

'We could bring them thram poddle eden.'

'Okay, give me that again?'

'Thram poddle eden.'

'Go again?'

'Thram poddle eden.'

'Still not getting it?'

'Thram poddle eden.'

'Once more?'

'Thram poddle eden.'

'Once more?'

'Thram poddle eden.'

'One more time?'

'Thram poddle eden.'

'Trampoling! Yes! I knew I'd get it in the end!'

'Rihatta-Barrogan's mad into it, so she is. There's a place in Sad-denyfowurd calt the Jump Zowunt.'

'I'm proud to say that's one place they haven't been banned from yet, mainly because they've never focking been there.'

'We'll sort it, so. Hee-or, how's Sudeka, by the way?'

'Sorcha? Yeah, no, she's sort of pissed off with me at the moment for one or two things. Okay, answer me this, Ro. If you had a wife and she came to you and said she thought you should stort dating again, would you think that meant dating *her* or dating other people?'

'Dating *her.*'

'Think about it.'

'I doatunt neeyud to think abourrit. I'd think she meddent dating *her.*'

'Okay, that's what most people seem to be saying. I'm storting to understand why she reacted the way she did now. Then there's a whole thing about Honor deciding not to make her Confirmation and me not telling her.'

It's hilarious because Ronan storts giving me *relationship* advice then? He goes, 'Look, it's bowunt be heerd at the steert, Rosser – especially arthur her habbon a babby wir anutter fedda.'

'The thing is,' I go, 'we're not actually *properly* back together yet? As in, we haven't actually sealed the deal yet.'

'You're saying you habn't had sex wirrer?'

'She doesn't know whether she trusts me enough to be intimate with me yet.'

'Moy Jaysus.'

'Direct quote.'

'It'll alt come togedder, but. You and Sudeka are meant to be togetter. Thrust me, Rosser.'

'I don't know how much longer I'm going to last without having sex.'

And then, as if on cue, a bird walks by. She looks like – and I'm not exaggerating here – an Irish version of Mikee Quintos, except with a little bit more bork on the trunk.

'I'll tell you something,' I go, 'if you take my advice, Ro, you'll stay single for the rest of your time in this place. The women here are even nicer than they were in my day.'

Ro goes, 'You caddent say that, Rosser.'

'Why not? It's a compliment to them.'

'Dudn't mathor. You caddent go arowunt thalken about wooben in that way addy mower. Especiady out hee-or.'

I'm like, 'What do you mean, out here?'

And it's not long before I end up finding out.

Standing outside the restaurant, in the middle of a group of angry-looking fellow students, is a good-looking bird – compliment – holding what looks very much to me like a *placord*? If I was allowed to describe her physical appearance – which, apparently, I'm *not* any more? – I'd say she looks like Camila Cabello except with smallers thrups and a slight underbite.

When she spots Ronan, she goes, 'Hi, Ro!'

And *he's* there, 'Howiya, Huguette? How's things?' and then he ends up introducing us. He's like, 'Huguette, this is Rosser, me ould fedda. Rosser, this is Huguette, a veddy good friend of moyun. She's in me Constitutionoddle Law tutordial.'

Huguette! Yeah, no, I thought I'd heard them all before, but it's definitely a new one on me.

I'm there, 'Yeah, no, nice to meet you.'

Ronan goes, 'So what's the demonstrashidden about, Huguette?'

She goes, 'We're picketing the restaurant to try to force them to take sushi off the menu.'

I'm there, 'Sushi? Why?'

'Why do you think?' she goes. 'Because Western people eating it represents cultural appropriation.'

I'm there, 'It represents what?'

Ronan goes, 'Culture doddle appropryashidden is where a pribileged commudity boddows the thradishiddens and symbols of anutter, often marginalized commudity wirrout permishidden or regeerd for the consequedences.'

I end up just staring at him. I've never heard him talk like this before.

Huguette goes, 'It's the reason we don't wear sombreros at Hallowe'en any more.'

I'm there, 'What are you talking about? I wore a sombrero last year – to a house porty in Glenageary. Actually, that was the year before. Last year, I blacked up and went as Mel B.'

I can tell from the way she looks at me that Huguette has taken an instant dislike to me.

'Or was it Mel C?' I go. 'No, it was definitely Mel B. Will I tell you a handy way to tell the difference? Just think Mel Black and Mel Caucasian!'

Ronan goes, 'See, that's anutter exampiddle of it, Rosser. You caddent do things like that addy mower.'

'Are you talking about blacking up or dressing up as a Mexican bandit?'

'Either,' Huguette goes. 'Both are *equally* offensive?'

'Even though the taxi driver who drove me to the porty was black himself and he thought it was hilarious?'

'Maybe he only laughed because you made him feel uncomfortable?'

'No, he found it genuinely funny. I was doing the voice and everything: "Oooh, I'm Scaaary Spice!"'

Ronan's like, 'It dudn't mathor if he laughed or not, Rosser. It's still offedensive.'

'Okay,' I go, 'I can see how it might be offensive to people who don't know my sense of humour. But you can't say that eating sushi is the same thing.'

'We have our own culture,' Huguette goes. 'We shouldn't be allowed to mine other people's – just to adopt things that we consider cool or of the moment.'

I'm there, 'If you're going to tell people they can't eat sushi, you might as well tell them they can't eat lasagne, then. Or spaghetti.'

Huguette turns around to one of the other protestors – a dude – and goes, 'Is lasagne on the menu?'

The dude checks his phone. 'No,' he goes, 'but *spaghetti* is?'

Huguette is like, 'Okay, we need to put spaghetti on the banned list.'

I'm standing there, thinking, What the fock is happening to UCD? These people are kids. They're, like, nineteen, twenty years old. Why aren't they drunk? Or in bed, riding each other?

Of course my next thought is, How are we going to get past the picketers because I am literally *storving* here?

I'm there, 'What if we go in and promise not to have the sushi? Do you know do they do a burger?'

But Ronan lets me down in a big-time way. He goes, 'You caddent pass the picket, Rosser. Thee woatunt chayunge the medu in theer udless we hit them where it hoorts – in the bleaten pocket!'

And then he goes, 'Gib us one of them soyuns theer, Huguette. Ine godda join yous.'

And I only have to look at him for a split second to realize that my son is smitten in a big-time way.

Sorcha sort of, like, sad-smiles me across the table. 'I never got to tell you,' she goes, 'how sorry I was.'

And I'm like, 'Sorry? What do you have to be sorry for?' pretending that I *don't* have a list?

'It's just I know you had your hort set on taking over Hook, Lyon and Sinker,' she goes.

I'm there, 'Hey, I just feel bad for telling JP that his old man thought he wasn't up to the job.'

'You weren't to know the man was going to suddenly drop dead, Ross.'

'Yeah, I know. But I still feel like shit. Maybe I'm not as emotionally switched off as JP's old man thought I was.'

'Yeah, that's kind of a *good* thing, Ross?'

We're having the early bird in Hortley's in Dún Laoghaire – having another crack at the whole date night thing.

I'm there, 'I'm worried about JP, though. I'm scared he's going to do something stupid.'

She goes, 'Like what?'

'I don't know. It was just the way he was acting at the funeral. I've never seen him so low.'

'You'll all have to watch him very closely, Ross. Grief can affect people in all sorts of ways.'

'Jesus, do you remember me when Ian Madigan moved to France? I sat on the side of the bed for three hours one morning, crying my eyes out because I couldn't make up my mind what colour socks to wear!'

'I remember when Brian O'Driscoll retired, you drove the wrong way around the Glenageary roundabout!'

In my pyjamas. Yeah, no, I never told her that detail. God, I've kept a lot from her over the years.

Sorcha goes, 'This is nice, isn't it, Ross?'

I'm like, 'What?'

'I'm talking about *this!*' she goes. 'As in, us having dinner! Just me and you!'

I'm like, 'Yeah, Eabha said she might try and join us for the dessert course.'

She laughs, in fairness to the girl.

She goes, 'I still can't believe you thought I wanted us to date other people!' but she's sort of, like, shaking her head, like she's beginning to see the funny side of it.

I'm there, 'I'm thick as shit, Sorcha.'

'I accept that,' she goes. 'Anyway, like I said, I'm happy to write it off as a misunderstanding and move on.'

That's big of her. It's been focking weeks.

I'm there, 'That's, em, a relief, Sorcha. It's a definite relief.'

'The great thing about date nights,' she goes, 'is that it's a chance to check in with each other.'

'Er, right.'

'Just to talk about things. For instance, I want you to know that I appreciate how difficult our whole – let's just say – *domestic* situation must be for you. I'm admitting that it's, like, not *ideal?*'

'As in?'

'As in, having a baby sleeping in our room – a baby that isn't yours.'

'It's a bit random alright.'

'I notice that you never look at him. Hillary, I mean.'

'I look at him the odd time. There's not a whole lot to see. He looks like Fionn. Poor kid.'

'It'll get easier, Ross.'

'Ugly kids get bullied, Sorcha. It's just a fact.'

'I'm saying it'll get easier for you.'

'Oh. Right.'

'I mean, look at me and Ronan. It took me a long time before I could get my head around the fact that you had a son with someone else.'

'It's hordly the same thing.'

'It's very nearly the same thing.'

'The difference is that Tina isn't living in our spare room.'

'Like I said, it's not ideal, but it'll all resolve itself eventually. And, again, I just want to say thank you for being patient with me – in relation to the other thing.'

'Do you mean the sex?'

'Ross, you don't have to spell it out – but yes, I mean sex.'

And that's when, totally out of nowhere, she goes, 'I need you to do something for me, Ross – as in, like, a favour?'

I'm there, 'What kind of favour are we talking?' realizing that this entire conversation was building up to this.

She goes, 'I need you to persuade Honor to make her Confirmation.'

I'm like, 'Me?'

'She listens to you.'

'She doesn't really.'

'You know she does, Ross. You're the only one who can get through to her.'

'I'm still trying to figure out why everyone's making such a big deal about her not making her Confirmation.'

'Because it's a *thing*, Ross.'

'Is it, though?'

'It's a massive, massive thing – especially in Mount Anville. How's it going to look if she ends up being the only one in her class who doesn't make it?'

'Is that not her choice, though?'

'No, Ross, it's *not* her choice. This is Mount Anville we're talking about – not Newpork Comprehensive. We're not the kind of parents who give their children wine with dinner and let them call us by our first names.'

We let them call us motherfocking shitclowns, though. I could point that out, but I don't.

I just go, 'Honor doesn't believe in God, Sorcha.'

But she's not ready to hear it. She's there, 'Of course she believes in God! How could she *not* believe in God?'

I'm like, 'Hey, you heard her. She actually has the whole thing figured out. I mean, some of the stuff that's apparently in the Bible, I'm beginning to think the whole thing is possibly horseshit myself.'

'I was talking to Sister Dave on the phone today and she thinks Honor is just looking for attention by saying that stuff. I explained the situation to her. A new baby in the house – blah, blah, blah.'

'Did you mention that it wasn't mine?'

'Why would I do that?'

'I don't know – just if she thought it was maybe relevant. Make sure she has all the facts.'

'She said that she *expects* Honor to make her Confirmation. That's how she put it, Ross.'

I'm there, 'Er, right.'

'And I do as well. I've had the caterers booked since last September. And the morquee. The Save the Dates have already been sent out for the porty afterwards.'

She takes a deep breath then – like she's getting ready to say something very important.

'Look,' she goes, 'I told you – didn't I? – that I'm getting to the point where I'm very nearly ready to, you know –'

'Have sex with me?'

'You don't have to say the words out loud, Ross. Okay, I hate sounding like a politician, but what I'm saying is this. You still have a little bit of work to do in terms of winning back my trust and also my respect. But this would definitely help. Do you understand?'

I think I do. Although given my record for getting the wrong end of the stick, it's probably still worth running it past her.

I'm there, 'Are you saying that if I can persuade Honor to make her Confirmation, you'll stort putting out again?'

She goes, 'I wouldn't have put it as chormingly as you did, Ross, but yes, that's basically what I'm saying, yes.'

And I'm just like, 'Happy focking days! Leave it with me!'

*

'Oh my God,' Honor goes, nearly losing it she's laughing so hord, 'that is *so* funny!'

Yeah, no, we're in Brian, Johnny and Leo's room and we're playing with this basically toy bird that Honor bought them for Christmas called Pirate Pete – the Repeat Parrot. Yeah, no, it's got this, like, voice-activated tape recorder inside it and it repeats everything you say. And there's no prizes for guessing what use the boys have found for it.

'I'll eat your focking head,' Leo goes, 'and shit your eyes out my focking hole,' then a second later the parrot goes, 'I'll eat your focking head and shit your eyes out my focking hole.'

And Honor cracks up laughing again. I do as well. It *is* funny.

I'm there, 'You got new batteries for it, then?' because Sorcha's old man took the last set out and focked them in the bin.

'Yeah,' Honor goes, 'it keeps them busy while I'm reading my comments. Hey, I was thinking we should do a video on Ten Items I Would Rescue from My Wardrobe if the House Caught Fire Tomorrow!'

I'm there, 'That sounds great, Honor. But I was wondering first could I maybe have a word with you about something?'

'What's wrong?'

'Okay, don't look so worried. It's just, look, I know you're not one hundred percent keen on the whole making your Confirmation thing.'

'Er, there's no such thing as God. The whole thing is a pack of focking bullshit.'

'And some of the stuff you told me that's in the Bible, Honor, has me asking one or two questions of my own. But, look, I'm having a pretty hord time of it at the moment, trying to fit back in here. Me and your old dear haven't exactly *clicked* yet? Even though you're too young to understand what that means.'

'It means she's not having sex with you.'

'Okay, you're obviously *not* too young.'

'You can tell by just looking at her – focking uptight bitch.'

'Yeah, if we could just bring the conversation back to the whole Confirmation thing, Honor.'

'The answer is yes, Dad.'

'What?'

'I'll make my Confirmation – if it'll make *your* life easier.'

I just smile at her. It genuinely upsets me that I'm the only one who can see how much good there is in her.

I'm there, 'It'll make me look good in Sorcha's eyes and – again, without going into the whys and the wherefores – I really, really need that right now.'

She's goes, 'I'm not going to say the bit about rejecting Satan, though.'

I'm like, 'Hey, I'm sure that's fine.'

'Or about rejecting his works and his empty promises.'

'Look, if it's anything like the Communion, it'll just be a day out for the moms. A chance to show off their Veneers and drink their weight in Prosecco.'

Brian goes, 'Fock you, you motherfocking fockstick!' and Pirate Pete – the Repeat Parrot goes, 'Fock you, you motherfocking fockstick!'

We all laugh our heads off, then I head off to tell Sorcha the good news. I put my head around our bedroom door to see if she's in there. It turns out she's not, but I end up being glad that I check because something is wrong. I can hear straight away that – Jesus Christ! – Hillary is having trouble breathing. I race over to his cot and I look in. He's been sick again and he's sort of, like, *choking* on it?

Instinct suddenly takes over. I reach in there and I lift him out, going, 'It's okay, little goy! It's okay! It's okay!' just trying to talk calmly to the little dude. Then I hold him to my chest and I pat his back and I make sort of, like, *soothing* noises? I'm there, 'It's okay! I'm here! Your Uncle Ross is here!'

I step out onto the landing and he ends up vomiting all over the shoulder and down the back of my Ireland training top.

I'm there going, 'That's it, little chap – get it up! Don't worry, I can wash my shirt! Just get it all up!'

Suddenly, Honor steps out of Brian, Johnny and Leo's room. She stares at me for a few seconds without saying anything. Then she goes, 'Fock's sake!' like she's – I don't know – disappointed, then she storts shouting down the stairs: 'YEAH, YOUR BABY IS SICK AGAIN – THAT'S IF EITHER OF YOU *GIVES* A SHIT?'

A second or two later, Sorcha comes chorging up the stairs, followed by *him*. Sorcha is frantic. She's going, 'WHAT HAPPENED? WHAT HAPPENED?'

I'm there, 'I looked in on him and he was puking his ring up. He's fine now. I'm wearing most of his lunch on my Ireland training top, though!'

Sorcha takes him out of my hands. Fionn raises his voice to me as well. He goes, 'WHY DIDN'T YOU CALL ME? WHY DIDN'T YOU CALL ME STRAIGHT AWAY?'

Honor rushes straight to my defence. She goes, 'Yeah, he just saved your kid's life. The least you could do is focking thank him.'

Sorcha's there, 'Honor's right, Fionn. If Ross hadn't looked in on Hillary – oh my God! – I dread to think what would have happened!'

Sorcha, in fairness to her, throws her free orm around me and goes, 'Oh my God, thank you, Ross! Thank you so, so much!'

Fionn can't bring himself to either thank me or apologize, though. He wanders into the bedroom, going, 'I can't understand why I didn't hear him if he was choking.'

Honor – totally out of the blue – goes, 'Mom, I've decided to make my Confirmation after all.'

Sorcha is a bit thrown by this news, coming so soon after the emergency with Hillary. It actually takes a second or two to sink in. Then she's like, 'Oh my God, Honor – really?'

Honor nods her head. She's like, 'Dad persuaded me. He explained to me why it was so important.'

Sorcha seems happier than I've seen her in a long time. She goes, 'That's amazing news, Honor!' and then she smiles at *me*.

Yeah, no, I seem to be very much the hero of the hour.

Honor goes, 'I was trying to think of what *name* I might choose? For my *Confirmation* name? And I was thinking of maybe Madeleine?'

'Oh my God,' Sorcha goes, 'after Madeleine Sophie Barat – the founder of the Society of the Sacred Hort?'

Honor's there, 'Yeah, if it wasn't for her, there wouldn't be a Mount Anville today.'

'I was actually going to pick Madeleine myself except I changed my mind at the very last minute and chose Mary instead – after Mary Robinson? And obviously the *Virgin* Mary? Oh my God, Honor, I'm so happy that you're going to make your Confirmation!'

'Jesus Christ,' Fionn goes, stepping out of our bedroom, 'someone's taken the batteries out of the baby monitor.'

Sorcha's like, 'Excuse me?'

'Look!' he goes, holding up the empty box up for all of us to see. 'Someone's removed the batteries!'

There's, like, silence on the landing.

Sorcha's there, 'Oh my God, I'm wondering was it possibly me?'

Fionn's like, 'Why would it have been you?'

'Well, maybe I took them out to change them and forgot to put the new ones in. I've got, like, total Baby Brain at the moment!'

But Fionn is just staring at Honor and it's pretty obvious that he thinks it was her.

She's just standing there, all innocence, looking at her phone, going, 'Okay, if I'm going to do this, I want a really, really expensive dress for the day,' and she has no idea that Fionn is giving her major filthies.

I feel like nearly throwing a punch at the goy. But then, out of Brian, Johnny and Leo's room, I hear Pirate Pete – the Repeat Parrot go, 'I'm going to split your head like a focking coconut, you focking prick with ears!'

So we're sitting in the Jump Zone in Sandyford – me and Ronan – watching our kids wear themselves out on the trampolines and I'd be a liar if I said I wasn't giving myself a little pat on the back at how well my son has turned out.

It seems like no time since we were enjoying our own unsupervised access days together – him kicking the fock out of the coin cascades in Dr Quirkey's Good Time Emporium to try to make the money fall into the chute and me being morched up to Wes Quirke's old man's office to write a cheque for the damage to the machines.

He goes, 'It's mad, idn't it, Rosser – the way toyum floyuz?'

I'm there, 'I was just thinking the same thing, Ro. Rihanna-Brogan's, what, five now? That's nearly the same age as you were when I first met you.'

He goes, 'Fooken mad, so it is.'

I'm watching his daughter playing away happily with Brian, Johnny and Leo – seeing who can jump the highest – and it gives me a really happy feeling inside. I'm there, 'The boys really love their auntie, don't they?'

But Ro goes, 'She's not their addenty, Rosser. They're her udden cuddles.'

'They couldn't be her uncles – they're younger than her.'

'It dudn't go by age, Rosser. Ine your sudden, which means moy kids will be your childorden's nephews and nieces.'

'Okay, I can't even think about that. I think I'd have a focking stroke or something. Still, it's nice that they obviously look up to her. Kids need role models. I've always said that.'

Rihanna-Brogan tips over to where we're sitting. She's out of breath and red in the face. She goes, 'Daddy, cad I have muddy for a thrink? Ine, like, *so* thoorsty.'

Her accent is hilarious. A bit like Saoirse Ronan's in the sense that it hasn't a focking clue where it's supposed to *be* from? Which is down to her spending the first two years of her life in Killiney and the rest in focking Nova Scobia.

The boys follow her over to us – shoes missing and their hair all over the shop.

Brian goes, 'I want money. Gimme some focking money.'

I end up having to laugh. That's exactly how I used to talk to *my* old man? Actually, it's *still* how I talk to my old man. It's the whole nature versus nurture thing. I'm a firm believer in the whole DNA thing. I genuinely think we don't know the half of what's going on with that shit.

I whip out a roll of fifties. 'Okay,' I go, 'get yourselves a Coke or something. And get one for your auntie – or whatever she is – as well.'

'Er, I actually don't *drink* Coke?' Rihanna-Brogan goes. 'So I doatunt?'

I'm like, 'Really? Seriously?'

Ronan's there, 'Sugardy thrinks is bad for kids, Rosser.'

I laugh. I'm like, 'The first time I met you, you had a John Player Blue between your fingers and another one behind your focking ear. You were, what, just turned six?'

'We ditn't know about the dangers of smoking in moy day, but.'

'That was in, like, 2003!'

'If it's all the same to you,' Rihanna-Brogan goes, 'I'll joost hab an odange juice.'

It's comical. It'll be a genuine shock if she doesn't end up on the *Late Late Toy Show* one day.

I peel off a Five-Oh and I hand it to Brian. 'Get R&B there an orange juice – obviously Tropicana, if they have it – and get yourselves whatever you want.'

Off to the shop they fock.

I'm there, 'I think there's a lot of horseshit talked about things that are supposedly good for kids and things that are supposedly bad for them. They've been drinking Coke since they were, like, six months old. I used to put it in their beakers for them. Although don't ever tell Sorcha that. She's a terrible one for putting two and two together and getting four.'

My phone suddenly rings and – talk of the devil – my wife's face fills the screen.

Ronan goes, 'Do you want to take that, Rosser?'

And I'm like, 'Not really, no. It'll be something to do with the Confirmation.'

'What Conferbation?'

'Honor's making her Confo next week.'

'She toawult me on the phowunt that she wadn't godda make it.'

'Yeah, no, I managed to change her mind – even though she's not going to say the lines about rejecting Satan. God, I'm a great father when you think about it.'

But he just gives me a look and goes, 'Mebbe you should an-sodder yisser phowunt, Rosser,' and he ends up shaming me into taking the call.

I'm just like, 'Fine – whatever!' and then I'm like, 'Sorcha, what's up?'

She goes, 'Oh! My God! Ross, you are not going to *believe* where I am?'

'Dundrum?'

'No, I'm in Havana!'

'Havana – the, I don't know, country?'

'No, Havana in Donnybrook. It's this, like, amazing, amazing boutique, where they stock, like, Haider Ackermann, Comme des Garçons, Maria Grachvogel . . .'

'Why are you telling me this, Sorcha? It's actually a bit boring.'

'The reason I'm telling you is because I'm here with Honor!'

'Honor?'

'We've just bought her a dress! For her Confirmation!'

I'm like, 'Seriously?' feeling a little bit jealous if I'm being honest. I thought *I* was her shopping buddy?

'It's a tulle flower appliqué dress by Simone Rocha,' she goes, 'and she looks ah-mazing in it! I *actually* cried? And I bought a dress for the day from the same collection, which complements hers, even though it's not, like, matchy-matchy? And guess what, Ross? She filmed the whole thing! Oh my God, I'm going to be on her You-Tube channel! Her mom!'

'What the fock is she up to? That's probably what you're wondering, is it?'

'Oh, don't worry, I *know* what's going on, Ross!'

'Do you?'

'It's the Holy Spirit coming down on her!'

I actually laugh. I shouldn't, but I do.

She goes, 'Ross, the *exact* same thing happened to me about a week before *my* Confirmation? I was suddenly filled with this overwhelming sense of, like, goodness and – oh my God! – *grace*?'

Fock. I'm wondering now is Honor maybe laying it on a bit too thick? Sorcha might not see through it, but her old pair almost certainly will.

She goes, 'I genuinely think it's a miracle! Honor reaffirming her commitment to God has finally given me the relationship with my daughter that I've always dreamed of having! I know I've said this loads of times before, Ross, but we should stort going to Mass together as a family.'

I'm there, 'Let's keep it in perspective, Sorcha.'

'We're going to the Dylan now for afternoon tea! Oh my God, mother–daughter fun!'

And then she hangs up on me.

Ronan goes, 'Hee-or, Rosser, I've been meadon to ast you –'

I'm like, 'Money?' and I whip out my roll again.

'No, Ine alreet for muddy. I was godda ast you for yisser opidion about sometin.'

'Okay, continue.'

'What do you think of Huguette?'

'Huguette? Is that the bird who wants sushi taken off the menu in the UCD restaurant?'

'We gorrit taken off, Rosser! The restordoddent agreeyut that thee woultn't seerb it addy mower!'

'We?'

'I was peert of the campayun.'

'Okay – and you want to know what I think of her?'

'That's why I ast you.'

'Honest opinion? Not much.'

I can tell from his face that this isn't the answer he wanted.

I'm there, 'She looks like Camila Cabello – I'll give her that – albeit with an underbite like an open cash register. But she's clearly no fan of mine.'

He goes, 'It's joost I really like her, Rosser. I'd luvven for you to meet her again.'

'No, thanks. Once was enough for me. More than enough.'

'It's joost I've steerted sort of seeing the geerdle.'

'For fock's sake, Ro! I thought the whole idea of you breaking up with Shadden was so you could ride all around you. Instead, you're hitching yourself to a bird who – okay, she's got a great set of, for want of a better word, bongos –'

'Mebbe that's why she dudn't like you, Rosser.'

'Excuse me?'

'You could mebbe do wit leardon about the koyunt of things you cadden and caddent say these days. The wurdled's chayunged.'

'She's zero crack, Ro. That's my point. I'm no fan of sushi, but I wouldn't consider it racist.'

'She's the President of the Students' Youn Yodden, Rosser. She's throying to make her meerk is all. Huguette was the wooden what got clapping baddened in UCD.'

'Clapping?'

'That's reet.'

'You're saying clapping is banned in UCD?'

'It's joost in case it thriggers some wooden to hab an anxiety attack.'

'So what do people do instead of clapping?'

'Thee do jazz haddens.'

Ronan demonstrates for me, even though I already know what jazz hands are – I was a showman back in my kicking days, bear in mind.

I'm there, 'So what do they do when the rugby team are playing?'

He goes, 'Sayum thing. Jazz haddens.'

'But they're in the All Ireland League! Jesus Christ – Division 1A!'

'Huguette persuaded them to put soyuns up alt over the growunt, aston the crowud to respect the clapping badden.'

'And they do?'

'It's just good maddors, Rosser. It's showing respect for people who are diffordent.'

'Seriously, Ro, you'd have been better off marrying Shadden. At least she's a bit of fun – especially when she drinks while she's on antibiotics.'

Of course, it's at that exact moment that a security gord arrives over to us. He's holding Brian by the scruff of the neck with one hand and Leo with the other. Behind them, I can see a boy, about the same age as them, crying his eyes out and his mother – early forties, total fox – telling him that it's okay, the nasty boys have gone now.

I notice Rihanna-Brogan apologizing to the woman, telling her that the boys are good but they just drink too much Coca-Cola.

Where's her focking loyalty? That's what I want to know. I can't believe Ronan raised a tout.

'Are these your children?' the security dude goes.

I'm like, 'No,' just to put the focker on the back foot. 'I've never seen them before in my life.'

'Fock you,' Leo goes.

And I'm like, 'No, fock *you*, Leo – how about that?' and that's how I end up giving myself away. 'I can't even enjoy an hour with my son. What have you been accused of doing now?' because I was raised never to admit liability early on.

The security dude goes, 'They pushed a little boy over.'

I'm there, 'I wasn't talking to you. I was talking to my – allegedly – son?'

Brian's like, 'He was standing in my focking way!'

And I'm there, 'See?' proud of the boy for trying to put a positive spin on it. 'Two sides to every story.'

But the security dude isn't in the mood to see it from *his* POV? He just goes, 'If I ever see these children in the Jump Zone again, I'll call the Guards.'

'Ross,' Sorcha goes, 'sit down here with me and help me figure this out, will you?'

She's sitting at the island in the kitchen with her Seanad Éireann diary open in front of her.

I'm like, 'I was just about to do something, em . . . something *else*?'

'Well, now you're not,' she goes. 'You're going to help me figure out this scheduling problem I have for Thursday.'

Thursday, by the way, is the day of the Confirmation and Sorcha is treating it like it's basically a dry run for Honor's wedding.

'No matter what way I look at it,' she goes, 'there are literally not enough hours in the morning to do all of the things I have to do.'

Jesus Christ, she's got the highlighter pens out. It's worse than I thought.

She's there, 'I've moved my spray tan and my pedicure to the night before. I thought that might free up some time, but it actually *hasn't?*'

I'm like, 'Okay,' sitting down beside her, deciding to just go with it – like drowning.

'So, at seven thirty a.m.,' she goes, 'I'm getting my hair done in Glasthule.'

I'm there, 'And does your hair actually *need* to be done?'

'Is that a joke?'

'No, it was a genuine question. I think it looks actually nice.'

'Okay, I'm just going to ignore that. After the hairdressers, I've got to rush from Glasthule to Blackrock to get, like, my make-up and nails done at nine. Then I've got to drive to Stillorgan to collect my Simone Rocha dress from the alterations place. It was, like, an inch too *long?* Then I have to go to Dún Laoghaire to collect the cake. But – oh my God – I have to be back home by half ten because the window cleaner is coming!'

'The window cleaner?'

'Ross, we're having, like, one hundred and twenty people over in the afternoon, including some of Dad's former law colleagues. I am not having dirty windows.'

'Could the window cleaner not come, I don't know, the day before?'

She laughs – like *I'm* the one being ridiculous?

She's like, 'Do you know how difficult it is to get a window cleaner in South Dublin in the Confirmation and Communion months?'

I'm there, 'I've never given it much thought, Sorcha.'

'Yes, that much is obvious, Ross. It's like getting a hair or make-up appointment. I actually booked it last *September?* Then the photographer is also coming at twelve.'

'We've hired a photographer?'

'Of course we've hired a photographer. We want a permanent record of Honor's Confirmation. These are the days, Ross.'

When you wished you'd stayed focking celibate. I'm very tempted to say it, but I manage to somehow stop myself.

'So it's, like, hair at seven thirty,' she goes and she's talking faster than Eabha Barnes now. 'Make-up and nails at nine. Collect my dress at ten. I don't even know if I'll have time to try it on. Then the cake. Then back here in time for the window cleaner and the photographer. And then the caterers are arriving at half twelve and so is the marquee. There'll be just enough time to put it up before . . . Oh! My God!'

'What?'

'I haven't actually scheduled in the whole churchy-churchy part of the day!'

'The what?'

'The churchy-churchy part!'

'Do you mean the *actual* Confirmation?'

'I'm talking about the Mass, Ross, yes! Oh my God, *how* do the other moms make it look so easy?'

I can see how worked up she is, so I take her by the two hands and I tell her to breathe. Which she does.

'Now,' I go, 'let me see this schedule.'

It's obvious from looking at it that more planning has gone into this Confirmation than the hunt for Osama bin Laden. The pages are, like, a confusion of times and notes highlighted in yellow and orange and green and Post-its stuck here, there and literally everywhere. It's classic Sorcha to, like, overthink everything. I end up looking at it with my rugby brain – in other words, tactically. And I figure it out straight away.

'Okay,' I go, 'you get your hair and your nails done as planned. Then go and have a nice champagne breakfast somewhere with Lauren or Chloe or Amie with an ie.'

'What?' she goes. 'I don't have time for that!'

'I'll collect your dress and I'll collect the cake. Then I'll come back here and I'll deal with the window cleaner, the caterers and the marquee. The only thing you need to do is get back in time for the photographer. Then we can all go and enjoy the churchy-churchy bit without anyone needing to be stressed.'

For a few seconds, she thinks about what I've said, then it's like a weight has suddenly been lifted from her shoulders.

'Oh my God,' she goes, 'you're an actual genius!'

I'm there, 'I see the world through the eyes of an outhalf, Sorcha. I'm like a rugby version of Russell Crowe in *A Beautiful Mind.*'

She's like, 'Oh my God, you're amazing!' and she puts her two orms around my shoulders and kisses me. And that kiss very quickly turns into a proper snog – to the point where it suddenly feels like we're finally about to do it, here and now, in the middle of the kitchen.

'We probably shouldn't,' Sorcha goes, pulling away from me.

I'm like, 'Do you want to maybe pop upstairs? I'll be quick.'

'No, let's wait until Thursday night.'

'Okay.'

Fock's sake!

'When all the pressure's off,' she goes.

I'm like, 'Fair enough. If that's how you feel.'

She kisses me again. And it's at that exact point that Fionn walks into the kitchen. He stares at us for a few seconds in silence, then he goes, 'I've just put Hillary down, Sorcha, if you want to say good-night to him.'

And Sorcha's like, 'I do! Then I might check with Honor to see if she's posted the video of us in Havana! I can't wait to read the comments!'

She heads upstairs with a definite skip in her step. Fionn watches her go. He's obviously raging because he still can't bring himself to thank me for saving his son's life.

I'm there, 'It looks like Thursday night is going to be my lucky night in terms of hopefully sealing the deal with Sorcha. I'll make sure the volume on the baby monitor is up nice and high for you.'

'Just make sure there's batteries in it,' he goes. 'That's all I care about.'

'Okay, what's that supposed to mean?'

'Do you really need me to spell it out for you?'

'If you're alleging something, then maybe you *should?*'

'I'm just saying that you and Sorcha might be fooled by Honor, but I'm not.'

'You think she took the batteries out, don't you?'

'You don't want to know what I think, Ross.'

'Say it.'

'All I'm interested in is protecting my son.'

'Protecting him? You'd swear that someone here was deliberately trying to hurt him.'

He goes, 'You would, wouldn't you?'

And I am right on the point of decking him. In other words, there's about to be a decking and he is going to be the subject of that decking. I'm going to be the decker and he's going to be the deckee.

But then Sorcha comes running into the kitchen in a total panic, holding Hillary in her orms, going, 'He's getting sick again, Fionn! Oh my God, what's wrong with our beautiful baby?'

So it's, like, Thursday morning and I'm in Dún Laoghaire with Honor. We've just collected the cake and I'm putting it into the boot of the cor when my old man suddenly texts me. He's like, 'Big day today, Kicker!'

I text him straight back. It's nice to be nice. I'm there, 'What the fock are you talking about?' and I'm presuming it's the Confirmation.

Except he texts me then, going, 'Haven't you seen my last tweet?' and, like a focking idiot, I check his Twitter feed. It's just like:

Charles O'Carroll-Kelly √ @realCOCK – 20m

Today Theresa May triggers Article 50! An historic day as the UK begins the process of taking back its country from the same EU that forced YOU to repay billions of euros in debts that had nothing to do with you! We should follow our friends out the door! #Brexit #Irexit

Reply 971 Retweet 5,426 Like 13,018 ✉

I'm thinking, who the fock is Theresa May? I don't even bother giving him a Like – wouldn't give him the pleasure. Instead, I stick my phone back into my pocket and get into the cor. I stort her up and point her in the direction of Stillorgan.

Honor's like, 'Where are we going now?'

I'm there, 'The alterations place – to pick up your old dear's dress.'

She goes, 'Eugh! I can't *believe* me and her are going to be wearing pretty much the same outfit today.'

'Sorcha said they weren't actually matchy-matchy.'

'They're close enough. You owe me big-time for this, by the way.'

'I know.'

'I mean, it's *actually* painful listening to her at the moment. You know she thinks the Holy focking Spirit is upon me?'

I laugh. It's just the way she phrases it.

I'm there, 'I've heard her mention the Holy Spirit once or twice alright. You're doing great, Honor.'

'I honestly don't know how I've managed to keep biting my tongue.'

'You're still going through with it, aren't you? The Confirmation, I mean?'

'I'm showing my face in the church and that's it. They can fock off if they think I'm saying any of the words.'

'That's great, Honor. I just want you to know that I really appreciate it, okay? I'm back in Sorcha's definite good books.'

'You should be – er, you saved her baby's *life*?'

There's, like, silence between us then. There's something on my mind and Honor knows it. She's sensitive like that.

'What the fock is wrong with you?' she goes.

And I'm there, 'Look, can I ask you a question, Honor?'

'What kind of question?'

'Okay, don't get all defensive. You're going to think I'm being ridiculous even asking this. As a matter of fact, you'll hopefully laugh. But you didn't, by any chance, take the batteries out of the baby monitor in Hillary's room, did you?'

She doesn't answer me either way. But I can feel her just staring at me while I'm focusing on the road ahead. There's just, like, twenty seconds of silence, of neither of us saying shit as I take the turn onto Patrick Street.

I'm there, 'That's good enough for me, Honor,' because I honestly can't bear that kind of silence. 'Not that I ever doubted you.'

She goes, 'Did *she* tell you to ask me that question?'

I'm like, 'No, I just wondered did you possibly borrow the batteries to put them in Pirate Pete – the Repeat Parrot and that's the reason they didn't hear Hillary basically choking?'

I can hear the fear in my voice. I really am terrified of my daughter.

'Oh my God,' she goes, 'it was *him*, wasn't it? *He* thinks I did it!'

I'm there, 'He didn't say it in so many words. But – yeah, no – he as *good* as said it? If it's any consolation, I came very close to decking him. *Very* close.'

'Why would I take the batteries out of the baby monitor?'

'Again, he didn't make any specific allegations. He just kept banging on about how Hillary needed to be protected.'

'Protected?'

'That was the word *he* used – the exact word.'

'Protected from me? He thinks I have something to do with him being sick, doesn't he?'

'He never said that.'

'Hillary is my brother.'

'I know. It's ridiculous – the whole thing.'

She becomes genuinely upset then.

She's like, 'I mean, yes, I'm a bitch. Yes, I've done a lot of things over the years that were genuinely horrible. But do you honestly think I would do anything to physically hurt a member of my own family?'

I go, 'I think you've answered your critics, Honor. Even though they're not here at the moment. Do you know something? I actually think I'll deck him when we get home. I'll just walk into his room. Won't say a word. Bang! Just deck him and leave. Let him figure out when he finally wakes up why he's been on the wrong end of a decking –'

I suddenly stop talking. Because I spot something halfway up Patrick Street that causes me to suddenly slam on the brakes.

I'm like, 'What? The fock?'

Even Honor goes, 'Isn't that your friend – what's his name?'

Yes, it *is* my friend. It's JP. And he's doing something I never thought I'd see any former teammate of mine ever do. He's walking out of a builder's providers, carrying – quite literally – a lorge sheet of wood, we're talking six feet by four feet, which he then storts trying to secure to the roof of his BMW X5 using rope.

I pull up in the middle of the road and I stick the hazards on. I get out of the cor and I walk over to him.

I'm like, 'Dude, what the fock are you doing?'

And he goes, 'What does it look like I'm doing? I'm buying some wood!' and he says it like it's the most natural thing in the world.

I'm there, 'You say that like it's nothing.'

'It *is* nothing,' he goes. 'It's just some wood.'

'Dude, I see you walking out of a builder's providers and you expect me to just drive away and pretend I haven't seen anything? What the fock is going on?'

'I'm building a prototype, Ross. Of the Vampire Bed.'

'Are you serious?'

'You better believe I'm serious. I've patented the idea and I'm going on the *Late Late Show* to talk about it.'

'Dude, you thought it was a stupid idea. You laughed in your old man's face.'

'And I shouldn't have. Maybe that's why he never believed in me – because I never believed in him. I mean, I laughed when he said that Camden Street was Ireland's Greenwich Village. I laughed when he described Sean McDermott Street as Dublin's Brick Lane.'

'JP, you're grieving. Look, I'm sorry I ever told you what your old man said about you.'

'Actually, I'm not. I mean, I was, but I'm not any more. Because it's given me the kick in the orse I needed to go and do this.'

'Dude, you've got an estate agency to run.'

'Fock the estate agency. I'm going to put all of my energy now into making the old man's Vampire Bed dream a reality.'

There's a real buzz outside the old Church of St Thérèse in Mount Merrion. The cor pork is full of excited children, proud fathers and heavily botoxed mothers. And it's big smiles all round, except in the case of the heavily botoxed mothers, who obviously can't smile, but you can tell from their eyes that the *intention* is there?

Honor looks great in her dress. I turn around to her and I ask her if she's okay.

'No, I'm focking not,' she goes, through gritted teeth. 'I feel like a total focking hypocrite.'

. And I'm there, 'I wouldn't let it bother you – it doesn't seem to be an issue for anyone *else* here? If you could just hold it together for one hour, though, I'll owe you in a major way.'

Sorcha waves across the cor pork at Cloud Gorvey's mom and mouths the words, 'Oh my God, your outfit is beautiful!' and the woman mouths back, 'Oh my God, look at *you*!'

'This is some focking prickfest!' Leo goes, looking around him.

Me and Honor laugh. But Sorcha's old dear just tuts. I turn around and I'm like, 'What the fock is your problem? Focking tutting!'

'I don't know *why* you insisted on bringing those boys,' she tries to go.

And I'm there, 'Yeah, *those boys*, as you call them, are Honor's brothers. They're entitled to be here – unlike you two focking dicks.'

Sorcha's old man looks like he wants to throttle me. But at the same time, he doesn't want to cause a scene outside a church – values his rep too much, so he just goes, 'Sorcha, I'm going to ask the priest if he needs assistance in ministering the Eucharist today.'

Because that's the kind of knob you're dealing with here.

And Sorcha's old dear goes, 'I'll come with you, Edmund,' and she makes sure to give me a filthy before they thankfully fock off.

It's a beautiful, spring day. It's one of the social events of the year in South Dublin and we all stand around outside the church to soak up the atmos and make comments about each other out of the side of our mouths.

'Oh my God,' Sorcha goes, 'Susan Gorvey wore that exact same skirt and top to the last Mount Anville Past Pupils Networking Brunch!' and then a few minutes later she's like, 'Oh my God, Ross, don't *ever* let me go out wearing what Currer Bell Whelehan's mom is wearing!'

Yes, it's nice to see that the old traditions are alive and well in Mount Anville. Money, insincerity and faces stuffed with filler – these people were doing it long before anyone had ever heard of the Kordashians.

Mallorie Kennedy tips over to us with her daughter, Courage. 'Oh my God!' the woman goes. 'Sorcha, look at you and Honor in your matching dresses!'

Sorcha can't figure out whether that's a dig or a compliment. That's the thing about dealing with Mount Anville moms – sometimes the truth only dawns on you weeks later.

'They're not, like, *matchy*-matchy?' Sorcha tries to go.

'Well, you both look absolutely fabulous,' Mallorie goes. 'What name is Honor choosing?'

Sorcha's like, 'Madeleine.'

'Oh,' Mallorie goes, unable to hide her disappointment. 'Courage was thinking about that one as well. Sister Dave was saying there'd be no Mount Anville today if it wasn't for this Madeleine person. Although Courage is still thinking about double-barrelling it – maybe with something French. She's still got two or three options in mind. Oh, look at your lovely boys, Sorcha!'

'Fock off,' Leo goes, 'you ugly focking bitch!'

I laugh. So does Honor. His comic timing is un-focking-believable.

Mallorie pretends that it doesn't bother her. She just smiles at Sorcha and goes, 'So did you get a morquee?'

Sorcha's like, 'Yeah, we've got, like, a hundred and twenty people coming this afternoon.'

'*We've* got a hundred and fifty. You stole our caterer, by the way.'

'Excuse me?'

'*We* booked him last August. But my husband forgot – or, more likely, didn't bother – to pay the deposit, then *you* came in and snapped him up. I don't want you to feel bad about it. Is he doing his quince, ham and blue cheese pintxos?'

'No, he's doing mango and crayfish *vol-au-vents* and then mini ginger burgers with lime mayo and arugula.'

'The pintxos are the thing he's famous for – again, not being a bitch. Oh my God, here comes Bishop Brannigan!'

Yeah, no, the dude who's going to do the actual *confirming* – if that's the right word? – gets out of the back of a black Merc and everyone ooohs and awwws and claps like it's Michael focking Bublé, then we all shuffle into the church.

Sister Dave greets us at the door. She's like, 'Hello, Honor!' and there's a real, I don't know, smugness in her voice, like she's reminding her who won the battle of wills between them and she's determined to rub her basic *nose* in it?

Inside the church, I spot Roz Matthews and she gives me a smile and a wave – obviously not one to hold a grudge – then Sincerity tips over and asks Honor if she wants to sit beside her and Honor just shrugs like she doesn't give a fock one way or the other.

Sorcha's like, 'Good luck, girls!' as Sincerity follows Honor up the aisle and they sit in the third pew back. 'We're so proud of you, Dorling!'

And I'm there, 'Bear in mind, Honor, it'll be over before you know it!'

And – yeah, no – then the whole thing kicks off. Sorcha spends most of the actual Mass dabbing at her eyes with a handkerchief and whispering, 'Our little girl, Ross!'

And I'm like, 'Yeah, no, definite fair focks.'

She slips her hand into mine while we're singing 'Praise, My Soul, the King of Heaven'. To her immediate left, I can see her old man staring at our two sets of fingers knotted together and I can tell that it kills him. I'm looking sideways at him and he accidentally makes eye contact with me and I run my tongue over my top lip just to let him know that I'm probably going to be – for want of a better phrase – banging his daughter's back out later on tonight.

Seriously, if that man ever puts his hands around my throat, he won't let go until I'm actually dead.

Anyway, the whole thing is going pretty well. Even the boys manage to behave themselves, except for one sort of embarrassing moment when Susan Gorvey is reading the Second Letter from St Paul to the Thessalonians and Leo shouts, 'Fock you! And fock the Thessalonians!' and the people in front of us stort looking back over their shoulders to find out where the comment came from.

I tell one or two of them to turn the fock around, then normal service resumes.

Yeah, no, like I said, the whole thing is going pretty much swimmingly until about forty-five minutes in, when we get to what I would call the whole 'Do you this?' and 'Do you that?' port of the Mass.

Bishop Brannigan is standing behind the altar and he's going, 'Do you reject Satan and all his works and all his empty promises?'

And all the girls are like, 'I do!'

He goes, 'Do you believe in God the Father, the Almighty, maker of Heaven and Earth?'

Again, they're all there, 'I do!'

Sorcha smiles at me, as if to say, So far, so good.

The bishop's there, 'Do you believe in Jesus Christ, His only Son, our Lord, who was born of the Virgin Mary, was crucified, died and was buried, rose from the dead, and is now seated at the right hand of the Father?'

They girls are all like, 'I do!'

But then the dude suddenly stops – as in, he doesn't say shit for about twenty seconds. There's something obviously wrong. He steps out from behind the altar and he walks over to the first pew. He goes, 'There's one little girl there and I don't see her lips moving.'

I'm thinking, Oh, fock!

There's, like, muttering throughout the church. Everyone's hoping it isn't *their* kid who's being singled out?

'I bet it's Courage Kennedy!' Sorcha goes.

The dude goes, 'The renewal of our Baptismal promises is an essential part of the Sacrament we are gathered here to celebrate today. Is there a reason why *you* see fit not to affirm these beliefs in words?'

He's staring directly at Honor and he's trying to embarrass her in front of the entire church. Not a good move with Honor. Someone should have warned him.

'Yeah,' Honor goes, suddenly standing up. 'Because it's all focking *bullshit*?'

There's, like, gasps in the church. Sorcha puts her hand over her mouth and I watch the colour drain quickly from her face.

'Pack! Of! Focking! Bullshit!' Brian shouts.

'I *beg* your pardon?' Bishop Brannigan goes.

Honor looks back over her shoulder at me and she's like, 'I'm sorry, Dad!'

I'm there, 'It's cool, Honor. I raised you to never be afraid to call it. So call it.'

She turns back to Bishop Brannigan. 'It's all focking bullshit,' she goes. 'God. The Devil. The Virgin Mary. The Resurrection. You standing up there in your stupid focking hat. All religious belief is just superstition. Like focking horoscopes. And deep down no one in this church actually believes it.'

Again, more gasps.

She goes, 'They're all just doing it for the day out. How many of them go to actual Mass?'

Sorcha's old man is suddenly up on his feet. 'Sit down,' he goes, 'this instant! And repeat the vows along with everyone else!'

'It's quite alright,' the bishop goes, pretending that he's not secretly bulling. 'Our faith should be sufficiently strong to withstand a little girl's questioning, however vulgarly expressed!' and he says it in a really patronizing voice to try to make her look small in front of her classmates. 'What do *you* know about Theology, child?'

Honor goes, 'Er, I've read enough to make up my *own* mind?'

'Oh, have you, indeed? Well, what have you read?'

'I read that in the year 312, before the Battle of Milvian Bridge, Emperor Constantine dreamt that he saw a cross in the sky.'

'The basis of our Roman Catholic faith.'

'Well, when he woke up the next morning and told everyone, someone really should have said, "Yeah, you just focking dreamt that." And if they had, none of us would be standing here today.'

I turn to Sorcha and I'm like, 'Is that true? Is the whole thing genuinely based on some focking dream that some dude had?' but the woman is in tears and she's being comforted by her old man.

The bishop turns suddenly angry. So much for his faith withstanding a little girl's questioning. He points at her – his face all red – and goes, 'You wicked child! You dare to stand up in the house of God and question the faith held by more than a billion –'

'Oh, please!' Honor goes. 'No one is born believing this bullshit. That's why you insist on filling our heads with it before our brains are properly developed. Oh my God, you baptize us before we even know we're born, then you tell us when we're, like, eleven or twelve years old that we're old enough to believe in God but we're not old enough *not* to?'

There's quite a few girls sobbing in the church. It kind of reminds me of a certain Christmas morning when Honor was five years old, when she picked up the microphone at the children's Mass in the Church of the Gordian Angels on Newtownpork Avenue and announced that there was no such thing as Santa Claus. I'm seeing definite parallels here. But, just like the last time, not everyone in the congregation appreciates her telling – as they call it – her *truth*.

Mallorie Kennedy is suddenly on her feet, going, 'Why are you here, then? Why are you even *making* your Confirmation if you don't believe in God?'

Honor's there, 'Because focking Dave there said I *had* to make it?'

'It's *Sister* focking Dave to you,' Sister focking Dave goes.

Mallorie goes, 'You should leave if that's how you feel!' and the woman turns around and glowers at Sorcha and it's obvious that she's thinking, What a waste of a good caterer.

I stand up and I step out of the pew. The three boys come with me. I'm like, 'Come on, Honor, let's go home!'

And, from the front of the church, Honor looks at me the way every father dreams his daughter will one day look at him – like I'm her actual hero. A second or two later, she comes running down the aisle towards me, a big smile on her face.

'Horrible girl!' I hear Susan Gorvey go.

And I'm like, 'Yeah, that's the same skirt and top you wore to the last Mount Anville Past Pupils Networking Brunch. And everyone's focking bitching about you behind your back!'

I give Honor a hug, then I kiss her on the top of the head. I can honestly say that I've never been prouder of her.

And that's the moment Brian chooses to put his hand down the back of his trousers again, catch a fart in his little fist, then blow it, like a kiss, at the congregation.

As we're leaving, I steal a sort of sideways look at Sorcha. The girl is absolutely devastated, bawling her eyes out and looking at Honor like she thinks the girl is, I don't know, possessed by the – allegedly – *devil*? And while the debate about the actual existence of God and the Virgin Mary and that entire crew is bound to continue, one fact is definitely beyond doubt.

I will not be getting sex from Sorcha tonight.

5.

What to Pack in Your Going-Away Bag!

I'm there, 'I really don't think we should make a bigger deal out of this than it *needs* to be?'

I'm chancing my orm with a line like that. I know it and they know it.

'A bigger deal than it needs to be?' Sorcha's old man goes. 'It's on the front page of the *Irish Times*! Do you have *any* idea how embarrassing this is for me professionally?'

That's his biggest concern, of course.

I'm there, 'Er, she's not actually *named* in the story?'

'Don't be ridiculous!' he goes. 'Everyone will know who it's about. And I've got to show my face in the Law Library with everyone no doubt sniggering behind my back.'

'A girl of not even twelve yet,' Sorcha's old dear goes, 'speaking to a bishop like that! In front of all those people!'

I'm there, 'I don't know what business it is of yours anyway. Why don't you take your husband and fock off back to the woodshed? Pair of bell-ends. Focking Bell-end and Sebastian.'

Sorcha cried for about six hours after we left the church. She was up all night crying as well. Then she storted again when she saw the headline in his morning's paper: 'What Did the Mountie Say to the Bishop?' – which *I* thought was quite *clever?* – and then when the school rang to say they were suspending Honor for two weeks.

Now Sorcha's just sitting at the kitchen table, staring into space, like a woman traumatized.

Her old man goes, 'You're being very quiet, Dorling.'

And she's like, 'I just don't know what to say. And I have no more tears left to cry.'

Seriously. When it comes to drama, Meryl focking Streep has nothing on the girl.

I'm standing in front of the open fridge, by the way, horsing into the mango and crayfish *vol-au-vents* and the mini ginger burgers with lime mayo and arugula.

Hey, they were paid for.

Sorcha's old dear stares out the window, where three Polish dudes are dismantling the morquee. 'All those people we had to ring and tell not to come,' she goes, 'can you imagine what they're saying today? The whole of South Dublin will be talking about it.'

Sorcha goes, 'I think we're missing the point here. I don't care what anyone in South Dublin thinks.'

Yeah, this coming from the girl who can't take a flight anywhere without telling everyone in her email inbox how many native broadleaf trees she going to plant to offset the carbon emissions. She's changed her tune. That's all I'm saying.

She goes, 'The point is that Honor is a very disturbed little girl.'

I'm like, 'No way! I'm not having that!'

'She's possibly even a sociopath.'

'What, just because she doesn't believe in God?'

'It was the pleasure she took in announcing it, Ross. It was like that time in Foxrock Church when she told all the little kiddies that there was no such thing as Santa Claus.'

'I don't think it was like that at all, Sorcha. I genuinely don't see the comparison.'

'And both times she waited until the middle of Mass to do it.'

'Hey, the dude tried to embarrass her in front of everyone. You shouldn't stick your neck out if there's a chance you might just get it slapped.'

'I was *so* embarrassed. And – oh my God – to think that I actually believed the Holy Spirit had come down on her?'

'Spare me, would you? She told you weeks ago that she didn't believe in God. But you were having none of it. You heard what you wanted to hear.'

Sorcha just shakes her head. She's really laying it on thick. 'She used the F-word,' she goes, 'in front of a bishop.'

Her old man's there, 'She's out of control. Your mother and I have been trying to tell you that for years. And there's no mystery as to who is to blame.'

I'm there, 'I can't listen to any more of this.'

Sorcha goes, 'Ross, come back here! We need to talk about what we're going to do about her!'

But I straight walk out of the kitchen – although not before grabbing six or seven mini ginger burgers in my hands and stuffing two or three more into my mouth.

I tip upstairs, where I find Honor lying on her bed – not a care in the world.

She goes, 'I was thinking, I should stort using my YouTube channel to get, like, *free* stuff?'

I'm like, 'Er, yeah, good point,' a bit thrown by how not bothered she is about the whole thing. It's like she doesn't properly understand the *hugeness* of what actually happened yesterday? She certainly doesn't give a fock about being suspended from school. 'You should definitely, definitely do that, Honor.'

She goes, 'I was talking to Erika on, like, FaceTime the other day. I was telling her that Love Honor and Obey has, like, 70,000 followers and she said I needed to stort thinking about it as, like, a brand?'

'Did she?'

'She said I should be looking for ways to, like, *monetize* my fame? Kind of like Pippa O'Connor has with the whole Fashion Factory thing.'

God, I love Pippa O'Connor. I know it's slightly off the point, but I remember making a move on her in Tramco after Leinster lost the Heineken Cup semi-final to Munster in 2006. She looked me up and down and told me that she valued herself more than that. Still drank the appletinis I bought for her and her mates, though.

I'm like, 'Honor, do you want to maybe talk about what happened yesterday?'

She goes, 'Er, not really? Do you?'

'You've been suspended from school, Honor. You're on the front page of the *Irish Times*. And I think your mother would probably want me to say something to you, in terms of hopefully trying to get you to see that what you did was wrong.'

'But *you* don't *think* I was wrong – do you?'

'Yeah, no, definitely not.'

'So why are we having this conversation? I mean, why does everyone have a problem with me not believing in God?'

'Hey, if I'd known the entire thing was based on some dude having a dream hundreds and hundreds of years ago, I would have been a bit Scooby Doobious myself. I certainly would have had one or two questions for Father Fehily back in the day.'

'The whole Bible is like that. *God appeared to Abraham in a dream.* Er, no, he didn't? Abraham focking dreamt it.'

'Well, you have me convinced. The point is, if you could maybe pretend to Sorcha that me and you had the big chat, that would definitely help me.'

'Fine.'

'She hasn't said anything, but deep down I think she's probably worried about what this might do to her political career.'

'What political career?'

'Good one, Honor!'

'Seriously, though – what focking political career? She's in the Seanad. No one cares.'

'That's actually a very good point. Just to warn you, though, she might take your devices away for a week or two – your phone and your laptop.'

'For fock's sake. Seriously?'

'Don't worry, I'll let you use mine on the sly. She might also stop your pocket money. Although, again, don't worry. I'll slip you cash. I'll take it out of her birthday present.'

'Thanks, Dad. Er, by the way?'

'What?'

'Bell-end and Sebastian?'

'Did you hear that?'

'Oh my God, that was *so* funny!'

'Yeah, no, it was one of those lines that just came to me in the moment.'

'I'm sorry, you are *actually* the funniest person in the world!'

It's impossible to be angry with this girl.

I'm there, 'Thanks, Honor. Although I doubt if either of them has ever heard of the band. I was thinking I should have maybe kept it for Fionn. He's got everything they ever put out.'

'So how long do you think *she's* going to be pissed off for?'

'Until they let you back into Mount Anville would be my guess.'

'Sister Dave is such an overreactor.'

'I wouldn't worry about it, Honor. As a matter of fact, I firmly believe that this is the kind of thing we'll be laughing at in a few weeks.'

'Really?'

'Or maybe months. And just to tell you, I did *way* worse than this in my day!'

'Did you? As in?'

'Okay, did I ever tell you about the time we egged a group of girls from Sion Hill – focking Pill Hill, in other words – and one of them ended up being allergic to eggs? Her head blew up like a focking Pilates ball!'

'Oh my God, that is *so* funny!'

'Oisinn had to stab her through the sternum with a focking epi-pen.'

'That's, like, way worse than telling a bishop that there's no such thing as God.'

'Trust me, Honor. One day this will just be an anecdote that'll bring the house down in my Father of the Bride speech.'

'Do you really believe that?'

'One hundred percent. Like that girl who nearly died of anaphylactic shock.'

'Thanks, Dad.'

'Don't you worry, Honor. I'm in your corner – even if I'm the only one.'

*

So it's, like, Friday night. And after the forty-eight hours I've just had, I'm looking forward to having my usual eight or nine quiet pints in Kielys of Donnybrook Town.

Except none of the goys has shown their faces yet, aport from Oisinn, who's already four or five pints down the road when I arrive.

He goes, 'Hey, Ross,' a definite note of concern in his voice. 'How's Honor doing?'

I'm like, 'Er, why are you asking about Honor?'

'Dude, the whole country is talking about what happened at the Mount Anville Confirmation.'

I end up just shaking my head.

I'm like, 'Why does everyone automatically assume it was Honor?'

He's there, 'It's just I got that text from you telling me that the porty was cancelled at, like, an hour's notice. Then it said on the front page of this morning's *Irish Times* that a girl had walked out of the church after openly questioning the existence of God and launching a foul-mouthed attack on the bishop.'

'And you joined up the dots and decided it was my daughter?'

'Sorry, Ross, I didn't mean any offence.'

'Jesus Christ – talk about give a dog a bad name.'

'So it *wasn't* her, then?'

'Yeah, no, it *was* her. It's just I hate the way people always assume.'

He hands me a pint of the obvious.

He goes, 'Is she okay?'

I'm like, 'She's fine. Suspended for two weeks. Her old dear's obviously not happy. She thinks Honor is a . . . What's that word that *sounds* like a psychopath but hopefully isn't as bad?'

'A sociopath?'

'That's the one. She thinks she's a sociopath.'

'Poor Honor.'

'Actually, I was telling her today about the time we hit that girl from Sion Hill with the eggs and you had to stab her with the epi-pen – we're talking *Pulp Fiction*-style.'

'What about it?'

'Yeah, no, I was using it as an example of something that seemed very serious at the time but then became a funny anecdote. I think her telling the bishop to go fock himself will eventually fall into that category. By the way, where *is* everyone tonight?'

'No idea where Fionn and JP are. Christian is on his way. And Magnus is working.'

'On a Friday night? I thought working in Facebook was a piece of piss?'

'It *would* be a piece of piss if he just went in, did his job and came home. It's just there's all this, like, *other* stuff, you know?'

'Yeah, no, he was telling me all about it at the Ireland v France match. I actually found it really boring.'

'I mean, he's working away on something, then someone says, "Oh, you're up next, Magnus! You're playing the Head of Compliance in the Facebook Dublin Air Hockey Championship." Or "You're playing someone from the Data Protection Team in the Facebook Dublin Fussball World Cup."'

'Jesus, that sounds like college.'

'It *is* like college. The only problem is that he still has his work to do, so he ends up having to stay late to do it, which means it's eating into *our* time?'

'I had to move away from him. That's how focking dull I found the whole thing.'

'Don't get me wrong, it's great that he's making new friends. He doesn't know that many people in Ireland. But it'd be nice for me to see him once in a while. Like, just as an example, he never comes to the gym with me any more.'

'Jesus! Didn't you get him membership of David Lloyd Riverview for Christmas?'

'Exactly. But any time I suggest going, he says he's going to work late and use the Facebook gym at lunchtime.'

'Shit one. I genuinely mean that.'

'It's the same with dinner. On the rare occasions he *is* home before ten o'clock at night, I ask if he fancies going out to grab something to eat – the other night, I suggested Mulberry Gorden.'

'Sorcha loves Mulberry Gorden.'

'And he says, "No, I actually ate in the Facebook canteen."'

'Like I said, Sorcha would bite your hand off.'

'I know I'm storting to sound incredibly needy, but it's like that place has become his life. As in, it's *all* he ever talks about now. We were having sex the other night –'

'Whoa! Too Much Information, Dude! And I hope that's not me being homophobic.'

'We were having sex and right in the middle of it, he said something about Google.'

'Google?'

'Something about how they were supposed to have a great softball team this year.'

'Jesus, that would put anyone off their stroke – again, *not* homophobic?'

'Google are, like, their nemesis. Everyone in Facebook hates Google and everyone in Google hates Facebook. They both hate LinkedIn, but LinkedIn pretend to be above it – except they're not above it, they're just too busy hating eBay. And everyone, by the way, hates PayPal.'

'So it's sort of like the schools rivalry thing – except obviously it doesn't matter a fock?'

'Nail on head, Ross. Nail on head.'

All of a sudden, Christian shows up. He's like, 'Hey, goys,' and I make a big show of looking at my wrist, even though I'm not actually wearing a watch, just to let him know how *late* he is? He goes, 'We need to turn on the TV. Mary, can you turn on the TV?'

Me and Oisinn are like, 'Dude, what's wrong?' because he seems upset about something.

He goes, 'JP is going to be on the *Late Late Show*. Mary, will you turn on the TV?'

Mary turns on the TV and we all look up at the screen. And sitting there, on the famous couch, is the man of the moment.

'Okay,' Oisinn goes, 'that explains why *he* was a no-show tonight.'

I'm like, 'Yeah, no, I met him yesterday in Dún Laoghaire, coming out of – quite literally – a builder's providers. He said was going to be on the *Late Late*, but I didn't think he meant, like, *this* week?'

Tubs is going, 'Now this bed – you *are* going to demonstrate for us, in just a moment, how it works – but, first of all, tell us the story behind it. Where did the idea come from?'

JP doesn't seem nervous at all.

'Well,' he goes, 'I've spent most of my working life, I suppose, in the property business. My father had his own estate agency – Hook, Lyon and Sinker. I believe he sold you your current house, Ryan.'

'He did,' Tubs goes. And from the big, empty smile that he gives him, you can tell instantly that he must have stung the dude in a big-time way. I just hope he's professional enough not to take it out on JP.

'And I suppose in the last few years,' JP goes, 'I was becoming a little bit restless. I was staring down the barrel of my forties, thinking, is this what I want to do for the rest of my life? And it was becoming more and more of an urgent issue for me because my father was planning to retire and I had to decide if I wanted to take over the business or not.'

Okay, *that's* a lie?

Tubs goes, 'And then your father died – very suddenly, wasn't it?'

'That's right, Ryan,' JP goes. 'He had a heart attack – doing what he loved, but that was just a small consolation. He was an amazing character –'

'He was certainly that. From my own dealings with him.'

'I remember the day of the funeral, sitting in the church, listening to speaker after speaker pay tribute to my father. For instance, he was the first estate agent ever to use the phrase "bijou" to describe a house that was simply small.'

'He was very fond of that word alright.'

'He was a visionary in so many ways. And, I suppose, listening to those tributes, I started to think, you know, how will *I* be remembered? What will *my* son say about *me* at *my* funeral? And that's when I realized that I didn't really exist in my own terms, that all I'd really done in life was – I suppose like a lot of South Dublin people – work for my old man.'

I end up shouting at the TV. I'm there, 'You won a Leinster Schools Senior Cup medal as well!'

For a second or two, I'm sure that Tubs is going to remind him of that, but in the end he doesn't, of course, because he's Blackrock College through and through.

It's no wonder they're considered the PayPal of rugby schools.

'So you decided to pursue your own dream,' Tubs goes. 'And you had an idea for an invention called –'

JP's like, 'The Vampire Bed.'

I turn around to Oisinn and Christian and I'm like, 'It wasn't his invention at all! You heard him laugh when his old man mentioned it in the Aviva that day.'

Tubs stands up and JP stands up at the same time. 'So,' Tubs goes, 'let's take a look at it and you can explain how it works.'

They walk across the floor of the studio. JP's supposed invention is standing there just in front of Paddy Cullivan and the Camembert Quartet, covered with a white sheet.

JP's there, 'Well, I suppose, being an estate agent for such a long time, I was especially interested in the concept of space – especially how to maximize it.'

'Yes,' Tubs goes, 'I seem to remember your father's measurements included the cavity wall spaces.'

I'm thinking, Get over yourself, Tubs. Everything doesn't have to be about you.

Thankfully, though, JP doesn't take the bait. He's there, 'As an estate agent, you spend a lot of time thinking about wasted space. And it always struck me that the biggest waste of space in any house or aportment is the amount of room given over to beds.'

'Beds,' Tubridy goes. 'Right.'

'A standard single bed is three feet wide and six feet and three inches in length. A double bed is four feet and six inches wide and – again – six feet and three inches in length.'

'And you've come up with a bed that takes up half the space. Do you want to remove the cover there?'

'Yeah,' JP goes, 'this is a prototype that I put together last night, just to show your viewers what it'll look like.'

JP grabs a hold of the sheet and he whips it off. Underneath is, well, as you'd expect, a bed that's standing up at an angle of whatever it is.

The audience bursts out laughing.

JP doesn't get flustered, in fairness to him. 'It's fine,' he goes, 'I can fully understand that reaction.'

Tubs is there, 'You can, can you?'

'Absolutely.'

'Because you're suggesting – are you not? – that people can sleep just as comfortably standing up as they can lying down?'

The audience cracks up laughing again. I've got a hell of a lot of time for Ryan Tubridy, but I have never wanted to give another human being a wedgy as much as I do right now.

JP's there, 'Well, actually, Ryan, would you believe me if I told you that humans are evolutionarily hordwired to sleep upright?'

'Er, no,' Tubs goes – and he pulls a face, much to the audience's amusement. 'I have to admit, I'm struggling with that idea.'

People who go to Blackrock College believe fock-all unless they hear it from a teacher in the Institute, where most of them end up eventually repeating.

'Well, it's true,' JP goes. 'It dates back to the time when man was a *flight* rather than *fight* animal. As a matter of fact, sleeping horizontally is a relatively recent phenomenon.'

'Right,' Tubs goes, nodding along dubiously. 'I'm going to have to take your word for it.'

JP doesn't let him throw him off his game. Back in the day, he was probably the best full-back in the country under a high ball.

'As you can see,' he goes, climbing onto the bed, 'it's got a footboard at the end here, which, along with the angle of the bed, supports your weight while you sleep. The mattress is made of memory foam and it's got this pillow here, which is attached by Velcro to stop it falling off. And, of course, what I haven't mentioned yet, but should, are the health benefits that come from sleeping vertically, including improved vascular function, metabolic action and mental health.'

He puts his head on the pillow. The audience laughs again. Christian's there, 'He's dying on his feet – literally!'

'So what happens next?' Tubs goes. 'You're about to go into production, is that right?'

JP's there, 'That's right, Ryan. I'm planning to open a factory within a matter of weeks and hopefully produce the first one thousand Vampire Beds this summer.'

There's, like, more laughter.

'You can hear the reaction,' Tubs goes. 'They all think you're mad, as I'm sure a lot of people watching at home do, too.'

JP's like, 'People laughed at the idea of telephones, airplanes – even television.'

'Well,' Tubs goes, 'we've had zombie banks and ghost estates! We might as well have Vampire Beds!'

You can tell he's been dying to say that all night. Of course, the *Late Late* audience lap up jokes like that, just like they do free shit.

JP tries to go, 'We're living through a time of record homelessness, Ryan. We have to face the facts. We just don't have enough houses or apartments for all of the people who are looking for somewhere to live.'

'And you think we will if we can persuade people to sleep standing up?'

'I'm absolutely convinced that this bed is the solution to the homelessness crisis. And even beyond that, it could be used to ease overcrowding in our hospitals. Patients will no longer have to sleep in corridors if we can sort of, like, stack them in the ward. I genuinely think that one day we'll look back at the time when we slept on our backs and we'll say, "My God, what a waste of space! What were we thinking?"'

'And you're absolutely committed to this idea!'

'One hundred percent, Ryan. As a sign of how much I actually believe in this idea, I made a big decision this morning – to put Hook, Lyon and Sinker on the morket.'

Me, Christian and Oisinn all just stare at each other, our mouths open in just shock.

Tubs is like, 'You're selling your father's estate agency?'

'That's right,' JP goes. 'I'm putting Hook, Lyon and Sinker on the morket first thing on Monday morning and I'm going to invest all of the proceeds from the sale in my new business venture. That's how confident I am in it.'

'Well, good luck with it – I have a feeling you're going to need it! But thank you for showing us your Vampire Bed. Ladies and gentlemen, put your hands together for JP Conroy!'

The audience claps, except you can tell it's just out of, like, politeness?

'He's totally lost it,' Christian goes. 'Goys, we have to stop him making the biggest mistake of his life.'

So it's, like, the following Wednesday afternoon and Sorcha rings to ask me where I am? I tell her I'm in the Country Bake in Dalkey, enjoying a bit of Me Time, drinking coffee, flirting with the waitresses clearing the tables and scribbling down thoughts in my famous Rugby Tactics Book.

Although I don't actually *mention* the flirting bit – for obvious reasons.

She goes, 'Can you come home, please – as in, like, right now?' and she sounds upset about something.

I'm there, 'What's up?'

'Just come home, Ross. And come straight around to the back of the house to the Shomera. And don't tell Honor you're home. I need to talk to you about something.'

I'm straight away wondering, Okay, what fresh hell is this? And, as it turns out, there's no preparing me for what I'm about to be told, even after all my years of being a father.

I arrive home, then around the side of the house I trot, thinking to myself – yeah, no – whatever this ends up being, I'll somehow spin it. I'm good at that.

There turns out to be four of them sitting around the table in the little wooden grief hole that Sorcha's old pair call a home. We're talking Sorcha, her old pair and Fionn – and they've all got, like, big, serious *faces* on them?

It actually feels like I've walked in on a wake. Yeah, no, it's like someone died. Sorcha, I can't help but notice, is as white as a sheet.

You know the way sometimes you sort of *know* what's coming even before you *actually* know? But I still go on the straight away defensive.

I'm like, 'Okay, what has she *allegably* done now?' and I make the little quotation morks with my fingers.

Sorcha's old dear goes, 'Blind loyalty to the end. Didn't expect anything less from him, of course.'

I look at Fionn and I notice that he's got Honor's MacBook in front of him. I'm like, 'What the fock are you doing with my daughter's laptop?'

He goes, 'I took it from her room to look through her Google search history. I'm entitled to know what's going on, Ross.'

I end up totally flipping. I'm there, 'And my daughter is entitled to her privacy. This is a breach of her, I don't know, civil rights?'

Which is weak, I fully realize. As my old man says, civil rights aren't something that people in this port of the world need to *concern* themselves with?

'Tell him what you found,' Sorcha's old man goes, egging him on – and there's a definite note of satisfaction in the dude's voice. It's like he's been waiting for this moment for a long time.

Fionn goes, 'I'm sorry, Ross. I had to find out who took the batteries out of the baby monitor. And, more than that, I had to find out what was making my son ill.'

I'm like, 'This sounds like it's going to be total bullshit. Whatever you're about to say, I already know that it's total bullshit.'

'I had my suspicions that it was something other than gastroenteritis,' he tries to go, 'especially after it happened for the third time. And then when I discovered that the baby monitor wasn't working, I knew that something sinister was going on. So I checked Honor's internet search history – going back to just before Hillary got sick for the first time.'

'Get to the point, you focking glasses fock. I think we're all bored.'

'Your daughter was googling poisons!' Sorcha's old man goes – delighted to be the one to actually tell me.

Sorcha storts – I swear to fock – sobbing uncontrollably.

I'm like, 'No way. That's, like, total bullshit.'

Fionn goes, 'I can show you the sites she visited, Ross. Specifically, she was looking for poisons that act slowly and leave no trace.'

My entire body turns suddenly cold. I don't *know* what to say?

I'm like, 'There's no way. There's literally, literally no way that Honor would do something like that. Think about it.'

Sorcha picks up her phone and dials a number. A second or two later, still wiping her tears away with an open palm, she goes, 'Honor, can you come down to the Shomera right now, please? There's something your father and I wish to talk to you about.'

Honor obviously says something back to her and Sorcha ends up roaring at her. She's like, 'No, it can't wait until "focking never"! Get down here right now!' and then she hangs up on her.

I'm there, 'Before she gets here, I just want to say on the record that I refuse to accept that she's capable of poisoning a baby. I just refuse – point blank – to accept it.'

I know I'm clutching at straws here.

'Ross,' Sorcha goes, 'will you please open your eyes to what our daughter has become? Because if we refuse to see it, then we can't help her.'

All of a sudden, the door opens and in she walks, full of 'tude.

'Let me guess,' she goes. 'You've finally seen the funny side of what happened at the Confirmation last week?'

She's very like me in that way – she'll go all out when she has a one-liner that she thinks is funny. I end up having to laugh – no matter what they claim she's done. I'm like, 'Good line, Honor! High stakes humour!'

But then she cops her laptop resting on Fionn's knees and her expression suddenly turns. She's like, 'What the fock are you doing with that?'

He goes, 'I'm protecting my son's life.'

'Your son's life? Dad, what the fock are they talking about?'

Sorcha goes, 'We *know*, Honor.'

Honor's there, 'Know what?' and she seems to genuinely mean it. Either that or she's a very good actor.

Actually, I *know* she's a very good actor?'

Sorcha's old man goes, 'You've been poisoning a helpless baby – and you've been found out!'

Honor's like, 'No, I haven't. Dad, where the fock are they getting this from?'

'Fionn checked your Google search history,' Sorcha goes. 'We know you've been looking up poisons on the internet – in particular, slow-acting ones that don't leave a trace.'

Honor's there, 'Yes, I've been looking up poisons,' like it's the most natural thing in the world to say. 'But I was actually looking for ways to kill your parents.'

I let out a sigh of relief.

'Thank God for that,' I go. 'Thanks for clearing that up, Honor. I knew there'd be an innocent explanation.'

Sorcha's old man goes, 'She's lying.'

I'm there, 'There's one thing my daughter is definitely not and that's a liar. Well, she *is* a liar. But I definitely don't think she's lying about this.'

Honor stares at Sorcha's old man like she could actually kill him right now with her bare hands.

'Not that it's any of your focking business,' she goes, 'but I was trying to find a way to poison that big oak tree out there to make it fall on the Shomera and kill you both in your focking beds.'

I'm there, 'I'm sorry you were accused in the wrong, Honor. Someone was obviously too keen to join the dots.'

'This is such rubbish,' Fionn goes. 'She's been looking up poisons to make Hillary sick.'

'And *she* says she was trying to kill these two pricks,' I go. 'And I, for one, think we should give her the benefit of the doubt.'

But Sorcha doesn't want to hear it. And she says *the* most unbelievably hurtful thing to her then. She goes, 'Honor, all I know is that I can't bear to even look at you any more. This is on top of what happened at the Confirmation. I'm sorry to have to say this, Honor, but I'm actually *ashamed* to say that you're my daughter.'

Honor ends up going ballistic. She's like, 'Well, *I'm* ashamed that you're my focking mother! Because you're a focking slut!'

She storms out of the Shomera, slamming the door behind her, then goes back into the house.

I'm like, 'That last bit was obviously a reference to you having sex with focking Gogglebox Ireland there.'

Sorcha goes, 'Yes, I think we got the reference, Ross, thank you very much.'

'Incontrovertible evidence of malfeasance!' Sorcha's old man goes, loving the sound of his own voice. It's like he's in focking court or some shit. 'What are we going to do with this evidence? That is the question!'

And before I can suggest offering Honor as much support and understanding as we possibly can, Fionn goes, 'I'll tell you what *I'm* going to do. Tomorrow morning, I'm going to go to see my solicitor and I'm going to apply for full custody of my son.'

Sorcha's there, 'Excuse me?'

'Hillary is not safe in this house, Sorcha. Not with *her* here.'

I'm there, 'Goodbye and good riddance, then. To the two of you. We'll get them to throw that morquee back up and we'll have a focking porty to celebrate.'

But Sorcha – obviously being the kid's mother – goes, 'You are *not* taking my son away from me, Fionn?'

He's there, 'Ultimately, that will be up to a judge to decide.'

'Well, before you choose to go down that road, I have to warn you that my dad is one of *the* best family law solicitors in the country.'

But then her old man ends up totally pulling the corpet from underneath her by going, 'I can't support you, Sorcha. Because Fionn is right. That daughter of yours *is* a danger to Hillary – and probably to your mother and me as well. It's time to consider other options.'

I'm there, 'What other options?'

And Sorcha goes, 'Okay, I might have an idea.'

I'm like, 'Continue.'

'Erika said she'd love to take her, Ross.'

'*Take* her? What the fock is she – a dog?'

'Erika has said it to Honor and she's said to me as well. She'd love to have her in Perth with her.'

'We are not sending her away. And that's my final word on the matter.'

'It'll just be for a few months, Ross. She can't go back to that school, Ross – even *when* her suspension ends. Can you imagine what life would be like for her?'

'She doesn't give a fock what anyone thinks. I love that about her.'

'At least this way, she could go to Australia and wait for the whole thing to hopefully blow over, then stort the senior school in September with a clean slate.'

'No.'

'Ross, it might end up being the making of her.'

I'm there, 'It's not happening,' and I can hear my voice go all *wobbly*? 'You are not sending my daughter away to – I'd have to check the map – but I'm presuming the other side of the world.'

Fionn goes, 'Either she's out of this house by the end of this week or I'm going to court to apply for a Safety and Protection Order for my son.'

'And you'll get it,' Sorcha's old man goes, then he turns his head and looks at me. 'I'll make sure of that, Ross.'

Sorcha tries to give me a sympathetic smile. She's there, 'I'm sorry, Ross. But you can't say that this day wasn't coming. She's been out of control for such a long time now.'

I'm like, 'Please, Sorcha. Don't send her away. I'm the only person in the world she has a genuine connection with.'

But Sorcha's there, 'She's going to Australia, Ross – and that's the end of the discussion.'

I ask Sorcha to at least allow *me* to break the news to Honor about her going to Australia?

So on Thursday afternoon, I take her out in the cor with the intention of having the big talk with her. We drive along the Vico Road all the way into Dalkey, then we keep going through Sandycove and along the seafront to Dún Laoghaire and then Blackrock.

Honor is being unusually talkative. Yeah, no, Sorcha took all of her devices – including phone – off her last week and it's like she's suddenly discovered the ort of conversation. Plus, she's, like, bouncing around from topic to topic. One minute she's talking about how she hopes Sorcha's old dear develops early onset dementia and Sorcha's old man ends up having to be her carer, the next she's talking about how she hopes Sorcha's old man has a stroke and Sorcha's old dear ends up having to be his carer.

'Honor,' I finally pluck up the courage to go, 'I need to talk to you about something slightly off-topic.'

She's like, 'What?' her back already up.

'Look,' I go, 'your old dear is very upset with you at the moment.'

'I didn't poison her stupid focking baby.'

'I believe you.'

'Er, *tell* her that, then?'

'Unfortunately, I've tried. Believe me, Honor, I've argued your innocence until I'm blue in the literally face. But your old dear thinks you need to be possibly punished.'

'I've *been* punished. They took away my phone and my focking laptop. Do you have any idea what it's like to be an influencer without a phone or a focking laptop?'

'I don't – I can only imagine.'

'What about my subscribers? I've got, like, seventy thousand people who want to know what I'm wearing!'

'I feel for them. I genuinely do.'

'I mean, how many times do I have to say it? I wasn't *trying* to kill the baby! I was trying to kill her parents!'

'I believe you.'

'Thank you.'

'But bear in mind that Fionn is putting in the poison as well – pordon the pun.'

'Yeah, this is a man – a supposed *friend* of yours? – who gets your wife pregnant, then comes to live in your house and tries to tell you how to raise your children.'

'The focking nerve of the goy – now that you say it.'

I'm not getting very far here in terms of delivering the bad news. But then Honor – totally out of the blue – goes, 'Do you know what I'd *really* love to do?'

And I'm like, 'What's that, Honor?' expecting her to say, I don't know, beat Sorcha's old pair about the head with a tyre iron so that they both end up in a coma and Sorcha ends up having to be their carer. But she doesn't say that at all.

She goes, 'I'd love to go and live in Australia. With Erika.'

I'm like, 'What? Seriously?'

'She said it to me a few weeks ago that she'd love to have me out there. She knows – oh my God – *loads* about fashion. *And* business. She could actually help me establish my brand!'

Talk about something just falling into your lap.

I'm there, 'Hey, I'd be totally cool with you going to Australia for a few months – maybe even until the end of the summer. It's *your* choice, bear in mind.'

She's like, 'Are you focking mad? *She* won't let me go.'

'Who?'

'Er, your stupid bitch-whore of a wife?'

'I wouldn't be so sure of that, Honor. I wouldn't be so sure.'

'Dad, there's no *way* she'd let me go. Because she's a focking bitch. A dried-up, frigid, focking bitch.'

'Look, why don't you let me talk to your mother about it?'

'Really?'

'Yeah, no, leave it to your old man.'

It's a win–win situation. That's the point I'm trying to make to Sorcha. Except she's having a hord time getting her head around that basic fact.

'The whole reason for *sending* her to Australia is to punish her,' she goes. 'What good is it if she thinks we're sending her there as a treat?'

Fionn walks into the kitchen at that exact moment, carrying Hillary.

I'm there, 'I thought the whole reason for sending her to Australia was because this knob here threatened to move out and take his baby with him.'

Fionn rolls his eyes and – seriously? – huffs at me. He'll be lucky if I don't throw a punch at him between now and the time my daughter leaves.

He's there, 'The reason for sending her away is to protect my son.'

174

Sorcha goes, 'Honor told Ross, totally out of the blue, that she wants to go to Australia to spend the summer with Erika.'

And Fionn's there, 'That's good – that's what you wanted, wasn't it?'

'Yes, but I also wanted her to understand that she was being sent there as, like, a *punishment?*'

'That's between you and Ross. I don't care as long as she's no longer living under the same roof as my son.'

I'd love to break every pane of glass in his face.

I'm there, 'The thing is, Sorcha, if we let her think that it's *her* idea, there's a very good chance she won't end up hating us.'

Sorcha goes, '*That's* your main concern, Ross? After everything the girl has done – poisoning a baby, humiliating us in front of Bishop Brannigan and all those Mount Anville moms, tricking me into thinking that she wanted to have a proper mother–daughter relationship with me – the thing that *most* concerns you is that she actually still likes you?'

I'm there, 'I'm her best friend,' even though I know that makes Sorcha jealous. 'I'm probably the only friend she's got in the world.'

'And whose fault is that?' she goes.

All of a sudden, the back door opens and in walk Sorcha's old pair.

I go, 'I think I'd prefer it if you two dickheads knocked, then waited to be actually *invited* in?'

They wouldn't give me the pleasure of a response, of course.

'Mom and Dad,' Sorcha goes, 'I want to ask your advice about something.'

They both go, 'Oh?'

'Yeah, no, Honor told Ross that she wants to go to Australia to spend some time with Erika. This was before Ross told her that it was also what *we* wanted?'

Her old dear goes, 'So what's the problem?'

'The problem is that it was supposed to be a punishment. If she actually *wants* to go, then it's obviously not. It's suddenly a holiday, isn't it? A holiday that we're paying for.'

Sorcha's old man goes, 'I thought the whole point of sending her was that we're all sick to death of her and her carry-on.'

I'm there, 'Yeah, speak for your focking selves,' because I find the things she does very funny when I'm not at the wrong end of them.

'My advice,' Sorcha's old dear goes, 'is that if she wants to go, then let her go. Because if she finds out that *you* want her to go, then she probably won't go – just to spite you.'

'Oh my God,' Sorcha goes, 'that's a very good point. Okay, Ross, tell her she can go to Australia. And let her think it's her idea.'

She nods at Honor's laptop on the kitchen counter.

'You can book her ticket now,' she goes, and it breaks my hort because it's like she can't wait to be rid of her.

I pick up the laptop and I tip upstairs.

Honor is in Brian, Johnny and Leo's room. They're all watching TV together. Leo sees me, laughs, then goes, 'Here's this fockwit, look.'

I'm there, 'Sorry to interrupt, Honor. I've just been talking to your old dear.'

Honor goes, 'And did you ask her – if I could go to Australia?'

'I did, yeah.'

'And I bet she said no, didn't she? I focking hate her. I hope she focking dies. No, I hope she gets some kind of disease that doesn't kill her but makes her, like, *wish* she was dead?'

'Honor, you didn't let me finish.'

'The Ebola virus.'

'Honor, she said yes.'

'What?'

'She said yes.'

'Oh my God!'

'She said you can go to Australia.'

'Oh! My God!'

'Are you not pleased?'

'Yes, I'm pleased.'

'You're not worried that you might end up being possibly homesick?'

'Homesick? Yeah, whatever! Can I borrow your phone so I can FaceTime Erika?'

I'm there, 'Your old dear's already talked to her. She's really looking forward to having you.' And then I hold up her laptop. 'Remember this thing? Let's look at flights, will we?'

We log on to the Qantas website.

I'm there, 'Okay, so when do you want to go?'

She's like, 'As soon as focking possible. Is there a flight tonight?'

'Tonight?'

'That's what I said, wasn't it?'

'I was thinking more in terms of the weekend. What about, like, Sunday?'

'Sunday? That's, like, three days away!'

'That's not long, Honor.'

'Oh! My God! I couldn't stay here for three more days!'

'I just thought, you know, it'd be a chance for us to spend a little bit of time together before you're gone. We could do something fun – as in, me, you and the boys?'

She just goes, 'Fine.'

I turn to the boys. I'm there, 'What do you think, goys? How do you fancy going on a mystery tour this weekend?'

And Brian and Leo – at the exact same time – go, 'Ask. My focking. Hole.'

Ronan's like, 'Soddy?'

Yeah, no, I break the news to him over lunch in the UCD restaurant. He's pretty shocked, it has to be said.

'Australia?' he goes. 'Are you seerdious?'

I'm like, 'Yeah, no, she's going over to stay with Erika for a few months.'

'A few *munts*?'

'Until the end of the summer.'

'Is it cos of what happened at the Conferbation?'

'Yeah, no, *sort* of? As in, it was one of a build-up of things. Including possibly poisoning Sorcha and Fionn's baby – although I seem to be the only one who thinks she's genuinely innocent.'

'Hodor woultn't do sometin like that, Rosser. Hodor wouldn't be capable of hoorting an iddocent little babby.'

177

'You're preaching to the choir, Ro. I actually believe her when she says she was looking up poisons to try to kill Sorcha's parents. But Fionn forced Sorcha's hand. He said he was going to apply for full custody on the basis that Honor was a danger to Hillary.'

'So the solution is that Hodor gets sent off to Austradia?'

'It turns out that she wanted to go anyway. She was the one who suggested it. So we're letting her think it was her idea.'

The restaurant, by the way, is open again and the picket has gone. Sushi, spaghetti and all the other supposedly racist food items have been removed from the menu and now it's just, like, Irish stuff, most of which I've never focking heard of before. I end up ordering the Irish stew with a Waterford blaa, while Ronan goes for the boxty with bacon and a side of colcannon.

'How's yours?' Ronan goes.

And I'm there, 'It's absolutely focking revolting. This is what I imagine the Healy-Raes live on. How's the – what's it called again – boxty?'

He looks over both shoulders to make sure the famous Huguette isn't within earshot, then he goes, 'It's the woorst thig I've ebber eaten in me bleaten life, Rosser.'

We both laugh. He puts down his knife and fork and pushes the plate into the middle of the table. I do the same.

Totally out of the blue then, he goes, 'Hee-or, Rosser, did I tell you that Heddessy's arthur offerton me a job?'

I'm like, 'You don't need a job. You've still got another year of college left.'

'He's arthur offerton me an appredentership, but – as a solicitodder. When I fiddish me thegree.'

'When did all this happen?'

'I'd a thrink wit your ould fedda last week and Heddessy was theer as well. He says Ine the koyunt of fedda he's feerm is altwees looking foe-er.'

I get this sudden flashback to Transition Year, when I did work experience in Hennessy's office in Fitzwilliam Square and spent the entire month in the cor pork, burning documents in a barrel to stop them falling into the hands of the Criminal Assets Bureau. I was the only kid in Castlerock College who filled in his Work Experience Report Form at gunpoint.

I'm there, 'Ro, don't get sucked in by Hennessy and my old man, okay?'

He goes, 'Heddessy says he'd put me troo Blackhall Place and hab me on a fuddle toyum wage until Ine fuddy quadified.'

'Just be careful, Ro. They're up to something.'

'What are thee up to?'

'I don't know. It's something to do with Russia. Erika found out about it, but I forget the actual details. I just know that it was dodgy shit and it was the reason she focked off to Australia.'

'Heddessy ast me if I'd be inthordested in learden Rushidden alreet.'

'There you go, then. Just be careful, Ro. The old man has changed since he put that wig on his head. It's like he's on some kind of power trip.'

'You know he's thalken about habbon anutter kid, Rosser.'

'He's not having another kid. He's firing blanks.'

'He was tedding me he's on some bleaten diet to throy to improve the quadity of he's speerm. He wadn't thrinking the night I merrum – he was on the minner doddle wather.'

'The what?'

'The minner doddle wather.'

'Okay, I've no idea what you're saying and I'm not interested enough in that focker to ask you to repeat it again.'

It's at that exact point that I spot the famous Huguette walking across the restaurant towards the table. I was just about to ask Ro was he still seeing the girl, but I end up getting my answer straight away.

She goes, 'Hey, Ronan,' and – I swear to fock – the goy pulls his plate towards him, picks up his knife and fork again and goes back to eating his boxty.

He goes, 'Ah, howiya, Huguette! This stuff is lubbly, by the way!'

He's obviously got it bad for the girl. She doesn't even *look* at me?

She goes, 'Don't eat another forkful! We've decided to boycott the restaurant again!'

Ro's there, 'Seerdiously?'

She's like, 'Are you saying you haven't read my blog today?' and she says it in a real, I don't know, *accusing* way?

He goes, 'I, er, habn't got to it yet, Huguette, no. I'd leckchodders alt morden, so I did.'

'Er, I posted it, like, an *hour* ago?'

'I was joost habbon a birra luddench with the Ross lad here. Me sister's off to Australia and he was in inviting me out to the air-powurt on Suddenday to see her off.'

'Right.'

'Hodestly, I was godda read it in the arthur noon, but.'

He's totally focking whipped by her. It's very depressing to actually watch.

'Anyway,' she goes, 'when you read my blog, you'll see *why* we've decided to stort picketing the restaurant again.'

Ro's there, 'Addy chaddence of a preview, Huguette?'

'Well, we were debating it at a student union meeting last night and we actually agreed that an Irish restaurant that serves *just* Irish food is actually guilty of monoculturalism.'

'Reet.'

'And monoculturalism, as we all know, is a form of racism.'

'I hab to admit, I hatn't thought abourit like that befower.'

'So get up – both of you.'

Ronan actually stands up.

I'm suddenly confused. I'm there, 'Whoa, whoa, whoa – what the fock are you doing?'

Ro goes, 'You heerd the geerdle, Rosser. Ine not eating in a bleaten racist resterdoddent.'

I'm there 'But I thought *serving* sushi and spaghetti was supposedly racist.'

'It is,' Huguette goes – again, without even looking at me. 'But *not* serving sushi and spaghetti is even *more* racist?'

Ronan goes, 'So, what, we're going to do anutter picket, aston them to put them back odden the medu?'

'That's exactly what we're going to do. Come on, let's go. I find the diversity-hating atmosphere in this place *actually* toxic?'

'The fock *are* we?' Leo goes as I pull into the cor pork.

It's Honor who ends up answering him. She goes, 'We've arrived, Leo! This is where we're going on our mystery tour!'

She's great with her brothers. How could anyone believe she was capable of hurting a baby?

'There's a smell of focking shite,' Brian goes.

And I'm there, 'That's because we're in Meath!'

Johnny's face definitely dorkens. He goes, 'Daddy, I want to go home,' because he's a nervous kid and I've raised my boys to be wary of anything that happens north of Exit 13 on the M50.

Honor's there, 'You won't want to go home when you find out what we're doing today! Boys, this is Tayto Pork!'

Their little faces light up. And the screams out of them. At the top of his voice, Leo is like, 'Focking focking fock fock focking focker!' punching the back of the seat in front of him.

Honor laughs. She goes, 'We knew you'd be excited!'

I open the back door and they pour out of the cor like sailors on shore leave. They peg it towards the entrance – Brian and Leo snorling and spitting and borking out random swear words at the top of their voices.

I slam the cor door shut.

'By the way,' Honor goes, 'I talked to Erika on, like, FaceTime this morning. She's *so* excited about me coming. She has loads of amazing ideas for my YouTube channel.'

I'm there, 'I wonder will people miss *me*, though?' and I can hear the pettiness in my voice when I say it. 'I wonder will people stort unsubscribing in massive, massive numbers because they miss our whole vibe?'

'Oh my God, you should *see* the house where Erika and Helen are living! She, like, walked me around it while I was talking to her!'

'Nice?'

'Oh my God – huge! They've got, like, two swimming pools – one indoor and one outdoor!'

'I get very bored in swimming pools. I think I like the *idea* of swimming pools more than I like *actual* swimming pools?'

We stort walking towards the gates, where I notice the boys are terrorizing the poor dude who's dressed in the giant Mr Tayto costume.

'She's also going to bring me horse-riding!' Honor goes. 'She's got, like, *four* horses!'

I'm there, 'You've always hated horses. We took you to the Dublin Horse Show when you were, like, six and you laughed your head off every time a horse crashed into a fence. We were eventually asked to leave.'

'You were laughing as well.'

'All I'm saying is that the grass isn't always greener – and blah, blah, blah.'

We join the queue, then we watch – along with everyone else – as the boys manage to get Mr Tayto down on the ground. Brian gets down on his hands and knees behind him and Leo gives him a shove so that Mr Tayto falls onto his back. Then we all laugh – well, *I* certainly do – at the sight of him trying to get up again. It's genuinely comical.

He's still lying there on his back, his two little legs kicking in the air while the three of them set about him.

We eventually reach the top of the queue.

I'm handing my credit cord to the dude in the booth, going, 'Do you know is Heineken served anywhere on the premises?' when he turns around to me and goes, 'I'm sorry, your children can't come in here.'

I'm there, 'Excuse me?'

'They're barred from Tayto Park.'

'Borred? What are you talking about?'

He pushes a laminated piece of paper across the counter at me, featuring – yeah, no – CCTV images of various children, including, at the very top of the list, Brian, Johnny and Leo.

'You were here last year,' he tries to go.

I'm there, 'Whoa, whoa, whoa – does this have anything to do with Brian and Leo spitting off the top of the rollercoaster?'

'Spitting off the rollercoaster, spitting at the animals, spitting at other children.'

'Okay, you're beginning to sound like the manager of DL Kids now.'

'I'm sorry,' the dude goes. 'Your children will not be allowed in today – or any day.'

I decide to try to appeal to his better nature. I'm like, 'Dude, their sister is going away to Australia tomorrow. This was supposed to be a special day for us. Our last day together as an actual family.'

'Tell him he's a focking dick,' Brian goes. 'A focking dick with ears.'

And I'm like, 'Brian, you're not exactly helping your case here.'

'I'm sorry, it's a no,' the dude goes. 'I'm just obeying orders.'

I'm like, 'Dude, please. We've been borred from everywhere. We're talking Imaginosity. We're talking The Fun Factory. We're talking Stillorgan Bowl. We're talking Dublin Zoo. There's literally nowhere I can bring them to let them just run amok.'

He goes, 'Please step aside, Sir! Next in line, please!'

And that ends up being that. I turn around and I go, 'Come on, let's go,' and we walk back to the cor, stepping over Mr Tayto on the way.

The boys don't go quietly either. Leo's like, 'The fock are we going now?'

And I'm like, 'Home, Leo. Because you've spoiled the day for everyone.'

Brian goes, 'This is some focking bullshit.'

And that's when I end up totally losing it with them. I go, 'I'll tell you what's some focking bullshit – the fact that you ruin absolutely focking everything! The fact that we can't enjoy one last day out with your sister, who's going to Australia tomorrow!'

I realize that I'm pointing my finger at them and I'm roaring at them – this is in the middle of the Tayto Pork cor pork.

I'm there, 'I'm sick of you! I've had it up to here with you! The constant effing and blinding! The spitting! The bullying other kids! And I'm telling you that it stops! I'm telling you that it stops now!'

Oh, that does the trick. The three of them look at me with their mouths open in literally just, like, *shock*?

Honor goes, 'Boys, get in the cor. I want to talk to Dad for a minute.'

They do as they're told. Like I said, she's great with them.

'Okay,' Honor goes, 'what was that?'

I'm there, 'I can't believe you're going and leaving me with those focking idiot kids.'

'They're not idiots.'

'They *are* idiots. Let's call a spade a spade here.'

She goes, 'Dad, what's wrong?'

And that's when it happens. I had a feeling it was coming. Yeah, no, the floodgates just open and I'm suddenly standing there in literally tears.

Honor's like, 'Dad?'

And I'm there, 'I'm sorry, Honor. It's just you're going away tomorrow and it's like –'

'What?'

'It's like you're not even sad. It's like you're not even going to miss me. You're banging on about horses and Jacuzzis and what Erika's going to do for your brand.'

'Of course I'm going to miss you!'

'Horses are shit. I've always said it. They're probably the most overrated animals on the planet.'

She's like, 'Dad, I'm going to miss you, okay?' and then – holy shit – *she* ends up bursting into tears and just throwing her orms around me.

I'm there, 'Really?'

She looks up at me and goes, 'Dad, you're my best friend.'

'That's a lovely thing for me to hear.'

'You're the only one who doesn't judge me, even when I'm being really, really horrible.'

'And I'll go on not judging you, Honor. I can promise you that. Just don't go away.'

'I have to go away. I can't bear to live in that house any more. I'll focking kill someone.'

'I still don't want you to go.'

'I know.'

She breaks away from me and she dries her eyes with the palm of her hand. I do the same.

I'm there, 'I probably owe the boys an apology for the way I lost it with them.'

She goes, 'I'm sure they'll understand, Dad.'

'I just wanted today to be special, you know? A day we'll always remember.'

'We can go somewhere else.'

'They're borred from everywhere else.'

'We can do something outdoorsy, then. Let's go to Killiney Hill. We could have a picnic – then the boys could set fire to the gorse.'

I'm like, 'That's a great idea. Thanks, Honor.'

We stort walking back to the cor. I open the door. From the back seat, I hear Leo go, 'Focking crying, look!'

And Brian's like, 'What! A focking! Pussy!'

Honor is determined not to cry. She wouldn't give Sorcha's old pair the pleasure. So she pretends that she's not sad to be leaving. She practically sprints from the bag drop area to the deporture gate while Sorcha follows a few feet behind, saying shit to ease her own conscience.

She's going, 'This could be the best thing that ever happened to you, Honor. There's a saying that travel broadens the mind. It was visiting the European Porliament in Strasbourg when I was exactly your age that awakened my interest in politics.'

Honor just keeps walking. It's like she's terrified that her old dear might change her mind about letting her go. And Sorcha's old pair clearly have the same fear because they've decided to tag along just to make sure the girl gets on the plane.

He's in Sorcha's ear, going, 'It's the best thing for everyone, Dorling. You just need to keep your resolve for a few minutes more.'

I turn around to Ronan and I go, 'He'll be lucky if I don't deck him today. No one can say it hasn't been coming for years.'

Ronan goes, 'Joost keep the head, Rosser. Do you think Hodor wants that to be her last memody of howum – you belting her grandda?'

185

And I'm there, 'I do actually. I think that's exactly what she'd want.'

I'm suddenly looking around me for the old pair. They were supposed to be here to see Honor off but they're cutting it fine.

I'm there, 'Did the old man say they were definitely coming?'

And Ronan goes, 'He's joost arthur thexting me from the keer, Rosser. Thee'd an appointment in the clidic this morden. He said they're about foyuv midutes away.'

Up the escalator we go, me pulling Honor's gold Rimowa carry-on case behind me. Ro decides to give us a moment because when we reach the departures area he hangs back. Honor stops, turns around and tries to take her case from me.

She goes, 'Dad, let go.'

But I'm there, 'I can't.'

And I *literally* can't? I'm gripping the handle like it's glued to my palm.

Honor just smiles at me kindly and goes, 'Let's not give *them* the satisfaction, okay?'

I look over my shoulder. Sorcha's old man is stepping off the escalator just in front of Sorcha and Sorcha's old dear and it's genuinely the happiest I've ever seen him.

So I let go of the case and Honor takes it from me. I bend down and I give her a hug. I go, 'What am I going do without you, Honor?'

She's there, 'You'll be fine.'

I'm like, 'I genuinely don't think I will. Everything's shit when you're not around.'

She goes, 'You've got the boys,' and she looks over my shoulder, smiling into the mid-distance, where Brian, Johnny and Leo have spotted the foreign currency dump bin. They're, like, rocking the thing backwards and forwards, trying to knock it over to get at the notes and coins inside.

'They're focking morons,' I go. 'I hate to say it, Honor, but there's fock-all in their heads.'

Sorcha arrives over to us, her parents just behind her. She goes, 'And make sure you write to me, will you?'

Honor's there, 'Who the fock *writes* to anyone any more?'

And those end up being her final words to her old dear. Sorcha tries to hug her, but Honor just stiffens.

Then a woman in an Aer Lingus uniform, who isn't great – and that's me being kind – walks over to us and goes, 'Are you the little girl who's travelling to Australia alone?'

Honor's like, 'Yeah?' like she's ready for a fight. 'So?'

The woman crouches down to Honor's level. 'I'm Una Falvey!' she goes, in a really patronizing voice. 'And I'm going to be chaperoning you all the way to Perth in the absence of your lovely mummy! Me and you are going to have so much fun, do you hear me? And if there's anything you need, you just have to ask.'

Honor shoots her a look that would make a seagull think twice.

'What I need,' she goes, 'is lots and lots of shut the fock up. You keep that coming and you and me will get on just fine.'

That poor woman. That poor, poor woman.

Honor goes, 'Goodbye, Ronan.'

Ro gives her an unbelievable hug. He's there, 'Stay ourra thrubble, do you hear me? And give me lub to Edika.'

She's like, 'I'll FaceTime you tomorrow, okay?'

There's an enormous crash then. It's the sound of breaking glass. The boys have managed to tip over the foreign currency dump bin and it's shattered into about a million pieces. Sorcha's old man, out of the corner of his mouth, goes, 'I wonder could she take those three with her as well?' and Sorcha's old dear laughs and goes, 'I was thinking the exact same thing!'

Honor calls Brian, Johnny and Leo over. She's like, 'Boys?' and they instantly come running – at the same time stuffing fistfuls of notes into their already full pockets. They throw their orms around their sister and she gives them each a kiss on the top of the head. She goes, 'Look after your daddy for me, will you?'

And that should be that. Except right at the last second, who comes tearing up the escalator, going, 'Wait! Just a minute! Don't go yet!' but my old pair.

Honor goes running to them. I look at Sorcha's old man, who just rolls his eyes and goes, 'I mean, how long is *this* going to take?'

It must kill him to see how well she gets on with *my* old pair?

The old dear goes, 'We couldn't let you go without saying good-bye!' She *can* be alright, my old dear.

Honor's there, 'Thanks, Fionnuala!'

My old man hands her – honestly – a brick of bank notes. He goes, 'Just a little – quote-unquote – spending money from Fionnuala and I! And don't worry, Dorling, it's just below the amount that it's permissible to carry without it constituting laundering!'

You can see poor Una Falvey looking at us, thinking, They're some focking family.

Honor hugs my old pair – first my old man, then my old dear. Then she takes her case and she morches confidently through the deporture gate with Una running after her to keep up, not even looking back once.

It takes all the self-control I have *not* to burst into tears? I can't say the same for Sorcha. She ends up totally losing her shit. She turns to her old dear and goes, 'She's gone! My little girl has gone!' and her old man goes, 'It's for the best, Dorling. We'll all sleep easier knowing that she's not plotting to murder us in our beds.'

My old dear goes, 'You must be so sad, Ross,' and it's like she *wants* me to cry? 'But never mind. We had some wonderful news this morning about your father's semen.'

That's literally what she says.

I'm like, 'What?' as in, why the fock are you telling me this now?

The old man goes, 'That's right, Kicker! According to the clinic, my sperm count is now exactly where it needs to be!'

The old dear smiles at me – a smile of pure, pure evil. 'Isn't it wonderful?' she goes. 'It looks like you're going to be getting a little brother or sister after all!'

6.

A New and Exciting Interior Make-Over!

Sorcha is on the phone, inquiring about hiring – I shit you not – a bouncy castle. She wouldn't dream of doing that if Honor was still here. 'While the cat's away,' I go. 'It's a definite case of that.'

She covers the mouthpiece. She's there, 'What was that, Ross?'

I'm like, 'Nothing. Carry on ordering your bouncy castle there.'

'It's fine. They've put me on hold.'

'I'm just saying, I can't imagine they're going to be too happy around here when they see that monstrosity going up in the gorden. Not a good look for the Vico Road, Sorcha. Not a good look.'

'Which is why I called around to all the neighbours to tell them that my son was being christened this weekend and we were having a porty in the house afterwards with about twenty children there.'

This is Sorcha's way of trying to make up for having to cancel the big Confirmation bash. She's – what's the phrase? – over-compensating?

'And they've no issues with us having a bouncy castle?' I go. 'Even though they're very WC?'

She's like, 'I grew up on this road, Ross. They're not the snobs that you think they are around here.'

She goes back to talking to whoever's on the other end of the phone then. She's like, 'Yes, ten o'clock in the morning would be perfect for delivery. And do you think you could deflate it for us before eight o'clock in the evening? It's just a rule that the residents association has around here . . . Oh, that's great. Thank you so much.'

Then she hangs up. I look out the window of the kitchen. Fionn is out in the gorden with Sorcha's old man – the two of them thick as thieves, talking about fock knows what. Sorcha's old dear is holding Hillary and pointing out the names of various trees to him – yeah, like he's going to remember them!

Actually, he probably *will* remember them.

I'm there, 'I'd say they're already doing their nut around here about us having that Shomera out there. Focking eyesore of a thing.'

Sorcha goes, 'She's having the time of her life in Australia, Ross.'

'How do we know that?'

'I've been talking to Erika. On WhatsApp.'

Honor's been gone, like, two weeks now and I haven't heard a word from her, aport from a text to say that she'd landed safely; then, a week later, an email saying she was an important social media influencer with over 100,000 followers and if I didn't send her free beauty products she would absolutely rip me aport on her You-Tube channel; then, ten minutes later, another email saying sorry, that last email was meant for Ross at Estée Lauder and not me.

Other than that, it's been basically radio silence. I've phoned her and I've texted her I don't know how many times. I spent the whole afternoon yesterday WhatsApping her photos that I found online of celebrities without their make-up. Perrie Edwards was the funniest – walking back from the shops with a corton of milk and a box of Frosties. That girl would frighten flies off a focking corpse. But nothing back. Not even a smiley face or a 'lol'.

'Erika said Honor has fallen in *love* with horse-riding!' Sorcha goes.

I'm there, 'Honor hated horses. Do you remember the time she got us focked out of the RDS? I loved that day.'

'Well, she apparently doesn't hate them now. Erika says she's a real natural with them. They go horse-riding in the morning. Then they have lunch out somewhere and they go shopping in the afternoon. Then, in the evening, Erika is showing her how to put a proper business plan in place for her YouTube channel with a view to, like, *monetizing* it? It's exactly what Honor needs, Ross – discipline and structure.'

'Did she say if she got the picture I sent her of Perrie Edwards? The focking state of her.'

'She didn't say.'

'The odd text back would be nice. That's all I'm saying.'

'You have *other* children, remember?'

Yeah, no, I can hear them upstairs, absolutely killing each other.

I'm there, 'Yeah, they're no focking good.'

'Did you just describe your children as –'

'I'm sick of them, Sorcha. I can't even bring them out any more because we've been borred from everywhere.'

'What about Tayto Pork?'

'Yes, Sorcha – even Tayto Pork.'

'Well, you can't sit around the house moping all day. By the way, aren't you supposed to be meeting Ronan for coffee?'

'Yeah, no, he rang me about an hour ago and asked did I fancy meeting him and Huguette in the Orts Café. He's absolutely convinced that if I spend enough time around the girl that we're going to suddenly hit it off.'

Sorcha goes, 'Ronan seems really keen on her. I hear she's President of the UCD Students' Union!'

I'm there, 'She's a pain in the hole, Sorcha – she's a human tut.'

'What does that mean?'

'She thinks eating spaghetti is racist. But she thinks *not* eating spaghetti is even *more* racist?'

'Well, I can see her point.'

'She actually reminds me of someone, but I can't put my finger on who it actually is.'

The back door suddenly opens and in they walk – Fionn, holding Hillary, followed by Sorcha's old pair.

Fionn's going, 'Yeah, they say that dancing is a good way for a father to bond with his infant son or daughter. So I'm taking Hillary to our first Daddy Dance Porty in the Town Hall in Dalkey tonight.'

I can't believe my wife thought it was a good idea to let this man ride her.

Sorcha's old man glowers at me. 'Have you got something to say?' he goes.

I'm like, 'No.'

'You muttered something under your breath there.'

'I meant to say it in my head.'

He laughs, then goes, 'Oh, he's a lot less cocky now, isn't he? Now that he hasn't got his little friend here to fight his battles for him!'

I end up having to get out of there before I say something I regret. I turn to Sorcha and I'm there, 'I'm going to go and meet Ro.'

My eldest son is one seriously, *seriously* smitten kitten. He's sitting in the Orts Café with the famous Huguette and a big, dumb smile on his face. *She's* smiling as well, something I haven't seen her do in the, I don't know, two or three times I've met her.

I pull out a chair and I sit down with them. I'm there, 'How the hell are you?' deciding to make the effort, if even just for Ronan's sake.

Her smile disappears straight away.

Ro goes, 'We're great, Rosser. We're cedebraton, so we are.'

I'm like, 'Celebrating?' suddenly worried in case it's another engagement. I look at Huguette's left hand. No diamond to be seen. Thank fock.

'Thee've put sushi back on the medu,' Ronan goes, 'in the main resterdoddent.'

Back on the menu? Where it was three weeks ago? Before *she* stuck her focking hooter in? Still, like I said, it's nice to be nice. I'm there, 'That's, er, great news.'

'Spaghetti as well,' Ronan goes. 'They're calden them Foods of the Wurdled, Rosser.'

I'm like, 'Foods of the Wurdled? You'd have to say fair focks, wouldn't you?'

But Huguette goes, 'I don't think they deserve praise for abandoning their policy of what was essentially culinary aportheid. Because that's what it is when you push the cultural agenda of a single social or ethnic group to the exclusion of all others.'

'A focking disgrace,' I go. 'I'm totally agreeing with you.'

Ronan's like, 'What'll you hab, Rosser?'

And I'm there, 'Yeah, no, I'll just have a coffee.'

He goes, 'Amedicado?'

I'm like, 'An Americano, yeah,' and then of course I can't resist the temptation to go, 'That's as long as it's not racist to drink coffee! It's not racist to drink coffee, is it, Huguette?'

She gives me a filthy. She's a girl who seriously needs to learn to laugh at herself. Ronan goes up to the counter to order and there ends up being that awkward moment when you're left sitting with someone you don't really know and you have literally fock-all to say to each other.

I'm like, 'This place used to be called Hilpers,' because I wouldn't be a big fan of silence. 'I spent a lot of time in here back in the day . . . Hilpers. It's one of those words that sounds more and more random the more times you say it . . . Hilpers . . . Hilpers . . . Hil-pers . . . Hil-pers . . .'

She goes, 'Ronan's slept with a lot of girls, hasn't he?'

And I'm like, 'Excuse me?' because it comes, like, *totally* out of the blue?

She's there, 'We had a conversation the other night – about how many people we'd both slept with. He said he'd had sex with about forty women.'

I'm thinking, For fock's sake, Ro! You never give a girl your stats.

She goes, 'Forty just seemed like a lot for someone who's only just turned twenty.'

I'm there, 'You're very hung up on numbers, aren't you?'

'I'm just saying I was surprised. But then I was talking to my aunt – as in, my mom's sister – last night and it turns out that she knows you.'

Shit. I hate conversations that go this way. This city is littered with the unexploded mines of my past romantic misadventures.

I'm there, 'So who's your aunt? Not that I'm worried.'

And she goes, 'Croía Ní Chathasaigh?'

I end up just laughing in her face. I'm there, 'That's who you remind me of! Oh my God, it's been focking *killing* me!'

Okay, bit of background here. Croía Ní Chathasaigh was a friend of Sorcha's from her time in UCD – we're talking Vice-Captain of the Irish Debating Team, auditor of the LGBT Society and one of the Rossmeister General's horshest critics. Yeah, no, the girl hated my guts – and she fell out with Sorcha after performing a failed intervention to try to stop her from marrying me.

Anyway, she reappeared in our lives last year and Sorcha appointed her as one of her Special Advisers in the Seanad. Possibly *the* most special piece of advice that Croía gave her was that she should lead a campaign to have the name of Grafton Street changed to Markievicz Street. It got passed as well, but lasted only a few weeks until the traders refused to pay their rates and Dublin City Council saw sense and switched it back. It didn't end well between Croía and Sorcha.

But – yeah, no – I can see the physical resemblance now, especially the anger. And the underbite.

I'm like, 'You're so like her – do you know that?'

She's there, 'I'll take that as a compliment.'

'Don't,' I go. 'I'm saying she's zero craic – like you.'

'Well, she had a few things to say about you as well.'

'Oh, I'm sure she did. She's a bit of a role model to you, is she?'

'She's actually my godmother.'

'Yeah, no, it's all beginning to make total sense. I can see why you'd think spaghetti was racist now. *She* was full of shit as well. Still is, I'd imagine.'

Ronan arrives back with the coffees then. He goes, 'Look at you two, getting on great, what? Hee-or, Huguette, did you tell Rosser that your addenty knows him?'

I'm like, 'Yeah, no, she did – and I can see the definite similarities, Ro.'

'Small wurdled, idn't it?'

'It certainly *is* a small world.'

I sip my coffee and Ronan sips his. Huguette just sits there and lets hers go cold. Ronan asks me if I've heard from Honor and I tell him no, but Erika told Sorcha that she's having the time of her life, which I'm doubtful about because it sounds like it's mostly just horse-riding, which is obviously boring, and shopping, which she could just as easily do in Dundrum.

Then he asks after Sorcha and I tell him about the christening this weekend and the bouncy castle coming to the Vico Road. And all the time I can feel this girl staring at me – yeah, no – *hating* me?

All of a sudden I hear my name called from the other side of the Orts Café. It's like, 'Ross! O'Carroll! Kelly!' and I look up to see another face from my distant past. It ends up being Phinneas McPhee, a dude who was on the same – hilariously – Sports and Exercise Management course as me back in the day. He went to Michael's but he was still sound.

I stand up. I'm like, 'Phinneas! McFocking! Phee! How the hell are you?'

We high-five. We chest-bump. We hug and tap out. Yeah, no, it's just like old times.

He goes, 'How long has it been?'

And I'm there, 'It must be, what, sixteen or seventeen years?'

'It must be. So what are you doing with yourself these days?'

'Literally fock-all, I'm proud to say. What about you? Jesus, you're not still repeating, are you?'

He laughs. He's there, 'No, I'm actually lecturing here now. Strategy and Operations Management in Sport.'

I'm there, 'Jesus Christ, is that an actual thing?'

'Yes, it's an actual thing.'

'It does sound like an actual thing, in fairness to you.'

I make the introductions.

I'm like, 'Ronan, this is a goy I was in college with – we're talking Phinneas McPhee. One of the best second rows I've ever shared a pitch with and I'm saying that as someone who played against Devin Toner in a Castlerock Legends v Castleknock Legends match in aid of the IRFU Charitable Trust. Phinneas, this is my son, Ronan. And this is his friend – em, sorry, I've forgotten your name.'

She ends up being *seriously* focked off by that. She goes, 'It's Huguette.'

And Phinneas is like, 'Huguette?' and then he laughs as the penny drops. 'Ah, you're the sushi girl!'

And *I* end up having to laugh then?

I'm like, 'The sushi girl! There you are, Huguette – that's what people think of you around here now!'

Phinneas turns to Ronan and goes, 'Your father was some player. I still can't understand how he didn't go on to do something in the game.'

I'm there, 'Listen to the man, Ronan! Yeah, no, my son sometimes thinks I'm exaggerating when I tell him how much talent I had but unfortunately pissed away.'

Phinneas goes, 'Do you play rugby yourself, Ronan?'

Ro's like, 'I did when I was a young fedda. I geb it up, but. I play the odd birra Gah now.'

'Ah, for UCD?'

'Nah, joost for the local club – nee-or where I lib.'

'And where do you live?'

'Figglas.'

'Finglas? So your club must be –'

'Edin's Oiled.'

I'm there, 'He's trying to say Erin's Isle. You sometimes have to listen very closely.'

'Yeah, no, the only reason I asked,' Phinneas goes, 'is because I played a little bit of football with Naomh Mearnóg. We actually had some cracking battles with Erin's Isle. They've got a good set-up out there. Anyway, I better go. I'm supposed to be giving a lecture in fifteen minutes.'

A lecture? Hilarious.

He's there, 'Great to see you again, Ross.'

And I'm like, 'Yeah, you as well, Phinneas,' even though I'm a little bit disappointed to hear that he's been playing Gaelic football.

'The sushi girl,' I go, chuckling to myself. 'I'd have given him a round of applause for that – except clapping is obviously banned!'

Ro's there, 'Rosser, leab it, will you?'

Huguette just stares at the back of Phinneas's head as he walks out of the café. And under her breath, I'm pretty sure I hear her go, 'He's going to focking regret that!'

Sorcha's old man loves being the centre of the attention. He goes, 'My daughter – the good Senator – has very kindly invited me to say a few words to formally welcome our grandson into the Catholic community and also into the Lalor family. Hillary Pius Flannan de Barra has been a wonderful, if unexpected, addition to our family. In his short time with us, I think it's fair to say, he has enriched all of our lives in a whole multitude of different ways . . .'

Jesus Christ, you're supposed to be toasting the kid, I think, not proposing him for membership of Milltown Golf Club.

I feel a hand on my shoulder then. I turn around and it ends up being JP. I haven't set eyes on the dude since the night he was on the *Late Late*.

He goes, 'Hey, Ross, sorry I'm late.'

I'm there, 'Don't apologize to me,' because I skipped the – as Sorcha calls it – *churchy-churchy bit* myself.

'I've a got a gift here,' he goes, holding up – like he said – a present. 'I, em, probably should give it to Fionn, should I?'

Given that *he's* the father and that the kid has fock-all to do with me, yeah, maybe you should. I manage to say all of that with just a look.

Then I'm there, 'I saw you on the *Late Late*. I just wanted you to know that I saw Tubs in The Butler's Pantry in Monkstown the other day. I pretended to hold the door for him, then at the last minute I slammed it in his face. He dropped a Gateau Lawrence, you'll be happy to hear!'

He goes, 'What? Why?'

'Er, because he stitched you *up*?'

'I thought the interview went well.'

'Yeah, no, that wasn't the consensus in Kielys. Most people thought he made you look like a complete tit.'

'Ross, I expected people to laugh. People laughed at the idea of lightbulbs.'

'Did they, though? I mean, you keep saying shit like that but did they *actually*?'

'Yes, they did. I actually had quite a few inquiries about the bed after the *Late Late*. Although most of them turned out to be people just ripping the piss. I'm pretty sure one of them was Simon Zebo.'

Focking Zebo. I mean, I love him like a brother, but, at the same time, he can be one sick fock.

I'm there, 'Were you serious – about selling Hook, Lyon and Sinker?'

JP just shrugs. 'I have to sell it,' he goes. 'I need the money for the business. There's this, like, Trade and Innovation Show coming to the RDS in June, "What's the Big Idea?", and I want to showcase the bed there.'

I'm there, 'So why do you need money?'

'I have to have a stock of these things ready to go. What if I'm suddenly inundated with orders?'

'I don't think you're going to be, Dude. And that's not me being a prick.'

Christian obviously hears this port of the conversation because he steps over to us and he's like, 'What do you need, JP? In terms of money?'

JP's there, 'Well, each bed costs, like, fifty yoyos to make – and I'd like to have maybe a thousand of them ready, just so I can be confident of being in a position to meet orders.'

Christian goes, 'I'll give you the money.'

I swear to fock, he says it without even hesitating.

JP's there, 'Are you serious?'

Christian's like, 'I've got about that much in savings. I'll give it to you tomorrow morning. Just don't sell the estate agency.'

Rugby. I'll go on saying it until the day I die.

Everyone storts clapping. Sorcha's old man has thankfully stopped talking and now it's Sorcha's turn. Yeah, no, I forgot to mention, this is all taking place in the gorden of Honalee.

She goes, 'Thank you, Dad, for those gorgeous, gorgeous words. As you all know – or those of you who got the circular email we sent around – one of the things that Fionn and I thought would make today even more special was if people could bring a gift for Hillary of maybe a book that they themselves cherished as a child and hope-fully write a quote on the inside cover that will possibly *inspire* him one day? I don't know if anyone wants to read theirs out?'

Amie with an ie goes first. She's like, 'I brought *Chorlotte's Web* by

E.B. White and on the inside cover I've written, "Be the best you that you can be!", although I don't know who actually said it.'

Everyone goes, 'Awwww!!!' and they all clap.

Next up is Lauren. She's like, 'My book is *Guess How Much I Love You* by Sam McBratney and inside I've written . . .'

Little Ross Junior goes, 'Leth *me* reath it, Mommy! You thaid you'd leth *me* reath it!'

She's like, 'Okay, go ahead, Ross. You read it.'

Ross is there, 'If I cannot thoo great thingth, I can thoo thmall thingth in a great way. Thath by Morthin Luther King.'

'*So* cute!' everyone goes. 'That's, like, oh my God!'

Next up is Chloe. 'I didn't actually *receive* the email?' she goes, clearly not happy. 'But I heard about it from Sophie – almost by accident. Anyway, I brought *The Very Hungry Caterpillar* by Eric Corle and the quote I wrote on the inside cover is by Hillary Clinton and it's, "Human rights are women's rights, and women's rights are human rights," and it's only now as I'm reading it that I'm suddenly remembering that *your* Hillary is a boy! Oh my God, I am *so* embarrassed!'

'It's still a beautiful quote,' Sorcha goes, trying to rescue the situation. 'And it's something I definitely want my son to know – especially in the current climate.'

She gets a round of applause. People would clap for literally anything these days – except in UCD, of course, where they'll clap for literally fock-all.

Sophie goes, 'The book *I* brought is *The Cat in the Hat* by Dr Seuss, which I – oh my God – *loved* as a child. And inside I've written – it's kind of similar to Amie with an ie's quote – except it's, "Breathe. Believe. Become. And always live your best life." And I don't know who said it either, but it's one of those ones you see a lot on Instagram.'

I can't listen to any more. I decide to get the borbecue lit. I walk past the bouncy castle and I notice that Brian and Leo are using the thing as a sort of UFC octagon. They're inside, basically beating the stuffing out of each other, while all the other little kids – Johnny included – are standing outside just watching, their faces filled with fear.

I decide to leave them to it. I switch on the grills and I throw on my famously inappropriate borbecue apron. It says, 'I Can Recommend The Sausage!' and then – this is the funny bit – it has a finger pointing downwards to my, well, you-know-what.

All of a sudden, Magnus tips over to me. He's there, 'Hey, Rosh, how the hell are you? Your apron ish hilarioush!'

And I'm like, 'Yeah, no, it was a birthday present from Bláthnaid Ní Chofaigh back in the days when you could say shit like that. You know where that finger is pointing, don't you? At my dick!'

'Yesh, I got that, Rosh.'

'I have to say, I'm surprised to see you here today. I thought you worked basically seven days a week these days.'

'I took a few hoursh off for the chrishening. It'sh all good. I can make up the hoursh by working late tonight.'

Yeah, no, he's talking about *Saturday* night?

'Hey, Rosh,' he goes, 'I haff to show you shomeshing,' and he whips out his phone. 'Like your apron, thish alsho ish lotsh of fun,' and he storts showing me photographs of – I shit you not – a humungous Lego model of what turns out to be the Facebook building in Grand Canal Square.

I go, 'Who put this together?' when what I really mean is, 'Why the fock do you think I'd be interested in looking at this?'

He's there, 'We all did – everybody who worksh for Fashebook. Every time you pash through resheption, you haff to add one brick to the model. That'sh one of the thingsh I love moasht about working for a big tech company like Fashebook – feeling like you are a shmall but vital part of a big whole.'

It's a big hole alright. Working Saturday nights? I'd rather be dead.

'Another thing I alsho like about working for Fashebook,' he goes, 'ish jusht the number of people around the world who ushe our product in their everyday livesh. I am shitting at my deshk and I am thinking about the impact we are haffing on the world, the number of people we are helping to shtay connected – it'sh inshane.'

'Sounds like a waste of time to me.'

'Yesh, it can shreshful – there ish no doubt about that. But any time you like, you can ashk for a shoulder mashage at your deshk.

It'sh one of the other thingsh I love about Fashebook. They are alwaysh thinking about the happinesh of their employeesh. For instansh, when it ish your birthday, the chef will cook you a speshial lunch. And alsho when it ish your Workavershary –'

That's when I decide to suddenly get away from him. He's literally boring me to tears here.

I'm like, 'Dude, I just have to walk over here for a second,' and then off I fock away from him.

The formalities are finished – as in, everyone has finished handing over their books and their horseshit quotes – and now they're all looking at me, going, 'When's the food coming, Ross?' and 'Hurry up, Ross, we're storving!' and 'Should you be wearing an apron like that in the current climate?'

Into the kitchen I go to grab the meat from the fridge. But Fionn is there ahead of me and taking out a bottle of – let's call a spade a spade here – my wife's breast milk. He's holding Hillary in one orm and he goes, 'Hey, Ross.'

And I'm just like, 'Whatever.'

But then I happen to look at Hillary's little face and I get this sudden flash of memory of Honor when she was that age, lying helpless in *my* orms, with the light of the Bosch, two-door, American-style, fridge-freezer on her face, waiting for me to feed her – again – the juice of her mother's boobs. And in that moment, my hort feels literally empty and I hate Fionn more than I thought it was possible to hate someone you played rugby with.

He knows what I'm thinking as well because he's like, 'Sorcha says Honor is having the time of her life with Erika.'

'Don't,' I go, giving him a serious filthy. 'Don't *even*.'

We end up standing there, just staring at each other for a good, I don't know, twenty seconds – until I feel like I'm about to burst into tears.

It's at that exact point that Ross Junior – ridiculous – walks into the kitchen, doing his little butterfly thing, with his two hands crossed on his chest.

I'm like, 'What's wrong with you?' even though I know the answer is too much attention from his mother.

But that's when he says it – a line that turns my blood cold.

'Ith thothe awful boyth!' he goes, obviously referring to my sons. 'They're in your cor and they've thtorted the engine!'

It takes a good ten seconds for the words to properly sink in with me. As a matter of fact, my first instinct is to think, God, you usually have to wait until they're fifteen or sixteen before your kids stort taking the cor without permission!, but then a few seconds after that I'm thinking, Hang on, did he just *thay* what I thought he *thaid*?

Suddenly, I'm racing through the house. There's probably some little port of me that doesn't quite believe it – that is, until I throw open the front door and spot Brian sitting behind the wheel of my Audi A8, with the engine running, stretching his little neck to try to see over the dash.

I'm just like, 'Brian, get out of the cor! Get out of the cor now!' and I try to open the front door on the driver's side, except it ends up being centrally *locked*?

Brian looks at me through the window and goes, 'Fock off, you fock!'

I'm like, 'Brian, switch off the engine! I'm ordering you to switch off the engine now!'

But he doesn't. He just gives me the middle finger.

The cor storts revving like a roaring lion and I'm suddenly thinking, How the fock is he even doing that? There's no way his feet could reach the accelerator. But then I look down and I notice that little Leo is crouching in the footwell in front of him, pressing the pedals down with his two little hands.

Oh, Jesus, no! Oh, Jesus, no! Oh, Jesus, no!

I'm suddenly banging on the window with my open palm, going, 'Leo, don't touch those pedals! Come out of there! Come out of there now! I'll give you money!'

By now, of course, everyone at the porty has heard the commotion. Thirty or forty people have come through the house to see what's happening, including Sorcha.

And I'm there, 'Two grand, goys! Two grand for whichever one of you opens the door first!'

Sorcha's like, 'Oh my God, Ross, the engine's running!'

And I'm there, 'It'll be fine, Sorcha, as long he doesn't put the thing into –'

I don't even get to finish my sentence. I watch in horror as Brian reaches for the gear stick and puts it into Drive, just as Leo presses down on the accelerator. The cor lurches forward, then stops. Then, inside the cor, I hear Brian and Leo's delighted squeals at having actually moved the thing.

I look up, and for some reason I spot Fionn standing next to the rose bushes in front of the living-room window. He's holding Hillary in his orms and feeding him the bottle.

I all of a sudden shout, 'Fionn, *move!*'

But he doesn't get a chance to because Leo presses down on the accelerator again. The wheels spin, spitting up gravel, then the cor flies forward and I fly forward too, running alongside it. I cover the ground between me and Fionn in literally a split-second and I throw myself at him – think Sam Warburton on Vincent Clerc and you're in the right ball pork – sending him flying to the ground. In fairness to Fionn, like Vincent Clerc, he manages to hold onto the ball – or, more specifically in this case, Hillary.

I end up basically on top of the two of them, then I roll over in time to watch my beautiful cor drive over the rose bushes and crash through the front of the house – into the *actual* living room.

Holy fock!

Honor had posted a new video on her YouTube channel. It's the first for, like, weeks and I end up finding it by total accident. Yeah, no, I'm watching a hilarious compilation of rugby swan-dive fails set to Daniel Powter's 'Bad Day' when it pops up in my Recommendeds.

It's like, 'Love Honor and Obey: From Down Under'.

I click on the link and suddenly there she is – my daughter, who I haven't actually heard from in, like, weeks.

'Hi, everyone!' she goes. 'And welcome back to my channel! I'm sorry I've been so quiet for the last few weeks! So, I'll just explain my very exciting news! Which is that I've relocated to Perth in

Australia, which is going to be my home until the end of August! Yay! So exciting!'

She actually seems *genuinely* excited?

'I've got lots and lots of things that I want to show you today! We've got, like, *so* much catching-up to do! But first I want to introduce you to someone who has been – oh my God – my hero since I was, like, literally five years old! And maybe even before that! So, you all met my dad! And a lot of you were kind enough to leave comments saying how cool he is! Well, the person I want to introduce you to is his sister slash half-sister – my Auntie Erika!'

Erika steps into the shot. God, she looks fantastic, and I'm saying that in the way that any half-brother would pay a compliment to his half-sister. She's wearing a denim mini and white camisole and I can pretty much see her tay-tays through the thin, cotton fabric.

She waves at the camera and goes, 'Hi, everyone!'

Honor's there, 'Isn't she the most – Oh! My God! – stunning woman you have ever seen in your lives?'

'Definitely,' I hear myself go and my face feels suddenly hot. 'Definitely, definitely, definitely.'

Honor's like, 'So we're going to do a video together and, as I'm standing here, I am actually shaking with nerves! Because, for as long as I can remember, literally, one of my ambitions has been to spend a day in Erika's wardrobe!'

Like father, like daughter, I could say. Yeah, no, I used to love having a nose around Erika's bedroom whenever I got the opportunity. I actually used to steal bras and sometimes tights from her drawers, although that was before I found out she was a blood relative.

Actually, I think they're still in a box in my old pair's attic. I probably should get rid of them.

'So,' Honor goes, 'Erika and I are going to do a special video today, the theme of which is . . . are you ready, Erika?'

They both go, 'Best Friend Style Swap!' and they giggle like two teenagers.

'Now,' Honor goes, 'even though I *actually* worship this woman, our taste in clothes could not be more different! And right now, I am actually scared! We are, like, literally the opposite of each other in terms of the kind of stuff we like to wear! Which is why we thought it would be kind of fun to go shopping for each other and then to literally swap styles!'

'And it *was* fun!' Erika goes. 'But, like you, Honor, I'm very, very nervous about trying on the clothes you've chosen for me! Because we do have very different taste! Even though I *love* the kind of clothes you wear!'

'I would, literally, describe your fashion sense as classic with an edge!'

'I think I'd call yours girlie-cool – is that okay?'

'Oh my God, I'm literally delighted with that!'

Anyway, the video goes on like this for a good fifteen minutes before they basically stort handing each other hats and jackets and boots and jeans to try on.

And it's obvious that the two of them are getting on like a house on fire. And it makes me feel sad. I'm not going to deny it. It's like I've been, I don't know, *replaced*?

I watch it for another five minutes and it's actually like listening to Erika and Sorcha back in the day.

It's all, 'I actually get more compliments on my faux-leather pants than I do on my actual leather ones, which cost, like, nine hundred euros!' and 'Oh my God, I love that you don't hate the Baker Boy hat!' and 'I never thought a cream roll-neck would suit me, but it's actually insane how much I love this one you chose for me, even though it's just Zara!'

I press Pause because I can't watch any more of it. It's too painful. I scroll down through the comments. There's, like, hundreds and hundreds of them – a lot of them saying how gorgeous Erika is and asking if she'll be appearing in future videos? Very few people ask for me.

I give the video a Like. It'd be petty not to. Then – I know I'm storting to sound like *her* now? – but *literally* thirty seconds later, my phone storts ringing. It's a number I don't recognize – a long one. I answer the phone and it ends up being *her* voice on the line.

She's like, 'Dad?'

I'm there, 'Honor? Oh my God, how the hell are you?'

'I'm fine!'

'I just gave you a Like.'

'I saw that. That's why I rang.'

'I haven't heard from you. I thought I would have heard from you.'

'I'm sorry, Dad. I was, like, really jetlagged for the first few days. Then I've been – oh my God – *so* busy. I've been emailing companies asking them to send me stuff for free in return for a mention on my channel.'

'Yeah, no, I got the one that was intended for Estée Lauder. I'd say they focking shat themselves when they read it.'

'I'm already getting, like, boxes and boxes of free stuff. And Erika thinks I should set up my own lifestyle brand – kind of like Gwyneth Paltrow's Goop?'

'I fancy Gwyneth Paltrow. A lot.'

'So how are you? How are the boys?'

'Ah, you know yourself – same old, same old. They crashed my cor through the front of the house and into the living room.'

'What?'

'Yeah, no, they totally ruined Hillary's christening yesterday, you'll be happy to hear. We're going to have to get builders in to fix the damage. And the front of my cor is banjoed.'

She goes, 'Oh! My God!' but she doesn't laugh. It's like she's shocked by it.

I'm there, 'Maybe I didn't tell the story properly.'

'Are they okay?'

'They weren't hurt, if that's what you mean. But I genuinely thought you'd love that story. Maybe it was one of those, you know – you had to *be* there?'

She's quiet for a few seconds and then she goes, 'I really miss them.'

And I'm like, 'We really miss you, Honor. *I* really miss you,' and – oh fock – here come the tears. Yeah, no, I'm suddenly bawling. And *she's* trying to comfort me again.

She's like, 'Dad, come on, don't cry.'

I'm there, 'It's focking rubbish, Honor.'

'What's rubbish?'

'Everything. Life. It's boring without you. I feel like I'm missing an orm or something.'

'I miss you, too.'

'And everyone's taking the piss because they know I don't have you there to back me up. They're sensing that the Rossmeister General is weak and they're all suddenly loving it.'

'Keep a list, will you? For when I get home?'

'Oh, I will. I'm definitely going to do that.'

She's like, 'Anyway, Dad, I have to go. We're going horse-riding.'

And I'm there, 'Look after yourself. And say hello to Erika for me.'

But by then she's already hung up.

Sorcha's old dear is not a happy rabbit. She's there, 'Why is nobody talking about the elephant in the room?'

'It's not an elephant,' I go. 'It's an Audi A8 luxury sedan.' And it's going to be in the room until at least this afternoon, when the AA have promised to send a man with a tow truck to remove it.

'You know perfectly well what my wife means,' Sorcha's old man goes. 'Fionn and Hillary could have been killed.'

Sorcha's there, 'Let's just be grateful that no one was hurt,' because the two boys escaped without even a scratch and Brian seemed to even enjoy the experience of having an airbag go off in his face. It's actually something that's on my own bucket list.

I'm there, 'Let's also be grateful to me for actually *saving* Fionn's and Hillary's lives.'

Fionn goes, 'Yeah, I've already thanked you, Ross.'

'If it wasn't for my quick thinking – *and* quick feet, I could add. I was thinking of Simon Warburton on Vincent Clerc. Poor Alain Rolland would have had a decision to make if that was a match situation – even though I know he's a fan of mine. I'd have just walked. Made it easy for him.'

Sorcha's old dear practically explodes. She goes, 'Those boys are out of control!'

And I'm like, 'So what's your solution? Send *them* to Australia as well? Jesus, you'll have the house to yourselves at this rate. Which is probably your plan all along.'

Sorcha goes, 'They ruined the day for everyone. I've never been so embarrassed in my life.'

Which, again, is horseshit. I've embarrassed her worse than that on dozens of occasions – Jesus, I brought a lapdancer to her graduation dinner! – although I don't think anyone would thank me for reminding them.

I'm there, 'Sorry, I'm picking up on the vibe here that you all think this is somehow *my* fault? They're orseholes – I'm accepting that. What am I supposed to do about it?'

And Sorcha's old man goes, 'Try parenting them!'

'What, reading science shit to them like Fionn there? Chromium and Millennium and whatever the fock else there is?'

'I'm saying those boys are the most badly behaved children I've ever had the misfortune to meet. And that's down to *you* – and also *portly* down to you, Sorcha, I regret to say, because you came up with this ridiculous idea that their bad language would just stop of its own accord.'

Sorcha's old dear goes, 'Instead, they've graduated to this – stealing cars and *joyriding* them at people.'

I'm not going to stand here and listen to her try to blame me and Sorcha for the way our children have turned out.

I'm there, 'And who bought them a soccer ball two Christmases ago?'

The woman pretends not to know what I'm talking about. She's like, 'What does that have to do with anything?'

'Oh,' I go, 'so you're totally unaware of the link between soccer and petty crime? One is a gateway to the other! Look up the focking stats!'

'How dare you speak to my wife like that?' Sorcha's old man goes.

'And how dare you and your wife buy my children Manchester United Soccer jerseys and then act all innocent when they turn out to be – let's be honest here – little focking thugs?'

'They *wanted* those soccer jerseys,' Sorcha's old dear tries to go, which is poor from her. 'They *asked* for them.'

And I'm there, 'If Sorcha had asked you for a chainsaw at that age, would you have given her one? Or her sister? Okay, *somebody* tell me her name!'

My phone suddenly rings. At first, I just presume it's the old man again. Yeah, no, he's been ringing me every second day and leaving long, rambling messages about how everyone in the clinic is suddenly delighted with the quality of his fun gel. I don't even check that it's him. I just answer the phone going, 'Yeah, I'm sick of hearing about how wonderful your focking jizz is, okay?'

But it ends up not being my old man at all. It ends up being Phinneas McPhee. He goes, 'Er, Ross?'

And I'm like, 'Sorry, Dude, I thought you were my dad.'

'Oh, er, right. Anyway, how are you?'

And I'm there, 'Top of the world, Phinneas. If my life got any better, I'd begin to suspect that Richard Curtis was secretly directing it. What's the Jack?'

'Look, I hope you don't mind me ringing you. I got your number from Garry Ringrose.'

'I didn't know Garry still had it. It'd be nice if he returned my texts once in a while – especially when I go to the trouble of sending him pre-match motivational quotes that are specifically tailored to him. You can tell him that next time you see him.'

'The reason I'm ringing is because, well, I've got myself into a bit of trouble.'

'Trouble?' I go. I stand up and I walk out of the kitchen – just for a bit of privacy. 'What kind of trouble are we talking?'

He goes, 'Look, what are your memories of our conversation last week?'

'The main one was you putting Ronan's girlfriend back in her box. I should have high-fived you at the time. That's going down as a definite regret. That's not why you're ringing, is it?'

'Er, no, it's not why I'm ringing. Do you remember me asking your son where he was from? We were talking about Gaelic football at the time.'

'Yeah, no, I kind of zoned out for that bit of the conversation. I've zero interest in any sport other than rugby.'

'I asked Ronan if he played for UCD and he said no, he played for a local club near where he lived. And I asked him where he lived and he said –'

'Figglas,' I go. 'Meaning Finglas. Yeah, no, I remember that bit, weirdly enough.'

'The thing is, Ross, as a result of that conversation, I've been accused by the Students' Union of committing an act of microaggression.'

'Of what?'

'Microaggression.'

'Okay, I'm hearing the words – it must just be that I don't know what it means.'

'I'll just read this thing to you that I found on the internet. *Microaggression is an action or a statement –* or, in this case, a question – *that implies an indirect, subtle or unintentional discrimination against members of a marginalized group, such as a racial or ethnic minority or someone who comes from a socially disadvantaged area.*'

'Ronan *does* come from a socially disadvantaged area. Jesus, the magician at his tenth birthday porty was wearing a focking stab vest! They call him David Cop-a-Feel, by the way, because he can be a bit handsy around the moms, especially if he's had a few. Actually, that's probably why he keeps getting stabbed.'

None of this seems to put Phinneas's mind at ease.

He goes, 'A lot of people, especially young people, think you shouldn't ask where people come from.'

I'm like, 'What? Why?'

'Because to ask someone where they come from is to make an issue out of their socio-economic circumstances.'

'But say if it's a job interview situation – how are you supposed to know who you should or shouldn't hire if you're not allowed to ask where the candidates come from? You could end up giving the job to someone from – okay, I'm trying to think of somewhere really bad to make my point. The obvious one is Bray.'

'The thing is, Ross, with the way campus politics is now, I could be in a huge amount of trouble here.'

'Young people have definitely lost it. We haven't even talked about the whole jazz hands thing.'

'Ross, I could lose my job.'

'For asking someone where they're from? Are you shitting me?'

'I'm just saying, this girl could make life really difficult for me. I've been invited to attend a meeting of the Students' Union to explain myself.'

'*Explain* yourself? Jesus, I don't envy you that.'

'I was wondering would you mind if I called you as a witness for me?'

'Er, unfortunately, I don't have any wheels at the moment – long story.'

But then he plays the rugby cord.

'You know,' he goes, 'seeing as we both played for UCD.'

I'm there, 'Fine, I'll take my wife's Nissan Leaf. Although I *could* point out that we only played, like, two matches together, given that I was injured slash boozing for most of the year I spent in Belfield. So when *is* this trial?'

And he goes, 'Friday afternoon – and I'm not actually *on* trial, Ross?'

And in his innocence, he seems to genuinely believe that.

I'm searching the house for my Rugby Tactics Book, having decided to spend the morning picking my squad of thirty-one for Ireland's summer tour of, like, the States and Japan.

Except I've no idea where I put it. I mean, I've literally turned the house upside-down – the bedroom, the study, the kitchen – looking for the thing, but I can't actually find it.

So I end up just picking up a random piece of paper in the kitchen, then I sit down at the island and I scribble down the names of James Ryan and Rory O'Loughlin. It's important that we win all three Tests, but at the same time I'm keen to bring a few new faces in with the World Cup just two years away. Then I have a little smile to myself thinking how delighted the goys would be to get the call from me.

That's when Sorcha's old man walks into the kitchen and decides to burst my bubble.

'I thought it might interest you to know,' he goes, 'that two of your children are trying to stuff another one into a cement mixer.'

He says it in a really smug way as well. I stand up from the table and I go into the living room. And – yeah, no – he ends up being right. Brian and Leo are trying to shove their screaming brother head-first into a cement mixer, although, in their defence, there's no actual cement in it and it isn't switched on.

We've got the builders in, by the way, repairing the damage that the boys did when they drove my cor through the front of the house. I shove Brian and Leo out of the way, then I grab Johnny by the ankles and I pull him out.

Sorcha walks into the room then, carrying Hillary and with a concerned look on her face. She's like, 'Why have you written "James Ryan" and "Rory O'Loughlin" on the back of Hillary's Baptismal Certificate?' but then she sees me hugging Johnny and trying to calm him down and she goes, 'Oh! My God! What happened?'

I'm there, 'Brian and Leo shoved Johnny head-first into the cement mixer. I doubt if they'd have got the thing storted, though.'

Mind you, I would have said the same thing about my cor.

Leo picks up a shovel and tries to hit me with it, but I manage to dodge it easily enough.

'Focking push me,' he goes, 'you focking wanker.'

I take the shovel from him.

Sorcha's there, 'Ross, I asked you to watch them.'

And I'm like, 'Yeah, I was actually trying to get some work done. If anyone is to blame, it's the builders for going off on their lunch break and leaving all this shit lying around.'

'I can't believe you actually just said that.'

'I'm just making the point, Sorcha, why do I always have to babysit them?'

'Babysit them? Ross, they're *your* children. It's not called babysitting when it's your own children – it's called parenting.'

Ah, that old chestnut. It's obvious that her old pair have been in her ear again. I mention that as well – that this is all coming from them.

She goes, 'Maybe I've realized they're right, Ross. We *are* going to have to do something about their behaviour – otherwise, they're going to grow up worse than Honor.'

I'm there, 'They're already worse than Honor,' pissed off that I have to keep defending my daughter. 'At least a lot of the shit Honor does is funny. Hilarious, in fact – provided you're not the one on the other end of it. Brian, put that chisel down.'

'Shut the fock up,' he goes, 'and give your focking hole a rest.'

Sorcha's there, 'Like my dad, I'm storting to question whether we did the right thing in choosing to ignore their swearing.'

I'm like, 'Yeah, that was *your* idea, can I just point out?'

'Something needs to change, Ross.'

Brian focks the chisel straight at me. I manage to duck just in time – I've always had pretty amazing reflexes – and the thing ends up embedded in the wall behind me.

'Ross,' Sorcha goes, 'take them out.'

I'm like, 'Where, though?'

'Anywhere. Just get them out of here.'

I throw them into the back of Sorcha's Nissan Leaf and I drive through Dalkey, then Sandycove, then Glasthule, trying to think of a place that serves brunch and hasn't explicitly banned my children from the premises.

In the end, I decide to try the Cookbook Café in Glasthule, thinking they might not remember the last time we were in there. But when I arrive at the door, it turns out that we made a more lasting impression than I hoped. A waitress, carrying a plate in either hand, takes one look at the boys on their leads and just shakes her head at me as if to say, Don't even think about it.

So what I end up doing is, I tie their leads to the wooden bench outside and I tell them to pretend to be dogs for half an hour while Daddy pops inside for a crispy quesadilla with a side of ham hock hash.

The three of them get down on their hands and knees. 'Woof, woof!' Brian goes. 'Hey, I'm a focking pit bull!'

And Leo's like, 'I'm a focking Rottweiler! A focking Rottweiler would kill a focking pit bull!'

They really are morons. More to be pitied than anything.

Anyway, I sit near the window – the whole responsible parent thing – and I order my breakfast, then I borrow a pen from the waitress and on the back of a napkin I stort writing down the names of the lucky fifteen who are going to stort against the States.

I'm actually mulling over the dilemma of who to put in the front row when I notice someone – a female – chatting to the boys through the window. I say 'chatting to them', but she's actually petting them and Leo, in particular, is loving the attention because he's going, 'Woof-woof! Woof-woof-woof!' and the woman is cracking up laughing.

Outside I go.

'Be careful of that one,' I go, meaning Leo. 'He bites.'

She thinks it's hilarious but I'm not even joking. I've nearly lost fingers to the little focker.

I look at the woman. She's about my age. She's not great in terms of looks, even though we're not supposed to *notice* shit like that any more? There's very little wrong with her actual features – nice eyes, nice nose, *great* mouth – it's just that they add up to less than the sum of their ports, like if you drew a picture of Emilia Clarke on a potato.

Again, you probably can't say that any more either.

Suddenly, she's looking at me, going, 'Ross? Ross O'Carroll-Kelly?' and it tells you everything you need to know about the kind of life I've led that I end up having to go, 'No, sorry, it's a case of mistaken identity.'

She laughs. She goes, 'It *is* you! I'm Sasha Graham! Holy Child Killiney?'

I'm like, 'Sasha Graham Holy Child Killiney? Oh my God!'

Yeah, no, I recognize her now. She took me to her debs back in the day. One of the many.

I'm there, 'So what's the Jack?'

And she goes, 'Married. Two kids. Successful business. Degree and a Master's. House on Albert Road.'

Holy Child girls are like that. You ask them how they are and they end up reading you their focking LinkedIn profiles.

I'm there, 'That, erm, all seems in order.'

'And you married Sorcha Lalor?' she goes.

'I, er, did, yeah.'

I could be wrong, but it kind of feels like an accusation.

I'm there, 'I married her. Yes, indeed,' although I don't mention that we haven't had sex in months because that would be probably weird.

'And these are your kids?' she goes. 'Oh my God, triplets! They're gorgeous!'

I'm like, 'They're not really,' and she laughs – again, like she thinks I'm joking. 'Seriously, they're not. You can have them if you want them.'

'Oh my God, don't tempt me! I'd run away with them!'

'No, do. Please do. Just don't come back.'

She laughs again.

Brian and Johnny have entered into a borking contest to see who can do it the loudest. They're going, 'WOOF! WOOF! WOOF! FOCKING WOOF!'

Sasha goes, 'Have they storted in Montessori yet?'

And I'm there, 'You must be focking joking! There's nowhere would take them!'

And she must see the sadness in my eyes because she suddenly looks at me all serious. She goes, 'Oh my God, you're *not* actually joking, are you?'

I'm there, 'They're little fockers, Sasha. You must have heard the stories about them?'

'I've heard stories about three little boys who . . . Oh my God, this is *them*?'

'Yeah, no, it's all true. Every focking word. They're beyond help.'

'FOCKING FOCKING WOOF WOOF!' Brian shouts. 'FOCK-ING PRICK!'

Sasha shakes her head. She goes, 'No child is beyond help, Ross. And I'm saying that because this is what I do.'

I'm like, 'What?'

'Have you heard of Little Cambridge? It's a Montessori School in Ranelagh?'

Of course I've heard of it. The waiting list is longer than the one for Columba's.

I'm there, 'Are you saying that's you? As in, *that's* your successful business?'

'Yeah, I storted it ten years ago. And we pride ourselves on being able to unlock the potential in every child.'

'I mean, is there any chance you'd –'

She knows where I'm going with this because she suddenly cuts me off.

She goes, 'We're actually at full *capacity* at the moment?'

I look down. Oh, Jesus Christ. Leo is quite literally humping Sasha's leg, going, 'WOOF! WOOF! WOOF!'

'Like father, like son,' I go, trying to laugh it off, but I think she sees the resignation in my eyes when I say it. 'I'll just go in and ask for a bucket of water to fock over him.'

And that's when Sasha goes, 'I'll take them.'

I'm like, 'What? Really?'

'What can I say? I like a challenge!'

'Oh, they're definitely that. I could tell you some of the shit they've done even in the last few days, but I'd be scared you'd change your mind.'

'Give me your number,' she goes.

Which I do. I rhyme off the digits and she puts them into her phone.

She's like, 'As it happens, you're in luck. I'm going to have some vacancies coming up soon. I'll text you in a week or two.'

I'm there, 'You won't regret this, Sasha,' even though I'm ninety-nine percent sure she will.

I manage to peel Leo off her leg and off Sasha goes.

And I'm suddenly filled with this happy feeling. There is someone in the world who thinks she can unlock the potential in my kids. At the very least, this is going to mean a week of peace and quiet for me, giving me time to focus on picking the right team for the three summer Tests, before Sasha finally accepts that there's fock-all she can do for them.

Yes, I can't remember when I last felt this happy. But then, all of a sudden, a cor drives by. I look up and I recognize it as my old man's Bentley. Kennet is behind the wheel. He slows down and the window in the back opens and my old man sticks his head out of it and shouts, 'Wonderful news, Kicker! We! Are! Pregnant!'

*

Ronan is leaning against the wall of the Newman Building, smoking one of his famous rollies. I walk up to him and I'm like, 'What's the story? I've been ringing you for the last two hours.'

He goes, 'Rosser, what are *you* doing hee-or?'

'What am I doing here? I'm here as a witness. Your girlfriend has accused poor Phinneas of, I don't know, something or other.'

'Microaggreshidden.'

'That was it. Look, I played rugby with the dude – twice, as a matter of fact – and I can tell you that he's innocent, even though I don't properly understand what he's being accused of.'

'It's the casual and unthinking degradashidden of addy soshidilly deproyuved group by a member of the domidant culchodder.'

'He just asked you where you lived, Ro.'

'He shoultn't hab, but. It's like some wooden who's white complimenton a black boord or a black fedda on he's afro.'

'Are you saying *that's* not cool now either?'

'It's not heerd to wontherstand, Rosser. Aston somewooden from a disadvaddenteged backgrowunt wheer they're from – whether intentionoddy or unintenionoddy – sends a denigrating message to that peerson.'

'I don't think that was his intention. You told him Finglas and that was that.'

'He shoulta known bethor than to ast me, but – he's apposed to be a leckchodder.'

'Yeah, in Sports and Exercise Management. Give him a focking break, Ro. Are you saying you're going to give evidence against him?'

'Huguette says that this is how racism and discriminashodden throyuv – because we doatunt cawdle out the subtle prejudices revealed in eer evoddy day exchayunges.'

'The only reason we're here, let's be honest, is because Phinneas called her the Sushi Girl in the Orts Café last week.'

He drops what's left of his cigarette, twists it into the ground with a Nike Air Max and goes, 'I'll see you insoyut, Rosser.'

Then into the Newman Building he goes. A few seconds later, Phinneas arrives. He's wearing – quite literally – a shirt and tie. He looks nervous. I tell him not to be.

I'm there, 'The entire thing is a focking joke. We'll get this thing thrown out, then we'll go on the lash for the rest of the day. It'll be just like old times.'

Phinneas leads the way to Theatre C where the hearing – yeah, no, that's the word they're using – is going to take place. But a serious shock awaits us when he pushes the door and we step inside. There must be, like, two or three hundred students in there, filling every inch of the banked seating area, and a sudden hush falls on the place as the word goes around that we've arrived.

I look at Phinneas and Phinneas looks at me. Rugby or no rugby, I get this sudden urge to turn around and walk out of there – fock him, he dug his own grave – but then I hear Huguette go, 'Okay, let's get this hearing under way.'

She's sitting at a table at the front of the lecture hall with two other students – both dudes, and none of them yet out of their teens. Huguette beckons us forward and goes, 'Thank you for joining us.'

As we approach the front, some dude in a black hoodie stands up and goes, 'Respectfully, Madam President, I would like to request a suspension of the running order to discuss a matter of extreme urgency. Last night, while in the Clubhouse Bor, it came to my attention that the jukebox, which is in the middle of a public area, populated by students, contains a record by the artist David Bowie called – quite literally – "China Girl".'

There are gasps in the room and more than a few Oh! My God!s.

The dude goes, 'Why is it necessary, I'm sure we're all wondering, to point out that the girl is Chinese? I'm wondering do we, as a union, have to tell the college authorities that defining someone by their ethnicity in this way is not acceptable?'

'Or their gender!' a girl behind him shouts. 'Why is he choosing to make an issue of the fact that the subject of the song is a girl? Is that not a bit sexist – as well as binarist?'

'It's totally binarist,' the dude goes, 'as well as racist and – like you said – sexist. I'm proposing that we stage a picket outside the Clubhouse Bor until the manager agrees to remove this so-called song from the jukebox.'

The girl's there, 'Maybe we should also invite this David Bowie

220

here so we can explain to him how deeply offensive this kind of thing is and how it's also not cool.'

'Unfortunately,' the dude goes, 'I looked him up on Wikipedia last night and he seems to be dead.'

'That's a pity because I was going to say we should ask him to come here and then, on the day, no-platform him. Is he *definitely* dead?'

'Yeah, no, it says he died in January of last year.'

'*That's* convenient for him.'

Huguette calls the session to order. She goes, 'Can I suggest we deal with the issue of this David Bowie person at the end? It's just that we have a microaggression case that I want to hear now – and it's particularly serious because it involves a member of the university staff.'

I'm standing next to Phinneas. I look at him. He's literally shaking. I sit down behind him rather than next to him. It's just the atmosphere in the room is pretty focked up and I don't want people to think *I'm* the one on trial here?

Huguette goes, 'Mister McPhee,' and the dude steps forward. 'There has been a very serious allegation made that on a day last week you committed an act of microaggression against a student – microaggression being a verbal or behavioural act, whether intentional or unintentional, that communicates hostile, derogatory or prejudicial feelings towards a member of a marginalized group, including the economically disadvantaged. Do you have anything to say?'

The poor focker.

He goes, 'I just asked him where he was from?' and there's suddenly a huge, collective intake of breath in the lecture hall. These people need to get out more. And maybe spend less time on the internet.

'So you do admit that you asked the question?' Huguette goes.

He's there, 'You know I asked the question. You were sitting there at the time.'

'We will consider your confession as part of any plea for mitigation.'

'Mitigation? Who the hell do you people think you are?'

'Unfortunately for you, we're the UCD Students' Union.'

Shit. I look around. Everyone in the theatre is doing jazz hands. It's not looking good for the dude.

'So the facts of the case are not contested,' Huguette goes. 'In the interests of fairness, I think it's important that we hear from the student involved. Ronan Masters, where are you?'

He's sitting in the front row on the other side of the aisle from us. He stands up. He's besotted with the girl. You can see it in his face.

Huguette goes, 'Is there anything you wish to say?'

And he's like, 'It was like you said, Huguette – happent last week. I was habbon a cup of coffee in the Eerts Café and Mistor McPhee came in. Turdens out he's a friend of me auld fedda's. We were thalken about Gah – in utter words – Gaelic football. And says he to me, "Where are you libbon?" or woords to that effect.'

Everyone is just, like, shaking their heads like it's the worst thing they've ever heard.

Phinneas shouts, 'You said that you were playing for the local club and I just said, "Where do you live?"'

'Shame!' someone shouts, then there's suddenly a chorus of it – people going, 'Shame! Shame! Shame! Shame!'

Huguette bangs her little – I want to say – *gabble* on the desk?

'I understand that this is an emotionally chorged case,' she goes, 'but can I ask you to please consider those in the room with anxiety and sensory issues, including autism?'

That quietens everyone down.

Poor Phinneas – not unreasonably – goes, 'I asked a student where he lived. It was a request for information. I didn't mean anything by it.'

Huguette goes, 'Can I just point out that your intention is actually irrelevant? A microaggression is considered to have occurred when the victim *feels* that they've been casually degraded because of their identity as a member of a minority grouping.'

Phinneas goes, 'But that's entirely subjective. I'm sorry, but I don't accept that microaggression is even a thing.'

'If you refuse to believe that microaggression exists, then how do you know you're not guilty of it?'

More jazz hands. Phinneas is royally focked here and I suspect he knows it.

Huguette goes, 'Ronan, can I ask you, did you feel in any way degraded when Phinneas asked you where you lived?'

Ro goes, 'I ditn't at the toyum, to be hodest wit you, Huguette. It was oatenly arthurwords, when it was pointed out to me that it wadn't okay for a fedda in his posishidden to be aston them koyunt of questyiddens, that I steerted to feel a birra what you were thalken about.'

I stand up. I'm like, 'For fock's sake, Ro! The girl isn't even that good-looking!'

Well, you can imagine how that ends up going down. There's, like, roars of disapproval in the lecture hall and more shouts of 'Shame!' until Huguette reminds them once again to have a bit of consideration for people in the hall who might be feeling triggered.

Poor Phinneas has his face in his hands.

I walk up to the front of the lecture hall and I go, 'I'm sorry, I just want to say something here. I can vouch for this man. I played rugby with him. Unfortunately, I can't say the same for that goy over there, even though he's my son. I barely recognize him today. And as for her, I genuinely don't know what Ronan sees in her. But the only reason she wants Phinneas sacked is because he called her the Sushi Girl and I laughed because I thought it was hilarious and I still do. Eating sushi is racist – but not eating sushi is even more racist. You lot would want to cop the fock on. I look around this room and all I see is unhappiness. You're supposed to be students, can I just remind you? Why aren't you off getting pissed? Or laid? Instead, you're sitting around worrying about this shit. I rest my case.'

I look into the crowd. They're all just staring at me with these big, serious faces on them. I don't know what kind of reaction I was expecting.

'Yeah, thanks for that,' Phinneas goes, 'Amal focking Clooney.'

Huguette's there, 'Given that the evidence is uncontested, I'd like to forward a motion calling on the university to terminate Mister McPhee's employment. Do I have a seconder?'

I look across at Ronan while he just looks down at the floor. I'm thinking, At least he has the decency to feel bad about what he's done, even though he says fock-all while Huguette goes, 'Okay, let's take a vote on this, then we can move on to the matter of David Bowie.'

I turn to Phinneas and I go, 'Sorry, Dude, I made my points but they didn't seem to want to listen.'

He goes, 'Thanks a bunch, Ross. That's my job gone. And God knows what my chances are of getting another one.'

A lecturer in Strategy and Operations Management in Sport? I would have thought not very high.

I drive to Foxrock and I pull up outside the house. I don't even bother taking the kids out of the cor. I'll only be staying long enough to tell the woman exactly what I think of her in a few short, shorp sentences, then I'll be out of there.

I let myself in, using my key, which she can have back now because after today I want nothing more to do with her ever again.

Pregnant? In a way, I still don't believe it.

I stand in the hallway and I shout, 'Where are you, you focking . . . I don't know . . . you focking . . .'

But I can't even come up with an original name to call her. In the end, I have to settle for 'You ugly, scabrous, ratdog fock,' but only because I heard Brian shout it out the window at an old woman getting off the 59 bus on Ulverton Road this morning, which meant it was already in my head.

I hear her voice coming from upstairs. She goes, 'I'll be down in just a minute, Ross! Go into the kitchen!'

So that's what I end up doing. At the same time, I'm thinking, I don't give a fock what she's cooked for lunch, I won't be eating any of it. Even if it's her famous braised lamb shawarma that she used to make for me as a treat on a Friday night. Or her curried tomato bisque that she used to make for me whenever I had a cold. Or her crab cake sliders with mango salsa that she used to make for me when I was hungover. Or her gourmet Gruyère Mac and Cheese that she used to make for me whenever I needed corbs ahead of a big match. Or her spicy squash and feta frittata with mint yoghurt that she used to make for me if I was feeling down in myself because she knew it cheered me up.

She can shove it all up her . . .

I push the kitchen door and I head straight for the fridge, more out of curiosity than anything. And that's when I discover that I'm not alone. I'm very far from alone, in fact. There's, like, one, two, three, four, five, six women in there – all of them good-looking. It would be rude of me not to notice.

I'm like, 'Hey,' because – bear in mind – I haven't had a sniff of anything in months and I'm as focking horny as the last goat on Dalkey Island.

'Hullo,' one of the birds goes. She's from – Huguette would have kittens, no doubt, if she heard me say this – but Eastern Europe. It turns out they *all* are?

I just take it for granted that the old dear is interviewing for a new cleaner. I'm there, 'So she finally gave Salome the bullet, huh?' except none of them answers me. They might not have good English, which is just as well for them because the old dear tends to insult her staff right to their faces.

I'm there, 'A little tip, she has cameras hidden all over the gaff, including one in her walk-in wardrobe, which is designed to look like a thermostat.'

And that's when the old dear walks into the kitchen, looking like Dan Cole dressed as a woman.

She goes, 'Ross! I hoped we might see you today! I made one of my famous spicy squash and feta frittatas with mint yoghurt.'

I'm there, 'The old man said you were knocked up, preggers, whatever you want to call it.'

She goes, 'Not *quite* pregnant, Ross. We had a call from the clinic to say that the fertilization process has been successful!'

'That's not what he shouted at me on the Glasthule Road the other day.'

She smiles at me then and goes, 'I see you've met Lidia, Roxana,

Szidonia, Brigita, Loredana and – oh, yes – another one called Lidia.'

And I'm there, 'Yeah, no, I was just warning them that you're paranoid about your shit going missing. Whichever one ends up cleaning for you, there'll be eyes on her the entire time. The clock on the mantelpiece in the living room is also a camera, by the way, girls.'

I didn't know that until about a year ago. I shudder to think how many times I wanked off in that room while watching *Home and Away* over the years.

And that's when the old dear says it. She says it totally out of the blue. 'Dorling,' she goes, 'these aren't cleaners. These are the surrogates that your father and I have chosen to carry our babies.'

I'm there, 'You mean your *baby*.'

'No,' she goes. 'I mean our *babies*.'

'Why do you keep saying babies when you mean to say baby? You must have drunk your breakfast too quickly, did you?'

She goes, 'Yes, I had a fuzzy navel, Ross – but that was to celebrate the news!'

I'm there, 'What news?'

'That Charles and I have *six* viable embryos for implantation!'

I'm just, like, staring at her in total shock. I'm like, 'Six embryos? Does that mean – Jesus focking Christ – six babies?'

And she goes, 'Yes! And these beautiful, strong, young women have come to Ireland to help bring your little brothers or sisters into the world!'

7

Outfit of the Day is a Canterbury Drill Top!

The old man has spent the last two days avoiding me. He hasn't returned any of the abusive messages that I left on his voicemail *or* with his Dáil secretary. But I end up finally tracking him down – as usual – to Hennessy's office in Fitzwilliam Square.

The man has no shame whatsoever. His opening line is 'So the race is on, Kicker!'

And I'm like, 'What race?'

'The race to replace Enda Kenny as the so-called leader of the country! He's just announced that he's stepping down as the leader of Fine Gael at midnight tonight!' and he storts tweeting while he's talking to me.

I'm there, 'Can you put your focking phone down, please?'

He goes, 'I just wanted to send this, Ross, while it's still fresh in my mind!'

Charles O'Carroll-Kelly √ @realCOCK – 12m

I see @rtenews reporting it's Leo 'not another cent' Varadkar versus HRH, the Merchant Prince, Simon Coveney for the #FGleadership. The Haves against the Have-Yachts! Are these two boarding school Hall Monitors really the best we can do in the search for someone to represent our country at home and abroad? #irexit #NewRepublic #CO'CKforTaoiseach

Reply 1,302 Retweet 4,960 Like 13,811 ✉

Suddenly, Hennessy steps into the room. 'I just talked to Fyodor,' he goes. 'He's got all their emails. Whose do we want to read first?

I told him Varadkar and Coveney obviously. Donohoe. Harris. Flanagan . . .'

He suddenly stops when he sees me sitting there in the corner.

I'm like, 'Hey, don't worry, I don't give a fock what you're up to. I'm here to discuss something more important.'

The old man goes, 'Just give me a few minutes here, Old Scout! And tell Fyodor to put Micheál Mortin and Dara Calleary on the list as well!'

Off Hennessy focks.

'So,' the old man goes, sitting down behind Hennessy's desk, 'what's troubling you, Kicker?'

I'm there, 'What's troubling me? You're un-focking-believable! One baby has suddenly turned into six?'

He's like, 'Oh, yes, your mother said you popped in to see her! You met our very lovely surrogate mums, I believe! Fyodor got them through a contact he has in Chişinău!'

'That's racist.'

'Is it?'

'You're not allowed to say where people are from any more.'

'Why on Earth not?'

'I don't fully understand it myself. That's not my point anyway. My point is why the fock do you want to bring six kids into the world?'

'Well, the clinic rang and they said we had six viable embryos – and, well, you've seen your mother in action in Sydney Vard! Give her a choice between three fur coats and the chances are she'll choose all three!'

'This isn't fur coats. This is actual babies.'

'Don't you think it'll be wonderful, Ross? Six little brothers and sisters for you to play with!'

'I'm thirty-focking-seven. And I've got kids coming out of my focking ears.'

'Your concerns have been minuted!'

'Minuted?'

'Look, Ross, Fionnuala is supporting my dream of becoming Taoiseach and taking Ireland out of the European Union with its cruel austerity measures and its ridiculous rules relating to everything, including the size of bloody well cabbages. So it's only fair that I support *her* dream of becoming a mother again!'

'Even though I came here today to try to talk you out of it?'

'There's no changing our minds now, Ross! Fertilization has occurred! There's no turning back! A lot of New Republic's support base is Pro-Life, you see! Capital P! Capital L! It wouldn't play at all well with the grassroots were it to get out that we binned five perfectly viable embryos!'

I'm like, 'Have you even thought about what it's going to be like to have six babies in the house? The feeds? The nappies?'

He goes, 'Oh, we'll get people to do all of that! I'm thinking more of the future, Kicker! I mean, there's bound to be a boy or two among that lot! And I have to confess, I haven't quite given up on the hope of seeing a son of mine play rugby for Ireland one day!'

'I can't believe you just said that.'

'It's an ambition of mine that's never gone away!'

I stand up. 'That's it,' I go. 'You and me are focking finished.'

He's there, 'Just think of it, Ross! A brother of yours winning the Grand Slam – maybe even captaining the Lions one day!'

I'm like, 'Seriously, Dude. I'm doing an Erika. I don't need you any more. I don't need you for anything.'

Of course, I end up regretting being so firm on that point when I go back to Sorcha's cor and discover that I've been clamped. I remember my old man's arrangement with the Leinster Branch, then I ring Sean Cronin and I ask him to phone my old man and tell him that his Nissan Leaf has been clamped in Fitzwilliam Square. But Sean isn't keen. Sean says he'd rather chew the clamp off with his own teeth than admit to driving a Nissan Leaf.

In the end, after a lot of humming and hawing from a man who's done pretty focking alright out of my old man over the years, Tadhg Furlong agrees to do it.

I sit there and wait for the dudes in the yellow bibs to arrive and free my cor. And after about fifteen minutes, my phone rings. I can see from the screen that it's Magnus calling me, which is a bit random. For some reason, I end up answering.

I'm like, 'Magnus, how the hell are you?'

He goes, 'All ish good, Rosh. We're all shtill bushing here on the exshitement of our financial results from Q1. Alsho, I have joined the Fashebook Health Committee and we are shetting all teamsh with the goal of walking one hundred thoushand shtepsh every week until Sheptember!'

'You're losing me, Magnus.'

'Shorry, Rosh, perhapsh the shignal ish not sho good where I'm shtanding.'

'No, I mean in terms of my interest. You're not ringing me to tell me how well the company's doing presumably?'

He laughs. He's like, 'Shorry, Rosh, Oisinn shays the shame thing to me – all I sheem to talk about theesh daysh ish Fashebook.'

'It's just I find stories about how well other people are doing very boring to listen to. That's me being straight with you.'

'Okay, sho I will tell you the reashon I am phoning. What are you doing on Shaturday morning?'

I'm like, 'Saaatuuurrrdaaayyy . . .' dragging the word out, trying to come up with an excuse, except my head is – as usual – empty.

He goes, 'The reashon I am ashking ish becaush I am playing a match.'

I should point out here that Magnus is very much a soccer guy. I've always thought it was the thing that would eventually break him and Oisinn up. I don't fancy his chances of persuading me and the rest of the goys to watch him kick a ball around for however many minutes that ridiculous game lasts.

'Dude,' I go, 'the only time I've ever deliberately watched soccer was when *Bend It Like Beckham* came out – and that had Keira Knightley in a sports bra in it.'

He goes, 'Thish time, I am not talking about shoccer, Rosh. I am talking about rugby.'

I'm there, 'Rugby?'

'Yesh, I have taken up rugby – if you can believe it!'

'At last.'

'That ish what Oisinn alsho shays!'

'It'll help your marriage in the long run. So who are you playing for? Jesus, it's not Greystones, is it?'

I've never liked Greystones. I don't know why. It's probably because they pretend to be better than Bray, which they're obviously not. Greystones is a Southside Skerries for Protestant underachievers.

Magnus goes, 'No, I am playing for Fashebook, of coursh!'

And I'm there, 'Facebook? I didn't know they had a rugby team.'

'Absholutely we haff a rugby team! Alsho, we are unbeaten for sheven matches. But shadly right now we haff no one to coach ush.'

'I can't believe Oisinn didn't mention that you were playing the beautiful game.'

'So I shay to my bosh, who ish the captain of the team, we are Fashebook. We are the besht. Which meansh we haff to haff the besht coach in the bishnish.'

'Steve Hansen?'

'No, of coursh not Shteve Hanshen – I'm talking about *you*, Rosh!'

'Me?'

'Yesh, shometimesh I lishen to you when you are dishcushing rugby with Oisinn and the other guysh in Kielysh and I think, okay, thish ish a guy who knowsh what he'sh talking about. Thish ish a guy who knowsh hish rugby inshide-out.'

'Sometimes, when people ask me what I do for a living, I just say teacher. And I mean every word of it.'

'You can really help ush, Rosh.'

'Yeah, no, it's just if I do decide to go into coaching, I had it in my head that it'd be at, like, All Ireland League level? I've always liked Old Wesley as a club.'

'I should tell you alsho that the Shportsh and Shocial Committee has shet ashide a budget for thish.'

'No offence but coaching Facebook is going to do fock-all for my CV. It's beneath me.'

He goes, 'They are prepared to pay you ten thoushand eurosh per session.'

And I'm just like, 'So, er, where do we train?'

'Six kids!' I go. 'Focking *six*, Sorcha!'

Yeah, no, I'm still trying – *and* failing – to get my head around it.

We're in the Nissan Leaf on the way to Ranelagh for Brian, Johnny and Leo's first day at Little Cambridge.

I'm there, 'She's seventy years of age. What the fock does she think she's doing bringing six little groin-wreckers into the world?'

'Ross,' she goes, 'please don't refer to children as groin-wreckers.'

I'm like, '*Six*, though, Sorcha!'

She's there, 'I don't blame you for being upset. What on Earth are your mom and dad thinking?'

'They're *not* thinking. *He's* drunk on power and *she's* drunk on, I don't know, anything she can get her hands on. Usually gin, but I once saw her drink hand sanitizer while she was waiting for Molloy's Liquor Store to open on the Ballyogan Road.'

'I mean, I can totally understand her wanting to have a baby, especially if she regrets putting her career and her advocacy work ahead of having a larger family.'

'Advocacy work? You mean trying to run Funderland out of Ballsbridge?'

'I can get my head around her wanting to have *one* baby. But like you say –'

'Focking *six*!'

'I don't want to upset you, Ross, but your mom is very much in the autumn of her life.'

'Deep focking winter, you mean.'

'This isn't me being a bitch, but there's a very real chance that those children will be orphans before they're even teenagers.'

Brian is suddenly looking around him.

'The fock are we?' he goes.

Sorcha's there, 'We're in Ranelagh, Brian. Today is the day you're storting your new school. There's, like, an actual waiting list to get into this place. Isn't it exciting?'

Brian goes, 'Fock school! And fock you!'

'You're going to meet your new teacher,' Sorcha goes. 'She's called Sasha – she went to Holy Child Killiney – and she's going to help you find your potential.'

I'm there, 'She actually said *unlock* their potential.'

'Did you flirt with her, by the way?'

'Excuse me?'

'I don't mind if the answer is yes. Lauren tried to get Oliver in here but couldn't. And Chloe said Isa is number one hundred and thirty something on the waiting list.'

'I didn't *knowingly* flirt?'

'Well, you obviously did something right. Didn't you go to her debs?'

'Er, I can't remember if I did or not. She's very happily married now. A couple kids. Degree and Master's.'

'I do remember she was mad about you.'

'Hey, I have a way with people – what can I say?'

'Well, for once I'm not complaining.'

We find the school – it's in a massive gaff on, like, Elmwood *Avenue?* – and Sorcha parallel-porks the cor outside with, let's just say, her *usual* level of skill and spatial awareness?

'Can't drive for shit,' Brian goes.

And I'm there, 'Yeah, you can afford to talk. Four grand's worth of damage to my Audi?'

'Shut your focking hole,' he goes. 'You focking shitwad fock.'

We take the boys out of the cor and up the path we go. We don't even need to knock. Sasha is waiting at the door for us with a big smile on her face. She goes, 'Here they are! Look at these beautiful boys!'

Leo – I swear to God – goes, 'Hey, Gorgeous!' which is kind of a *me* thing to say, while Brian walks straight past her and goes, 'I need to focking hit someone.'

It doesn't seem to faze her in the slightest. She keeps on smiling and goes, 'Hi, Sorcha. I'm Sasha.'

And Sorcha's like, 'I remember you. You were an amazing debater.'

'I seem to remember you were a pretty amazing debater yourself.'

I'm there, 'What time do you want us to pick them up, Sasha?' pretty keen to be off. This seems to come as a surprise to the girl. She goes, 'You don't want to look around the place?'

I look at Sorcha and I'm like, 'Not really – do we? No offence, but I think we'll pass, Sash.'

I'm going to be honest with you, I'm just worried that Brian has already belted some kid in there. My plan is for me and Sorcha to switch off our phones – taking a leaf from Honor's book – and go to Cinnamon for a long breakfast.

Sorcha goes, 'Oh my God, Ross, this is, like, *the* most famous Montessori school in Ireland in terms of identifying young people's talents. We'd *love* the tour, Sasha!' and I end up being overruled.

So in we go. The place is like a spa. And by that I mean all the walls are painted white, it smells of mint and lavender and all the staff are smiling so hord that it makes you think they're either Mormons or up to something.

Sasha leads us into a lorge, open-plan room, which is full of boys and girls of all shades and colours – notice I'm being careful not to mention specific countries here – and they're all quietly reading or drawing or listening to presumably music on giant Beats.

I spot Brian. To my great relief, he isn't panelling the fock out some genius of tomorrow – he's just standing there, looking around the room with a slightly hostile look on his face.

'The fock is this shit?' he goes.

'As parents,' Sorcha goes, 'we chose not to correct our children when they used bad language for fear of actually *encouraging* it?'

'You did right,' Sasha goes. 'We don't correct them either. And I'm also putting inverted commas around the word correct. Most of what we consider to be *bad* behaviour in children comes as a result of intellectual boredom, usually because they haven't discovered their gifts yet.'

I'm there, 'What if they don't have any gifts? What if they're just – I'm pre-warning you here – focking dopes?'

She goes, 'All children have gifts, Ross. And our priority at Little Cambridge is to help them discover those gifts and engage their minds in positive and hopefully creative ways. Come on, let me show you some of the work the children are doing.'

So she leads us around the room, pointing out various kids and what they're up to.

'This is Shinya,' pointing out this little boy from you can probably guess where. He's the one wearing the humungous Beats and he's also writing something down in, like, a *copy*book? 'He can listen to a concerto, pick out the individual instruments and – as you can see – write out the notes that each member of the orchestra is playing.'

Brian goes to throw a punch at him, but I manage to block it before it hits the back of his head.

'And this is Rebecca,' she goes, pointing out this – I don't even know if I'm allowed to say the word *Irish* – girl, who's drawing what looks like a humungous church.

I'm there, 'She must have traced that,' because it's that good – unbelievable detail and everything. 'I think she's pulling the wool over all of your eyes, Sash.'

Sasha laughs. She goes, 'I can promise you that she didn't trace it. She's drawing Christchurch Cathedral. Her mom and dad took her there for the first time at the weekend and she's drawing the entire thing from memory.'

Sorcha's like, 'Oh! My God! Do you think our boys might be gifted like these children are gifted?'

And Sasha goes, 'That's what we're going to find out.'

My hopes aren't high. I'm there, 'We'll see you at, what, seven o'clock tonight?' and I reach into my pocket and switch my phone off.

But she goes, 'Well, the school day actually finishes at two thirty, Ross.'

I'm there, 'Two thirty? I think it's going to take a hell of a lot more time than that to fix the problem, Sash. But, hey, you seem to know what you're doing.'

'I've always thought that Johnny might be gifted,' Sorcha goes, 'because he's the quiet, sensitive one,' meaning the one who's been beaten down by the other two.

Sasha goes, 'Whatever his talent is, we will discover it here.'

Sorcha's there, 'Thank you so much, Sasha. On behalf of both of us. I can't tell you how much it means to find someone who doesn't just write off our children as thugs.'

That's aimed at me. I decide to just let it go. I turn to leave. And out of the corner of my eye – oh, Jesus, no! – I spot Brian, hunkered down, taking a shit in the middle of the floor.

*

So I'm standing in front of the full-length mirror in the bedroom in my Canterbury VapoDri drill top and I'm thinking about what I'm going to say to the players this morning. I've been up since – not a lie – eight o'clock, doing a lot of sit-ups, then having another search for my Rugby Tactics Book to try to dig out some inspirational quotes to give them. But I still can't find the focking thing.

I'm trying to make up my mind what kind of line I should take with the players when I meet them for the first time this morning. I'm torn between being a no-nonsense Eddie Jones character – I do love his quips – or a calm, steady, very little ego, Leo Cullen type.

I look at myself in the mirror and I try out different voices. I'm there, 'You will find me a tough coach but a fair coach! But if I see you giving me anything less than one hundred percent out there, I will drag you off the focking field myself!'

Yeah, no, it looks like it's going to be Eddie Jones, although I'll make sure to throw in some funny lines that'll hopefully come to me as I'm going along.

All of a sudden, Sorcha walks into the room. She sits on the edge of the bed. It's like she's got something on her mind.

She's there, 'You were up early this morning.'

I'm like, 'That's rugby, Sorcha. Makes me behave in all sorts of crazy ways.'

'I heard you doing your sit-ups.'

'Fifty of the things. I'm like a man possessed.'

In the mirror, I can see her smiling at me. She goes, 'I love seeing you like this.'

I'm there, 'It's just a Canterbury VapoDri drill top, Sorcha. The best thing about being totally deluded about your chances of being involved in the Ireland set-up one day is that you tend to have all the gear ready.'

That's actually true. I used to keep a Go Bag under the bed back in the day. I remember one day when Sorcha was pregnant with Honor, she had one of her many false alorms – she sat on a wet patio chair outside The Queens and thought her waters had broken – and I swung back to the house and grabbed what I *thought* was *her* hospital bag? When I opened it up in the ward, I couldn't focking believe it. Water bottle. Gumshield. Electrical tape. Kicking tees. I was like, 'Er, wrong emergency!'

Sorcha walks up behind me and puts her two hands on my shoulders. She goes, 'I'm not talking about your top, Ross. When I say I love seeing you like this, I mean excited about something.'

I'm there, 'It's rugby, Sorcha. It's what I was put on this Earth to do.'

Still standing behind me, she lays one hand flat on my abs and with the other she traces the outline of my pecs. She's kidding herself if she thinks it's not about the drill top.

'Listen,' she whispers in my ear. 'Can you hear that?'

I can't hear anything. I say that to her as well. I'm like, 'I can hear fock-all, Sorcha.'

She's like, 'Exactly. We have the house to ourselves.'

I can feel her hot breath in my ear. She smells of Jo Malone shower gel, the lime, basil and mandarin one she always uses when she has a shower pre-sex. I'm thinking, Oh my God, is this about to finally happen?

I'm like, 'Where is everyone?'

She's there, 'Mom and Dad have taken the boys out for a drive.'

'Jesus,' I go. 'I don't envy anyone in that cor.'

'And Fionn has taken Hillary to the, em . . . the Irish Emigration Museum.'

I realize that I'm hord. And it has nothing to do with the Irish Emigration Museum. I couldn't give a fock about the Irish Emigration Museum.

I turn around and Sorcha is looking at me with what can only be described as a hungry look on her face – *storving*, in fact? She throws herself at me, her lips on mine and suddenly she's all over me like a cat at a scratching post.

I'm not exactly a shrinking virgin in this situation and I'm giving every bit as good as I get. I put my two hands on her orse and I lift her up off the ground and at the same time she wraps her two legs around my waist. I carry her over to the bed, the two of us still wearing the face off each other, then we fall onto the bed with me on top of her.

'Oh, Ross,' she goes, 'I've wanted this for so long.'

And I'm thinking, You could have fooled me. And here I am walking around with balls like two focking motorcycle helmets.

She goes, 'Let's try to make it last for ages.'

And I'm thinking, I am going to disappoint you like I've never disappointed a girl before.

I whip off my shorts while she kicks off her slippers and pulls her jeans down over her legs. I go to take off my drill top but she goes, 'No, leave it on. I really like it,' which is what I suspected all along.

Imagine Fionn in a drill top! Actually, don't bother! I saw him wearing one loads of times back in the day and it did very, very little for the goy. Okay, I've got to stop thinking about Fionn.

We get down to it then in a serious way. She takes off her t-shirt and bra, grabs my head in her two hands and directs me to the drink station. And there – unfortunately – I'm going to bring the story to a close – out of respect for the sacred code of privacy that exists between a husband and wife.

All I *will* say is that I *do* last for ages – although not so long that I end up being late for training – and that the whole sweaty business comes to an end with Sorcha kneeling on the chair from her dressing table, shouting, 'I'm very nearly there! I'm very nearly there! Don't you focking dare stop!' and me looking at my face in her vanity mirror, one eye shut and one eye popping out of my head, my mouth forming a perfect O and my entire body shaking like a shitting dog as I gallop her to glory.

I've possibly said too much so I'm going to leave it there.

We both fix ourselves up. I go looking for my clothes. I'm like, 'I'd better head off – I don't want to be late for rugby training,' and I get this sudden flashback to us being teenagers again.

It's nice.

As she's putting on her bra, she goes, 'Ross, I love you.'

And I'm like, 'Er, yeah, no, I love you too, Sorcha. Definitely.'

She goes, 'I just want you to know that, okay? Whatever else happens, I really, really do love you.'

★

We're going to be training, apparently, in Herbert Pork, so that's where I head. I come up with a plan while I'm in the cor. I decide to put the forwards through a few drills, then teach the front row goys one or two of the, let's just say, dork orts of the scrum that I learned playing as a hooker for Seapoint – like, for instance, eating something like a lasagne or a prawn curry just before kick-off, then, just as you're coming in for the bind, sticking your fingers down your throat and throwing up on the jersey of your opposite number.

Then – my real calling – I'll do some serious work with the backs, including one or two moves from the still-missing Tactics Book that I *was* considering holding back just in case Leinster were ever looking for a new backs coach and I wanted to blow them away at the interview. I just think, Fock it, I can use these goys to prove to myself that the moves do actually work.

I pork up and I grab my kitbag out of the boot. It's a beautiful, sunny May morning and I feel genuinely good about life. Okay, on one the hand, I miss my daughter and my old pair are planning to give me half a dozen brothers or sisters that I don't actually want. But, on the other hand, me and Sorcha are back at it, the triplets are in an apparently great Montessori school, which means they're someone else's problem for five and a half hours every day, and I'm doing what I was born to do, which is coach rugby and get paid for doing it.

I sling the kitbag over my shoulder and I head for the pitch next to the adventure playground, which is where Magnus said they usually meet. I hear him call my name. He's like, 'Hey, Rosh! Rosh! Over here!'

I spot him. He's dressed – I shit you not – in what can only be described as tennis whites. As I move closer to the group, I notice that there's, like, twelve players, we're talking six men and six – it's impossible not to say this in a sexist way – but *women*?

I'm like, 'What the fock is this?'

And Magnus goes, 'Thish ish our team, Rosh. Everybody – this ish Rosh! He ish going to be our coach!'

I'm there, 'But there's, like, women here.'

One of the women – she must be, like, forty – goes, 'Oh, great – another sexist asshole.'

And that ends up hurting me a lot, because I was a supporter of women's rugby long before everyone else in this country jumped on the bandwagon. Yeah, no, I've been friends with Fiona Coghlan since we were, like, fifteen years old. I used to let her use me as a tackle bag, until one night, on the back pitch in Clontorf, when she hit me so hord I felt my liver move and she had to drive me to Beaumont for an MRI. She didn't even wait there with me. She dropped me off outside A&E and as I limped through the electric doors, doubled over at the waist, told me to 'focking grow a pair'.

I've always been a little bit in love with Fiona since that day.

The point I'm making – and Fiona would be the first to hopefully back me up on this – is that I am about as far from a sexist as it's possible to be. I just thought I was going to be training an actual rugby team, instead of . . .

And that's when I notice Magnus pulling on a belt that's got, like, two fluorescent yellow tags Velcroed onto the sides.

I'm like, 'Whoa, whoa, whoa – I thought you said you were playing rugby?'

He goes, 'Thish *ish* rugby!'

He actually has the balls to say that.

I'm there, 'This is focking *tag* rugby!'

And he's like, 'Yeah, shame thing!'

Which it's not. Which it most focking definitely is not.

I'm there, 'Jesus Christ, if this was *actual* rugby, you wouldn't be dressed up as Andy Murray and you wouldn't have six birds on your team wearing a full face of make-up.'

He has the cheek to look actually hurt. I can't believe I left my wife at home for this. Some dude steps up to me – some random accountant-type dude with side-ported hair and a white Slazenger polo shirt with the collar popped.

'I'm Chris,' he goes. 'I'm the Manager of SMB Accounts.'

And I'm there, 'I literally don't care.'

'Look, I'm sorry if there was some misunderstanding. But we

could still use your expertise. A lot of these guys have never actually played rugby before.'

'Dude, it's *tag* rugby. It's focking speed-dating for people who work in offices.'

And to think I was going to share some of my most valuable secrets with them – moves I invented with the likes of Joey Corbery and Jordan Larmour in mind.

Talk about feeding strawberries to a donkey.

The dude goes, 'We need help because we're about to play Google. Do have you any idea what that means?'

'It means fock-all. It's tag rugby. It matters to no one.'

'For global tech companies using Ireland as their tax and revenue base, Ross, Facebook versus Google is tag rugby's equivalent of *El Clásico* – or, as we call it, *El Taxico!*'

Yeah, no, I'd say that gets a few laughs in the breakout rooms and think-spaces of Barrow Street and Grand Canal Square. I give him fock-all back, though. I'm too pissed off.

He's there, 'We had a really good tag rugby team last summer. We beat everyone – eBay, Apple, Microsoft. Even Google. And do you know what they did? They poached everyone on the team.'

One of the men laughs. 'Yeah,' he goes, 'and they all went off to join a company where, according to Payscale, only sixty-seven percent of employees feel like their work has real meaning, compared to eighty-one percent in Facebook!'

They all laugh then.

'They don't even have a nail bar!' one of the women goes. 'Or a massage programme!'

Jesus Christ, it's like they live in their own little bubble – it's like meeting boarders from Clongowes.

Magnus goes, 'Rosh, you can shee how much it meansh to the guysh to win thish match.'

I'm there, 'How can you even *call* it a match? Dude, it's tag rugby! It's kiss-chase with a ball.'

This Chris dude goes, 'Ross, please. I've asked a few people about you. And I've been told you know the game inside-out.'

I'm there, 'Who said that?'

'A few people.'

'It'd be interesting to know whether any of those people are involved in the current Leinster and Ireland set-ups.'

'All I'll say is the phrase that kept coming up was "a rugby brain".'

'Yeah, that can be taken two ways. But, in this case, I'm going to take it as a compliment.'

Seriously. I'm suddenly thinking, What have you got to lose? Why not just take the focking moo? It's ten Ks per session. You can throw on a baseball cap while you're coaching them so that nobody recognizes you. And if anyone ever takes the piss out of you for doing it – I can see the likes of Shane Byrne having a focking field day if he ever found out – you can just deny everything point-blank.

I swear to God, I'm right on the point of saying okay when I hear one of the women – again, not sexist – go, 'Does the ball have to be thrown backwards or can it go forwards as well?' and that ends up being the last straw for me.

I once heard Sorcha's old man ask the exact same question at an Ireland versus South Africa match while sitting in a complimentary seat just two rows in front of Fergus Slattery. I nearly focked him over the edge of the Upper West Stand for disrespecting the great man, and I wasn't the only one who was sorely tempted.

No, I decide, I'm not wasting my knowledge on these people. Focking tag rugby.

I'm just there, 'I'm sorry, goys. I'm out of here.'

'The *fock* is wrong with you two?' Leo goes.

Yeah, no, it was probably hoping for too much to expect a major improvement in their behaviour after, like, a week in Little Cambridge. But I would like to see *some* change in the boys.

Brian's like, 'The *fock* are they smiling at?'

I gave Sorcha another good cordio workout this morning while Fionn was giving Hillary his morning feed downstairs. Twice in a week. That's what the fock we're smiling at.

Our happiness seems to piss Brian off most of all. He puts his hand down the back of his trousers, farts into his hand and blows it at me.

Little focker.

Johnny, by the way, is playing the violin. Or rather there's a violin sitting on the kitchen table in front of him and he's scraping the bow back and forth across its strings like he's trying to saw the thing in half. It's very focking annoying.

Sasha told Sorcha yesterday that she thought music might be Johnny's thing on the basis that he pointed at a violin and went, 'What the fock is that?'

Direct quote.

Of course, Sorcha rushed straight into Waltons to buy him one for three hundred snots. And while it's still early days, my guess is that music *isn't* going to be Johnny's thing.

Sorcha puts my breakfast in front of me. It's, like, smashed avocado toast with a poached egg on top – and this on a Monday morning, bear in mind. I tell her thanks and I grab her hand and we give each other a long, lingering look. She looks – honestly? – as beautiful as I've ever seen her and I'm thinking, Am I falling in love with my wife all over again?

'Get a focking room,' Leo goes. And me and Sorcha both laugh. No avoiding it. And that's when my phone suddenly storts ringing.

I'm there, 'That'll be Honor!'

Sorcha's like, 'Honor?'

'Yeah, no,' I go, 'she texted me last night and said she'd FaceTime me this morning.'

Sorcha goes, 'Em,' suddenly deciding she doesn't want to be in the room, 'I'd better go and put on my make-up. We don't want the boys to be late for Montessori.'

I answer the phone and up pops Honor's face. I'm like, 'Hey, Honor, how the hell are you?'

She goes, 'Hi, Dad! What the fock is that noise?'

I'm like, 'Yeah, no, Johnny's learning the violin – if you could call it that.'

I point my phone at them. I'm like, 'Hey, goys, say hello to your sister!'

They're all like, 'Hi, Honor!' and she's there, 'Hi, boys!' and it ends up being a genuinely lovely moment.

She goes, 'Are you boys being good for your daddy?'

And I'm like, 'Not really. They're still little pricks. But the big news since I last spoke to you is that they've storted in Montessori.'

'You mean someone actually agreed to take them?'

'I know, right? Focking mugs! So how have you been?'

'Oh my God, Dad – ah-mazing! Have you been watching my channel?'

'Yeah, no, I saw the last video you put up. My Favourite Everyday Ten-Minute Make-Up Looks.'

'Dad, we've got, like, 300,000 subscribers!'

We meaning her and Erika. I try not to come across as jealous, but I end up going, 'It was basically the two of you just putting make-up on. There's definitely less banter than when I was doing it with you.'

She goes, 'Oh! My God! You should *see* the stuff that arrives here for me every day!'

'What kind of stuff are we talking?'

'Oh my God, clothes! We're talking, like, jeans, tops, shoes, jackets, dresses. All from labels who want to be associated with the Love Honor and Obey brand. And then, like, beauty products – boxes and boxes of them. Erika has turned me into a proper influencer, Dad!'

'Yeah, no, that's great news, Honor!'

'I don't even need to threaten companies with bad reviews any more. Helen says they might have to give me a second room.'

'I'm genuinely delighted for you.'

'Anyway, I have to go. We're going out for dinner. I'll talk to you again soon, Dad. Bye, boys!'

They're like, 'Bye, Honor!'

And that ends up being that.

Johnny goes back to dragging the bow across the strings of his violin. It seems to somehow match my mood in a weird way because I feel suddenly sad.

I stand up. I'm there, 'Come on, goys, let's get you to Montessori. See can poor Sasha discover some genius in you that me and your old dear are somehow missing.'

'Fock you,' Brian goes.

And I'm like, 'No, fock *you*, Brian – fock you very much indeed.'

Anyway, twenty minutes later, we're on the N11 and we're passing UCD. Weirdly, Sorcha hasn't asked after Honor, so I go, 'So, er, our daughter's in cracking form.'

Sorcha's there, 'Is she?'

'Yeah, no, Erika seems to have had a really positive effect on her. She's up to, like, 300,000 subscribers now.'

And it's at that exact point that I hear my phone ring. I'm the one actually driving this morning, so I answer it on speaker and the cor is suddenly filled with the sound of a dude's voice, doing, 'Hoy! Is that Ross O'Carroll-Killoy?'

Whoever it is sounds definitely foreign, but at the same time the voice is weirdly *familiar*?

I'm like, 'The one! The only!' because it's a funny thing I sometimes say.

And that's when the voice goes, 'Ross, ut's Joe Schmudt.'

Now, you can probably imagine my response.

I'm like, 'Fock you, Zebo. I've got my wife and kids in the cor.'

He goes, 'Whoy?'

'Simon focking Zebo. I know it's you. And I know it was you who rang JP after the *Late Late* and pretended to be interested in one of his Vampire Beds.'

But the dude just laughs and goes, 'Yeah, ut's not Soymun Zoyboy, Ross! Ut's Joe Schmudt!'

Shit, I think it actually *is* him. I look at Sorcha and she's already mouthing the words, 'Oh! My! God!'

I'm there, 'Why would *you* be ringing *me*?' already doing the mental inventory of what's in my Go Bag.

He goes, 'Oym just kitchen up on moy correspondence – litters Oy've boyn moyning to reploy toy for a long toym. Oym ringing because I got one from your daughter.'

'What?'

'Honor – is that her noym?'

'Yeah, no, Honor.'

'She sint me a beautiful litter a luttle whoyle agoy – all abaaht her faahther, what a groyt goy he us, how much he knoys abaaht rugboy and what a groyt coych he'd moyk if someone would oynloy gave hum a broyk.'

It's a lovely thing to hear. Even though Honor knows very little about the game.

Then he goes, 'She sint moy your tactics book, Moyt.'

I'm like, 'My *Rugby* Tactics Book? I was wondering where the fock that had gone?'

'She aahsked moy to have a royd of ut.'

I'm suddenly embarrassed. I don't *know* why because it's obviously all good stuff.

I'm like, 'Don't take anything in it seriously, Joe. I'm usually shit-faced when I write stuff in that book.'

Sorcha puts her hand on my knee and gives me a disapproving look – she hates to hear me running myself down.

'Well,' the dude goes, 'Oym just runging to till yoy that the litter royloy moyved moy. You're obvoyousloy your daughter's heroy.'

I can suddenly hear Sorcha sobbing in the seat beside me.

'Yeah, no,' I go, 'I do pride myself on being an amazing, amazing father.'

'Fock you!' Johnny shouts at Brian – then I watch in the rear-view mirror as he swings his violin at him and smashes him across the face with the flat side of it, bursting open Brian's nose.

'Soy,' Joe goes, 'what are yoy gonna doy with ut?'

I'm like, 'What do you mean?'

'Oym talking abaaht your tactics book. What are yoy gonna doy with all these thungs you've written daahn?'

'I don't know.'

'All thoyse thoughts you have on the goym – they're woysted unless yoy actually sheer them with someone.'

'Are you saying you'd be interested? Because I've got a few ideas about the summer tour of the States and Japan. I think it's definitely time to introduce new faces – maybe one or two of the Michael's boys, even though they wouldn't be fans of mine.'

He laughs. I can tell he likes me. He goes, 'Oy've got a fyoy thoughts of my oyn abaaht the summer tour, Ross. Oy thunk Oy'll be foyne.'

I'm like, 'Yeah, no, course you do. You're the actual coach.'

'What Oy moyn us, what are your plaahns? Are yoy coyching a toym at the moyment?'

'Er, not one specific team, no.'

'Whoy the Hill not? You're obvoyously someone whoy thunks abaaht the goym a lot –'

'I can't *stop* thinking about the game, Joe. It's how my mind works. I can't switch it off.'

'Then yoy should be *doying* something with your knowledge. Otherwoyse, ut's woystud.'

'I *was* offered a job last week actually. Again – a coaching role. But – yeah, no – it wasn't quite what I had in mind.'

'Yoy have to staaht somewhere, Moyt. What do yoy thunk, Linstah are just gonna ring yoy up aaht of the bloy one doy and offer yoy a job?'

I laugh. I'm there, 'That's not what I think.'

That *is* what I think.

He goes, 'Doy yoy knoy where Oy stahted aaht?'

I'm there, 'Coaching schools rugby in Kawakawa. Yeah, no, there's a whole section in that book specifically about you – I don't know if you saw that – mostly facts about your life that I copied down from your Wikipedia page. You're probably thinking, er, *stalker* much?'

Sorcha whispers to me, 'You're doing great, Ross!'

'So what are yoy gonna doy?' he goes. 'Are yoy gonna koyp what's un thus book to yoursilf, then have ut buried with yoy when yoy doy? Or are yoy gonna put ut to the tist – and foynd aaht exactloy how much yoy doy knoy abaaht the goym of rugboy?'

I feel my eyes stort to tear up. I can't believe Honor did this for me. What an incredible kid she is.

I'm there, 'Yeah, no, thanks for saying all of that to me, Joe. It might just be the kick in the orse I need.'

And then, without saying another word, he hangs up on me.

I turn and I look at Sorcha. She's wiping tears from her face with her open palms.

She's like, 'Oh! My God! Oh! My! Literally! God!'

★

Ronan asks me where I am. I tell him I'm in the cor – I got my A8 back from the repair shop – on the way to rugby training.

He goes, 'You're not still playing, are you? Jaysus, Rosser, the bleaten soyuz of you!'

I'm like, 'No, Ro, I'm not still playing. If you must know, I'm doing a bit of coaching.'

'Ah, feer fooks to you.'

'Yeah, no, that's what Joe Schmidt said.'

'Who?'

'Er, Joe Schmidt?'

'The rubby fedda?'

'Yes, Ronan, the *rubby fedda*.'

'When were you thalken to *him*, but?'

'The other day. Yeah, no, he just happened to be flicking through my famous Rugby Tactics Book – as you do – and he had one or two questions he wanted to ask me.'

'How'd he get his haddens on that, Rosser?'

'Good question. It turns out that Honor sent it to him.'

'Seerdiously?'

'You know, I don't care if she doesn't believe in God, Ro. There's more goodness in her than in a lot of people who supposedly do – including Sorcha's old pair. Anyway, what's going on with you? How did the exams go?'

'Thee went moostard, so thee did.'

'And what are you doing for the summer?'

'Ine arthur offerton to woork in the Citiziddens Advice Centhor in Figlas.'

'Citizens Advice? Presumably that means for free?'

'It's voddun toddy, yeah.'

Focking mug, I think – although I don't say it.

I go, 'See, you're like Honor, Ro. There's so much good in you as well.'

And that's when he goes suddenly quiet.

I'm like, 'Ro, what's wrong?'

He's there, 'I feel teddible, Rosser.'

'As in, hungover?'

'No, Ine saying I feel teddible about that pooer fedda – what did you say he's nayum was?'

'Are you talking about Phinneas?'

'Phiddeas, yeah. He's arthur been sacked.'

'You're shitting me.'

'Or mebbe he resoyunt. Huguette no-platfordemed him.'

'What does that mean?'

'She picketed he's leckchodders. And now he's gone. And I feel teddible abourrit, because if I hadn't gibbon ebidence against him . . .'

'You sold him down the river, Ro.'

'It was joost he embadassed Huguette. He calt her the Sushi Geerdle. She was veddy upset – she said she wanthed to gerrum back – so I backed her up.'

'You were thinking with your dick, Ro. Don't worry, I do the same myself.'

'I thought thee were joost godda warden him about he's fuchodder behabiour. I ditn't think he'd end up losing he's job.'

'I wouldn't sweat it, Ro. I'm sure there's loads of jobs in the whole lecturing in Sports Management area.'

He'll never focking work again.

He goes, 'I reedy hope so.'

I'm there, 'Ro, do you really think this girl is the one for you?'

He's like, 'Ine cutting me ties wirrer, Rosser.'

And I'm like, 'Are you?' unable to hide my delight.

He goes, 'Ine arthur seen a soyut to the geerdle I doatunt like.'

Jesus, that was the *only* side *I* saw to her. She must have been a real focking sweetheart when they were alone together.

I'm there, 'So you told her it was over?'

He goes, 'I broke it off wirrer, yeah.'

'And how did she take it?'

'Veddy weddle.'

'Veddy weddle?'

'She went a bit quiet. She ditn't cry, but.'

I don't know what that means. But I don't have time to think about it right now because I've arrived in Herbert Pork.

'Ro,' I go, 'I'll give you a shout tomorrow, okay?'

He's there, 'Feerd enough, Rosser. Enjoy yisser thraining.'

I hang up, then I pork. A minute or two after that, I'm walking past the adventure playground again, then I hear Magnus going, 'That'sh it, Fashebook! Let'sh show theesh Google ash holesh who ish the besht! Or are we going to loosh thish match to a company that doeshn't even provide full healthcare for friendsh and family ash a shtandard term of employment?'

'Exactly!' one of the women goes. 'And they don't even have an ice-cream station for their staff in the summer!' and there's real bitterness in her voice when she says it.

I stand there and watch them from a distance. Jesus Christ, they're a focking state. They're making every basic error in the book. We're talking knock-ons. We're talking hospital passes. We're talking handling errors. The men are as bad as the women and the women are focking hopeless.

Then they stort fighting among themselves. One man accuses another of carrying on running after he'd been tagged and they end up having a pushing and shoving match. One of them goes, 'This is exactly the kind of thing I'd expect from someone from Regional Trade and Customs Compliance!' and they end up having to be pulled aport by Magnus, who shouts, 'Come on, guysh! Rememeber what we shay in the offish! One team, one dream!'

I end up actually chuckling to myself. I'm thinking, What are you doing, Rossmeister? Do you honestly think you can improve their skills in, like, one or two training sessions?

Then I suddenly hear myself shout, 'You're doing it all wrong!'

And every head suddenly turns in my direction. I watch their faces light up, one by one. It's like when the Ag Science girls used to see me coming back in my UCD days.

'Is that the same wanker who was here the other day?' one of the women goes.

Okay, not everyone is doubly pleased to see me.

But I look her straight in the eye and I go, 'It's a focking rugby ball. Stop treating it like it's a cake you've just taken out of the oven . . . And you – what did you say your name was? Chris? Put some spin on the ball when you throw it. That's why the receiver keeps dropping it. There's no actual traction . . . And Magnus – what in the name of fock are you wearing?'

They're all just looking at me. I have their attention.

I'm there, 'Okay, everyone, I'm Ross – we're talking Ross O'Carroll-Kelly?'

They're all like, 'Hey, Ross!'

And then they all introduce themselves to me, telling me not only their names but also the deportments they work for, which is possibly unnecessary. But here, standing in front of me, are the players I must fashion into a team capable of beating Google.

We're talking Chris from SMB Accounts. We're talking Tarek from Data Analytics (Europe, Middle East and Africa). We're talking John from Security, Risk and Compliance. We're talking Belinda from Anti-Abuse, Trust and Safety, Incorporating Spam. We're talking Donna from Abuse Investigation (Sexual Harassment, Hate Speech and Overseas Election Meddling). We're talking Phenola from Quality Assurance. We're talking Karim from Content Moderation (Happy Slappings, White Nationalism and Islamic State Executions). We're talking Li from Capacity Planning. We're talking Ciaran from Regional Trade and Customs Compliance. And we're talking Derek, who works in the cor pork.

'Okay,' I go, clapping my two hands together, 'let's do some work.'

And, just like that, I'm suddenly a rugby coach.

So JP's big day is finally here.

Yeah, no, he's showcasing his Vampire Bed at the 'What's the Big Idea?' Trade and Innovation Show at the RDS. He's still convinced that it's going to suddenly take off, despite the fact that he hasn't even sold one yet.

And even though the whole thing is doomed to failure, me and the goys decide that we're going to go along to support him. Because that's what people who played rugby together do.

Me and Oisinn are walking through the Simmonscourt Pavilion, trying to find where he's set up.

We're looking at some of the other crazy inventions that people have come up with. There's a Segway-and-baby-stroller hybrid that allows you to take your baby out for a walk without getting any exercise. There's an umbrella with a glasses-shaped clear plastic window in it, which comes in various prescription strengths. There's a robot razor that shaves your face while you sleep. There's even adult nappies that allow you to work at your desk all day without the annoying necessity of having to take a toilet break. Oisinn says he might buy Magnus a pack of twenty.

I laugh.

'So,' he goes, 'I hear you're coaching the Facebook tag rugby team.'

I'm like, 'Yeah, no, coaching is probably too strong a word. I've done three two-hour sessions with them this week – mainly trying to improve their skills. One or two of them aren't bad: Tarek from Data Analytics and Li from Capacity Planning.'

'Three two-hour sessions,' Oisinn goes. 'That means you've seen more of Magnus this week than I have.'

'Seriously?'

'Dude, he never comes home.'

I can actually believe that. I saw him Wednesday night, Thursday night and last night – and all three times the dude was going back to the office afterwards. All of them were, as a matter of fact.

I try to put a positive spin on it for him. I'm there, 'I know he's pretty nervous about *El Taxico*.'

He goes, '*El* what?'

'Yeah, no, they're playing Google on Monday night. Facebook versus Google is *their* equivalent of Terenure versus Michael's. You couldn't think of two groups of people who hate each other more even though there's basically no difference between them.'

'Coaching tag rugby, though? No offence, Ross, but I would have thought it was a bit beneath you.'

'Hey, I did, too. That was until I got a call from Joe Schmidt.'

'What?'

'He rang me. Talked a lot of sense to me as well.'

'Are you sure it wasn't –'

'It wasn't Simon Zebo.'

'I was going to say Fergus McFadden. He's unbelievable at voices.'

'It was definitely Joe Schmidt. Honor sent him my Rugby Tactics Book and told him she couldn't believe that he'd never found a role for me within the set-up. He pretty much told me that he would if I got myself some experience first.'

I suddenly spot JP then. He's standing with his – yeah, no – vertical bed, surrounded by people who seem to be mostly just ripping the piss out of him. They're all trying out the bed and taking photos of each other on their phones, which they're presumably then posting on social media. There's one dude taking a selfie with JP in front of the bed and he's giving him bunny ears and laughing.

And standing there, I notice, just watching it happen, is Fionn.

I give him an absolute filthy. I'm there, 'Yeah, well done, Fionn – you're supposed to be his focking friend.'

Fionn goes, 'Ross, I've got Hillary here,' which he does, sleeping in his little papoose, but it's still weak in terms of an excuse. 'What am I supposed to do?'

And I end up showing him by walking up to the dude who took the selfie and going, 'If you and your mates don't get the fock out of here now, you're going to be decked.'

The dude doesn't even look at me. He's too busy uploading the photo to Instagram, so I grab his phone out of his hand, drop it on the floor, then stamp on it. Oh, that grabs him.

He looks up. He's like, 'What the fock?'

His mates say the same thing. They're all like, 'What the fock?'

I grab him by the scruff of the neck and I'm there, 'You have literally five seconds to fock off. Otherwise, I'm going to beat you to death with that "As Seen on the *Late Late Show*" sign.'

One of his mates goes, 'We were thinking of buying one of the beds,' and he's got a big smirk on his face.

And I'm like, 'No, you weren't. You were ripping the piss out of a goy I played rugby with – and that's not something I'm prepared to allow happen on my watch. So pick up your shitty phone there and get the fock out of here.'

The dude does as he's told – the phone is focked – and him and his mates head off.

JP goes, 'Ross, was that really necessary?'

I'm there, 'What, you're happy to let people just rip the piss out of you?'

'The more people that take selfies, the more it gets around on social media. Actually, Christian is trying to get Leo Varadkar to come along?'

Oisinn's there, 'Why Leo Varadkar?'

'Well,' JP goes, 'you know the way he says he admires people who get up early in the morning? Well, with this bed, you're technically up all the time. Sleeping vertically means you're ready to get up and go to work the second you open your eyes in the morning. I think it's the kind of thing that Leo would definitely approve of.'

The poor dude – he's head-in-the-fridge crazy at this point.

Christian arrives over. He goes, 'I spoke to one of his people. He's obviously got the leadership contest going on at the moment, but he's going to try and get down in the afternoon.'

I'm like, 'Fair focks to you, Christian,' because he's what I would call a *real* friend? Mind you, he's also got fifty focking Ks invested in this bullshit idea, so it's in his interests to get the word out there.

Shit. My old man is here. I spot him coming. He's with Hennessy and – yeah, no – that little, bald Russian mate of theirs, Hodor or Fyodor or whatever the fock he's called.

I'm like, 'What the fock are you doing here?'

The old man goes, 'As a porty, Ross, New Republic believes that business, enterprise and innovation will be the keys to Ireland's future once we leave the entrepreneurship-averse, creativity-strangling, compliance culture of the European Union! These people here represent the future of our country post-Irexit!'

God focking help us, is all I can think.

Hennessy storts talking to Christian about Lauren in that awkward way that fathers-in-law talk to sons-in-laws. I can't help but overhear the conversation.

Hennessy goes, 'There's fifty thousand euros missing from your joint savings account.'

And Christian's there, 'So?'

'Where is it?'

'That's none of your business.'

'Does my daughter know?'

And it's obvious the answer is no because Christian goes, 'That's none of your business either.'

He cleared out their savings to give the money to a friend to invest in an idea that's doomed to failure. And he didn't tell his wife. I'm going to say it again.

Rugby.

The old man goes, 'So Joe Schmidt will be taking the chaps off to Japan and America any day soon – I expect you've been taking quite a few notes in that famous tactics book of yours, Kicker!'

I think about telling him about my call from the great man, but in the end I don't.

I just go, 'Hey, I'm not interested in having the big chats. Like I told you the last day in town, you and me are done. I don't need anything from you.'

'It's funny you should say that, Ross, because after you left the office that day, I had a call from young Tadhg Furlong, would you believe? Wanted to know could I have the clamp removed from his Nissan Leaf! Parked in Fitzwilliam Square, he was!'

'A lot of people drive Nissan Leafs. It's not just a woman's cor.'

It is just a woman's cor.

'It was a 161D registration,' he tries to go, 'just like your good lady wife drives!'

And I'm there, 'A lot of people drive 161D Nissan Leafs – what's your point?'

'Well, about twenty minutes after it was declamped, I had a call from Dan Leavy, asking me to unclamp the exact same cor!'

Fock. Yeah, no, I left voice messages for a few other players before I finally talked Tadhg into doing it.

'This continued for the rest of the day!' the old man goes. 'Jack McGrath! Dave Kearney! Jamison Gibson-Pork! All requesting that I remove the clamp from the same 161D Nissan Leaf!'

I'm there, 'I don't know what you think any of this proves?'

'Devin Toner! I mean, how would Big Dev even fit into such a cor? He'd have to remove the bloody well back seats!'

I decide not to get into it with him. And anyway, our attention is suddenly drawn to Fyodor, who has his phone clamped to his ear and he's talking excitedly to someone in what I'm *presuming* is Russian?

When he finally hangs up, he points at one of JP's vertical beds and goes, 'This! I want this!'

JP smiles. It's obviously a relief for him to finally get a sale. He goes, 'Congratulations! You are the very first owner of a Vampire Bed!'

Fyodor turns to the rest of us and goes, 'This bed! This is miracle!'

We're all, like, looking at each other.

He's there, 'Biggest problem in the world today is space. Too many people, not enough room. This, my friends, is miracle. You invent this?'

JP's like, 'It was originally my old man's idea, but – yeah, no – I own the patent, yeah.'

Fyodor turns back to us. He goes, 'I hear on radio, Ireland has not enough homes. I hear, not enough room in hospitals. I hear, too many people in prisons. Here is answer.'

JP goes, 'I'm glad you like it. Let me find my order book and you can tell me where you want me to deliver it.'

Fyodor goes, 'No, no, you do not understand. How many of this do you have?'

JP looks at Christian, then goes, 'I've got, em, a thousand of them, some singles, some doubles.'

The dude's like, 'I will take all.'

Our mouths just fall open.

JP goes, 'You know they're, em, three hundred euros each? Five hundred for the doubles?'

Fyodor's there. 'I will take. Also, my friends in Moscow would like to buy patent.'

'Unfortunately, the patent isn't for sale. It's not about money. For me, it's about honouring my late father and providing for my son's future.'

Fyodor just nods, then goes, 'I can arrange for you to have accident. I can arrange for your son to have accident.'

256

Hennessy laughs. I haven't a clue who this dude is, but he's definitely Hennessy's kind of goy.

The old man puts his orm around Fyodor's shoulder. He goes, 'I'm sure there'll be no need for that, Old Chap! Look, why don't we arrange to sit down with JP – we'll book a room in the Stephen's Green Club – and see if we can't come to some kind of arrangement! I'm a firm believer in that old truism – quote-unquote – that business always finds a way!'

There ends up being a far bigger crowd for the Facebook versus Google match than I was expecting – we're talking two thousand people – and it has all the atmosphere of a Leinster Schools Senior Cup final, which is amazing given that there is literally fock-all at stake.

Although you wouldn't know it standing in Herbert Pork. The Facebook staff – I suppose you could call them *our* fans? – are mixed in with the Google staff slash fans and you only have to listen to the conversations going on in the crowd to know that there's a real edge to this fixture. People are literally bickering among themselves over which company is the best to work for.

'Google has better maternity and paternity benefits,' I hear one girl tell another girl. 'We're talking eighteen weeks of paid maternity leave and between seven and twelve weeks of paid paternity leave.'

'You're not comparing like with like,' the girl from Facebook snaps back. 'We have a seventeen-week-paid-leave policy that's available to both men *and* women.'

Most of the crowd are wearing branded t-shirts with either the Facebook or the Google logo on the front. Quite a few of them are also wearing glasses, security swipe cords and bluetooth headsets and I honestly haven't seen this many geeks since Fionn's twenty-first birthday porty.

It feels great to be finally coaching, though. I thought I was possibly overdoing it wearing my IRFU ThermoReg padded jacket tonight, but I don't actually *feel* overdressed?

Magnus is in a state of what can only be described as high

excitement. He's clapping his two hands together, going, 'Come on, Fashebook – thish ish for the pride of the company that we are playing! One team, one dream! One team, one dream!'

I'm thinking, Okay, it's time for me to do some actual coaching here. I'm walking among them as they perform their stretches and I'm going, 'Magnus, just defend our line like I showed you all week, okay . . . Derek from the cor pork, keep your eye on the ball when it's coming to you and try to cut out the handling errors . . . And all of you, just try to get the ball as often as you can to Li from Capacity Planning,' because she's an absolute flier.

I give them one last shout of 'Come on, Facebook – let's do this thing!' and then I step off the field.

The referee blows the whistle and the match – and let's be honest, I'm using that term very, very loosely – gets under way.

The first couple of minutes go by in a flash. A lot of players are keen to get their hands on the ball, presumably to try to impress whichever colleague they're hoping to get off with later on in Slattery's or The Gasworks.

This is especially noticeable in the case of Ciaran from Regional Trade and Customs Compliance and Belinda from Anti-Abuse, Trust and Safety, Incorporating Spam, who decide to ignore every pre-match instruction they were given and just do their own thing, which means basically only passing the ball to each other – a form of toss-and-catch foreplay that causes us to turn over possession three times in the opening ten minutes.

They're not alone either. As a matter of fact, none of our players is doing a single thing I told them to do. They're all just running around excitedly after the same ball – like they do in children's rugby. And grown-up Gaelic football.

I'm going, 'Come on, goys, this isn't the gameplan we worked on!' but it's obvious that that's gone out the window.

There's, like, fifteen minutes gone when some little dude on the Google team, who looks like Peter Stringer except with hair, gets the ball in his hands, slips in between Karim from Content Moderation (Happy Slappings, White Nationalism and Islamic State

Executions) and Donna from Abuse Investigation (Sexual Harassment, Hate Speech and Overseas Election Meddling) and manages to ground the ball for a try – or at least the tag rugby *equivalent* of a try?

Then he throws the ball into the air and shouts, 'Congratulations! You have just been GOOGLED!' right in the face of Tarek from Data Analytics (Europe, Middle East and Africa).

Magnus ends up totally losing it. He shoves the dude in the chest and the referee ends up having to step in between them to separate them.

I'm there, 'Dude, I told you to keep the head!'

I look over my shoulder and I happen to notice that Oisinn is standing in the crowd just behind me.

I'm there, 'I'm being totally focking ignored?'

'Welcome to my life,' he goes.

Magnus storts giving out instructions then. He's there, 'Come on, guysh, let'sh go in hard on them!'

And I'm like, 'That's the exact opposite of what I want you to do! Get the ball to Li from Capacity Planning – we need to utilize her pace!'

Sixty seconds later, in all fairness to him, Magnus takes a pass from Chris from SMB Accounts and runs past three women – one of them good-looking – to score a tag rugby try. He turns around to Peter Stringer with Hair and goes, 'Perhapsh now you can shee how Fashebook rollsh, Mishter Google Man – yesh?'

This time, it's their teammates who end up having to pull them aport. I'm like, 'Magnus, keep the head! Come on, let's stort using some of the moves we worked on in training.'

Oisinn goes, 'He's not listening, Ross. It's like they've stolen his mind or something.'

The crowd is going ballistic. There's a definite sense that this could turn nasty.

Ten minutes before half-time, a woman from Google – *not* the looker – gets the ball in her hands and takes advantage of a lapse in concentration in the Facebook defence, when Ciaran from

Regional Trade and Customs Compliance takes his eye off the ball and asks Belinda from Anti-Abuse, Trust and Safety, Incorporating Spam if she has a boyfriend and if she's going to The Gasworks later on.

I'm like, 'For fock's sake, Facebook!' because everything I said about tag rugby is being proven spectacularly right.

A minute after that, Magnus gets the ball from Derek from the cor pork and makes a break for the line. And that's when, out of nowhere, and totally against the rules, Peter Stringer with Hair tackles him – as in full-on *rugby* tackles him?

The referee blows the whistle for a foul, but Magnus jumps to his feet and he's absolutely livid with the dude. He shouts, 'Thish ish typical for Google to show contempt for the rulesh!'

Oh, that doesn't go down well with the Google crowd, who are getting seriously stirred up. They all stort booing him and telling him to fock off back to Grand Canal Square and take his low-skilled and poorly motivated colleagues with him.

Peter Stringer with Hair makes the mistake of telling Magnus to chill out. He goes, 'It's only a game!'

'Yesh, for shure,' Magnus goes, 'everything ish jusht a game for Google! Like, for inshtansh, forshing shellphone makersh to ushe your shoftware on Android phonesh!'

The Google dude suddenly sees red. He grabs Magnus by the front of his branded t-shirt and goes, 'You're out of order!'

'Perhapsh I am not sho out of order!' Magnus goes, shoving him away. 'Becaush your company wash fined five billion dollarsh for thish by the European Union!'

'Oh,' the Google dude goes, 'do you want to talk about Facebook's market abuses and lack of social and political accountability?'

There's a really ugly atmosphere developing in the crowd. I haven't seen this many *angry* geeks since I set off the fire alorm at a meeting of the UCD Harry Potter Society while they were doing a marathon reading of *The Goblet of Fire*. Half of them are screaming abuse at Magnus while the other half are egging him on to hit the goy and – as one girl standing behind me puts it – 'send him back to Barrow Street in a focking wheelchair'.

This provokes an argument in the crowd over whether Facebook or Google provides the most accessible working environment for those with mobility issues and I notice one or two punches thrown.

On the field, Magnus and Peter Stringer with Hair are really going at it now. They have a hold of each other's branded t-shirts and they're pushing and pulling each other all over the pitch, even though the other players are trying to break it up. Magnus is going, 'Google people are all ash holesh!'

And Peter Stringer with Hair is like, 'Hey, at least our company only hires the brightest and best!'

'The brightesht and the besht? Ha! That ish what *you* shay! But everyone knowsh that moasht of your Google shtaff wishes they worked inshtead for Fashebook!'

'And why would they do that?'

'Becaush Fashebook ish the besht company to work for!'

'Not according to *Glassdoor*, which recently placed Google ahead of Facebook in terms of employee satisfaction! And that was based on a survey of three thousand worldwide employees!'

'Thish ish shuch bullshit. The *Shunday Bishnish Posht* had a shimilar shurvey which showed that Fashebook's Irish employeesh were far more likely to recommend their company to othersh, bashed on key workplashe factorsh shuch ash career advanshment opportunitiesh, compenshation and benefitsh, culture and alsho valuesh!'

There are similar rows happening everywhere in the crowd. I hear two girls having an absolute screaming match and it goes like this:

'You don't even have a focking hairdressers in your building!'

'Er, yes, we do, actually – and a focking nail bar!'

'Well, we have a dentist! I get my teeth whitened there twice a week!'

'How would you like me to smash them down your focking throat?'

'It wouldn't bother me! I could get them fixed again first thing in the morning – no chorge!'

'Well, we have two doctors *and* a full-time nurse in our building.'

'We have a midwife! I gave birth to both of my children in the Google building and I was back working that night!'

'Well, my boyfriend, who's also my Team Leader, had a stent put in his heart last year! It was done *in* the office and he was sitting up in one of the sleep pods working on his laptop an hour later!'

Five seconds later, the two of them are rolling around on the ground, pulling out handfuls of each other's hair. The hairdressers in both companies are going to be rushed off their focking feet tomorrow.

All hell breaks loose then. There ends up being a pitch invasion and Herbert Pork turns into a pretty much *riot* zone? People are throwing and aiming kicks at each other while boasting about their working conditions and their levels of employee satisfaction.

The referee announces that he's abandoning the match – proof, if proof were needed, that it actually doesn't matter to anyone – and he's heading to The Bridge 1859 for a pint.

I decide that, on balance, my time coaching Facebook is over. It was only ever about – as Joe Schmidt said – putting a first line down on my CV. I'm actually on the point of joining the referee in The Bridge when I notice Oisinn rush onto the field of play to try to separate Magnus from Peter Stringer with Hair.

Yeah, no, they're now rolling around on the ground and Magnus is going, 'Fashebook ish the besht!' while Peter Stringer with Hair is going, 'Google is best! By a mile!'

Oisinn somehow manages to drag Magnus off the dude before he kills him. He's like, 'What the fock are you doing?'

But Magnus goes, 'Perhapsh I musht ashk *you* what the fuck *you* are doing!'

Oisinn just shakes his head. It's like he doesn't even recognize the man he's married to any more. 'Magnus,' he goes, 'you're fighting over which American multinational tech company is the best! What the fock is happening to you?'

And Magnus goes, 'I might alsho ashk what the fock ish happening to you? I haff found shomewhere where I feel really valued. And let me tell you shomeshing, Oisinn – I don't feel that way any more when I am around you.'

Oisinn looks about as hurt as I've ever seen him.

He goes, 'That's because you're never around me any more.'

'Well,' Magnus goes, 'perhapsh we haff to acshept that there ish a reashon for that.'

Oisinn's like, 'What are you saying, Magnus? Come on, spit it out!'

And Magnus looks him in the eye and goes, 'I'm shaying, Oisinn, that our marriage ish over!'

8.

How to Style a Surgical Collar!

So – yeah, no – I'm in the cor with Sorcha on the way to collect the boys from Montessori when JP rings.

He goes, 'Hey, Ross.'

And I'm like, 'Dude, how the hell are you?' because I haven't heard a word from him since the Trade and Innovation Show in the RDS. 'I've got you on speaker and Sorcha is in the cor . . .'

So keep it clean.

He goes, 'How's Oisinn?'

And I'm like, 'I presume you heard the news? Magnus has left him – for Facebook.'

'Yeah, Christian told me. Poor Oisinn.'

I'm there, 'Where are you, by the way?'

'Yeah, no,' he goes, 'that's actually the reason I'm ringing. I'm at the airport. I'm on the way to Moscow.'

'Moscow? The one in, em –?'

'The one in Russia, yeah. It turns out that Fyodor is, like, super-serious about acquiring the patent for the bed.'

'I thought you weren't interested in selling it? I thought it was your way of, like, honouring your old man?'

'I thought about it. I mean, I could spend the next ten years of my life dragging it around from trade fair to trade fair, selling the odd one here or there. EZ Living in Sandyford have said they'll take five on sale or return. But what Fyodor is talking about is mass-production. He's talking about selling it all over the world.'

'Why do you need to go to Moscow, though?'

'He wants me to meet his boss.'

I don't know why, but I get an instantly bad feeling about it.

I'm like, 'Dude, are you sure it's safe? How do you know you can even trust this goy?'

He goes, 'Your old man knows him.'

'Yeah, I wouldn't consider that any kind of character reference. Hang on, didn't Fyodor already threaten to kill you? And your son? I mean, I heard that with my own ears.'

'He said that was just a joke, Ross. Apparently, Russians have a very dork sense of humour. Hey, my flight's about to board here. I'll talk to you soon.'

And with that, he hangs up.

I turn right onto Sandford Road. I'm there, 'I have a really bad feeling about this.'

Not about Sandford Road. It's in Dublin 6, but aport from that, there's very little wrong with it. The bad feeling I have is that I'm never going to see JP again.

But Sorcha's there, 'I'm sure he'll be fine, Ross,' and she puts her hand on my leg and says she really enjoyed that earlier – *that* meaning the sex we had?

Yeah, no, Fionn took Hillary to – get this – a Daddy and Baby Dance Porty in the Town Hall in Dalkey, while her old pair went into town – her old man is checking out semi-furnished office space available to let in the Distillers Building in Smithfield – and me and Sorcha celebrated by riding ourselves bow-legged on the floor of the kitchen.

We pull up outside Little Cambridge and we get out of the cor. As we're walking to the door, Sorcha reaches for my hand. I can't remember the last time we held hands in public. She gives me a sort of sideways smile, then gives my hand a little squeeze and goes, 'Oh my God, we are so smug!'

And I'm there, 'I know – what are we like?'

Sasha gives us a big smile when she sees us. She's like, 'Brian, Johnny, Leo – your mom and dad are here!'

Sorcha goes, 'How did they do today?'

Sasha's there, 'They did great. They've fit in so well here.'

We both just smile and raise our eyebrows and wait for her to say something else. You don't pay five hundred yoyos per week per child for them to just fit in.

I'm there, 'I think what Sorcha meant was how are they doing in terms of, like, achievements?'

She seems to find this hilarious. 'I wouldn't expect to identify their unique gifts in just a few weeks,' she goes. 'It's something that takes time. Although Brian and Leo seem really drawn to ort.'

'Ort?' Sorcha goes.

Sasha's like, 'Yeah, come and see,' and she leads us over to a table where – yeah, no – the two boys are sitting quietly and drawing on paper with colouring pencils.

I take a look over their shoulders and I have to admit that I end up struggling to hide my disappointment. Brian is drawing a picture of Santa Claus – fock's sake, it's June – and Leo is drawing a picture of – worse – two soccer men. I don't want to be too critical but – honestly? – they're both shit.

Sorcha goes, 'Oh my God, Ross, look at what they've drawn!'

'Santa!' Brian goes.

And Sorcha's like, 'Yes, Santa! We might even send this to him along with your list this year!'

Sorcha is one of those South Dublin mothers – if her kid pissed on the floor of the Vatican, she'd be looking for evidence of genius in the splash patterns. I'm not as fast and loose with the compliments, of course.

I'm there, 'Come on, boys, let's hit the road,' because I'm double-porked outside. I find Johnny. He's playing with a bucket of building blocks – no evidence of genius to report there either. I pick him up and Sorcha takes Brian and Leo by the hand.

Sasha goes, 'Do you want to bring their drawings home?'

And I'm there, 'No, I don't think we'll bother, Sasha. I honestly don't see what you see when I look at them.'

But at the exact same time, Sorcha goes, 'We'd love to! We'll put them on the fridge, won't we, boys?'

We step outside. All I can hear are cor horns beeping. Like I said, I porked in the middle of the road with the hazards on and the traffic is backed up all the way to the end of Elmwood Avenue and presumably Ranelagh Main Street. They keep leaning on their horns even while me and Sorcha are trying to strap the boys into their booster seats, so I stand behind the cor and give them the middle finger of both hands, then I make sure to take my time driving away – putting on my seatbelt, checking my mirrors, indicating to pull out, all the shit they tell you to do when you first take up driving.

'Mom,' Leo goes, 'can we play football when we go home?'

And I'm like, 'No, you can't. I burst that soccer ball that your grandmother bought you and I stuck it in the focking bin.'

I carry on driving. I'm suddenly in foul form. I'm remembering the drawing that other kid did of Christchurch Cathedral and I'm thinking, Why are we wasting our money sending these three – I'm sorry – but dopes to a place like Little Cambridge?

Then I hear Sorcha whisper something. 'Ross,' she goes, 'can you hear that?'

And I'm like, 'No,' because all I can hear is the dude behind me in a silver Volkswagen Passat, still leaning on his horn because I'm deliberately driving at ten miles per hour to basically piss him off.

'It's the boys!' Sorcha goes. 'Oh my God, Ross, they've stopped swearing!'

I'm watching Ronan from across the room and I can't tell you how proud I am of my son.

He's going, 'Where does it hoort?'

And the woman sitting opposite him is like, 'In me neck.'

'Wheerabouts in yisser neck, but?'

'All oaber me neck.'

He's wearing – believe it or not – a shirt and tie and he's sitting behind a desk in the Citizens Advice Bureau above the vape shop on Mellowes Road. It makes me actually happy that this is how he's choosing to spend his summer, helping people in his own local community.

'And ted me again,' he goes, 'when did it happidden?'

The woman's like, 'Abourra munt ago. I was on the bus and I was stanton up to the press the beddle cos me stop was cubbing up, so it was. The thriver hit the brakes and I went floying forwoods.'

269

'Did you say athin to the thriver at the toyum? Did you compla-yun to him?'

'I ditn't, no.'

'So it was oatently, what, a munt later that yisser neck steerted hoorting you?'

'That's reet. But Ine in agony wirrit now, so I am. So do you think I've a case?'

'It sowunts veddy like it to me, Mrs Muddigan.'

'Calt me Brentha.'

'Brentha, so. What Ine godda suggest to you is get yisser self to A&E and get a coddar on that neck of yooers. And hee-or's a list of locaddle solicitodders who look arthur personoddle injurdoddy claiyums on a no win, no fee basis.'

'Thanks,' the woman goes – then she focks off.

Ronan presses the button and the counter changes to thirty-four. He goes, 'Thoorty-foe-er! Who's number thoorty-foe-er?'

I'm number thirty-four. I stand up and I'm like, 'That'd be me!'

And it's the first time he notices me in the waiting room.

He's there, 'Ah, howiya, Rosser? What the bleaten hell are you doing here?'

I'm like, 'I just popped in to see how you were getting on,' and I sit down in the seat opposite him. 'Very well seems to be the answer to that question. I've been listening to you for the past twenty minutes.'

'Ine lubbin it, Rosser, so I am. I caddent ted you how much it meadens to be gibbon sometin back to the commudity.'

'Can I just ask you, though, is it just people who've sustained whiplash injuries or tripped over things or had things fall on top of them?'

'Mostly, Rosser, yeah.'

'How's Rihanna-Borgan?'

'She's getting big. Big and bowult. How's the boyuz?'

'You're not going to believe this, but they've stopped actually swearing.'

'You're pudding me woyer!'

'I'm not pulling anything. Remember I was telling you about

this very expensive Montessori we're sending them to in Ranelagh? I don't know what goes on in there, but I literally haven't heard them use a bad word in a week. And they've stopped kicking the shit out of each other as well.'

'Where are thee, Rosser? Are thee not wit you?'

'Yeah, no, I left them outside in the cor. I just thought there'd probably be a fair a bit of effing and blinding in here and it might trigger a relapse. How did your exams go, by the way?'

He goes, 'Ah, thee went moostard, so thee did.'

'And what about Huguette? What's she up to for the summer? Not that I give a fock?'

'I doatunt know. I, er, habn't hoord from her.'

Something's up. I see it in his face. I know my son better than I nearly know myself.

I'm like, 'Something's wrong. I know it just looking at you.'

He sighs. He knows he can't hide anything from his old man. He goes, 'I ended up with wood of her mates, Rosser.'

I'm like, 'You did what?'

'Her best mate, as a mathor of fact. A boord called Racher Doddle.'

'I'm going to go out on a limb here and guess you're saying Rachel?'

'It was the night we were all out cedebraton fidishing eer exaddoms. There's been a birra fleerting between me and Racher Doddle oaber the last few munts. Then, that night, we weddent back to her place . . .'

'Does Huguette know?'

'No, she dudn't.'

'You better hope it stays like that. You saw what she did to poor Phinneas.'

'That's why Ine detormiddened that she's nebber godda foyunt out.'

'Well, good luck with that,' I go, then I stand up. 'I'd better hit the road.'

I walk back to the cor. The boys are sitting in the back of the cor. There isn't a peep out of them. It's going to take a lot of getting used to.

'Daddy,' Leo goes, 'can we go to McDonald's?'

And I'm like, 'Of course we can go to McDonald's! Just let me think where's the nearest one to home that we haven't already been thrown out of. It might have to be Bray, of all places.'

'McDonald's!' Johnny goes – and the three of them clap their hands together with the excitement of it all. And I have to say, I love them like this. It doesn't even bother me that they're focking useless at everything. They're actually bearable to be around.

Sorcha says she has a surprise for me.

She goes, 'Take a left at the end of the road.'

It's, like, date night and we're in the cor, but where we're heading is an actual mystery. She's all chat, though. She goes, 'I was saying to Fionn this morning that it might be time for Hillary to move out of our room and into the nursery.'

I'm like, 'Yeah, no, that'd be great.'

'Things are finally coming together – do you think that as well, Ross?'

'As in?'

'As in, the boys are behaving so well. It's like living with three totally different children. Dad is back working – and him and Mom are saving for a place of their own, hopefully before the end of the year, although I've told them they can stay for as long as they want.'

'You're slipping that into the good news category, huh?'

'And then me and you are getting on probably better than we ever have, don't you think?'

'Yeah, no, I suppose we are.'

'There's trust. But there's also friendship. And we're getting there with the sex as well!'

'Do you not miss, Honor, though?'

She's like, 'Sorry, what?'

Seriously, that's what she says.

I'm there, 'Er, your daughter? It's just you never seem to mention her. It's like she's no longer a port of the family.'

'That's not true.'

'Have you even spoken to her since she went?'

272

'Erika keeps me up to date on all the things she's been doing. I've watched one or two of the videos they've done.'

'So you're saying no?'

'She doesn't want to talk to me. It's taken me a long time to come to terms with this fact, Ross, but Honor hates me.'

'Hate is a very strong word.'

'And God forgive me for saying this, but I don't think it's a coincidence that everything in our lives seems to be suddenly falling into place now that she's off the scene.'

'That's horsh.'

'There's peace in our home. You can't deny that. Turn in here.'

She wants me to pull into the cor pork next to Kingsland in Glasthule. I'm like, 'Random,' but I do it anyway and I find a porking space.

She goes, 'Okay, do you know where we are?'

'Er, Glasthule?'

'What used to be here, Ross?'

And then the penny finally drops. I'm like, 'The cinema?'

She goes, 'The Forum. Do you remember? This is where we had our first actual date.'

'Was that not Eddie Rocket's in Donnybrook?'

'No, that was where I first plucked up the courage to talk to you. This was where we had our first, like, date date? Do you remember what movie we went to see?'

'Was it *Titanic*?'

'Er, that was, like, our fourth? I thought you'd remember that night of all nights. That was the night we both said "I love you" for the first time.'

I remember I'd watched *Titanic* with another girl the night before and I had to pretend I didn't know what happened at the end.

She goes, 'On our first date, we went to see *Jerry Maguire*!'

I'm like, 'Yeah, no, I remember now.'

I don't. Like I said, I had a lot of names on my dance cord around that time.

'So here's the surprise,' she goes, then she reaches across me and presses the little button that pushes my seat right back.

She goes, 'Just give me a second,' and she reaches around and takes a blanket off the back seat. Then she pushes her own seat back and spreads the blanket over us. We're both just lying there, staring at the ceiling of the cor. Then she storts fiddling with her phone.

'I bought this, like, thing,' she goes, 'that lets you turn your phone into a projector.'

Suddenly – yeah, no, she's right – a picture appears above us and we stort watching the movie. And I'm going to be honest with you, it's actually very nice. It also takes me back, even though I don't actually remember seeing the movie with her?

She goes, 'Do you remember I said I'd love a little boy like the boy with the glasses and you said it'd never happen if we ended up together because you had perfect vision and if that's what I wanted then –'

She stops talking. We're both suddenly thinking about Hillary, the poor little half-blind thing.

She goes, 'I'm sorry, Ross, I didn't mean –'

I'm like, 'It's cool, Sorcha. In a weird way, I'm actually storting to get my head around it.'

She smiles at me. It's actually really nice lying there in the cor. She goes, 'I love you, Ross.'

And I go, 'I love you, Sorcha,' and even though it's not the first time I've said it since we got back together, it's the first time I've genuinely meant it.

The kid's up on the screen going, 'Thid you know the human brain weighth eighth pounth?'

And I'm there, 'Jesus, he talks like Christian and Lauren's little lad!'

Sorcha laughs, in fairness to her, and tells me I'm terrible and that's when my phone suddenly rings. I whip it out of my pocket and I can see that it's Honor.

I swear to God, Sorcha goes, 'Don't answer it.'

I'm there, 'It's Honor, though.'

'Ring her back later. When we get home. Ross, this is supposed to be our time.'

I'm like, 'Just pause the movie. I can't believe you're not excited that she's ringing.'

I answer the phone. I'm like, 'Hey, Honor!'

She goes, 'Hey, Dad. What are you doing?'

'Watching *Jerry Maguire*.'

'Oh my God, Mom never shuts up about that movie. That was what you went to see on your first date, by the way.'

God, I must get Honor to write me out a list of these.

I'm there, 'Hey, the big news this end is that Joe Schmidt rang me.' She's like, 'What?'

'Yeah, no, he got your letter, Honor. And my Rugby Tactics Book.'

Which he still hasn't sent me back, by the way. He's possibly taken it to Japan with him.

'And what did he say?' she goes.

I'm there, 'He just said he was pretty blown away by the things you wrote. He said you obviously loved your daddy very . . . Okay, I'm trying not to cry here.'

'I don't mind if you cry.'

So I cry for a little bit and I can tell that Sorcha is rolling her eyes and shaking her head beside me.

I'm there, 'He's amazing, Honor. It's like talking to a holy man. He told me that I obviously had a lot of deep thoughts about the game and that it was an actual crime that I hadn't been snapped up by a club.'

'Oh my God,' she goes, 'did he give you a job?'

'No, but he encouraged me to say yes to a coaching offer that I happened to be considering at that time. And even though it didn't work out, I've decided that it's only going to be the stort of it.'

Suddenly, out of nowhere, Honor goes, 'Dad, there's something I need to talk to Mom about – is she there?'

I'm like, 'Your mother?' and I look at Sorcha, who just shakes her head in tight, little movements. 'She's, em, unfortunately not here at the moment, Honor.'

She knows I'm lying. 'It doesn't matter,' she goes, sounding really disappointed.

I'm there, 'Is it not something you can talk to me about?'

'No, it's nothing,' she goes. 'I'll talk to you again soon,' and then she hangs up.

★

So I'm in Brian, Johnny and Leo's room and we're lying on the bed, watching a DVD in – believe it or not – silence.

At some point, I happen to look at my voicemail and I notice that I have four missed calls from JP, then a text message asking me to ring him urgently – and the word 'urgently' is in, like, capital letters.

So I step out of the room and I call the dude back. He answers on the third ring. He's like, 'Ross . . . Ross, is that you?' and I can hear straight away that his voice is trembling.

I'm like, 'Dude? Dude, what's wrong?'

He goes, 'Ross . . . Ross . . .'

Jesus Christ, it sounds like he can hordly breathe.

I'm there, 'JP, what's going on?'

'Fyodor and his boss . . .' he goes. 'They took me . . .'

'Took you? Where did they take you?'

'They took me . . . out to lunch . . . A seafood restaurant . . . They said it was . . . one of the best in . . . Euuugghhh . . .'

'Dude, are you about to vom? You sound like you're about to vom.'

'When we finished eating . . . Fyodor's boss . . . said he wanted the bed . . . and he'd do anything . . . to get it . . .'

I suddenly realize what's going down here. I'm there, 'Holy fock, did they poison you? Dude, did they poison you?'

He goes, 'Ross . . . I'm going to . . . have to hang up on you . . .' but before he does I hear him spewing – as in, like, seriously spewing? He's like, 'BLEEEUUUGGGHHH!!! BLEEEUUUGGGHHH!!! BLEEEUUUGGGHHH!!! BLEEEUUUGGGHHH!!!'

I'm going, 'JP . . . JP . . . Dude . . . Dude?' before the line goes suddenly dead.

I drive out to Foxrock in an actual rage. I let myself into the gaff, then down to the kitchen I go. I push the door. And while my head is obviously all over the place, the sight that greets me still manages to pull me up short.

They're all sitting around having dinner together – we're talking the old man and the old dear, one at either end of the table, then the six surrogates, or whatever they're called, three on either side.

The old dear pretends to be pleased to see me. She goes, 'Ross! How lovely! Sit down! You're just in time for dinner!'

She's made her grilled halibut with peach and pepper salsa, I notice.

But I'm there, 'I'm not focking staying. This isn't a social call.'

The old man goes, 'Don't worry, Dorling, I think I know why Kicker's here!'

I'm there, 'Is he dead? Just answer me that.'

'Oh, he's not dead!' the old man goes. Then he has a little chuckle to himself. He's like, 'At least not yet anyway!'

I literally don't know what to say to that. I end up just staring at him, speechless.

The old dear, meanwhile, is looking around the table, checking out everyone's plates.

'Szidonia,' she goes, 'you haven't touched your fish.'

Szidonia's there, 'I not like fish,' and I suddenly feel like I'm not actually in the room, like this is a scene I'm watching on TV or something.

'Whether you like fish or not is irrelevant,' the old dear goes. 'You signed a contract when you agreed to carry one of my babies – and when you signed that contract you agreed to abide by a diet plan. That goes for the rest of you as well.'

'What the fock did you mean,' I hear my voice go, 'when you said he wasn't dead yet?'

He's there, 'His demise will be a slow, drawn-out affair! With a bit of luck, he'll be gone by the end of the summer!'

I'm like, 'What? You're saying you're involved in this?'

'You must understand, Ross, it's nothing personal! It's just that he has something that we want! And, with Fyodor's help, we're going to take it from him!'

I'm just like, 'You focking . . .' but I can't find the words to describe how I feel about him in that moment and I end up just bursting into tears.

He goes, 'Well, this is a fine how-do-you-do! Why are you so concerned for the chap's welfare, Ross, as a matter of interest?'

'Are you joking me? He's one of my best friends!'

'Is he?'

'I love the goy.'

'You love him?'

'Yes, I love him. Hord as that might be for someone like you to understand.'

'Well, this is a turn-up for the books and no mistake!'

The old dear looks at me. She's like, 'I'm trying to talk to the girls here, Ross. Why on Earth are you crying?'

The old man goes, 'It seems he's in love with Leo Varadkar!'

I'm like, 'Excuse me?'

'Has he given you any indication that he feels the same way about you, Kicker?'

'I'm not talking about Leo Varadkar. For fock's sake, I'm talking about JP!'

'JP? You mean, JP, your pal?'

'Yes, JP, my focking pal.'

He laughs. He thinks it's suddenly hilarious.

He goes, 'It seems we've been talking at cross-purposes! I just assumed you'd seen young Leo being sworn in as Taoiseach today and raced over here to try to draw me into one of our famous political debates! *Post hoc ergo propter hoc!* There! I said it before you did, Ross!'

'I came here because JP just rang me. From Moscow. They focking poisoned him.'

'Poisoned him? Who poisoned him?'

'Your mate – whatever he's called? Fyodor.'

'I have to say, Ross, this differs rather markedly from the account I heard! I was talking to Fyodor not two hours ago! It seems they had a very productive meeting with one of Fyodor's oligarch pals! This chap has a theory, Fionnuala, that the most valuable commodity in the world of the future won't be oil and it won't be clean water, it'll be room in which to move!'

I'm like, 'Dude, I'm telling you, when JP rang me, he was choking to death.'

'I rather think your imagination is getting the better of you, Ross! Give him a call!'

'Who?'

'JP, of course! Give him a call!'

I take out my phone and I ring the dude's number again. I'm not expecting him to answer. But he does – this time after only one ring.

He goes, 'Hey, Ross, I'm sorry I had to hang up on you there.'

I'm like, 'Dude, you need to get to a hospital – and fast.'

'I don't need a hospital. There's nothing wrong with me.'

'I was talking to you twenty minutes ago. You could hordly breathe. You were spewing your ring.'

He laughs. He goes, 'That was, em, shock, Ross.'

I'm like, 'Shock? Dude, is Fyodor holding a gun to your head there? Cough twice if the answer is yes.'

But he doesn't cough twice. He doesn't cough at all. He just goes, 'What I was trying to tell you was that Fyodor's boss took me out for lunch. He said he wanted the Vampire Bed and was prepared to do anything to get it. He offered me –'

I'm like, 'What?'

'– ten million euros.'

'Ten million yoyos?'

The old man smiles at me and nods knowingly.

I'm there, 'You're focking shitting me! And what did you say to him?'

And JP's like, 'I said yes, of course!'

Of course there ends up being an awkward atmos in the kitchen when I hang up. The old man has another little chuckle to himself.

He goes, 'Poison JP? I don't know what kind of people you think we are, Ross!' then he picks up his phone and storts presumably tweeting.

Charles O'Carroll-Kelly √ @realCOCK – 8m

Leo Varadkar is part of the same middle-class ruling elite that rewards bankers and is happy for YOU to pay for their greed! A boy who joins Fine Gael at the age of 16 is not a boy who is looking to change the world – he's a boy who's already thinking about his place in it!

Reply 2,880 Retweet 6,406 Like 28,993 ✉

The old dear is just, like, glowering at the girls. 'Your contracts say no alcohol,' she goes. 'Roxana, did you sign a contract that said you would refrain from drinking alcohol for the full term of your pregnancy?'

I notice the girls exchanging nervous looks across the table.

Roxana's like, 'I not drink alcohol!'

'You had two mouthfuls of Grey Goose vodka last night,' the old dear goes – the focking hypocrite – 'after I went to bed.'

I did warn them about the hidden cameras. There was bound to be one in the drinks cabinet.

Roxana's there, 'I drink because is too much pressure. Always you say to me, "Eat this!" and "Don't eat that!", "Take folic acid", "Take vitamins". You say, "You take exercise yet?"'

'Brigita hasn't stepped on the treadmill in days,' the old dear goes. 'And don't bother lying to me, Brigita, because I know what goes on under my own roof.'

Brigita goes, 'I try – but I am out of breath.'

The old dear's there, 'Perhaps it's all those cigarettes you've been smoking?' and Brigita just looks away – busted and disgusted. 'I want my babies to be born healthy. That's why I'm warning you now that unless you stick to the instructions I've given you with regard to diet and exercise – and that means taking your folic acid, Lidia Two – then you won't receive your balloon payment at the end of your pregnancy. And I'm sorry you've forced me to do this, but from now on I'm going to have to insist on breathalysing you all three times daily.'

We're having a few cheeky Friday afternoon pints in Madigan Square Gorden to celebrate JP's big news.

'Be honest,' he goes, 'how many of you really believed that the Vampire Bed was a good idea?'

Me and Oisinn exchange a look over the top of our pints and we both burst out laughing.

'Don't get me wrong,' Oisinn goes, 'I still think it's a terrible idea. I just can't believe they paid you – what was it, ten million for it?'

'Plus a percentage of the profit on each bed sold,' he goes. 'They're talking about selling it into China, Japan, Mexico, Brazil – anywhere that's overpopulated really.'

I laugh.

He goes, 'I would have liked to hang on to the patent myself, but I just don't have the resources to bring it to the market in the numbers they can. I mean, they're actually convinced that in twenty years, this is how everyone in the world will sleep, even in this country – stacked like plates in a draining rack.'

I'm there, 'Your old man would be proud of you, JP,' and I genuinely mean it. 'Very proud.'

He's like, 'Thanks, Ross.'

Fionn arrives then. Glasses. Everything.

I'm like, 'I can't get a break from you. It's bad enough that I have to live under the same roof as you – now I can't have a few pints without looking at your big, stupid head.'

He has no answer to this, so he decides to just blank me.

Then Oisinn makes the mistake of going, 'Hey, Fionn! How's Hillary?'

And Fionn reaches straight for his phone to give him the full focking picture show. I don't have a single photograph of the triplets in my phone and I've got more than five hundred of Emily Blunt.

I rest my case.

'So is he talking yet?' JP goes, pretending to take an interest in his stupid pictures.

Fionn's there, 'No, he hasn't said anything, but I can tell he's right on the point of verbalizing. Which would actually be early. A lot of the books I've read say that how early they speak is an indicator of intelligence.'

I'm like, 'Yeah, the only question is what focking language it'll be in – right, Fionn?'

Again, he lets it just wash over him.

I call the lounge girl over and I ask for four pints of the obvious, then a 7-Up for Christian, who arrives just at that moment. He looks like shit – the weight of the world and blah, blah, blah.

I'm like, 'Are you okay?'

'Yeah,' he goes, 'I just had a massive row with Lauren.'

I'm there, 'Another one? Would you not be better off single?'

He goes, 'She found out about the money,' and then he looks at JP. 'I might need that fifty Ks back at some point. No pressure, but even if you could stort paying me back in instalments over the next, say, two to three years?'

JP just laughs.

Christian obviously hasn't heard JP's good news yet because he goes, 'What's so funny?'

And JP's like, 'The Russians bought the patent from me, Christian. Ten million snots.'

'Ten?' Christian goes. 'Million?'

'Out of which I'm giving you two.'

All of our jaws just drop. Including Christian's, by the way.

He's like, 'Sorry, say that again?' because none of us can actually believe what we're hearing.

JP goes, 'You can tell Lauren. I'm giving you two million euros. To say thank you to you both.'

Christian's there, 'You don't have to do that.'

'I know I don't have to do it. But I'm going to do it. Because you were the only one who believed in the idea.'

Christian laughs. 'Jesus, I didn't believe in it,' he goes. 'I thought it was the stupidest idea I'd ever heard in my life. I just didn't want to see you throw everything away.'

'You gave me all that money,' JP goes, 'to invest in an idea that you thought was going to fail?'

Christian just nods.

'Then you're taking the two million,' JP goes, 'and there's going to be no arguments.'

Christian just stares off into the distance with a look of just, like, shock on his face? It'll take a long time for this to sink in. But I'm delighted for him. It's actually years since the dude has had something good happen to him.

I'm there, 'Can I just interrupt here and say the word "rugby"?' because someone has to say it and it might as well be me.

'Rugby,' everyone agrees.

But then I catch a glimpse of Oisinn looking sad and I feel suddenly shit that we've been standing here toasting JP's good fortune and no one has asked him how he's doing?

So I'm like, 'Any word, Dude? From, like, Magnus?'

Oisinn goes, 'We've spoken on the phone once or twice.'

JP's like, 'Where's he sleeping?'

Oisinn goes, 'In work.'

'What? They've got actual beds in there?'

'They've got actual everything in there.'

Fionn goes, 'I read a long-form article about this whole phenomenon. It might have been in the *New Yorker*. It was all about how big companies are creating such happy workplace environments that many employees grow resentful, even mistrustful, of the world outside.'

'It's the focking *Truman Show*,' Christian goes. 'But that can't be it, Oisinn. That can't be your marriage over?'

Oisinn's there, 'He's not the Magnus I fell in love with, Christian. It's like he's joined a cult. Ross, you saw him at the tag rugby. He's been indoctrinated into a way of thinking that I just don't understand. I rang him the other day and he agreed that we needed to talk. But he said he didn't have any capacity at the moment and it'd have to wait until the end of Q3. Then he said he had to go because he was taking on Debbie from Strategic Planning and Operational Excellence in the basketball hoop-shoot final.'

I'm there, 'Okay, this has gone on long enough.'

Oisinn's there, 'What do you mean?' because he can tell by my tone – and by the fact that I've put down my pint – that I'm suddenly deadly serious.

I'm there, 'Dude, Magnus is as much our friend as he is your husband.'

'Shit! The Bed! You've got an idea, don't you?'

'You're damn right I've got an idea. Although you'll have to give me the weekend to work out the finer points of the plan.'

'What does it involve?'

'We're going to break into Facebook and we're going to . . . what's the word, Fionn?'

Fionn goes, 'Exfiltrate?'

And I'm like, 'That's right. We're going to exfiltrate the dude. The five of us. We'll do it on Monday afternoon.'

'Ohmygod, ohmygod, ohmygod!' Sorcha goes. 'Ohmygod, ohmygod, ohmygod! Ohmygod, ohmygod, ohmygod!'

And while it's never been my style to discuss what goes on in the bedroom, all I will say, for the purposes of the story, is that I'm lying on the flat of my back and my wife is bouncing up and down on me like Daenerys Targaryen riding one of her dragons into battle.

She puts one hand on my chest and the other one over her mouth to stifle the screams that I'm expecting to stort any second now, while I'm keeping the mast up by running through the names of the Ireland storting XV who beat Japan in the First Test this morning. We're talking Healy, Scannell, Ryan, Roux, Toner, Ruddock, Leavy, Conan . . .

Sorcha goes, 'Stop naming rugby players. I can't concentrate.'

I'm there, 'Sorry, I thought I was saying them in my head.'

'Oh my God!' she goes. 'Oh my God! Oh my God!'

And it's at that exact moment that I look over her left shoulder and find myself staring at my old dear's face.

I'm like, 'Okay, what the fock?'

And Sorcha goes, 'Ross, don't stop. I'm so close! Oh my God, I'm so close!'

I'm there, 'Sorcha, get off me! Get off me now!'

She – there's no better word for it – dismounts me and goes, 'What the focking hell is wrong with you?' and then she looks over her shoulder and sees exactly what I see. My old dear. Looking like a badly beaten porpoise squeezed into a navy velvet pantsuit.

Sorcha goes, 'I knew I should have switched off the TV instead of just muting it.'

I'm like, 'What the fock is she doing on TV?'

'She must be on *Saturday with Miriam*. Oh my God, I love her velvet tux. I've seen Cara Delevingne wearing something very similar.'

'Jesus Christ.'

'I'll turn it off and we can go back to what we were doing.'

'Seriously, Sorcha, I doubt very much if I'm going to be in a position to achieve and sustain again tonight having seen that face. Jesus Christ.'

Sorcha grabs the TV remote and sticks the sound on. Yeah, no, it's *Saturday with Miriam* alright. And the old dear is laying it on factor-fifty thick.

She's going, 'I had an experience last Christmas, Miriam. A near-death experience. I almost choked to death on a Kalamata olive and I wouldn't be sitting here tonight if it wasn't for this man sitting beside me.'

Yeah, no, it turns out that *he's* there as well – as in, the old man?

'Charles,' Miriam goes, 'you saved Fionnuala's life, didn't you? Tell us what happened?'

He's there, 'Well, it's not the kind of thing you even need to think about, Miriam! You see someone you love lying on the floor, turning blue, airways blocked, etcetera, etcetera – your first instinct is to do whatever is necessary to save that person's life!'

My first instinct was to let nature take its course.

'So I performed the Heimlich manoeuvre on her and, well, the olive shot out,' he goes, 'and she could suddenly breathe again!'

'And what,' Miriam goes, 'were the lessons you learned from that experience, Fionnuala?'

I'm like, 'Have your mid-afternoon Mortini with a twist of lemon instead.'

Sorcha shushes me. She goes, 'Ross, I never knew anything about her nearly dying!'

I decide to keep my mouth shut then.

The old dear goes, 'Lying on the floor, waiting to die by suffocation, gives you time to think, Miriam. Time really does slow down in that moment. And, as I was lying there, I began reflecting on my life and asking myself whether I had spent my time on this Earth wisely.'

'And the answer?' Miriam goes – she's worse for encouraging her.

The old dear's there, 'The answer was no, Miriam. And I know that will probably shock a lot of people in your audience and a lot of people watching at home. People look at me and they see the successful literary career and the role I've played as an advocate for those with no voice and they think I have the complete life. But I realized, in that moment, that I didn't. My life was utterly meaningless. Because I was dying, Miriam, and I was alone.'

She pretends to be upset then. The old man puts his hand on top of hers. It's an IFTA-winning performance.

'Was there anything specific,' Miriam goes, 'that you regretted doing or perhaps not doing in your life?'

The old dear's there, 'It's going to sound selfish, Miriam, because I know I've helped a great many people with my charitable work and I've brought pleasure to millions of lives with my books. But in that moment, I regretted leading a life of such selflessness. I wished I'd had a family.'

Sorcha goes, 'Oh my God, Ross – she has a family! She has you!'

And I'm there, 'I didn't hear Miriam jumping in there to correct her either.'

'So come on,' Miriam goes, 'I know you're bursting to tell us this wonderful news.'

The old dear's like, 'Charles and I have decided to have children.'

You can nearly hear the audience thinking, Someone's made a pig of themselves with the gin in the green room.

'Explain to us,' Miriam goes, 'how that's even possible, Fionnuala, because you're –'

'Sixty,' the old dear goes.

'Oh, I've got seventy here in my notes.'

'No, Miriam, it's sixty. You might want to change your researchers. But to answer your question, back in the 1980s – when I was torn between having a family and dedicating my life to helping, as well as entertaining, others – I had some of my eggs frozen in the Ukraine.'

Miriam's there, 'And, Charles, you knew literally nothing about this?'

He's like, 'Nothing whatsoever, Miriam! Until last Christmas!

The business with the olive! Fionnuala was upset and she said, "Who's going to look after us when we get old, Chorles? We're all alone in this world!" And that's when she told me about her secret trip to the Ukraine, where she had various things removed and – like you said – refrigerated!'

Miriam goes, 'Now, you're not talking about having a baby, are you?'

The old dear's like, 'No, we're having six!'

I'm expecting to hear boos from the audience – except they actually stort clapping?

I'm there, 'How the fock can people think this is good?'

'Six?' Miriam goes. 'And you're using surrogates to carry them for you. And we're going to meet them in just a moment. But first I want to ask you, Chorles, where are you going to find the time to be a father to all these babies? I mean, you are still intent on becoming Taoiseach one day?'

He's like, 'Yes, I am, Miriam! And I have to tell you that just the thought of bringing these six new lives into the world has fired me with an energy I haven't known since I was a much younger man! You see, now I have a very real stake in this country's future! It is now incumbent on me to do everything I can to ensure that these children of ours grow up in an Ireland that is both happy and prosperous – and not a country whose citizens are asked to foot the bill for a failed –'

Miriam cuts him off. She's there, 'I'm not going to allow you to make a party political statement, Charles O'Carroll-Kelly, but I am going to ask you about Leo Varadkar, who received his seal of office from President Michael D. Higgins this week. Do you wish him well as Ireland's youngest ever Taoiseach?'

The old man goes, 'You're doing the chap a disservice there, Miriam! He's not only Ireland's youngest ever Taoiseach, he's also our first leader who has openly admitted to going to a second-tier private school! But of course I wish him – and all his Head Prefect pals – well! I'm rather looking forward to taking Leader's Questions from the chap when he's the leader of the Opposition in the very near future!'

The audience laughs, then gives him another round of applause. It always amazes me how easily swayed people are by his bullshit.

Miriam stands up and goes, 'Okay, will we meet the six lovely women who are helping Charles and Fionnuala to have the family of which they've always dreamed?'

The audience is like, 'Yaaaaaayyyyyy!!!'

Miriam goes, 'Okay, here they come – the six women who are pregnant with Charles and Fionnuala's babies! They are Szidonia, Roxana, Loredana, Brigita, Lidia and then another Lidia!'

Out they walk. They're wearing identical, shapeless, grey smock dresses. Even Sorcha's like, 'Oh! My God! They're like actual clones!'

Miriam goes, 'Now, Fionnuala, when you look at them, do you know who is who?'

The old dear's like, 'Not really, Miriam. I've given them name badges but they refuse to wear them. I know the one with the big nose is Brigita. And that one's either Roxana or one of the Lidias.'

Sorcha goes, 'It's like something from *The Handmaid's Tale*.'

Miriam turns around to the six birds and goes, 'So how does it feel to be helping Fionnuala and Charles to have the family they've always wanted?'

'It feels very nice,' Roxana – one of the ones I definitely fancy – goes.

Brigita's there, 'They are very good to us,' and she says it like she's memorized it from an actual script. 'They give us food and roof and we also do housework.'

'Oh my God,' Sorcha goes, 'they look actually terrified, Ross!'

Miriam's there, 'Fionnuala, will you come on the show again after the babies are born and maybe bring them with you?'

The old dear's like, 'It would be my pleasure, Miriam.'

'And Charles,' Miriam goes, 'do you have any particular preference in terms of their gender? Would you take three and three?'

And he's like, 'I don't mind what they are, Miriam, as long as they're six future Ireland rugby internationals!'

That gets a great laugh from the audience.

I'm there, 'He had to say that, didn't he? He had to mention rugby.'

Sorcha goes, 'Oh my God, Ross, I'm so, so sorry.'

And I just think to myself, I am going to get him back for this.

I'm beginning to wonder is Sasha drugging my children – and I'm saying that as a compliment to the girl? It's, like, ten o'clock on Sunday morning and there hasn't been a peep out of them. And I end up having to check on them to make sure they haven't climbed out the window and taken the cor for another spin.

But, no, when I stick my head around the door, Johnny is sitting on the floor, playing away happily with his Lego, while Brian and Leo are sitting at their little desk, drawing with their crayons.

I'm like, 'What are you drawing, goys?'

Brian shows me his picture and goes, 'Wayne Rooney!' and it takes all the strength I have to stop myself from snatching it from him, scrunching it up in a ball and focking it in the bin.

Instead, I go, 'Two out of ten, Brian,' because he'll never learn otherwise. 'And just to let you know, it would have been eight or nine out of ten if you'd drawn Dan Leavy. Er, two tries on his debut yesterday? You'd know that if you'd bothered to watch it with me.'

Sorcha walks in, holding Hillary in her orms. She goes, 'Oh my God, look at them, Ross! Three busy little beavers!'

I'm just there, 'Just don't go over the top with the praise is what I'm saying.'

She goes, 'Are you okay?' because she knows I barely slept after watching the old pair on TV last night.

I'm like, 'Yeah, no, I'm fine.'

Johnny is trying to attach a Lego brick to a sticky brick and he can't understand why it's not happening for him. He's definitely not going to work in construction – maybe I should be relieved.

'No, Johnny,' Sorcha goes, 'the sticky bricks only work with the other sticky bricks. Mommy will show you. Ross, will you hold Hillary?'

And before I get a chance to say anything, she's plonked Hillary in my orms. I try not to make eye contact with him – I've no idea why – but I can feel him just, like, staring at me intensely, so I end

289

up looking at him and his face suddenly breaks into a smile and he claps his two little hands together.

And suddenly all I can think is, Oh my God, what a beautiful baby he is. I mean, he didn't ask to be Fionn's kid. But thankfully there's very little of his father in him except – like I keep saying – the weak little eyes.

I feel my own face break into a smile. And then the most random thing happens. He storts going, 'Dadadadadadadadada!' basically trying to talk to me.

Sorcha looks over. She's like, 'Oh! My! God! Ross, he's verbalizing!' and then she runs to the door and shouts, 'Fionn! Fionn! He's verbalizing! He's verbalizing!'

'Dadadadadadada!' the kid goes.

And I'm like, 'Dadadadadadada!' and he sort of laughs and hiccups at the same time.

He goes, 'Dadadadadadadadadadadada!'

Sorcha's there, 'Oh my God, he's trying to have an actual conversation with you!'

All of a sudden, Fionn bursts into the room. He sees Hillary trying to have the deep meaningfuls with me and he's straight away jealous. The first thing he does is he takes him from me and goes, 'Regardez ici, mon enfant! Ton papa est ici!'

And you can actually see the joy disappear from the poor kid's face.

Fionn looks at me and he goes, 'What were you saying to him?'

And I'm like, 'I didn't say shit. He just storted chatting away to me. You know, maybe if you just chilled the fock out, Fionn, and stopped trying to fill his head with stupid languages, you might get a smile and the odd Dada out of him yourself.'

'I'll tell you what,' he goes, 'why don't I raise my child the way I want and not the way you tell me – given that your record in this area is far from exemplary.'

I try to think of a comeback, but I can't. If Honor was here, she'd tear him a new one, but she's not here. I can feel myself about to burst into tears again, so I end up just storming out of the room.

I hear Sorcha go, 'Fionn, I think that was uncalled-for.'

Downstairs, I spot Fionn's Dubes by the fireplace in the kitchen and I decide to go old school on him. I pick them up and I bring them into the jacks. I'm just about to whip down my chinos and boxer shorts when my phone all of a sudden rings? I check the screen and – holy fock! – I end up having to do a double-take.

Because Joe Schmidt is ringing me. Again.

I answer by going, 'Hello?'

His voice is muffled, like he's not talking directly into the mouth-piece. I can only make it out faintly. He's going, 'Could Oy git the chickin teriyakoy with froyed royce, ployse? And actually Oy moyt git a staahtah – Oy'll have the froyed toyfoy.'

The dude has obviously orse-dialled me by accident.

I'm there, 'Hello? HELLO? HEEELLLOOO?'

And then I hear him go, 'Can yoy hear that?' and then, a second or two later, I hear his voice, as clear as a bell. He goes, 'Helloy?'

I'm there, 'Yeah, no, sorry, Joe – you must have accidentally orse-dialled me.'

He's like, 'Oy thought Oy was going croyzoy for a munnet – hearing voices! Whoy's thus?'

'You must have sat on your phone or something. This is, like, Ross O'Carroll-Kelly?'

'Whoy?'

It kills me that the Ireland rugby coach doesn't even know my name. No wonder the old man is so keen to try again.

I'm there, 'Yeah, no, my daughter –'

'Aw, yeah, she wroyte moy thit litter!' he goes. 'That's royt! It was a groyt litter!'

'Yeah, no, she also sent you my Rugby Tactics Book.'

'Aw, I forgot to sind it beck to yoy! Is thit whoy you're ringing moy?'

'Yeah, no, I didn't ring you. I think you possibly orse-dialled me – in other words, sat on your phone.'

'Aw, dud Oy? Hey, we were talking abaaht coyching, weren't we?'

I'm there, 'We, er, were, yeah.'

He goes, 'So dud yoy soy yis to that toym that wanted yoy to coych them?'

'Yeah, no, I did actually. We had our first match a couple of weeks back.'

'That's groyt – and haahd yoy goy?'

I'm there, 'Er, I'd say there were pluses and minuses? Let's just say the match ended up being a lot more physical than I expected it to be.'

'Look,' he goes, 'we all goy into goyms with expictoytions – and you prepeer accordingloy. But what moykes a groyt coych is the ability toy react toy circumstaahnces as they onfoyld – do yoy git moy?'

God, his voice is so soothing.

I'm there, 'Yeah, no, I do get you, Joe. I definitely do.'

He goes, 'Yoy doyn't soym toy happy toy moy, Moyte. What us ut?'

He's just so easy to talk to – that's how it all ends up coming out about my old pair on the TV last night.

I'm there, 'They're trying to replace me.'

He's like, 'Reployce yoy? What, they've alriddy moyd up their moynds that you're not what thoy want?'

Yeah, no, Joe thinks we're still talking about rugby.

I'm there, 'I'm not sure I ever was what they wanted, Joe. I think I've turned out to be a major disappointment to them.'

'Un what woy?'

'I just didn't achieve all the things they wanted me to achieve. And now they think they can do better. They want to bring in, let's just say, new blood.'

'Lit me till you something, Moyt. You're looking at ut all wrong.'

'Am I?'

'This craahd you're wuth – they're troying toy till yoy that you're not the royt fut for them. Think abaaht ut another woy. Moyboy they're not the royt fut for yoy.'

'That's actually a good point.'

'Uf they think they can doy bitter than yoy, then moyboy troy spinding your toym around those whoy approyciate yoy – doy yoy git moy?'

'I do get you.'

'Lit moy aahsk yoy something else. What's the moyst important thung un the world to yoy?'

I don't even hesitate. I'm like, 'My wife and kids,' because that's what you're expected to say.

Joe goes, 'Your famloy. That's your number one toym, Ross.'

Well, I'd still put Leinster on a por with them, but I do accept the point he's trying to make.

He's there, 'Lusten, Moyt, Oy've gotta goy – moy moyle's arroyved. It's boyn noyce talking toy yoy agin, Moyte.'

And I go, 'Yeah, well done against Japan yesterday. I thought Jack Conan did very well, even though Dan Leavy obviously took all the headlines . . . Hello? Hello?' but by that stage the dude has already hung up.

I sit down on the jacks and I'm in just shock? That Joe Schmidt would accidentally ring my number but then stay on the line and give me, like, life advice is a bit surreal. And he's totally right. My priority now has to be my own family.

Sometimes it just takes a wise head to help you see the bigger picture, even if he thought we were talking about something else completely.

I look at Fionn's shoes and I think, Do you know what? Don't bother. Take the high road. You don't need to do this. Think of all the things you have going for you that Fionn doesn't have? Shitting in his shoes is actually beneath you.

So I go back out to the kitchen and I put them back where I found them. And I suddenly feel good about myself. I wouldn't be the first rugby player to say that Joe Schmidt has made me want to be a better person.

But then a minute or two later the good feeling passes, and I decide to shit in Fionn's shoes after all.

So the day finally arrives. We're standing outside the Facebook Ireland building in Grand Canal Square – the five of us staring up at this dork, glass structure, wondering how do we get inside?

'So what happens next?' Oisinn goes.

Then, automatically, they all turn to me for the game plan. It's just like old times. Once a ten, always a ten.

I'm there, 'It's very simple. We're going to morch in there and we're going to ask them very nicely if can have our friend back.'

'And if they say no?' Oisinn goes.

'Then, goys, we're going to have to resort to Plan B.'

I don't actually have a Plan B. I just figure I'll think of something if it comes to it. So up the steps, then into the building we go. I walk straight up to reception and – with the goys standing behind me – I go, 'Hi, I'm looking for Magnus, em – shit, I can't remember his second name.'

'Laakso-Sigurjónsson,' Oisinn goes.

I'm like, 'That's easy for you to say!' and I crack my hole laughing.

Okay, lunchtime pints might have been a bad idea before doing this and I definitely drank the last two a bit too quickly.

The receptionist storts eyeing us warily. 'Do you have an appointment?' she goes.

I'm there, 'Do we look like we've an appointment?' probably stinking of booze.

'I'll, em, try his extension,' she goes, picking up the phone. She presses some numbers, listens for a few seconds, then goes, 'Sorry, there's no answer.'

Oisinn's there 'You didn't dial a number. I watched you. You just touched the keys.'

All of a sudden, a voice behind us goes, 'I'll take it from here, Rebecca.'

We all turn around and there's a dude standing there. It ends up being Chris, the Manager of SMB Accounts. He goes, 'Can I help you gentlemen with something?'

He doesn't even recognize me.

I'm there, 'Er, Ross? As in, Ross O'Carroll-Kelly? I coached your tag rugby team – so-called.'

'Ah, yes,' he goes, 'I remember you now.'

'I focking hope so. It was, like, two weeks ago.'

'What can I do for you?'

'Yeah, no, we're looking for Magnus.'

'Which Magnus? We have a lot of Magnuses working here.'

I'm there, 'Over to you, Oisinn.'

'Laakso-Sigurjónsson,' Oisinn goes.

The dude just smiles at us. Perfect teeth. Not a hair out of place. He goes, 'I'm afraid Magnus is unavailable at the moment.'

'Unavailable?' Christian goes. 'What does that mean?'

He's there, 'It means he's not available,' and there's a definite change in his tone. 'Now can I ask you to leave? Or do I have to call someone?'

I'm staring at the security barrier, wondering could I jump over it? And if I did, how far would I get? Then I spot the Lego model of the Facebook building and I'm thinking, What if one of us shoved that over and smashed it into a million pieces just to create a distraction? Would that give me enough time to reach the lifts? And when I reach the lifts, would I need an access cord to choose a floor?

Like I said, once a ten . . .

'Come on,' Oisinn goes, flicking his head in the direction of the door, 'we don't want any trouble.'

So we all follow him outside, feeling a little bit deflated, to be honest. It's very unlike us to just give up like this. I say that to Oisinn as well as we're tipping down the steps.

'And just to let you know,' I go, 'I don't actually have a Plan B?'

He's like, 'I do,' because he always had a good tactical head on his shoulders himself. He stops walking and goes, 'I hope you goys have a head for heights.'

I follow his line of vision. He's staring at this window-cleaning – I want to say – rig that's porked on the ground floor a few feet away.

I laugh. I have no head for heights, but I'm just about pissed enough not to give a fock.

We all walk over to it. Fionn is lagging a few feet behind us, going, 'I really don't think this is a good idea.'

I'm there, 'Are you still in a snot over me shitting in your shoes?'

'I can't believe you're still doing that.'

'And I can't believe you're still leaving your shoes lying around when you know what I'm capable of.'

I jump into the thing first, followed by Oisinn, then JP and Christian. Then me and Oisinn just grab Fionn and drag him over the bor into it, while JP fiddles about with the controls to try to figure out how it works.

After a few seconds, the motor roars into life, then the rig sort of, like, lurches violently and we all end up nearly falling out of it.

'Here,' Christian goes, 'give me the controls. It needs someone with sensitive hands.'

In all my years playing rugby, I don't remember Christian ever knocking the ball on.

Suddenly, we stort moving slowly but steadily upwards. We're about ten feet off the ground when I stort to feel sick and I tell myself not to look down. Instead, I stare straight ahead into the actual building as Christian takes us up through the floors.

We literally have a window into the world of Facebook.

We're suddenly seeing men and women in preppy clothes having what looks like a pretty serious meeting while sitting cross-legged on the floor in a room with no furniture in it. We see a dude in a suit taking a call on his mobile phone while sitting in a tyre swing. We see a woman in a dentist's chair texting someone while one of her back teeth is being ripped from her head.

We see a lot of things that I can never *unsee*? And then we see Magnus. Or, actually, Oisinn does.

He goes, 'There he is! Christian, stop the rig!' and we come to a jolting stop.

He's standing very near the window, having a chat with Karim from Content Moderation (Happy Slappings, White Nationalism and Islamic State Executions).

Oisinn thumps the window with the side of his fist and Magnus turns to see us. We watch him mouth the words 'What'sh going on?' and then he walks over to the window.

He opens it. He's like, 'Guysh, what are you doing?'

And I'm there, 'We've come here to rescue you!' at the same time climbing in through the window.

I'm thinking this would make a cracking final scene in an actual romcom.

'Reshcue?' Magnus goes. 'I don't need to be reshcued!'

I'm there, 'Well, I say you do.'

The rest of the goys climb in through the window as well. We're talking Oisinn, then Christian, then JP, then Fionn.

'Oisinn,' Magnus goes, 'what do you hope to achieve by thish?'

Oisinn's there, 'I want to save my marriage. I want to save our marriage.'

But Magnus sort of, like, stares through him. He goes, 'I have a preshentation to make thish afternoon to the EMEA Regional Training Team, then I am partnering Karim from Content Moderation in the Facebook Inter-Departmental Piggy-Back Competition. We've jusht been going over our shtrategy.'

A look passes between me and Oisinn. And between Oisinn and Christian. And between Christian and Fionn. And between Fionn and JP. And between JP and me. That's all that's ever necessary between people who played rugby together.

I tackle Magnus around the waist and knock him to the ground. He goes down easily. I'm tempted to say like a typical soccer player. Then the other goys are straight on him. Me and Fionn each take an orm, and Christian and JP each take a leg, while Oisinn takes his swipe cord from around his neck.

Magnus is shouting, 'Guysh, no! Pleash! I have sho much work to do! Alsho, it ish Alan from Affiliate Referralsh Workavershary drinksh tonight!' but we run down the corridor with him while Oisinn uses his swipe cord to open any doors we encounter along the way.

We reach the lift and in we go. Oisinn hits the button for the ground floor. Magnus is still roaring, 'Pleash, guysh! Jusht take me back to my deshk!'

The lift doors open and we're suddenly running with him through the lobby. Various people stop and stare at us in shock. Then I notice Chris from SMB Accounts on the other side of the barrier. He's got his phone to his ear and my suspicion is that he's trying to alert security.

'Oisinn!' I go, trying to draw his attention to him.

And Oisinn's like, 'I'm on it, Dude!'

He throws me the swipe cord, then he leaps over the barrier and he tackles Chris from SMB Accounts – high, but who gives a fock? The dude hits the deck.

I open the barrier and we go through it, then through the lobby

and out onto Macken Street, where Oisinn – by some miracle of timing – manages to flag down a seven-seater taxi.

The driver doesn't seem to mind that we have a man in a head-lock who's begging to talk to his Operations Leader.

'Google?' the driver goes, like a man who's seen it all before.

Oisinn's like, 'Facebook.'

'Fuck Google!' Magnus manages to go. 'That'sh a fucking inshult!'

The driver's like, 'Where to, fellas?'

And Oisinn puts his hand over his husband's mouth and goes, 'Home.'

9.

Every Woman's Absolute Must-Have!

Honor rings me as I'm on the way to Little Cambridge to collect the boys. It's always lovely to hear her voice. I stick her on speaker phone and I go, 'Hey, Honor! Is everything okay?'

She goes, 'Why do you always say it like that?'

'Like what?'

'Like you think I might have done something wrong?'

'I find it's easier all round to just expect the worst, Honor. Then when it turns out to be nothing, it actually feels good. You'll be a parent yourself one day. I'm loving your and Erika's videos, by the way – although I still think me and you made a better double act. But that's just me being biased.'

'Dad, I need to talk to you about something.'

'Okay. Go ahead.'

'I've decided to stay in Australia.'

I end up nearly running a red light on Morlborough Road – that's how in shock I am?

I'm like, 'Say that again?'

She goes, 'Oh my God, I knew you'd overreact!'

'I haven't overreacted yet because I can't believe what I'm actually hearing. Why do you want to stay in Australia?'

'Because I love living with Erika and Helen. And we're about to relaunch Love Honor and Obey as an actual lifestyle brand. We're going to be doing, like, wellness summits. We're going to be doing, like, fashion factories, where we offer, like, styling sessions, skincare advice, tanning demos, then a fashion show, followed by afternoon tea and everyone goes home with a luxury goodie bag.'

'Yeah, no, it sounds definitely exciting, Honor.'

'Well, there's no point in me launching it and then suddenly leaving Australia, is there?'

'God, I don't know, Honor. What does Erika say?'

'Erika says I should talk to you. That's the reason I'm ringing. And I want an answer right now.'

'I can't give you an answer now, Honor. I'll have to talk to Sorcha.'

'Er, why?'

'Because she's your mother.'

'Erika's been more of a mother to me in the last two months than *she's* ever been.'

'Don't say things like that.'

'Er, she hasn't spoken to me since I left Ireland?'

'What? Is that true?'

'Yes, it's true. And, by the way, I know she refused to talk to me the last time I rang because I could hear her in the background.'

'The thing is, Honor, I don't want you to stay in Australia. The only thing that's got me through the last couple of months is the thought that you're coming back home at the end of August.'

She ends up totally losing it with me then.

She's like, 'Fock you! I knew you'd say no! You're worse than her! You focking orsehole! I focking hate you! Fock you!'

Then she hangs up on me.

My ears are still ringing when I pull up outside Little Cambridge. I pork the cor, then in I go to collect the boys. They look like they're having the time of their lives, by the way. Brian and Johnny are doing finger-painting – they're shit at it – and Leo is trying his hand at the piano – also shit – but the point is they're behaving themselves.

Jesus, Brian is even smiling!

I'm like, 'Come on, goys, let's hit the road,' and that's when Sasha appears and asks me if she can have a word.

I'm like, 'Is everything okay?'

She goes, 'Can we talk in private?'

And I'm there, 'Er, okay?' and I follow her into her office.

She shuts the door behind her.

I'm like, 'What did they do?' expecting her to tell me some story in which, I don't know, another kid lost an eye or worse.

She goes, 'They didn't do anything,' and she locks the door.

I'm there, 'So why am I here?'

'Because I want to ask you a question.'

'Okay.'

'When are you going to stop playing games with me?'

'Games with you?'

'Drop the little boy lost act, Ross. It doesn't suit you.'

She pushes me down onto a swivel chair, hitches up her skirt and sits – I want to say – astride me?

She's like, 'We both know this is going to happen. It's just a bit rude that you keep making me wait.'

Now, I've been around some corners in my life, but this is possibly the most lost for words I've ever been?

I'm there, 'Sasha, I hope I didn't give you the impression that –'

But before I can finish my sentence, she's thrown the lips on me. She kisses me for a good thirty seconds and – to be fair – I definitely respond a little bit before she pulls away.

I'm there, 'Sasha, I'm married.'

'Yeah,' she goes, 'to Sorcha focking Lalor. Do you know how much we all hated her in Holy Child Killiney?'

'Yeah, no, I've heard that from a few people over the years.'

'She used to put on that ridiculous Mary Robinson voice whenever she debated. And the stupid focking hand gestures.'

She kisses me again.

I'm there, 'I'm not a hundred percent sure that I should be doing this. You're also married?'

'Matthew's an asshole,' she goes, then she puts her hand between my legs and storts going at my understuff. 'Er, you don't seem to care as much as you're pretending to?'

I go, 'I can't do this. Seriously, Sasha. Me and Sorcha have only just got back together,' but at the same – me being me – I stort unbuttoning her blouse, then I pull up her bra.

'Of course it had to be Mount Anville,' she goes as I'm giving Bert and Ernie a bit of love. 'She was too good for Holy Child Killiney, even though it was only up the road.'

And it's her slagging off Sorcha that eventually brings me to my senses. I tell her to get off me, which she does. I go, 'I'm sorry, I can't do this. I know it's a word I hordly ever use – but it's, like, inappropriate?'

'Inappropriate?' she goes, red-faced, not happy. 'Seriously, do you know how long the waiting list is for this place?'

I'm there, 'Yeah, no, I've heard it's long alright.'

'Do you want me to give you the names of all the actual celebrities whose kids I've turned away? And I took three of yours. You must have known there was going to be a quid pro quo, Ross.'

I'm there, 'What are you saying?'

She walks over to the door and she opens it for me. She goes, 'I know you're famously slow on the uptake, Ross, so I'll spell it out for you. I'm giving you two weeks to think about it. Either have sex with me or you can find another Montessori for your boys. And let me tell you, Ross, that won't be an easy job.'

Sorcha says she can't believe what Sasha told her this afternoon. And I go, 'She's lying, Sorcha. Whatever she's claiming happened, it sounds like total horseshit to me.'

Sorcha just laughs. She's there, 'She paid me a compliment, Ross!'

'Sorry, I thought it was going to be . . . Okay, keep going, Sorcha.'

'She said that when I debated it always made her think of Mary Robinson! Isn't that – oh my God – such an amazing thing to say?'

'Yeah, no, it's definitely that alright.'

I've let Sorcha do the school run for the past week or so in the hope that Sasha's passion for me would somehow cool? But it obviously hasn't because I got a text message from her an hour ago saying that she had sex with Matthew last night and she thought about me the entire time they were doing it.

It's one of those ones where you don't know whether to delete it or save it.

Sorcha goes, 'She really is amazing, isn't she, Ross? Even though I still think she fancies you!'

I'm there, 'I've never seen any evidence of that. If it's true, she hides it very well.'

'Hey, you might not have noticed it, but girls pick up on these things. Not that I'm complaining!'

'What do you mean?'

'She's helping our children to discover their unique gifts, Ross – I don't care if it's because she fancies their dad!'

'Yeah, no, I was thinking about that, Sorcha. It's storting to look like they don't actually have any unique gifts? Maybe we should take them out of there and let three other kids have their place?'

'Sasha says she hasn't given up yet. And, anyway, look at the change in them since they storted going there.'

We're in the cor – I should have mentioned that – and Sorcha is driving. Yeah, no, I've agreed to go with her to a live taping of Muirgheal Massey TD's new feminist podcast in a room above The Glimmer Man in Stoneybatter.

I know, right? What the actual fock?

I'm there, 'I didn't think Muirgheal was a feminist anyway,' trying to subtly put her off the idea of going. 'I remember she said some horsh things about you when she was, like, deputy leader of my old man's porty. I wonder should we just go for a few drinks in town instead – and I'm saying that out of loyalty to you?'

'I think it's fine for people to change their minds on issues,' she goes. 'Politically, she's obviously matured. No offence, Ross, but I think the time she spent in New Republic opened her eyes to the way women in public life are treated. There's no doubt there was an element of sexism involved in her being dumped from the porty by your dad.'

My old man booted her out because she was plotting to take over the porty behind his back. Not that I'd ever defend him. All I'm doing is stating the facts.

I'm there, 'So are you two, like, bezzy mates again? I'll bring you back to all the shit she said about you.'

'She reached out to me by email,' Sorcha goes as she porks the cor – badly, as usual, even though I don't want to seem sexist. 'She said she had regrets about a lot of things that happened.'

I'm there, 'Doesn't sound like an actual apology.'

'Well,' she goes, 'I just thought, okay, I'm going back to the

Oireachtas in September. I'm going to be bumping into her all the time. And I remembered that thing that Hillary Clinton said – we are stronger together. So we agreed to bury the hatchet. And she invited me to her next live taping. She's actually interviewing Croía tonight!'

'Jesus Christ. We should have gone for pints first. Four sounds like a good number.'

Into The Glimmer Man, then up the stairs we go. We're late. It turns out that Sorcha got the time wrong and the thing has already storted. Muirgheal and Croía are sitting on two hord chairs at the top of the room and there's a crowd of, like, fifty or sixty people – all women – sitting there listening to them. Sorcha spots two empty chairs in the middle of the third row and we take them, apologizing to the people who have to move their legs slightly to let us past. There's a lot of tutting and eye-rolling going on.

Stronger together, my hole.

Croía is saying something about the white cisgender patriarchy and how they're basically all assholes and the entire audience claps. I sit down and look over my shoulder. I'm there, 'I wonder are they serving drinks up here?'

Sorcha shushes me. Actually, quite a few people shush me.

'I should probably tell you,' Muirgheal goes, 'that Croía and I know each other very well. She was, in a large way, responsible for awakening my own feminist consciousness and I'm proud to say that, in my capacity as a member of Dáil Éireann, she is an adviser to me on Women's Issues. Croía, tell us about this exciting new venture that you're involved in.'

'Thanks, Muirgheal. Yeah, so I've started a publishing company called Woke Reads. And what I'm planning to do – obviously crowd-funded – is to republish classic works of literature from a feminist perspective. And when I say a feminist perspective, I obviously mean with all the casual misogyny removed.'

Everyone laughs, then claps – even Sorcha. I suddenly feel very, very male.

Muirgheal goes, 'Because there is a lot of – let's be honest – sexism in these books, isn't there, even if it's too subtle for a lot of people to see it?'

'I mean, it storts with *Sleeping Beauty*,' Croía goes. 'A children's story, in which a woman is awoken from a coma by the uninvited sexual attentions of – surprise, surprise – a man of privilege. Let's set aside the highly offensive cisgender-white-male-as-rescuer trope for a minute and just focus on the message that this so-called fairytale sends out to young boys and girls on the issue of consent.'

Again, more clapping.

'I'm not saying I'm planning to rewrite *Sleeping Beauty*,' she goes. 'I think there are problems with it that are beyond fixing. I would just focking ban it.'

Muirgheal goes, 'So tell us which books you think could be made less offensive to women.'

'Well, *Jane Eyre* is the obvious one. Mister Rochester locks his wife away in the attic because of her mental health issues, yet Charlotte Brontë tries to persuade us that this man is some kind of romantic hero. Which is highly insulting to women. So in the version I'm planning to rewrite, it won't be, "Reader, I married him." It'll be, "Reader, I told him that his attitude towards mental illness made him a focking asshole and I discovered that it was preferable to be alone than to be married to a misogynist creep."'

The crowd love that.

'*Rebecca* would be another one,' she goes. 'A timid, weak-minded woman falls in love with a man who murdered his first wife because she refused to adhere to a set of man-made rules governing how women should act within a marriage? And don't even get me started on *Little Women!*'

Again, there's more laughter and more clapping. The interview eventually, thankfully, ends and Sorcha tips up to her two former mates to say hello and fair focks. I'm standing just behind her.

Sorcha air-kisses Muirgheal and tells her that was amazing. Then she turns to Croía and goes, 'Hi, Croía!' but Croía doesn't answer her – instead, she just stares at me.

'So it's true,' she goes. 'You took the asshole back.'

Sorcha's there, 'We're very happy, Croía.'

Croía goes, 'Your very own Maxim de Winter,' whatever the

fock that even means, then she finally hugs Sorcha and goes, 'How are you, beautiful?'

'I'm really, really good, Croía. That sounds like an amazing, amazing project you're working on. It's so needed.'

'How's your baby? A boy, wasn't it?'

'Yeah, we called him Hillary, after, obviously . . .'

She doesn't mention that I'm not the father. I'm being totally ignored, by the way?

'Muirgheal,' Sorcha goes, changing the subject, 'your podcast is also amazing. I've downloaded and listened to, like, nine of them already! They're great to listen to while driving the boys to and from Montessori!'

Muirgheal goes, 'Thanks, Sorcha. When are you coming back to the Seanad?'

'I'm thinking probably September.'

'That's good. Because we need strong women in both chambers right now. Especially if we're going to take on that sexist, racist –'

Muirgheal stops and looks at me.

I'm there, 'Hey, you can say his name. I hate my old man as much as the rest of you.'

'I doubt that,' Croía goes. 'I seriously focking doubt that.'

All of a sudden, someone walks up behind me and I hear them go, 'I really enjoyed that.'

And Croía goes, 'Thanks. I believe you've met my niece, Ross?'

I turn around and – yeah, no – it ends up being, hilariously, Huguette. I actually laugh in her face. I shouldn't, but I'm possibly cranky due to not having had a drink tonight. I'm there, 'How the hell are you, Huguette? I hope the clapping didn't upset you too much!'

She's pissed off, but she has no comeback, except, 'I thought this was supposed to be a safe space, Croía? Why have we let male energy into the room?'

I'm there, 'Sorcha, this is Huguette – do you remember I told you. She's Ronan's, er –'

'I'm not Ronan's anything,' the girl goes.

And I'm there, 'I know. I was going to say ex –'

I tell myself to shut the fock up.

'What I mean is,' she goes, 'I'm not defined by my relationships with anyone, especially men.'

That's weak. I let her know by pulling a face.

Then Croía decides to get involved. She goes, 'I hear your son is a misogynist wanker like you.'

I'm there, 'Excuse me?'

In fairness to her, Sorcha tries to defend Ronan's honour. She goes, 'He's actually a lovely, lovely goy, Croía.'

But Croía's there, 'When it comes to men, Sorcha – no disrespect – but you're a bit of a *Jane Eyre*-head.'

Huguette is clearly still hurt by Ronan dumping her orse because she goes, 'Only someone who really hates women would sleep with forty girls while still in their teens.'

I should keep my mouth shut. But I'm suddenly remembering what she did that day to poor Phinneas McPhee and how she basically destroyed a good man – albeit, St Michael's – just for sport. A voice in my head is just going, 'Don't say it, Ross! Don't say it, Ross! Don't say it, Ross!'

But, unfortunately, I do say it?

I go, 'I'm just delighted to hear that my son has moved on. Oh, I don't know if you know this, Huguette, but he rode your mate, Rachel.'

I walk into The Fumbally and I spot Oisinn and Magnus straight away. They wave at me across the floor, then they stand up – a nice touch – just as I reach their table. It ends up being hugs all round and I tell Magnus that he looks well. Which he does.

Or certainly better than he did.

He goes, 'I want to shay thank you again, Rosh, for helping to shave me.'

He means save. I've never shaved another man in my life and I don't intend on storting now.

I'm there, 'Don't mention it, Dude,' and I sit down opposite them. 'It's what friends do for each other.'

He's like, 'I totally losht it, Rosh. There ish no doubt about that.

It wash jusht the exshitement of working for a multi-nashional tech giant that really knowsh how to treat itsh shtaff well. I got totally shucked in.'

I'm there, 'It was like you'd joined a cult, wasn't it, Oisinn? Except one where you become really, really, really boring. And you're shit at rugby, by the way – even the tag kind.'

Oisinn laughs, in fairness to him.

Magnus goes, 'Well, you shaved me, Rosh. And I owe you for thish.'

And I'm there, 'Friends don't owe each other shit. But I am going to let you buy me lunch.'

They've just come back from the South of France, where a couple of weeks in the sun, sipping piña coladas, managed to fix the damage that working in Facebook did to his mind. Gaycation Ireland is reopening for business in a week's time and all is suddenly well with the world again – for them, anyway.

Oisinn goes, 'Seriously, Ross – thanks.'

I'm like, 'Dude, we're a team, aren't we? Father Fehily told us we'd always be a team. I know sometimes it seems like I'm the only one who remembers that – what with certain ex-teammates who shall remain nameless getting my wife pregnant – but it's still a fact.'

'Let'sh order shome food,' Magnus goes, trying to attract the attention of a passing waitress.

I'm there, 'I've heard good things about the pulled porchetta.'

And that's when my phone all of a sudden beeps. It's a text message and it's from Ronan. It just says, 'Need to talk to you Rosser.'

It's, like, three days later and I'm watching TV with the boys in their room. The door suddenly swings open and in walks Sorcha with Hillary in her orms. She goes, 'Oh! My God!'

And I'm like, 'What?' because it could be literally anything.

Bear in mind, I haven't even told her yet about Honor wanting to stay in Australia. But it's not that. It ends up being something totally random instead.

She goes, 'Have you been watching the news?'

I laugh – portly out of relief and portly at the idea of me watching the news. Even when Sharon Ní Bheoláin's reading it, I watch it on mute.

I'm there, 'Er, no, I haven't, Sorcha. What happened?'

She goes, 'Someone's leaked a load of emails – showing that Fianna Fáil are considering pulling out of their Confidence and Supply agreement with the Government!'

I must stort actually following what's going on in the world. It would mean I wouldn't have to keep pretending to understand what people are talking about half the time.

I'm there, 'That is a real bummer, Sorcha. That has seriously, seriously bummed me out now.'

She's there, 'Do you know what this means?'

'Being honest, Sorcha, no.'

'Leo Varadkar said he considers it a major breach of trust. Oh my God, thousands of Micheál Mortin's emails have been dumped onto the internet. In one of them, he calls Varadkar smug, arrogant and smormy.'

'Yeah, he went to King's Hos, Sorcha. This is news to absolutely no one.'

'There could end up being a General Election! Oh my God, I wonder who hacked his account?'

'That'd be my old man.'

'What?'

'Yeah, no, I was in Hennessy's office a few months ago and the old man was reading Leo Varadkar's emails. And your mate Coveney's.'

Yeah, no, Sorcha loves Simon Coveney – she's always had a weakness for a strong jaw – and has a folder on her laptop full of pictures of the dude, which she thinks I don't know about.

Sorcha goes, 'Oh! My God, Ross! Are you actually serious?'

I'm there, 'Yeah, no, it was that Russian mate of his who did it. I heard him saying he'd hacked the email accounts of everyone in the Dáil.'

'And do you know did he hack the emails of Seanad members as well?'

What would be the point? I don't want to say it to her face but I'm thinking, What would be the actual point?

I go, 'Er, I didn't hear the Seanad specifically mentioned, Babes. I think yours might be safe.'

She's like, 'Oh my God, Ross, why didn't you tell me about this?'

'You know me, Sorcha. I'm not really interested in current affairs. Plus, you were on your holliers.'

'Holliers? I'm on maternity leave, Ross!'

'Exactly. And you didn't want to be thinking about work.'

'This isn't work. Ross, this is an attack on our actual democracy!'

'Is it?'

'Yes!'

'Well, I genuinely didn't realize that. I've had a lot of other shit on my mind. So what are you going to do about it?'

'I don't know.'

'As in, you don't have actual proof?'

'Oh my God, I don't need actual proof if I say it under Oireachtas privilege. Oh, hang on . . .'

'What?'

'The summer recess storted yesterday. The next sitting is in September. Ross, you should have told me about this!'

She storms off.

I'm thinking about tipping downstairs to grab a stick of Heine-mite from the fridge when my phone all of a sudden rings. It's Ronan's number. I'm thinking, Oh, fock!

What I wouldn't do for just one simple day.

I decide to just bite the bullet. I answer it by going, 'Ro, how the hell are you?' deciding to just front it out and deny everything.

He's there, 'She knows, Rosser.'

I'm there, 'Knows? As in?'

'Huguette. She knows about me and Racher Doddle.'

'What makes you think that?'

'Ine arthur been cheerged by the Students' Youn Yodden wirrer a rashidilly motivated act.'

'Racially motivated? As in, like, racism?'

'She's arthur going troo me Facebuke, Rosser. She's arthur thrawling back troo me feeyut – tree or foe-ur yee-ors ob it – look-ing for sometin odden me.'

'And?'

'She fowunt a video I sheered tree year ago.'

'What kind of video are we talking?'

'It was Nudger what took it. He fillumed these tree Muslim wooben.'

'Muslim women? Are we even allowed to say that?'

'He saw them in the Ilac Centodder. Thee had the fuddle hajeeb on – all tree of them. Alls you could see of addy of them was their eyes. One of them took a pitcher of the utter two . . .'

'Okay, I think I know where this is going.'

'Then one of the wooben in the pitcher says, "Hee-or, I'll take wood of you two now."'

'Even though the second picture was going to look the exact same as the first one?'

'It was a fuddy video, Rosser. I joost liked it, then sheered it.'

'I'm not surprised. I'm cracking up laughing here.'

'Huguette's not, but. She says it's racist.'

'And you think she's only doing this just to get you back for riding her mate?'

'Why edelse would she do it, Rosser?'

'How would she have found out, though?'

'Racher Doddle moost have toawult her.'

'They can't hold their piss, can they, women? Much as I love them.'

'I've been throying her mobile, but there's no ansodder.'

'Probably wise not to dig too deep into it. Just accept what's happened and get on with your life, Ro.'

'I caddent joost gerron wit me life, Rosser. Ine godda hab to face the same crowut as Phiddeas when I go back in September. Except I caddent go back now.'

'What do you mean?'

'I've no utter choice. Ine godda hab to throp ourra coddidge.'

Oh, fock. I'm suddenly blaming myself – which is me all over, of course – and I feel this sudden, unbelievable urge to come clean.

I'm there, 'Look, Ro, Rachel – or Racher Doddle – didn't tell Huguette about you two.'

He's like, 'Soddy?'

'Okay, one night last week, Sorcha dragged me along to this feminist podcast live taping. I don't know what she was thinking bringing me somewhere like that.'

He doesn't respond. He clearly wants more.

'Okay,' I go, 'while I was there, I ran into Huguette and let's just say that words were exchanged.'

He's there, 'It was you, Rosser! It was you opent yisser bleaten mowt.'

I'm there, 'My biggest regret of that night, Ro, was not having a few pints before we went in there.'

But he's not ready to see things from my POV.

He goes, 'I should nebber hab listened to you, Rosser. If I'd nebber of listened to you, I'd be a happy madden today.'

'I want to go to school!' Brian goes.

He literally says that. If I was a suspicious man, I'd be wondering is he one of Fionn's as well?

I'm there, 'It's, er, closed today, boys. It's a holy day of obbledy-gobbledy.'

Which it's not, of course. It's, like, a regular Monday morning, but I can't bring the boys to Little Cambridge because the two-week ultimatum that Sasha gave me is up.

She ends up texting me when I don't show up with them. She's like, 'U avoiding me?'

And I text back, going, 'Sory the boys r a bit sick this am, both ends, blah blah blah.'

And then she texts me back and it's like, 'Remember our conversation, don't come back here again unless the answer's yes.'

'Daddy,' Leo goes, 'why is the sky so low?'

And I'm like, 'It's because we're in Finglas, Leo. We're going to visit your brother Ronan.'

Five minutes later, I'm knocking on the door of Tina's gaff. She answers. Still in her dressing gown. Ten o'clock in the morning. This time there's no comment from me. I'm just laying out the facts for others to draw their own conclusions.

I'm there, 'Hey, Tina, is he here?'

'No,' she goes, 'he's not hee-or. Ine presuming he's gone back howum.'

I'm like, 'What? Are you saying he's back with Shadden?'

'All's I know is he toalt me last neet that taking relashiddenship advice from he's fadder was the woorst mistake he ebber made in he's life. Then I came from work this morden and all he's clowuts was gone ourra the warthrobe.'

'Fock.'

I jump back in the cor and I point it in the direction of his gaff.

Five minutes later, I'm banging on his door – literally, because there's no actual knocker. The letter box has been blocked up to stop the local kids putting bangers through it.

Shadden answers. I can't say whether she's wearing day clothes or night clothes because around here it's not always easy to tell. I don't bring it up with her.

I just go, 'Where's Ro?'

She's like, 'He dudn't wanth to thalk to you, Rosser.'

I'm there, 'Don't give me that,' and I push past her into the gaff. 'He's my son.'

Ronan's sitting at the kitchen table, finishing his breakfast – yeah, no, he's stubbing it into the ashtray when I walk into the kitchen. We look at each other through a fog of John Player Blue smoke. He doesn't say shit. I suddenly spot what I think is Rihanna-Brogan sitting next to him. Like I said, it's pretty hord to see anything.

She goes, 'Hi, Rosser!'

And I'm like, 'Hey, Rihanna-Brogan – how the hell are you?'

Ronan's there, 'Rihatta-Barrogan, lub, why doatunt you go up to yizzer roowum and watch a birra teddy while I thalk to me auld fedda?'

She goes, 'Okay, Dad. Mustard,' and then off she focks.

I'm there, 'Ro, look, I'm sorry for sort of accidentally landing you in it.'

He's there, 'You ditn't sort ob accidentoddy land me in it, Rosser. You opent your bleaten mowt and sold me down the ribber.'

'Down the –'

'Ribber.'

'Got it. River.'

'And now I caddent go back to coddidge in Septembor cos I'd hab to face one of Huguette's heardons.'

'You won't, Ro. I'll fix it.'

'You've dud enough, Rosser.'

'Leave it to me. Just promise me you won't do anything stupid in the meantime. Like getting back with Shadden. I couldn't live with myself if I thought I'd done something to push you back into the orms of her and her scumbag family. No offence, Shadden.'

Shadden just glowers at me. It reminds me of the look Sorcha gave me once when I let another girl's name slip while we were having sex. It's, like, pure hatred.

I'm there, 'I'm just making the point that he can do better.'

Ronan goes, 'Gerrout, Rosser.'

'Just guarantee me that you won't do anything rash until I at least try to fix this thing?'

But he just roars at me then. He's like, 'I said gerrout!'

So I end up leaving. I tip back to the cor and get the fock out of the old Costa del Fingal as fast my Goodyears can carry me.

Despite my promise to fix the mess that – let's be honest here – I helped create, I haven't a clue what I'm going to do next. I get back onto the M50 and I drive as far as Dundrum Town Centre. I pull into the cor pork.

'Daddy,' Johnny goes, 'can we go to McDonald's?'

And I'm like, 'Yeah, just give me a second, Johnny,' because an idea is suddenly forming in my mind.

I whip out my phone and I ring Joe Schmidt's number, then I leave the phone on the seat beside me. A second or two later, I hear him answer. He's like, 'Helloy? HELLOY?'

And I'm there, 'So what are you going to have in McDonald's, goys?'

And they're all like, 'Big Mac! Quarter Pounder! Nuggets!'

And in the background I can still hear Joe going, 'HELLOY? HELLOY?'

I'm like, 'Who's that? Can anyone else hear that? Hang on, I think it's my phone.'

I pick it up. I'm like, 'Hello? Who's this?'

He goes, 'Ut's Joe Schmudt – yoy rang moy, Moyte.'

'Sorry, Dude. I must have accidentally orse-dialled you.'

'Not a problem – goodboy.'

I'm like, 'Wait! Don't hang up! This is Ross O'Carroll-Kelly!'

He goes, 'Whoy?'

Seriously? And they say this man has a memory like focking Santa Claus?

I'm there, 'Ross O'Carroll-Kelly? As in, my daughter wrote you a letter and then sent you my famous Rugby Tactics Book, which I wouldn't mind getting back at some stage?'

'Oy've just funished royding ut,' he goes.

I'm like, 'What?'

'Yeah, Oy oynloy flucked throy ut before. But Oy've just had a chince to royd ut from cover to cover.'

He sort of, like, chuckles to himself then. He goes, 'Yoy've roy-loy got ut un for Warren Gitland, doyn't yoy?'

I'm there, 'Does that come across?'

'Just a little! Some of the comments yoy've wrutten abaaht hum un the maahgins!'

'Yeah, no, there's history there.'

'Yoy've wrutten something abaaht hum on pretty much evroy poyge.'

'The mad thing is, Joe, if he walked into Kielys tonight, I'd be the first one buying him a drink. I'm tempted to say that's rugby.'

'Oy was looking at what yoy wroyte before the England mitch. When we lost Joymoy Hoyslup, yoy rickoned Oy should've put Poyter O'Mihony in ut number oyt?'

'I just thought he could do a lot of damage if you played him there.'

'Well, thit's what Oy dud doy.'

'I know. For me, he was man of the match.'

'Un a lot of woys, yoy and Oy thunk very similarloy abaaht the goym.'

317

'Jesus Christ,' I go – and I can hear my voice crack.

He's there, 'Not abaaht Warren, thoy. Oy'm very fond of the goy.'

'Just to let you know, you've just literally made my life by saying what you said to me a second ago.'

'Moyd your loyf? What doy yoy moyn?'

'Doesn't matter. Look, Joe, can I admit something to you?'

'Yeah, what us ut?'

'Do you remember I told you I was coaching a team? I was talking shit. It was actually a tag rugby team I was coaching.'

'Teg rugboy?'

'You don't have to say it, Dude, I already know. Don't worry, though, I quit after one match. I have another confession to make. I didn't accidentally orse-dial you just now. I rang you on purpose.'

'Okoy. Whoy?'

'I don't know. You're just so, like, wise or something. You're like Father Fehily, Mister Miyagi and Yoda all rolled into one.'

He laughs. He seems to find me funny even though he can't remember my name ten seconds after he last spoke to me.

I'm there, 'The thing is, Dude, my life is a bit all over the place at the moment and I just like hearing your voice. That's not me being weird. I just find it very soothing.'

He chuckles at this. Then he says the most incredible thing. He goes, 'Loyfe us loyk rugboy un a lot of woys, Ross. Ut's just a seeroys of moyves, all of them connicted. Toyk keer of yoursilf, Moyte.'

Then he hangs up on me.

I'm sitting there in the cor thinking about what he said. Life is a series of moves. And suddenly – just like that – the answer comes to me. I know exactly what I'm going to do. And I'm going to do it right after I take the boys to McDonald's.

Sorcha is in the Shomera when we arrive home, still gabbing away with her old man. When he sees me, he goes, 'Oh, there he is! You must be very proud of your father, are you?'

There's things I could say but I choose not to.

Sorcha's there, 'More emails have been leaked this morning, Ross. It turns out that Leo Varadkar was also thinking about pulling out of the Confidence and Supply agreement. He said Micheál Mortin has a chip on his shoulder because he got an average Leaving Cert, which is how he ended becoming a school teacher and not studying Medicine in Trinity like him. Micheál Mortin has issued a statement saying he actually got a reasonably good Leaving Certificate, but now Simon Coveney has challenged him to produce his results. The Fianna Fáil porliamentary porty are meeting tonight, Ross! They've all been told to return from their holidays!'

'There's still time to stop it.'

'Dad thinks I should request a return of the Seanad, then make a personal statement under Oireachtas privilege detailing how your dad has been colluding with Russian interests to undermine our democracy and make himself Taoiseach.'

'It'll sound better coming from me, Sorcha.'

Her old man laughs. 'Of course it will!' he goes. 'The man who heard his father talking openly about reading the private emails of members of the Cabinet and the opposition front bench and didn't think to mention it to a soul!'

Sorcha goes, 'Dad, can we just hear what Ross has to say? He's still an actual witness, even though he didn't really understand what was going on.'

I'm there, 'Thanks, Sorcha. What I was going to suggest was that I make the statement?'

'How can you, Ross? You're not a member of Seanad Éireann!'

She still thinks that's something to brag about. She definitely slipped into the Mary Robinson voice when she said it as well.

'Yeah, no,' I go, 'I was going to make the statement to Muirgheal. On her feminist podcast.'

Sorcha's there, 'Oh my God, Muirgheal hates Chorles!'

Hey, I'm not too wild about him any more either. And this is my chance to settle a lot of scores. Him and the old dear having a rake of kids to try to replace me. That shit he said about wanting a son who played rugby for Ireland. Him and his Russian mates burning down Erika's gallery and driving her away to Australia.

Yeah, no, he's had it coming ever since he put that stupid wig on his head. It's time that someone destroyed him once and for all.

I'm like, 'It'll definitely mean more coming from me, Sorcha.'

But her old man goes, 'I still think you should request that the Seanad be recalled. This is the kind of watershed moment in our history that you want to be associated with, Dorling.'

But Sorcha goes, 'They're not going to recall the Seanad, Dad, just because one of Enda Kenny's nominees wants to say something. They're all getting ready for a General Election.'

I'm there, 'Ignore him, Sorcha. We're wasting time here. Let's go and find Muirgheal. Come on, I've got the boys in the cor.'

She's like, 'In the cor? Why aren't they in Montessori?'

'Yeah, no, let's deal with one problem at a time, will we?'

Ten minutes later, we're in the cor and we're heading for town. Sorcha manages to get Muirgheal on the phone. She's having lunch – happy focking days – with Croía in the Pig's Ear on Nassau Street. We throw the cor into Merrion Square, then we run all the way there – Sorcha carrying Johnny, me carrying Leo and Brian.

Up the stairs we go, then over to the table where the two of them are sitting.

'Eugh!' Croía goes when she sees me and the boys. 'I suddenly can't taste my Pot Roast Cauliflower for the overwhelming stench of testosterone in here.'

Sorcha's there, 'Please, Croía! Believe it or not, Ross has something to say that's actually in the national interest?'

Yeah, no, it's a definite first, I admit.

'Let me guess,' Croía goes, 'is it the names of more girls his ass-hole son slept with behind my niece's back?'

'My old man hacked Leo Varadkar's emails,' I go. 'And Micheál Mortin's. And basically everyone else's in the Dáil.'

Oh, that rocks them back on their heels.

'He doesn't know about the Seanad,' Sorcha goes.

I do, though. I think, deep down, we all know.

Muirgheal goes, 'How do you know about this?'

I'm there, 'Because I was there in his office when he was talking about it. He's got some dude working for him called Fyodor, although it's his bosses in Russia who are pulling the old man's strings.'

320

'Russia?'

'Yeah, no, he's got all these dodgy business interests over there. It's all connected to this, like, foundation that my old dear set up – so-called.'

'Erika was looking into it,' Sorcha goes, 'before she went to Australia. She said he was basically pre-selling all of Ireland's natural resources in expectation of becoming Taoiseach one day. And they were using Fionnuala's foundation as a front to launder the money.'

That definitely shocks Muirgheal. She goes, 'Sorcha, why didn't you bring this up in the Seanad?'

Sorcha's there, 'Yeah, I was actually on maternity leave, Muirgheal? Plus, I didn't think he was ever going to be the Taoiseach.'

Croía goes, 'We can't let that misogynist asshole become the leader of the country.'

I'm like, 'None taken.'

Sorcha's there, 'Ross is prepared to go on the record about what his dad has been doing, Muirgheal – if you want to interview him for your podcast?'

Muirgheal's face lights up. And why wouldn't it?

'Oh my God,' she goes, 'this is a chance to finish Charles O'Carroll-Kelly off once and for all.'

And that's when Croía suddenly reads the look on my face. 'He wants something,' she goes. 'Something in return.'

No one ever said Croía was stupid. Just focking irritating.

I'm there, 'It's quite small, you'll be happy to hear. I'll give you the goods on my old man – everything you need to bring him down – but first, Croía, you need to call off Huguette.'

Croía goes, 'What do you mean by call her off?'

'You know what I'm talking about. She's put the Students' Union on Ronan's case for sharing some video on Facebook that was hilarious but also supposedly racist. He's been chorged.'

Croía smiles. You can see that she admires her niece – probably reminds her a lot of herself.

'I'll talk to her,' she goes. 'I'll get her to drop the chorges.'

I turn around to Muirgheal. 'Okay,' I go, 'you've got yourself an interview.'

Sorcha goes, 'Ross, I'll drive the boys home. I might actually ring Erika later on to find out what else she remembers. I think she said your dad was selling off Ireland's gas, petroleum and peat reserves, as well as our forests.'

And I'm like, 'Yeah, no, you go and do that. And I'll see you later, Babes.'

At the mention of the B word, I can see that Croía wants to stick her thumbs in my eyes.

I'm there, 'Okay, Muirgheal, let's do this interview. I've got a lot of shit to get off my chest.'

Muirgheal books a room in Buswells on Molesworth Street. The interview lasts for four hours and she barely gets a word in edgeways except when I stray off-topic.

'Why do you always end up talking about your mother?' she goes. 'I don't give a fock if she was cold and withholding when you were a child. It's Charles I'm interested in.'

So I tell her everything. About how the old man has all these dodgy Russian interests who want to buy up our – quoting Sorcha – natural resources. About the – again – Russian dudes working out of Hennessy's building and how I overheard them talking about hacking the email accounts of everyone in the Dáil. I mention the Seanad as well – just to throw Sorcha a bone. I mention my old dear's trips to Russia and her supposedly charitable foundation and how it's apparently dodgy as fock. I mention my sister, Erika, and how she found out a lot of this shit but all the evidence she gathered was stolen and her ort gallery was mysteriously burned to the ground.

I mention the six women that my old pair are using as hosts for their babies and the way the old dear treats them. I mention all the plastic surgeries she's had, how much she drinks in an average morning and how the plots for her books were all ripped off from other writers.

It's, like, seven o'clock in the evening when I finish and I'm absolutely wrecked from talking.

Muirgheal thanks me. 'Weird as it sounds,' she goes, 'I think you've actually done an amazing thing for the country today.'

Which is why I decide that I deserve a drink. I grab a cheeky pint –
two, if I'm being totally honest? – in Café en Seine. And while I'm
finishing the second, I leave Ronan a voice message telling him that
I've fixed everything. He won't be having any trouble from Huguette
in September. I tell him he should maybe think about getting the
fock out of that house before Shadden gets her claws back into him.

Of course, then I realize that I left the message on Shadden's
actual phone – I must have been thinking about her when I went
into my phonebook – but I think, Fock it, she already knows how I
feel about her family. I'll ring him in the morning and have a proper
chat with him.

I grab a taxi and I tell the driver Killiney. I'm in much better
form, it has to be said, so much so that I end up actually chatting to
the driver, which ends up being a massive, massive mistake. He
says he's got nothing against women or people from Cork, but that
Charles O'Carroll-Kelly says things that we all secretly think but
are too scared to say any more.

We're on Ballinclea Road when I suddenly have an idea.

'Change of plan,' I go. 'Drop me at the top of Albert Road instead,'
which he does.

I get out, then I whip out my phone and I call up Sasha's number.
She answers on the third ring.

She's like, 'Ross?'

I'm there, 'I need to talk to you.'

'So talk.'

'I mean in person. I'm on Albert Road. What number are you?'

She tells me the exact gaff. Sixty seconds later, she's opening the
door to me, a glass of white wine in her hand. On a Monday night.
Hey, I know I'm one to talk, being two pints down the road to
Sloshington DC.

I'm there, 'I need to talk to you.'

She goes, 'Do you want to come in?'

'What about what's-his-name – as in, your husband?'

'Matthew's taken the kids to Bits and Pizzas in Dún Laoghaire,'
she goes, opening the door wider to invite me in. 'They won't be
back for another half an hour.'

I think, half an hour? Okay. So in I go. It's a nice gaff. Sasha is obviously a bit of a neat freak because there's, like, literally nothing out of place?

'How are the boys?' she goes.

I'm like, 'They're great. They miss you, though. They miss Little Cambridge.'

'Well, you know how to fix that, Ross.'

'I came here tonight to try to appeal to your better nature.'

'Seriously?' she goes, dubious. 'That's why you're here?'

I'm like, 'Please, Sasha, hear me out here. Look, I really appreciate what you've done for the boys. Me and Sorcha do. I mean, they've genuinely changed. They're not violent any more. And they've stopped effing and blinding every second word.'

'I know. It's such a pity that I'm going to have to give their places away to three other children.'

'I'm here to beg you not to do that.'

'Beg me? You don't have to beg me! You just have to have sex with me!'

'I'm not going to do that. Like I told you that day in your office when you kissed me —'

'You mean the day when you kissed me back, unbuttoned my shirt and fondled my breasts?'

'Okay, that day, yeah. I told you that nothing was going to happen between us and I meant it. I'm married, Sasha. And, while that might not have meant a whole heap to me in the past, me and Sorcha have very much clicked recently. And it's made me think that I'm finally capable of being hopefully loyal to the girl.'

'You know what's hilarious?' she goes, pouring herself another glass of wine. 'You almost sound like you actually mean it.'

I'm there, 'Yeah, no, that's because I do mean it.'

'And yet when I mentioned that Matthew wouldn't be back for half an hour, I could see you doing the calculations in your head.'

'No, I wasn't.'

'You were thinking would that be enough time for us to do it?'

'That's habit more than anything.'

'Because you still get off on that thrill, Ross. The danger excites you. It's like the night of my debs when I came back in from having a cigarette outside and I was nearly sure you'd just been getting off with my friend, Amanda.'

'I never got off with your friend, Amanda.'

I did get off with her friend, Amanda.

She goes, 'I could taste Malibu on your mouth.'

I'm there, 'I didn't get off with her, Sasha. May God strike my mother down dead if I'm lying.'

She smiles. She doesn't believe me. She takes a sip of her wine. She goes, 'So what did your brain tell you, Ross? Half an hour? Would it be enough time to do the deed?'

And – yeah, no – I'm suddenly having visions of the two of us going at it, we're talking angry, clear-the-air sex, me with my chinos around my ankles, Sasha sitting on the kitchen table with her legs wrapped around my orse and her nails dug into the back of my neck, me catching an ugly reflection of my face in that photograph of Matthew and his mates having just completed the Camino de Santiago, my two eyes turned outwards, my tongue flapping about like a focked roller blind, while Sasha, between thrusts, curses Sorcha for choosing to go to school in Goatstown despite living so close to Military Road.

'Stop it!' I suddenly shout because I'm getting definitely turned on here and she knows it. 'Just stop it, okay?'

'Stop what?' she goes. 'You're the one who's standing in my kitchen with an erection.'

But then the most surprising thing of all ends up happening. I turn around and I head for the door. She can't actually believe it. For what it's worth, I can't either.

She goes, 'Seriously? You're turning me down again?'

I'm there, 'Like I said, my cheating days are over, Sasha. I'm ready to be finally faithful to Sorcha.'

'What,' she goes, 'the girl who got her daddy to drive her half an hour to school every day because she was too good for Holy Child Killiney?'

God, it really is an issue for her.

I'm there, 'I love her, Sasha. She's my wife. And I know you have a problem with her – and obviously a thing for me – but I'm asking you please don't take it out on my kids. Especially when they've made so much – I want to say – progress?'

She looks at me coldly, then goes, 'I don't want to see those boys anywhere near Little Cambridge again.'

I'm like, 'You don't mean that.'

'Ross,' she goes, 'your children are idiots.'

And I'm there, 'What? I thought you said they were possibly gifted?'

And she laughs in a really, like, cruel way?

'They're not gifted!' she goes. 'That's just something we say because we know how much parents love to hear it.'

I'm there, 'But the change I've seen in them since they storted going to you. They've stopped swearing and being violent.'

'I'll tell you my secret, will I? I just shouted at them.'

'You did what?'

'I just shouted at them: "Stop swearing! And stop fighting!" And they did. All they needed was a firm voice to tell them what was acceptable behaviour and what was unacceptable. But, beyond that, there's nothing more I can do for them. They're not good at any-thing, Ross.'

'They must be good at something.'

'Trust me, they're not. They're not good at music. They're not good at ort. They're not good at problem-solving. They're three of the stupidest children I've ever had the misfortune to teach. And, unfortunately for you, I don't want them dragging down the edu-cational standard of the rest of the class.'

'Yeah, no, you're just lashing out now. I thought you said that all kids were gifted?'

'Not yours. Now get out of my house. I never want to see you or those idiot boys of yours again.'

I walk up to the roundabout at the top of the road, then I whip out my phone, the plan being to Hailo another cab. But I see that I've got two missed calls from Muirgheal, so I ring her back straight away.

She goes, 'I've been trying to get Sorcha on the phone but she's not answering.'

I'm there, 'Is everything okay?' at the same time managing to wave down a taxi that happens to be passing.

I hop into the back of it.

'I'm not going to use the interview,' she goes.

I'm like, 'Vico Road, Dude. Sorry, Muirgheal, say that again?'

She's there, 'I've decided not to podcast the interview I did with you tonight.'

'Is it because I kept crying when I was talking about my old dear? Because you said you could edit those bits out.'

'It has nothing to do with the crying. I had a chat with Croía tonight. I told you she's advising me on Women's Issues.'

'And?'

'She thinks we should just let the Government fall.'

'Let it fall? Do you mind me asking why?'

'To let people see how utterly focking useless our male politicians are. To let them see how the likes of Leo Varadkar and Micheál Mortin are prepared to put their egos ahead of the challenges facing our country. If there ends up being a General Election, Croía thinks there'll be a massive swing towards women candidates.'

'But what if my old man ends up winning?'

'Oh, don't worry, we've got something planned for him that's way better than exposing him for hacking the email accounts of everyone in the Dáil. And the Seanad.'

'Only one of those was absolutely definite, by the way. What about Ronan – do you know does that deal still stand?'

She goes, 'Don't know, don't care. That's between you and Croía's niece. I'm sorry, I have to go,' and she just hangs up on me.

I'm thinking, Oh, fock it.

I arrive home a few minutes later. The second I open the front door, I can hear Sorcha sobbing. I'm wondering, do I even want to know what this is about? I follow the sound to the kitchen. She's sitting at the table with Fionn and her old pair.

I honestly haven't seen her this upset since, well, the last time she was this upset.

I'm there, 'Is this about Honor not wanting to come home from Australia? Because if you're wondering why I didn't tell you . . .'

But something very random happens then. Sorcha gets up from the table and runs towards me, going, 'I'm so sorry, Ross! Oh my God, I am so, so sorry!'

And she throws her orms around me.

I'm like, 'Sorry?' and I look at the others. 'What the fock is going on?'

I reach behind me and I tear off a piece of kitchen roll and give it to Sorcha to dry her eyes.

I'm there, 'Seriously? What's the Jack?'

'I rang Erika,' she goes. 'She told me something about Honor.'

I'm there, 'Yeah, no, I'm trying not to take it personally, Sorcha. It's just she doesn't want to have to come home just as her Fashion Factories and her Wellness Summits are taking off.'

Sorcha goes, 'She had her first period, Ross.'

Jesus Christ. Okay, that's not something I was expecting. Or something I'm interested in discussing.

I'm there, 'Did you see Leinster got Montpellier and the Exeter Chiefs in the Heineken Cup draw, Fionn? I'd be happy enough with that.'

Sorcha goes, 'It happened that night, Ross. Do you remember we were watching *Jerry Maguire* in the cor? She asked you to put me on the phone but I didn't want to speak to her? In the end, she had to go and talk to Erika about it.'

'I presume she gave her – I'm sorry, I feel a bit icky saying this – but whatever she needed.'

'You don't understand, Ross. I've missed one of the most seminal moments in the life of my only daughter. She's transitioned from childhood into womanhood – and I wasn't there to talk her through the changes happening to her body.'

'Munster got Racing and Castres, by the way – good enough for the fockers!'

'And it's all my fault, Ross. It's all my fault for sending her away.'

Sorcha's old man goes, 'Dorling, I would think very, very carefully about what you say next.'

And suddenly I'm getting the feeling that something massive has happened and I'm the last person to know about it.

I'm there, 'Is someone going to tell me what the fock is going on?'

'We accused her in the wrong,' Sorcha goes. 'She wasn't poisoning Hillary at all.'

There's, like, silence then. I'm in, like, shock. Sorcha storts sobbing again to the point where she can't actually talk, so Fionn ends up having to pick up the story.

'I was walking past your bedroom,' he goes. 'Hillary was in his bassinet, sleeping. The boys were in the room with him. And they were –'

I'm like, 'What?'

He goes, 'They were dipping his soother into the toilet, Ross, then giving it to him to suck. And we think that's what was making him sick.'

I'm there, 'So you're saying it wasn't actually Honor?'

He goes, 'No, it wasn't Honor.'

'And presumably she didn't take the batteries out of the baby monitor either?'

He can't even look me in the eye. He goes, 'No. I watched them do that as well. They took them out to put them into –'

'Pirate Pete – the Repeat Parrot.'

'Yeah.'

I find myself getting suddenly angry. I'm there, 'How long have you all known about this?'

Sorcha goes, 'A few months.'

I'm like, 'A few *months?*'

'Since just after Honor left.'

Something suddenly occurs to me. I let go of Sorcha and I take a step backwards. I'm there, 'So that morning, when you said Fionn had gone to the –'

'The Irish Emigrant Museum,' she goes. 'I panicked, Ross. I just said the first thing that came into my head.'

Fionn's there, 'We took Hillary to the hospital. He was vomiting. But they gave him fluids and then he was fine. I stayed with him while they kept him under observation for a few hours –'

'And I came home,' Sorcha goes, 'to look after the boys. But Mom and Dad ended up taking them to the pork because I was so angry with them in the moment. I was genuinely scared of what I might do.'

I'm there, 'You basically seduced me. I mean, that was the day you finally decided to let me have sex with you. So what was it – a sympathy ride?'

Sorcha's old man goes, 'Do we have to listen to him talk like that?'

'It wasn't a sympathy ride!' Sorcha tries to go. 'You have to believe me, Ross! It wasn't a sympathy ride!'

'So you've all known about this,' I go, 'for the entire summer? And Honor's been in Australia that entire time, knowing her family were on the other side of the world thinking the worst possible thing about her – that she would try to hurt a defenceless little baby? And you had no intention of telling her that you accused her in the wrong?'

Sorcha's old dear decides to have her say then. She goes, 'Oh, come on, she's hordly an innocent. Fine, she didn't do that but she did plenty of other things. Am I the only one who remembers the way she spoke to that poor bishop?'

'For God's sake,' Sorcha's old man goes, 'she was looking for ways to poison us, Sorcha! Your mother and I! She admitted as much herself!'

I'm just staring at the dude. It's funny the things that pop into your head at, like, random moments. I'm suddenly remembering him that day at the Aviva when he asked that question about throwing the ball forwards in front of poor Slats. I'm remembering he was wearing a scorf that was half Ireland and half South Africa, like the focking day-tripper that he was. And his focking opera glasses.

And I realize that the reason I'm suddenly thinking about it is because I want to kill him now as much as I did that day.

Fionn is trying to make them all feel better about what they did, of course. He goes, 'Look, I feel just as guilty about it as you do, Sorcha. But Honor wanted to go to Australia. She actually asked if she could go.'

I'm there, 'But *I* didn't want her to go!' and I shout it at the top of my voice. 'Sorcha didn't want her to go. We only agreed to let her go because you were threatening to apply for custody of Hillary.'

Sorcha closes her eyes. She has tears spilling down her face. She goes, 'I did want her to go, Ross. And, yes, I am ashamed to say it because that probably makes me a bad mother. But after the way she embarrassed us at the Confirmation, I couldn't bring myself to even look at her. I wanted her out of the house. I wanted all her unpleasantness and her nastiness and her hostility and her cruelty gone.'

I'm there, 'You don't mean that.'

'Ross, I don't like her. And I know how awful that sounds. But at the same time it's true. I love her because she's my daughter. But I don't like her – not even a little bit.'

'I can't believe I'm actually hearing this.'

'You can't deny how nice it's been having her out of the way, Ross. Think about the lovely summer we've had. There's been no atmosphere in the house. The boys have stopped swearing. You and I have finally clicked. We both said it – it's like we're teenagers again.'

'I'm wondering if you felt any of that. I'm still wondering did you only let me up on you out of pity?'

Sorcha's old dear goes, 'Can you please stop talking about our daughter like that?'

Sorcha's there, 'Ross, I didn't lie to you – not about that. I really do love you.'

But I'm there, 'I have to get out of here. Otherwise, I won't be responsible for what I say slash do.'

I open the kitchen door and I hear a shout from upstairs. It's Brian. He goes, 'Shut the fock up and give your focking hole a rest.'

10.

The One Piece I Couldn't Live Without!

The big news this morning is that there's going to be an election. But the even bigger news in this house is that my wife is a lying, scheming cheat – although I'm saying that as someone who's slept with her sister and most of her friends over the years.

I walk into the kitchen. She's feeding Hillary mashed-up something or other while Fionn's shaking a little rattle at him and going, '*Buenos días*, Hillary! *¿Cómo estás?*'

They both turn and look at me at the exact same time. Sorcha looks terrible. I'm pretty sure she got zero sleep last night because every time I woke, I could hear sobbing in the bed next to me.

She goes, 'Ross, will you have some breakfast?'

And I'm there, 'I'm not hungry,' which is total horseshit. But then, it's so rare for me to find myself in a position where I'm not the actual bad goy that I decide to milk it for all it's worth.

Sorcha goes, 'Ross, I'm so sorry.'

And I'm there, 'Yeah, no, so you said. I'll have some French toast with bacon if it'll make you feel any better. And a pot of coffee if you're looking to take your mind off what you did to me.'

Fionn snorts – he actually *snorts*? 'Yeah,' he goes, 'you're really milking this, aren't you, Ross?'

And I'm there, 'How would you like it if I put Hillary on a plane and sent him to the other side of the world?'

He doesn't answer me. The back door suddenly opens and in her old man walks. He's all, 'You've seen the news, I take it? Micheál Martin says there's no way he's going to be bullied into releasing his Leaving Cert results and Leo Varadkar is going to the Park this morning to ask the President to dissolve the Dáil.'

Sorcha goes, 'Dad, I've got more important things on my mind this morning.'

He's like, 'More important than the future of your political career?' Then he looks at me. 'And what happened to your intervention? Weren't you supposed to tell the world that your father and his Russian friends were behind all of this?'

I'm there, 'I did the interview. They just decided not to run with it.'

Sorcha goes, 'Croía and Muirgheal actually *want* there to be an election? *Oscail do bhéal*, Hillary. *Maith an buachaill!* They think women could do very well in it.'

His face lights up. He goes, 'There's the answer! You've got to run, Dorling! We always said we'd treat your time in Seanad Éireann as an apprenticeship before having a second run at a Dáil seat! We might even think about Dún Laoghaire this time!'

'Dad,' Sorcha goes, 'I'm not sure it's what I want any more.'

'Well, you'd better make up your mind. They're saying it's likely to be a very short election campaign.'

'Dad, you're not listening to me. I think I need to step away from politics to spend more time with my family.'

She smiles at me, waiting for my approval. It's hordly a huge sacrifice. She wasn't in the place a wet day.

He's raging with me, of course. He goes, 'Oh, you think it's something to smirk about, do you? A brilliant young woman, who could make a difference to the lives of millions of people both here and abroad, is turning her back on politics – and for what?'

The back door opens and in walks Sorcha's old dear. She goes, 'One of your sons just called me a shitting ugly focktard.'

I laugh. In a focked-up way, I've kind of missed the swearing.

'So much for that school,' she goes, 'that was supposed to unlock their genius.'

It suddenly dawns on Sorcha that they're not actually there this morning. She goes, 'Ross –'

And I'm like, 'Yeah, no, they got expelled. Cords on the table – Sasha said she tried everything, but in the end she just had to accept that she was pissing into the wind with them.'

I look out the window. They're booting a – yeah, no – soccer ball around the gorden. It looks like we're back to square one with them.

Sorcha goes, 'In a way, I'm glad they were expelled. I realize now that I've been trying to fix the problems of the world while out-sourcing the problem of my own children to Sasha, Erika and whoever else would take them.'

Her old dear goes, 'You're not still beating yourself up over send-ing that girl away, are you? She was out of control!'

Sorcha's like, '*She* has a name, Mom. It's, like, *Honor?*'

For me the questionmork has always been silent.

I'm there, 'So presumably you're going to apologize to her?'

Sorcha doesn't love the sound of that. 'Apologize to her?' she goes.

I'm like, 'Yeah, for accusing her of trying to poison a baby. And you can apologize to her for sending her away as well.'

Sorcha's old man sticks his ample hooter in then. He goes, 'Thankfully, she has no idea she was sent away.'

And I'm there, 'She's going to – because I'm going to tell her everything.'

Sorcha goes, 'Ross, please! She's had the time of her life in Aus-tralia! If we tell her that it was a punishment, she's going to end up hating me even more than she already does!'

I'm actually thinking about this when there's suddenly a loud crash – the sound of breaking glass – then Sorcha and her old pair scream as a soccer ball comes flying through the window, then bounces across the floor of the kitchen.

Leo looks at us through the broken window. 'Pack of focking fockpricks!' he goes.

Fionn's there, 'For God's sake, Hillary could have been hit by that glass! He could have lost an eye!'

And Sorcha's old man goes, 'Those three boys are on the same path to ruin as the other one.'

The *other one* being my daughter. I just decide, that's it. I'm not listening to this shit any more.

I'm there, 'Sorcha, you don't want me to tell Honor the truth, right?'

She goes, 'I just don't think it would be helpful in terms of my relationship with her going forward.'

'Okay, if you want me to keep the truth from her, this is what it's going to take. Honor's coming home in, what, three weeks' time? I want these two focking knobs gone by then.'

I flick my head in the direction of Sorcha's old pair.

Her old dear goes, 'How dare you speak about us like that!'

I'm there, 'I don't want them in the house. I don't want them in that shed out there. I want them gone.'

Sorcha's old man goes, 'Good luck with that. I expect you're about to be very disappointed.'

Then I flick my thumb at Fionn and, without even looking at him, I go, 'Same with him. He's caused nothing but trouble since he moved in here. I don't want him here when Honor comes home either.'

He's there, 'I'm not moving out.'

I'm like, 'Dude, you can't threaten us with protection orders any more. You've got fock-all to borgain with. That's the deal, Sorcha. You either fock these three jokers out of the gaff or I'm telling Honor the full story.'

And Sorcha – without even looking at Fionn or her old pair – goes, 'Fine, Ross. They're gone.'

'Oh my God, Mark Twain – you are such a sexist prick!'

Woke Reads operates out of a room in the basement of Tallant, Gammell and de Paor Solicitors in Merrion Square, where Croía's old man happens to be a portner.

I tip down the steps and I realize that it's actually Huguette's voice I can hear coming through the open window.

She's like, 'He says here, "I think I could write a pretty strong argument in favour of female suffrage – but I do not want to do it."'

I hear gasps from a few people.

Croía's there, 'It doesn't surprise me even a little bit. *The Adventures of Huckleberry Finn*, for instance, is full of misogyny. *And* racism. I'm going to put it on the list.'

'Well, I'm going to tweet this quote,' Huguette goes. 'We need to get everything he ever wrote removed from the shelves of our libraries until we can produce, like, *clean* versions?'

I press the buzzer.

I hear Croía go, 'Who's that?' and then another voice – not hers *or* Huguette's – go, 'Oh my God, it's a focking *man!*'

Seriously?

A few seconds later, Croía opens the door with an already angry look on her face. She's like, 'Oh, for fock's sake!'

I'm there, 'I want to know does the deal still stand?'

'What deal? What are you talking about?'

'As in, you telling your niece to get off my son's case.'

'I can't *tell* Huguette to do anything.'

'Can you ask her, then?'

She goes, 'Why don't you ask her yourself?' and she opens the door to let me in.

It's a pretty poky office with, like, six or seven desks, each with a – not sexist – but *woman* sitting behind it? They all look at me like I'm an alien.

'I thought this was supposed to be a safe space,' one of them goes.

I'm like, 'Don't worry, I'm not staying.'

I look at Huguette. I'm there, 'Putting the Students' Union on my son – that was a nice touch.'

She goes, 'He shouldn't be using social media to spread hate messages. He might find women in burqas funny, but to hundreds of millions of women all over the world it's an instrument of male oppression.'

I'm tempted to comment on that, but I don't really know what she's talking about.

Instead, I'm there, 'I was hoping you might lay off him. Ronan, I mean. Give him a break.'

'And why would I do that?' she goes.

'Because he's a good person.'

'He slept with my friend Rachel.'

'He's a horny person. I'm not denying that. I *could* say it takes two to tango and blah, blah, blah. But I won't. I'm just going to say this. What Ronan has come through in his life, Huguette, is pretty amazing. He was raised by a single mother in – I know you don't want to hear the word – but *Finglas*? You wouldn't believe the disadvantages he's had to overcome in his life – he got my genes, for fock's sake. But thankfully he didn't inherit my brains. You see, he's super smort, as you already know. And he's decided to study Law because he wants to use his brains to help the people in the community where he lives – the poor, the vulnerable, the accident-prone. Man or woman, it doesn't matter a fock. He's a good goy. And he could make a serious, serious impact on the world as long as you don't destroy him. Because that power is in your hands.'

The office is just, like, silent. I'd love to think that I've got through to them all, except then I hear a woman go, 'Look, everyone, the white cisgender male is showing he has a heart after all! You woman-hating, Ernest Hemingway asshole!'

But I notice Huguette's face definitely soften. She looks at Croía and goes, 'What do you think?'

Croía's there, 'I told you, he was happy to give us all that stuff about his dad.'

Huguette looks back at me. 'Okay, I'll give him a break.'

I'm there, 'You mean you won't put him on trial in September?'

'We don't have trials. We have hearings.'

Tell poor Phinneas McPhee that. I don't say that, though. I'm just like, 'Thanks, Huguette. I'm, er, pretty grateful to you.'

'Yeah,' she goes, 'like I *need* your focking gratitude.'

Everyone goes back to work then. 'Your tweet about Mark Twain,' one of the women goes, 'has already got eighty-five Likes and thirty-two retweets, Huguette. Oh my God, someone says that the N-word is mentioned 219 times in *Huckleberry Finn*! Oh my God! That is, like –! Unless he's black, of course. Do we know if he's black?'

'Mark Twain?' Croía goes. 'No, he's white. He's also dead.'

'Right. Because my next question was whether we could call out this racist asshole on Twitter?'

I'm there, 'I'll, er, leave you ladies to it,' and I head for the door. I end up running into Muirgheal on her way in. She's wearing, like, a white suit, with a humungous blue-and-white rosette – and on it are the words 'Massey – An Independent Voice for Dublin Bay South'.

She's there, 'Is Sorcha running?' because they were, like, constituency *rivals* last time? 'Please tell me she's not.'

I'm there, 'No, she's decided to concentrate on her family.'

'That's good. I was going to say it would end up splitting the Independent vote. I always thought she was more suited to Dún Laoghaire anyway. Thanks again for doing the interview.'

'Hey, I meant every word I said about the wanker. The focking pair of them. My only regret is that you're not going to end up using it.'

She goes, 'Oh, don't worry. Like I said, we've got something even better planned for your father,' and then she looks at Croía. 'The ropes are going to need to be pretty thick if they're going to hold him down.'

Okay, that gets my attention.

'Jesus Christ,' I go, 'what are you planning to do with him?'

Croía's there, 'We're going to tie the racist, misogynistic asshole up and throw him in the focking sea.'

I stare at her. She's actually serious.

I'm there, 'I'm not sure I one hundred percent agree with that,' surprised at myself for actually *giving* a shit?

But then ten seconds later, she laughs and I realize that – yeah, no – she's not serious after all. She looks at Muirgheal and goes, 'Will I show him?'

Muirgheal's there, 'Why not? He hates him more than we do.'

Croía grabs this, like, photograph from her desk – it's of a giant balloon version of my old man, with a mobile phone in his hand, and he's naked except for a nappy.

'It's the Charles O'Carroll-Kelly Baby Blimp!' she goes.

And I'm like, 'Right,' at the same time wondering what the fock they're planning to do with it.

Croía obviously reads my mind because she goes, 'Your dad is having a rally in the Phoenix Pork the Sunday before the election. All his supporters are going to be there.'

I'm there, 'Er, okay.'

'And we're going to launch this in the middle of the pork so that everyone can see it.'

Muirgheal's there, 'Oh my God, can you imagine how pissed off he's going to be when he sees it?'

I look at Muirgheal, then back at Croía.

'Er, obviously I know fock-all about politics,' I go, 'but is this definitely better than telling the world that he's in league with the Russians?'

And Muirgheal's there, 'You're one hundred percent right, Ross. You know fock-all about politics.'

I ring Ronan but there ends up being no answer, so I leave a message on his voicemail to tell him he has nothing to worry about, that I've squared it with Huguette and he can go back to college in a few weeks' time without having to worry about facing a trial.

I'm there, 'I hope it hasn't put you off the idea of playing the field. I'd still hate to see you settling down too young. Especially with someone from that family. Anyway, give me a shout back, will you? We haven't properly talked in ages.'

I tip downstairs, then into the kitchen I go. Fionn's in there, feeding little Hillary from a spoon. He's going, '*Das ist gut*, Hillary! Yum-yum! *Ja?*'

I'm there, 'I'm not going to miss *that* when you finally move out,' and I laugh. 'My head is full of stupid foreign words that I have literally no use for.'

He goes, 'You're enjoying this, aren't you?'

'You're spot-on I'm enjoying it. I haven't seen my daughter for months and that's down to you. So if you're asking me to feel sorry for you, you're borking up the wrong tree.'

'I accept I should have told you when I found out.'

'Yes, you focking should have – but you didn't. When are you moving out, by the way?'

'My parents said I could have their spare room until –'

'I didn't ask where you were going? I couldn't give a fock if you end up living on Killiney Beach.'

'Hey, I said I'd be gone by the time Honor comes home from Australia and I will, okay?'

'What, so you're going to drag it out until the very last minute?'

'I'm going to spend every second I can with my son, yes. And I'm sorry if that inconveniences you, Ross.'

'Well, Honor's back at the end of next week. Just make sure you're out of here before I go to the airport to collect her. Otherwise, I'll tell her that you accused her in the wrong.'

And that's when Hillary's face suddenly lights up. He points at me and – I swear to God – goes, 'Dada!' and I end up having to laugh.

I'm there, 'It sounds like you've got a lot of explaining to do to the kid, Fionn. I'm just going to go out and check when these two other fockwits are going.'

Out into the gorden I go. The boys are kicking a ball around. A *soccer* ball, I probably don't *need* to add? There's a rugby one lying on the ground next to the fence – an actual Gilbert – but it might as well be a focking Sudoku book for all the interest they have in it.

Sorcha's old dear is looking up into the branches of a tree. I don't know what kind it is – I find trees boring and a bit pointless, to be totally honest.

I'm there, 'Are you two still here?'

She goes, 'I'm just thinking that's very unusual, isn't it? That ash has already shed its leaves,' obviously trying to change the subject.

I'm like, 'So focking what?'

'I'm just saying it's very unusual,' she goes, 'for August, I mean.'

I'm there, 'Yeah, thanks for that, Diarmuid Gavin. Should you not be out flat-hunting or something?'

'We've found a place, if you must know.'

'Where is it? Please say the Beacon South Quarter,' because I know they absolutely hated living there. 'That would make my literally day.'

'It's in Smithfield – very close to Edmund's new office.'

'It's probably a focking dump, is it – hopefully?'

'It's very small –'

'Good.'

'There's only one bedroom, but it's perfectly sufficient for our needs. You'll be pleased to know that we'll be moving out tomorrow.'

I'm there, 'At long focking last!' and then I tip over to the Shomera to find her husband and have a gloat.

He's actually in there with Sorcha. She's going, 'Dad, I'm not going to change my mind, okay?'

I'm like, 'Dude, you're wasting your breath. You're out of here. Get focking packing.'

Sorcha's there, 'We're not talking about the move, Ross. Dad is still trying to persuade me to run in this election.'

The dude flicks his head at me. '*His* father,' he goes, 'was on *Morning Ireland* this morning saying all sorts of hateful things about women drivers, about members of the Travelling community, about people from Cork. And the response he got from the public was overwhelmingly supportive. Who is going to counterbalance these arguments, Sorcha, if not you?'

'There are plenty of good people out there – for instance, Muirgheal Massey.'

Yeah, I wouldn't hold your focking breath, I think.

He goes, 'But, Sorcha, this is your moment! Don't you see that? Just as Mary Robinson was born to lead the Campaign for Homosexual Law Reform, so you were born to lead the fight against this new breed of hateful populism that's sprung up everywhere.'

She goes, 'There are other ways of fighting it, Dad, without standing for the actual Dáil.'

'How exactly?'

'The best way to fight Fascism is to raise children to know better.'

That's pretty weak, in all fairness. I don't know how I manage to keep a straight face.

He goes, 'Sorcha, you are giving up the chance to make a difference – a *real* difference – to the Ireland in which your children will grow up.'

'I'm sorry, Dad, but I already have a very important job. And that's being a good role model to my children.'

Outside, through the open door of the Shomera, I hear Brian go, 'Shut your focking whore mouth!'

And that's when Sorcha suddenly stands up. She looks at me and goes, 'I'm really sorry, Ross. I should have done this a long, long time ago.'

She walks over to the door and she goes, 'Brian, please don't use bad language like that!'

And Brian looks at her – I swear to God – like he thinks she's lost her mind. He's like, 'What are *you* shitting on about?'

'Brian,' she goes, 'we don't use bad words like that in this house, okay?'

Brian looks at me then. He goes, 'Stupid focking bitch.'

I just burst out laughing. I know I shouldn't but there you go.

And that's when Sorcha all of a sudden *loses* her shit. And I mean loses her shit in a *major*, major way. She roars at Brian. Her face is, like, proper Munster red. She goes, 'Don't you *ever* speak about me like that again!' and Brian – I swear to God – kacks himself. 'I am your mother and you will show me some respect! That goes for the rest of you as well! If I ever, *ever* hear a word like that out of your mouths again, I will scrub them out with soap and water! Do you understand me?'

She doesn't wait around for an answer. She doesn't need one. From the looks on the faces of the boys, it's pretty obvious that she's coming through loud and clear. Brian and Leo actually burst into tears. But I also know at that moment that the swearing has stopped for probably good.

It's, like, twenty minutes later when Honor rings. Tempted as I am to tell her that we know that she was innocent all along, I keep my promise to her old dear to say fock-all.

Instead, I dance around the subject of her having got her first you-know-what, trying to sound sympathetic but not so sympathetic that she decides to confide in me.

It's a minefield for any father.

I go, 'I was really sorry to hear about, you know – blah, blah, blah. Just to let you know, we're all thinking about you and hoping that you're on the mend.'

She's there, 'Are you talking about me getting my first period?'

I'm like, 'Jesus Christ, Honor, can we maybe talk about it without going into actual specifics?'

'It's not an illness, Dad.'

'It's kind of an illness. Jesus, if you saw your mother doubled over with the hot-water bottle clutched to her stomach, horsing into the Ben & Jerry's and losing her shit with me for literally nothing, you'd say it was a definite illness. Although they don't seem to be any closer to finding out what causes it. You'd have to wonder how hord they're trying. Sorry, I'm babbling here.'

'Would you prefer not to talk about it?'

'I would, Honor, if it's all the same to you. My face is really hot all of a sudden.'

'You were the one who brought it up.'

'And I regretted it straight away. I just wanted to check were you okay now?'

'Yes, I'm fine. Anyway, I was just ringing to tell you that your stupid focking bitch of a wife has totally ruined my chances of staying in Australia.'

'Has she?'

'Er, she rang Erika and said she wanted me home because I'm going to be storting secondary school in a few weeks.'

'You'll be going to *actual* Mount Anville. That'll be some day, Honor. Sorcha driving you there for the first time. There'll be tears. I'm just warning you in advance.'

'I told Erika to tell her to go fock herself.'

'Right.'

'I have no intention of going home. But now Erika is saying that I don't have any choice in the matter – that I have to do what my mother says and that's final.'

'Am I detecting one or two cracks in your relationship? I'm sure your subscribers will pick up on it – yeah, no – if it storts to affect your on-screen chemistry.'

All of a sudden, I hear this, like, sobbing on the other end of the phone.

I'm like, 'Honor? Honor, what's wrong?'

She goes, 'Dad, I don't want to go home.'

I'm there, 'Why not, Honor? Don't you miss us?'

'I miss you and I miss the boys.'

'Well, then. Aren't you looking forward to seeing us again?'

She goes, 'I don't want to go back to living in that house where they all hate me.'

'They don't all hate you, Honor.'

'They do,' she goes – and then she ends up *really* losing it. She's suddenly crying so hord that her voice goes all high-pitched. 'They think I poisoned . . . a baby, Dad . . . They think . . . I poisoned . . . a baby.'

And I'm there, 'They don't, Honor,' and the words are out before I can stop myself from saying them. I'm just trying to comfort the girl – as her father. 'They found out it wasn't you after all.'

There's just, like, silence on the other end of the phone. It seems to go on forever.

I'm there, 'Anyway, Honor, it's been lovely talking to you.'

But she won't be so easily fobbed off. She goes, 'What do you mean they found out it wasn't me?'

I take a deep a breath. I know I'm going to possibly regret opening my mouth.

I'm there, 'Yeah, no, Fionn found out that it was actually the boys dipping Hillary's soother into the jacks, then sticking it into his mouth. That's what was actually making him sick. So you're off the hook. Anyway, I'm going to let you go.'

'When did they find this out?'

'Er, you're kind of breaking up there, Honor.'

'We're both talking on landlines, Dad. When did they find this out?'

'Okay, don't go ballistic, but it was a few months ago.'

'*Months* ago?'

'Yeah, no, it was just after you left for Australia apparently. Although they didn't tell me about it until last week.'

'So why didn't *she* ring me to apologize?'

'Good question. Very good question.'

'Well, what's the focking answer?'

'I don't know. You've been pretty hord to get a hold of. You've been up to your eyes with the YouTube channel, then the whole Wellness Summit and Fashion Factory things.'

She goes, 'Dad, stop lying for her!' and she roars it at me. 'She accused me of trying to kill my brother. They all did. Why didn't she ring me to say sorry?'

I'm there, 'I presume it was because she felt bad about sending you away.'

Oh, shit.

She goes, 'Sending me away? What the fock are you talking about?'

I'm there, 'Look, I've said way too much already.'

'Tell me!'

'Okay, basically, they decided between them – we're talking Sorcha, Fionn and her dickhead old pair – that they were packing you off to Australia. But then you decided that you actually *wanted* to go?'

'So they let me think that going away was my idea?'

'You wanted to go and they wanted you gone. Everyone was a winner.'

She's suddenly not crying any more.

She just goes, 'Thank you for focking telling me,' and then the line goes suddenly dead.

So it's, like, a few days later and I'm walking up Grafton Street and I pop into Brown Thomas for one of my famous shit-and-runs.

'Toilets are for the use of customers only,' the dude in the top hat goes, staring at me stony-faced, then he holds the door open for me and laughs. It's been a running joke between us for as long as I've been coming here to snip one off.

Up three flights of escalators I go. I'm thinking about my conversation the other day with Honor. She's not replying to any of my WhatsApp messages. I'm just hoping she'll have calmed down by the time she comes home next week. It'll be a nice surprise for her when she finds out that Fionn and those other two fockwits are moving out.

The gaff that Sorcha's old pair are moving into is tiny. There isn't room to turn over in your sleep apparently. And I'm focking delighted, of course.

I reach the top of the final escalator and that's when I see the massive queue of people, snaking from one end of the homewares floor to the other, then back again, then doubled over on itself a third time. There must be, like, six or seven hundred people here. I haven't seen a queue like this in Brown Thomas since the height of the Celtic Tiger, when Michael Bublé was helicoptered in to launch his own range of paleo, refined sugar-free macarons in association with Ladurée.

And that's when I spot JP and Christian smiling at me across the floor of the homewares deportment.

I'm like, 'No focking way!' quickly walking towards them. 'No! Focking! Way!'

JP just nods and goes, 'Yes focking way, Ross! Yes focking way!'

A high-five turns into a chest-bump turns into a hug. Christian gets the same.

'You did it!' I go. 'You actually did it!'

Technically, he did it when he flogged the patent for ten mills plus a percentage from each bed sold. But seeing people queuing up in BTs to buy his Vampire Bed is the real confirmation that he's arrived.

'Your old man is up there and he's smiling down on you, Dude. And I'll tell you something else. I'd be shocked if Father Fehily isn't standing next to him, saying, "The boy did good!"'

I look at Christian then. I'm there, 'You as well. You back your friends and look what happens. Did he give you your two mills, by the way?'

Christian laughs. 'Yes, Ross,' he goes, 'he gave me my two mills.'

'Well, I hope Lauren apologized to you for doubting you. That girl would want to get off your case and stort appreciating what she has. Seriously, this thing couldn't have happened to two nicer goys even if it happened to George Clooney and Ryan Gosling.'

JP goes, 'Will we tell him our other news?'

I'm like, 'Other news?'

'The Russian firm that bought the bed have asked me to head up the operation for Europe, the Middle East and Africa. And guess who I've just hired as my Head of Morkeshing?'

'Christian?'

'You got it.'

'Whoa, whoa, whoa – what does this mean for Hook, Lyon and Sinker?'

'I'm selling it, Ross.'

'Seriously?'

'It's time to move on. I'm just so buzzed about the future. Look at the queues, Ross. There's a piece in the *Irish Times* this morning that says the Vampire Bed will allow developers to build aportments up to fifty percent smaller in size. Which means they'll be able to provide up to twice as many homes every year.'

'And all because people came around to the idea of sleeping standing up.'

'This is what the Government meant when they said they trusted the morket to fix the problem of homelessness.'

'I'm going to buy one.'

'What?'

'I came in to take a shit, but that can focking wait now. I'm joining this queue and I'm buying a bed.'

Christian laughs. He's there, 'Do you think Sorcha will be cool with sleeping vertically?'

And I'm like, 'It's not for us. It's for Sorcha's old pair. Yeah, no, they're moving into a gaff in Smithfield that's so small, apparently you can't fart and brush your teeth at the same time.'

I say goodbye – and fair focks – to the goys again, then I join the queue. While I'm standing there, I end up ringing Sorcha.

I'm like, 'Hey, Babes, I've decided to buy your old pair a little moving-out present – just to show there's no hord feelings.'

She goes, 'That's, em, really decent of you, Ross.'

'Hey, it'll be worth it just to see the look on their faces.'

'Oh my God, did you hear the RTÉ News this morning?'

'Er, you do know who you're talking to, Sorcha, don't you?'

'Your dad is, like, five points ahead in the latest opinion poll, with, like, a week to go until the election. I'm still waiting to see what Muirgheal and Croía's big plan is going to be.'

'Yeah, I wouldn't invest too much hope in that. You're not storting to suddenly regret it, are you? As in, not standing?'

'A little bit. I would love to be a member of Dáil Éireann, pointing out the factual inaccuracies in all the statements that your dad and members of his porty make in the House. But then I look at the boys – and that includes Hillary – and I think, oh my God, I already *have* a job? We don't need expensive Montessori schools to teach our children how to behave, Ross. That's our job as parents.'

Who would have thought that stopping your kids from swearing was as easy as just telling them to stop focking swearing?

I'm there, 'There's no right and wrong way to raise kids, Sorcha. A lot of it, I've learned, is just making it up as you go along.'

All of a sudden, I hear this woman's voice behind me, go, 'Can we skip ahead of you in the queue? These ladies are pregnant . . . Thank you so much!' and then, a few seconds later, the same thing again. 'Can we skip ahead of you in the queue? These ladies are pregnant . . . Thank you so much!'

There's no mistaking that focking voice.

I'm there, 'Sorcha, I'll see you at home,' and then I hang up on her.

'Can we skip ahead of you in the –'

I turn around and I'm like, 'No, you focking can't.'

She gets a fright when she sees me. It's not half as big as the fright that *I* end up getting? She's standing, like, six inches away from me – invading your personal space is a tactic she uses when she wants something – and I can see her face close up, the cracks and wrinkles showing through her foundation, her chin covered in patches of grey hair like blackberries on the turn.

'Ross?' she goes. 'What are you doing here?'

I'm there, 'Er, I'm buying a bed – what do you think I'm doing?' and then I look at her six surrogates. Szidonia. Roxana. Loredana. Brigita. Lidia. And then another Lidia. Again, they're in identical smock dresses – this time black – and they're all beginning to show. I'm like, 'Hang on a second, you're not putting them in Vampire Beds, are you?'

She goes, 'We haven't the space for them all any more. We have the decorators coming to turn all of the spare rooms into nurseries for the children. So the girls are going to have to share a bedroom for the duration.'

'You are seriously twisted. And I don't mean twisted as in drunk. Even though you're that as well. I can focking smell it off you.'

'You've probably heard that your father's streaking ahead in the opinion polls. Are you coming to the rally on Sunday?'

'I told you. I don't want anything to do with you – *or* him.'

'I was rather hoping that you and I could put all of our history behind us. These babies are going to be your brothers and sisters, Ross, whether you like it or not.'

'I don't want anything to do with them either.'

She bitch-smiles and goes, 'I'm sure you won't always feel that way, Ross,' and then she takes a step forward, taps the woman in front of me on the shoulder and – standing uncomfortably close to her – goes, 'Can we skip ahead of you in the queue? These ladies are pregnant . . . Thank you so much!'

The grunt at the security gate won't let me through. This six-foot-five Russian dude goes, 'If your name is not on list, then you cannot come in,' and I get a sudden flashback to being turned away from Club 92 back in the day and the long, drunken walk down the Leopardstown Road in search of a taxi.

I'm there, 'You're not listening to me. Chorles O'Carroll-Kelly is my actual father. Do you think I'd admit that if it wasn't focking true?'

Suddenly, I spot Kennet through the wire-mesh fence. I call his name. I'm like, 'Kennet!' except he just ignores me, even when I shout it three or four times. He actually goes to walk away. So I shout, 'The R . . . R . . . R . . . R . . . Rowuz of F . . . F . . . F . . . Finglas!' and that gets his attention.

He comes walking over, all smiles. He's wearing his driver's uniform and he's got a laminate pass hanging around his neck. He goes, 'Ah, howiya, R . . . R . . . R . . . R . . . R . . . Rosser. I ditn't see you theer.'

I'm there, 'You tried to ignore me, you mean – until I reminded you that I knew your sordid little secret. Talk to this dude and tell him who I am.'

Kennet nods at the Russian dude to tell him it's okay and the dude opens the gate and lets me into the backstage area.

The Phoenix Pork is absolutely rammers, by the way. Someone says that as many as one hundred thousand people might have come to hear what my old man has to say on the last Sunday before the actual election.

I go, 'I need to talk to him.'

And Kennet's there, 'He d . . . d . . . d . . . d . . . dudn't wanth to see addy wooden, Rosser. He's throying to s . . . s . . . s . . . sabe he's voice for he's sp . . . sp . . . sp . . . spee-itch.'

I go, 'How about I tell Dordeen that I saw you and her sister going at it like porn stors in my old man's cor?'

He's like, ''M . . .'M . . .'M . . .'Mon this way, so,' and he leads me through the throng of porty workers and hangers-on to the old man's trailer. I bang the door with my fist and the door opens. It's Hennessy. 'He's not seeing anyone,' he tries to go. 'He's saving his voice.'

But I just push past him. Saving his voice? That's a joke. He's smoking a cigor the size of Keith Earls and, at the top of his voice, he's telling Fyodor about the time he shook the hand of Greg Norman – 'the Great White Shork himself!' – at Mount Juliet in 1995, just before Greg told him to get the fock off the fairway.

He spots me and goes, 'Kicker! Just reminiscing about the good old days – quote-unquote! So you've come to hear your old dad make the speech that's going to decide the election, have you?'

I'm there, 'No, I've come to talk to you about the old dear.'

It's the fact that I *call* her the 'old dear' – and not, for example, 'that ugly, refuse sack of Botox, bitterness and animal organs that you for some reason married' – that convinces him that this is serious.

He goes, 'Okay, clear the room, people, while I speak to the famous Ross for a moment!'

When everyone has gone, I turn around to him and go, 'You've *got* to stop her before it's too late!'

He's like, 'Too late? What on Earth are you talking about, Kicker?'

'You can't let her bring six babies into the world. She's only doing it to get back at me for letting her choke on that olive.'

'I'm afraid the proverbial die has been cast, Kicker! Each of the girls is *with child* as it were! There's no turning back now!'

'You could let them go.'

'Let them go? Good Lord!'

'I mean, you could buy them each a plane ticket and send them back to –'

'Chişinău!'

'You said it, not me.'

'But they're carrying your brothers and/or sisters, Kicker!'

'Just because we have the same mother and father doesn't make us brothers and sisters.'

There's a knock on the door. Hennessy sticks his head around it and goes, 'Charlie, it's time!'

The old man stands up. He goes, 'I'm sorry to cut our little tête-à-tête short, Ross! I have a General Election to win!'

He walks out of the trailer and through the VIP area towards the makeshift stage. I spot the old dear, surrounded by her surrogates. The old man hugs and kisses her and she whispers something in his ear. Then – un-focking-believable – he kisses the bellies of each of the surrogates, presumably for luck, then he walks up the steps to the stage.

I hear his name announced by, I don't know, whoever. It's just like, 'Ladies and gentlemen, I'm proud to introduce to you . . . to the next Taoiseach . . . Charles . . . O'Carroll . . . Kelly!'

There's, like, a roar from the crowd – and – yeah, no – it *is* deafening – as the old man steps out onto the stage.

He's there, 'Ladies and gentlemen, I will be brief – although not quite as brief as Leo Varadkar's time in office!'

There's, like, howls of laughter from the crowd, then a round of applause that goes on for a good thirty seconds.

'Ladies and gentlemen,' he goes, 'in the coming week, the voters of this country will have a once-in-a-lifetime opportunity to do something that is truly revolutionary! We have a chance to boot out the career politicians who have helped turn this country into a vassal state! We have a chance to remove from office those politicians who stood around like eunuchs in a proverbial harem while unelected bureaucrats with cross faces told you, the people of Ireland, that you would have to cover billions and billions of euros' worth of debt that had nothing whatsoever to do with you! Because your children, and your children's children, and twenty generations of children yet unborn, will be paying for the greed of rich men and the incompetence of politicians who were elected to represent you but don't represent you at all!'

People stort booing.

'You're angry!' the old man goes. 'And you're bloody well right to be angry! You've lived through a decade of – inverted commas – austerity! And what was it all for! It was the price *they* decided you should pay to remain part of a club that doesn't care a bloody well jot about you – that would sell this country out at the first opportunity! And meanwhile, across the water, we see our wonderful friends, the good people of Great Britain, doing what we should have done ten years ago – standing up to the tyranny of Brussels in the same way they stood up to the tyranny of a certain Adolf Hitler! And this time, I say, let us be on the right side of history! This time, let us stand with them!'

There's, like, a huge roar of approval from the crowd. And that's when I see it in the distance, rising slowly from the ground – a blimp that looks, it has to be said, exactly like my old man.

He must see it as well, but he tries not to let it put him off his speech.

He goes, 'Unfortunately, we, in this country, do not have leaders of courage! We do not have leaders of substance! We have Varadkar! And Coveney! And Murphy! And Harris! The smartest boys in the Sixth Year Common Room! We have a Taoiseach who admires people who get up early in the morning, remember, to ensure we all keep chipping away at that debt burden like good little Europeans!'

The blimp storts to rise and suddenly it's blocking out the sun and casting a humungous shadow over the crowd. People are turning around and booing. There's, like, definite anger in the air.

The old man goes, 'And this is what happens, ladies and gentleman, when you challenge the authority of our smug, privately educated, ruling elite! Instead of answering your arguments, they try to ridicule you for having the courage to think differently from them!'

Behind me, I hear Fyodor go, 'Where is my gun?'

'We must not let them win!' the old man goes. 'We! Must! Not! Let! Them! Win!'

Kennet sidles up to me then and he says *the* most random thing. He goes, 'Sh . . . Sh . . . Sh . . . Sh . . . Shadden and Ronan seem to be habbon the t . . . t . . . t . . . t . . . t . . . toyum of their loyuvs, Rosser!'

I turn around to him and I go, 'What are *you* shitting about?'

'Thee weddent away, thee did. D . . . D . . . D . . . D . . . Did Ronan not ted you?'

'No, he didn't *ted* me. Where the fock have they gone?'

'Thee weddent to V . . . V . . . V . . . V . . . V . . . Vegas. With Rihatta-Barrogan – a p . . . p . . . p . . . p . . . proper famidy hodiday, wha? And alls Ine saying is thee l . . . l . . . l . . . l . . . looked veddy lubbed up in the ph . . . ph . . . ph . . . phoros that Shadden purrup on the F . . . F . . . F . . . F . . . Facebuke. Dordeen says to me sh . . . sh . . . sh . . . she wootunt be surproyzed if thee kem back m . . . m . . . m . . . m . . . maddied!'

That's when I hear a loud bang like a gunshot. I look over my right shoulder and I see Fyodor lowering a rifle. There's, like, screams in the crowd.

The old man goes, 'Don't be alarmed, people, this man is here for our protection!'

It turns out the dude missed the blimp but ended up hitting the rope that was, like, tethering it to the ground. Because suddenly the thing lifts off and storts blowing across the pork, sending screaming people scattering for cover. The entire crowd turns and watches in absolute horror as this ginormous, Chorles O'Carroll-Kelly-shaped balloon sweeps over the tops of the trees and towards Áras an actual Uachtaráin.

353

The old man's there, 'This is what they do, my friends, to people who disagree with their agenda! They try to sabotage them! They try to silence them! Good God, I can only hope, for his sake, that poor President Higgins isn't home and looking out the window! Imagine the fright the poor chap will get if he sees that thing coming towards him! Doesn't bear thinking about!'

'They're m . . . m . . . m . . . m . . . med for each utter,' Kennet goes.

I'm like, 'What?'

'Shadden and Ronan. They're a l . . . l . . . l . . . l . . . l . . . lubbly cupiddle. Bout t . . . t . . . t . . . toyum he made an hodest wooban ourrof her. And joost think ob it, Rosser – me and you and Ch . . . Ch . . . Ch . . . Ch . . . Ch . . . Cheerdles there will be famidy!'

There's an enormous crash then, like the sound of a building collapsing. The Charles O'Carroll-Kelly blimp has crashed into the front of the Áras, sending bricks and slates raining down on the lawn below.

The old man goes, 'They *must* not – they *will* not – be allowed to silence our movement!'

And then the crowd bursts into a chant of, 'CO'CK for Taoiseach! CO'CK for Taoiseach! CO'CK for Taoiseach! CO'CK for Taoiseach!'

Sorcha asks me if I've voted yet, even though I've actually never voted – as in, like, *ever*? Seriously, after twenty years together, sometimes it's like we've never even been introduced.

'Yeah, no,' I go, 'I'm, er, hoping to get out to do it at some stage.'

This is us in the kitchen, by the way. The boys are playing quietly with their Lego on the floor. They're very focking wary of their mother all of a sudden.

She's there, 'Because this is an important election, Ross. Possibly *the* most important? As my dad was just saying, this is the one that will decide whether we remain port of Europe or disappear down the same – oh my God – rabbit hole as Britain and the States.'

I'm like, 'I noticed this morning that we were out of Heineken. Yeah, no, I might vote on the way back from the off-licence.'

I don't even know *where* I'm supposed to do it? And aren't you supposed to be, like, registered or some shit?

I'm there, 'Are you looking forward to seeing Honor?'

She's arriving home tomorrow, by the way.

She goes, 'I am, Ross. I know you might not believe me, but I actually *am?*'

I'm there, 'And you definitely think that not telling her the truth about what happened to Hillary is the right way to go?'

'She would never, ever forgive me, Ross.'

'Yeah, you're, er, probably right there.'

'This way we at least have a chance to stort over again. I think the break from each other might turn out to be the best thing that ever happened to us. It gives us a chance to reboot our relationship – to be the best friends that I've always dreamt we *would* be?'

Yeah, good luck with that, I think.

I knock back the last of my coffee while she checks the news on her phone.

'Oh my God,' she goes, 'Muirgheal, Croía and her niece have been arrested and chorged with causing a million euros' worth of damage to the roof of the Áras.'

I'm there, 'I'm not surprised. Three dopes.'

'And endangering the lives of the public. That's, like, oh my God! It says here that when chorged, Croía refused to accept the validity of the chorge until it was put to her by a Bean Gorda. When a Bean Gorda put the chorge to her, she accused her of being a hapless stooge for a patriarchal organization that oppresses women and the right to free speech and freedom of expression.'

'Hilarious.'

'I'd say that's Muirgheal's seat probably gone as well.'

'Well,' I go, standing up, 'I can't say I feel sorry for either of them. Is Fionn finished packing up all his shit, by the way?'

She's there, 'Ross, please don't gloat. He's upset enough as it is.'

'I'm going to go out and grab that Heineken. It's a day of celebration.'

'Don't forget to vote on the way back.'

'Yeah, no, I'll go with the flow, Babes, and see what happens.'

All of Fionn's shit is piled up in boxes in the hallway, waiting for him to put it into his cor. He's standing there and he's saying his final farewells to Hillary. He's looking into the little lad's eyes and you can tell he's trying his best not to cry. He's going, 'I won't be here any more, Hillary, but I won't be very far away either. And I'll come and visit you all the time.'

And I'm like, 'Yeah, make sure and ring ahead first, Fionn,' as I walk past them, then as I'm going out the front door I stort singing Paul Brady's 'The Long Goodbye'.

I get into the cor. I feel actually good. I'm just about to stort the engine when my phone suddenly rings. I check my caller ID and I notice that it's Joe Schmidt. I answer and there's, like, five seconds of silence on the other end.

'Joe,' I shout, 'you've orse-dialled me again!'

Then I hear his voice – God, it's like honey – go, 'Nah, Oy actually mint toy ring yoy thus toym, Ross! How are yoy goying?'

I'm like, 'Er, yeah, no, cool.'

'Oy just wanted toy sind yoy back your Rugboy Tictucs Book.'

'Oh, right.'

'Oy wanted toy git your addriss.'

'It's Honalee, Vico Road, Killiney, County Dublin.'

'Got ut. Boy the woy, that mooyve on poyge eight – yoy knoy the one Oy moyn?'

I'm there, 'The one I designed for Garry Ringrose and Jordan Larmour?'

'That's ut. That was prutty smaaht.'

'Do you think?'

'Oy moyn royloy, royloy smaaht. Ross, Oy hoype yoy doyn't moynd but Oy talked toy one or toy poyple abaaht yoy.'

'Haters gonna hate, Joe. Was one of them your mate Gatland?'

'When are yoy gonna give yourself some cridit? Yoy've got all thoyse great oydeas abaaht the goym and yoy're doying nothing wuth them. All because yoy've got some koynd of chup on your shoulder.'

'Some of kind of –?'

'Chup.'

'I thought that's what you said. You *were* talking to Gatland then.'

'Look, Oy'm gonna sind yoy a tixt missage in a few munnets. It's just the noyms and numbers of a few contacts of moyn – AIL, one of toy Linster schools – whoy could use a coych with frish oydeas.'

I swear to fock, I suddenly feel like nearly crying.

I'm there, 'Why are you doing this?' because I honestly can't remember the last time anyone was this nice to me.

He goes, 'Because Oy think your daughter's royt – Oy think yoy've royloy got something. Nah, just ring thoyse numbers Oy'm sinding yoy. And lit thus boy the staaht of something, okoy?'

I tell him it will. We both hang up. And then about twenty seconds later, my phone beeps and it's a text message. I look at the names. DLSP. Old Belvedere. Newpork Comprehensive. Gorey Community School. Pres Bray.

I actually have a little chuckle to myself thinking about what Father Fehily would say if he knew I was thinking of coaching Pres Bray. And then it suddenly hits me. I'm thinking about Father Fehily and all these memories from my schooldays come suddenly flooding back. I'm remembering one time, against St Mary's, Fionn taking an unbelievably hord hit just so he could play a pass to me at exactly the right moment for me to score a try. I'm remembering him another time throwing himself into the middle of a group of Terenure players who objected to me flashing my sixpack at their supporters and taking a punch in the face for me. I'm remembering him another time trying to give me grinds the night before we sat Leaving Cert Maths Paper I and explaining everything to me without ever losing his patience, even though nothing actually went into my head in the end.

I stare at the door of the house and I think, 'What the fock have you become, Rossmeister?'

I get out of the cor and I walk back to the house. I let myself in. Fionn looks at me. He's got, like, tears streaming down his face as he says his last goodbyes to Hillary.

'Pick up all your focking shit,' I go, 'and put it back upstairs.'

He's like, 'What?'

I'm there, 'I'm going to end up tripping over it and breaking my focking neck. Then I'd be no use to any club. Put it back upstairs. In your room.'

Sorcha comes out of the kitchen. She goes, 'Oh! My God!'

Fionn's there, 'Are you saying –?'

'I'm saying you can stay,' I go. 'I'm saying you don't have to move out – if you don't want to.'

He's in shock.

He goes, 'What changed your mind?'

I'm there, 'The short answer is rugby.'

'Jesus, Ross.'

'The long answer is that I've just spent the entire summer separated from my daughter and I've missed her more than I have the words to say. And I wouldn't want to think of anyone else going through what I just went through – even you, Fionn.'

He goes, 'That's very decent of you – considering.'

We're just, like, staring hord at each other.

Sorcha's there, 'What about my mom and dad, Ross?'

I don't take my eyes off Fionn. I'm there, 'I didn't play rugby with your mom and dad, Sorcha.'

And she knows just to leave it at that.

I bend down and I pick up a box. It's got, like, a mobile inside with what I'm presuming are all the planets in the – I think it's the right word – but *sonar* system?

'Come on,' I go, 'let's get all this focking junk back up to your room.'

The same words keep getting used. Stunning. Shocking. Staggering. Chorles O'Carroll-Kelly's New Republic are on course to win an overall majority as counting continues in twelve constituencies and it's all anyone in the country seems to be talking about.

People are walking through the doors of Arrivals, having obviously read the news on their phones, and they're hugging loved ones and going, 'Is this for real?' and 'He's a Fascist lunatic.'

You'd genuinely have to wonder who actually voted for him because no one seems to be admitting it.

I'm looking up at the little monitor.

'Honor's flight has landed,' I go.

But Sorcha's not listening to me. Like everyone else, she's just glued to her phone. 'They're saying that Ireland leaving the European Union would require a change in the Constitution,' she goes. 'That's what my dad said this morning. So there's still a chance to stop it from happening.'

I'm there, 'Did you hear what I said? Honor's plane landed ten minutes ago.'

She puts away her phone. She goes, 'I'm sorry. I'm just nervous about seeing her again.'

Yeah, not half as nervous as *I* am? I literally haven't spoken to the girl since I let it slip that she was basically *sent* to Australia – and for a crime we now know she didn't commit.

Leo goes, 'Mommy, when is Honor coming?' and Sorcha smiles sweetly, leans down and kisses him on the top of the head.

'She'll be coming through those doors any minute now,' she goes.

The boys are holding the little signs they made that say 'Welcome home, Honor!' and they're genuinely giddy with excitement.

Out of the corner of my eye, I catch Sorcha looking at me with a big smile on her face. Yeah, no, things are getting back to nearly normal between us. A year ago, I wouldn't have believed we'd ever be this loved up again.

She stood next to me this morning when I made the phone call – a supportive hand on my shoulder. I said I'd heard rumours they were looking for a coach. They said they'd heard good things about me. I asked how good? They say *really* good. So I arranged to swing out there next week for a chat and a look at their set-up.

And when I say 'out there', I'm talking about – believe it or not – Bray. Of all places.

That's right. I've got an interview on Monday morning for the position of senior rugby coach in Presentation College Bray. I know a lot of people – my critics, mostly – will get a great kick out of that. I've said a lot of bad things about Bray over the years. And, while I stand over every focking word of it, the old romantic in me loves the idea of taking this school from – let's not dodge this – Wicklow and opening my Rugby Tactics Book to them.

361

Father Fehily, who spent a lot of his life doing missionary work in Botswana, used to say, 'You go where the need is greatest,' and I can't think of anywhere more in need than Bray.

I'm also conscious of the fact that twenty-something years ago, Joe Schmidt storted his coaching career in Ireland by leading Wilson's Hospital in Mullingor to victory in the Leinster Schools Senior Cup Section 'A' final, and there's a little bit of me that likes the idea of following in the great man's footsteps.

You never know, I might even give Phinneas a bell to ask him if he fancies being my assistant?

Yeah, no, things are finally coming together. Sorcha's old pair are moving out tomorrow. And aport from my old man threatening to lead the country into ruin and my old dear giving me six brothers and/or sisters that I don't want, it feels like things are returning to normal again. My only real worry now is . . .

'Honor!'

Brian, Johnny and Leo all shout it at exactly the same time. I look and I see my daughter pushing her trolley, loaded with baggage, through the Arrivals gate. The boys can't contain themselves. They run towards her, then they throw their orms around her waist and she laughs, then sort of, like, hunkers down to their level and gives them each a hug and tells them that she missed them.

She's definitely changed. She looks, I don't know, taller. Or maybe not taller. Just not a child any more.

Our eyes meet. I still don't know whether she's pissed off with me or not. Then suddenly she breaks into a run and she throws her orms around me and it's like the last few months never happened. It's like we were never even aport. She goes, 'Hey, Dad!' and she's crying.

And I'm crying, too.

I'm like, 'Hey, Honor! God, I missed you so much! Hey, I'm possibly going to be coaching Pres Bray in the Leinster Schools Senior Cup next year and it's all down to you. And I don't mean that in a bad way.'

And then *the* most random thing happens. She spots Sorcha standing behind me and she breaks away from me. Sorcha doesn't move. She just goes, 'Hi, Honor,' and her voice sounds, I don't know, cautious and uncertain. For ten seconds, I swear to fock, Honor doesn't say shit. She just stares at her old dear, then she walks towards her and I'm still half expecting her to slap her across the face. She doesn't, though. She does the same to Sorcha as she did to me – throws her orms around her waist and hugs her tightly.

Sorcha looks at me and mouths the words, 'Oh! My! God!' and she holds her daughter like I haven't seen her hold her in years.

Honor goes, 'I'm sorry, Mom! I'm so sorry!'

And that ends up setting Sorcha off. She goes, 'No, Honor, I'm the one who's sorry!' and *she's* suddenly bawling her eyes out.

I'm thinking, Oh, holy shit, she's not going to tell her, is she? But she *does* end up telling her? Yeah, no, it all comes out – there in the middle of the Arrivals hall.

'I accused you of trying to poison Hillary,' she goes, 'and I know that it wasn't true. Even worse, Honor, I found out weeks ago that it wasn't true and I never said anything.'

Er, try *months* ago?

But Honor's there, 'I don't blame you for not believing me, Mom. I did so many bad things.'

'That's not all,' Sorcha goes. 'I let you think that going to Australia was your idea, but the truth was I wanted to send you away.'

Again, Honor takes this better than she did when I told her on the phone last week, having had time to, like, *process* it?

She goes, 'Mom, I don't blame you. I'm horrible.'

Sorcha's like, 'You're not horrible, Honor. You're my little girl. And I love you so much.'

Someone's changed their tune. But now is not the time to pull her up on what she said a few weeks ago. Because mother and daughter are having a definite moment.

'Spending time with Erika was the best thing that ever happened to me,' Honor goes. 'She taught me to appreciate all the good things I have in my life and that includes you, Mom.'

Sorcha's like, 'Oh, Honor!'

'She just, like, talked to me all the time about how lucky I was to have a mother like you and I'm so sorry that I treated you so badly.'

'Hey,' Sorcha goes, 'we can stort again, Honor. You're going to be storting in *actual* Mount Anville in two weeks and it can be a whole new beginning for us. You'll be doing all the things I did, Honor. The St Madeleine Sophie Barat Prayer Circle. The Model United Nations. We can be, like, best, best friends.'

Honor's like, 'I really want that, Mom. I really do.'

'Come on,' Sorcha goes, 'let's go home.'

'I can't wait to see Hillary.'

'On my God, he's gotten *so* big, Honor!'

The two of them stort walking in the direction of the cor pork and I think to myself, Fock my old pair. Whether it's having kids or destroying the country, I don't care what they do any more. Because these people here are my priority – one, two, three, four, five, six of us, plus Ronan, whatever the fock he decides to do.

And plus – I'm going to say it – Hillary. Okay, he's not mine, but he's *theirs*? He's Sorcha's son and a brother to Honor, Brian, Johnny and Leo. And that makes him family. End of.

I grab Honor's trolley and I tell the boys that we're going. And, as I stort pushing it, I notice that Sorcha and Honor are holding hands and I think to myself, Okay, what kind of miracle is that? And then something else pretty miraculous happens. I'm aware of Brian and Leo sort of, like, bickering with each other – not effing and blinding and threatening each other with extreme violence like before. Yeah, no, they're just having a little orgument, the way normal brothers do. I turn back and I go, 'What's wrong, goys?'

And that's when Leo says the most incredible thing to me. He goes, 'Dad, who's the best – Johnny Sexton or Owen Farrell?'

And you get days like that in your life, where all your problems seem to just fall away of their own accord and you can suddenly see the future, bright and happy, stretching out in front of you.

'That's a stupid focking question,' I go. 'But I can't tell you how happy I am that you asked it.'

Epilogue: Don't Forget to Hit the Subscribe Button!

So he's done it. I hoped he wouldn't – and I didn't think he would – but the evidence is there, right in front of my eyes. And this is how I find out. A photograph on WhatsApp. Ronan and Shadden and little Rihanna-Brogan, all in their finest, standing outside the Happy Ever After Chapel in Hooters Casino in Vegas.

I just shake my head. I'm like, 'You must be focking mad, Ro.'

And Brian pipes up then. He's like, 'Must be focking mad, Ro. Focking prickfock.'

And I go, 'Remember, Brian, we don't use bad language, okay? And your daddy's going to try his best to stop as well, even though your big brother has decided to piss his focking life away.'

We're sitting in the living room, watching a DVD of – I can barely believe it myself – the 2011 Heineken Cup final between Leinster and the Northampton Saints. The famous Miracle Match that I dreamt of one day watching with my kids. And they're loving every minute of it. We're into, like, the final seconds and Leo is shouting, 'Johnny Sexton!' at the screen just like I do when I watch it.

I go, 'Johnny Sexton!'

And then Brian and Johnny get in on the act as well. They're like, 'Johnny Sexton!'

It's a lovely, lovely moment.

The match ends and Leo shouts, 'Again! Again!'

But I'm like, 'No, Leo. You can't keep watching the same match over and over again. It's important for you to get a broad education. I want to show you them beating Ulster the following year.'

God, they're going to love me out in Bray.

I press Stop on the disc and the TV comes on. The old man is on the RTÉ lunchtime news, saying that the Irish people have spoken and they have said loudly and clearly that they wish to take back control of their country.

'Granddad!' Johnny shouts.

And I'm like, 'It's not your granddad, Johnny, it's just someone who looks and sounds a little bit like him.'

The old man goes, 'What we have seen this week is a rejection of the same old careerist politicians who have served this country badly since Independence! I intend to make good on my promise to renege on our – inverted commas – debt obligations and follow Britain out of the European Union and towards a bright tomorrow!'

I mute the TV while I look for the DVD of the 2012 final.

There's a pretty much gale blowing outside. I look out the window. Sorcha is helping her old pair move all of their shit out of the Shomera and into the removal van that her old man rented for the day.

I bang on the window and her old man – who's carrying a morble-based arc lamp that he got in IKEA – looks at me through the glass.

I'm like, 'Did you get my goodbye-and-good-riddance gift?'

He did. The Vampire Bed arrived this morning. I saw it being delivered. He wouldn't give me the pleasure of acknowledging it, of course. I doubt if they'll even bring it with them. I don't mind either way. It served my purpose of giving me a good focking laugh as I watched him sign for it, only to then realize what it actually was.

He's absolutely fuming with me. He looks at me – he's practically being blown away in the wind – and he goes, 'I have better things to do than engage with the likes of you!'

Which is poor from him. I give him the wanker sign and he walks around the side of the house with the lamp. I feel like calling Honor. She should be here to witness this, except she's upstairs, preparing a video for her YouTube channel called Five Items in Your Wardrobe that You Think You Need But Don't.

I'm kind of hoping that she asks me to appear in it.

I find the DVD I'm looking for, except it's the wrong disc in the case. Instead of the Leinster versus Ulster match, it's the *Davina McCall Extreme Abs Boxercise* DVD that I used to watch practically five times a week when Sorcha was pregnant with the boys and had lost her sexual appetite. I stort looking through all the other cases for the right disc when all of a sudden I hear the most unbelievable crash outside. I'm not exaggerating – the entire house shakes – and the boys all scream with the fright.

And so do I when I look up and see what caused the actual noise. A humungous branch – we're talking thirty feet long – has snapped off a tree in the high wind and come crashing down on the roof of the Shomera, flattening the focking thing.

It says a lot that my first reaction is that it's a pity Sorcha's old pair weren't in there, because I just watched her old dear walk past the window carrying a Brabantia pedal bin.

But then all of a sudden I hear all this screaming and shouting and Sorcha's old pair come chorging around the side of the house into the back gorden, going, 'Sorcha! Sorcha!' and that's when I realize that my wife must have been inside the Shomera when the – practically – tree fell on top of it.

I race out into the hall, then outside, screaming her name. I'm going, 'Sorcha! Sorcha!' except there ends up being no answer.

I'm standing over this flattened mess of wood and steel and glass, screaming her name over and over again, listening out for a noise, for any sign of life and it's like time has suddenly stopped.

I'm going, 'Sorcha, can you hear me? Sorcha, answer me if you can hear me?'

And her old pair are shouting basically the same thing while running circles around what's left of what was their home until sixty seconds ago.

I'm like, 'Sorcha? Sorcha, can you hear me?'

And that's when I hear her voice – tiny and frightened – coming from deep inside the basically rubble of the Shomera.

She's there, 'Ross? Ross?' and – I swear to fock – I have never loved my wife the way I love her at that moment in time.

Her old man goes, 'Dorling? Dorling, are you hurt?' but I shoulder him out of the way like Rory Best clearing out a ruck.

I'm there, 'Sorcha, are you hurt?'

And she's like, 'I don't think so.'

'No broken bones?' I go, looking for a way to get into what's left of the thing.

She's there, 'No, I think I'm okay. Just a bit in shock. What happened?'

Sorcha's old dear goes, 'A branch fell onto the Shomera, Dorling!'

I climb up onto the wreckage and I find a big hole where the window used to be. I stick my head into it and I look inside. It's pitch dork in there. But I whip out my phone and I switch on the torch and I can suddenly make out a hand.

I'm like, 'Sorcha? I'm over here! Follow the light!'

I reach out my hand towards her. Ten seconds later, she grabs it and I pull her slowly out through the window towards safety. She was lucky and she knows it. She's suffering from nothing worse than a few cuts and bruises and – like she said – a little bit of shock.

Sorcha's old pair are all over her, hugging her and telling her how much they love her and how grateful they are that she's alive. There's not a word of thanks for me, of course.

Her old man goes, 'You've been saved for a purpose, Dorling! Oh, I'm fully convinced of that! It's to be a thorn in the side of Charles O'Carroll-Kelly and his efforts to take Ireland out of Europe!'

Meanwhile, her old dear is going, 'It was that tree! Do you remember the one I said had lost all of its leaves?'

I'm sort of, like, doubled over, trying to regain my breath. And that's when something all of a sudden hits me. You could call it a realization.

I look up at Honor's bedroom window and I see her standing there, just staring out, a blank expression on her face.

Into the house I go, then up the stairs, along the landing and into Honor's room. She doesn't even turn around when I push the actual door.

I'm like, 'You killed the tree, didn't you? *That's* why you were looking up poisons on the internet.'

She's there, 'Why did you have to tell them to move out? They'd probably be dead if you didn't.'

'Jesus Christ, Honor, you could have killed your mother.'

She sort of, like, laughs. She's goes, 'Oh my God, she's being such a drama queen about it. Loves the attention, of course.'

I walk over to her and I spin her around. I'm like, 'Honor, I thought you and Sorcha had agreed to let bygones be bygones.'

But she just smiles, then she does an impression of Sorcha. She's like, 'You'll be doing all the things I did, Honor. The St Madeleine Sophie Barat Prayer Circle. The Model United Nations. We can be, like, best, best friends.'

It's a pretty good impression, it has to be said.

'She was happy to send me away,' she goes. 'Her own daughter.'

I'm there, 'She seems to have genuinely learned her lesson, though, Honor. Why don't we just agree that it ends there?'

But she just laughs. She's like, 'I haven't even storted on her yet. She has no idea of the shit I've got planned for her.'

Acknowledgements

Grateful thanks as always to the brilliant team behind Ross, especially my editor, Rachel Pierce; my agent, Faith O'Grady; and the artist Alan Clarke. Thank you to Michael McLoughlin, Patricia Deevy, Cliona Lewis, Patricia McVeigh, Brian Walker, Aimee Johnson, Carrie Anderson and everyone at Penguin Ireland. Thanks to my family – Dad, Mark, Vincent and Richard. And, most of all, thank you to my beautiful wife, Mary.